An award-winning writer born in New Zealand, Sarah Quigley has a D.Phil. from the University of Oxford and is now based in Berlin, where she was the inaugural CNZ/DAAD Literary Fellow for 2000-1. Quigley's short fiction and poetry have been published widely. Her previous novel, *Shot*, is also published by Virago Press.

FIFTY DAYS

SARAH QUIGLEY

Virago

VIRAGO

First published by Virago Press 2004
This edition published by Virago Press in September 2005

Copyright © Sarah Quigley 2004

'The Lingerer' copyright © 1992 by Stephen Fowler. Reprinted from
Thing Happen Hole with the kind permission of Stephen Fowler

The moral right of the author has been asserted

A CIP catalogue record for this book is available from the British Library.

ISBN 1 84408 174 5

Typeset in Bembo by Palimpsest Book Production Limited,
Polmont, Stirlingshire

Printed and bound in Great Britain by Clays Ltd, St Ives plc

Virago Press
An imprint of
Time Warner Book Group UK
Brettenham House
Lancaster Place
London WC2E 7EN

www.virago.co.uk

To J. S.

In the beginning

One side of her apartment looks out on to trees, the other on to windows. This is all. This is all she has.

The situation

She is as close as you can come to the perfect woman. She has the hair, sleek and black. It falls quietly in line with gravity. And what about skin? She has the skin. If she were walking on a backdrop of snow, her skin would pick up its pure and pale texture. Against sand it would become a grainy fawn. As for her cheekbones – see her cheekbones? – they have the same slanting certainty as the first sun in a cold and breathless world.

In the 1920s the Surrealists would play a game. This game involved entering a movie theatre after the lights had gone down and the film had already started. (Plunging themselves into a state of incomprehension, this is what they were doing.) They would settle back in their hard seats and begin to watch lives in which many things had already happened. These could be big things, or small: chance meetings, stolen kisses, coat tails caught in revolving doors or bodies falling from buildings. These past events were things at which the Surrealists could only guess, establishing their likelihood by certain clues: the trembling of hands about to light a cigarette, for example. Such things were small flares in an otherwise encompassing darkness.

Here, now, we may believe that we are at the beginning of a story. We are entering a new setting, meeting a new woman. But this, of course, is our own game: is nothing more than our chosen point of entry. The woman we are watching has existed for far longer than two days, working quietly and unobserved in her high apartment. She existed before we came along. And should we step away, it is likely that she will go on breathing.

A question now. Do you remember that utensil used by your mother many long years ago, to prepare eggs for boiling? It was yellow and white, that tool, it was egg-coloured plastic, and with it your mother would make a tiny pin-hole in the more rounded end of the egg, and you could hardly believe it when you saw that the egg did not break, didn't splinter, crack wide, spill its runny guts and its sun-yolk over your mother's wrists and hands. There it was still whole in her palm: secretive, closed, holding on to its dark and determined heart.

When placed in the pan of boiling water, however, the egg would tremble, float, and leak a little. And you would turn your back on it then, turn your attention to a plastic egg timer (also yellow) which you would, neatly and immediately, turn upside down so that the white granules began counting out the minutes. Six perfect minutes, measured, limited, poured from one clear plastic pod to the other.

After this time had elapsed things had changed. When you fished the egg out you found it different. Its shell no longer had the cool texture of skin but had become shiny, slick, and coated with heat. When you tapped it with a teaspoon it spoke back in a different voice, and when you sawed its head off and peered inside you saw that its translucent liquid was now white and solid.

But then, you would have been astonished if this had not happened.

This was what the egg timer did for you: it gave you certainty. It gave you the perfect breakfast, it gave you time to comb your hair or make your bed or make a phone call, and it gave you certainty. All you needed to supply was faith: faith that, with the counting out of minutes, the nature of things would change.

When you got older you realized that the egg timer which you knew and trusted was a modern invention, developed from the traditional hourglass that trickled sand rather than synthetic granules through it, and had an altogether weightier responsibility. An hourglass had to hold sixty minutes rather than six within its curved glass sides, but the governing principle remained the same: trust, belief, call it what you will. You have no way of knowing if the glass-blower has correctly calculated the width of the funnel so that your hourglass is perfect, but you tip it up anyway. The internal clock is now running, and you run with it.

This woman in her echoing high apartment? She has what you might call an hourglass figure. She has curved hips that swell softly inwards to a perfect waist, and from this perfect waist her body swells out once again into perfectly curvaceous breasts. And the skin on her curved hips and flat stomach is as smooth as glass. On this day, the second we have seen her, she has already inverted her life. She has taken the plunge, started the journey in; from this point, whether or not we watch her, know this. She will go on.

She has skin that feels like cool glass to the touch. She has shards in her past. She has a measured step as she crosses her kitchen floor, steady, steady, so the empty space below her resonates and thrums: a spring within a clock.

Her apartment has a view of windows from one side, and from the other the surging tops of trees. We do not know her name – why should we? It is enough for now that we see her, all of her, perfect. Walking across bare linoleum, sand whispering through her.

The visitor

A girl comes to the apartment every day. She must climb seventy-two steps to reach the woman's door, and when she pauses on every second landing to catch her breath she thinks she hears the tread of feet, a faint booming through empty layers of ceilings and floors. Twelve steps to each flight, six flights of stairs, and even then she is not quite at the top of the building but this is high enough because now she is at the woman's door. See the sheen on the girl's lip, see her breasts under the large sweater rising and falling just as her feet have done.

She comes every day, this girl. She is not beautiful like the woman who waits for her, but she is reliable! As reliable as a Swiss watch, and there is a certain beauty about precision.

Odd that the Arab word for beauty is close to the English word for hour. *Houri.* Yet for Muslims the mark of beauty is held in the eye − not in the eye of the beholder, but the eye of the beauty herself. What makes a beauty for them? The starkest contrast between a pitch-black pupil and a bright white background: the negative image of a photographed desert moon against a clean black sky.

On this, the third day, we are allowed to watch from outside the apartment as well as inside. See the plain, reliable girl climbing seventy-two stairs and standing, panting, on the landing. See her raise her hand to the door. It could be the random sound of a tree branch on the window. *Knock!* But it is an anticipated sound, and so is interpreted correctly from the inside.

Now, with a flick of the lens, we are rushing through

5

the closed front door, squeezing lungs cracking ribcages squashing faces pushing our way through tight dense particles of two-inch wood to get to the other side. Here we see the beautiful woman putting her eye close to the peephole. She has the darkest pupils ever: they stretch further back than it is comfortable to see. Like a black hole in the ceiling of the universe: this is what it is like to look deep into her eyes.

When she peers out the peephole the girl's face appears, swelling larger in the middle and receding around the edges. The girl's eyes are in shadow, for the light fixture on the stairwell has been broken for some time and will never be mended; but her eager pupils pick up the daylight from the window on the landing and throw it straight at the door. *Ping*! This is the Candy Girl, arrived for her day's work.

They have known each other before this, it seems. Otherwise how do you explain the ease between them as soon as the woman (Gest) opens the door, and also the way that the girl (the Candy Girl) starts to speak right in the middle of a sentence.

Was terrible! she is saying. Just terrible!

She steps inside. Now we are all in the hallway together, waiting for the Candy Girl to put down her bags and finish her complaint.

She is talking about the traffic, the foot traffic: the long haul that it is to get from the train station to the front door of Gest's apartment block, weaving on her bicycle along the pavement, in and out of pedestrians who carry shopping baskets and push trundlers, with a silver thread of impatience spinning behind her.

And you know, she pauses, it goes on day after day!

Her voice is muffled and then clear again, because as she speaks she is taking off her jumper (too many layers, the heat, the climb) so that by this time she might not even be talking anymore about the hordes of pram-pushing women who slow the blur of her shining wheeling spokes.

Day after day, agrees Gest, although she too is no longer sure what the topic is. For the Candy Girl could equally justifiably be complaining about the humidity of this particular season, the way that once she has got off the stuffy train and wheeled her bike out into the street, the moisture rushes to coat the inside of her nostrils and sits heavily on her head so her hair must lie down dog-like, flat and disgraced.

There is an ease here, perhaps a friendship, which seems beyond what might be expected between an average employer and an average and reliable employee. And when Gest and the Candy Girl walk down the hallway in the direction of the workroom, of one accord they detour through a doorway on their left into the kitchen.

There is bound to be some difference, of course; this is a domestic situation, we are not in an office. But see how the Candy Girl puts her hand on Gest's arm in a familiar kind of way, and watch how, when Gest spills some milk on the table, she wipes it away with her sleeve instead of getting a cloth.

Secrets

Day four, and you are walking down a wide street, past kebab shops displaying turning sweaty torsos of meat in their windows just as brothels display teenage prostitutes.

7

Hungry for something? But you are not, you are after neither food nor sex, and you walk on, hurrying now.

Traffic screams beside you. Leaves litter the pavement, shuffling around with the balled-up rubbish and the coloured pamphlets of bad patio furniture. It may be spring, but it's an odd kind of spring, like nothing you've known before. You hurry, leaves rustle after you like rats. Hot meaty breath on your bare shoulders, chilly air on your neck, but at last you're there.

The movie has started. This is not deliberate (you are not an admirer of the Surrealists); you have simply been delayed in the bank and now you are here, too late, kicking the edge of the stairs with your feet. The white screen turns the audience into ghosts, the light and the dark are blinding you, and you walk on and up until finally, in the last row, you make out an empty seat right on the aisle. You sit.

Now you can enter the movie, but know this: know you have missed something. Not the sense of anticipation as the lights dim and the voices fall to murmurs – not only these things. Not the movie-maker's logo lifting you right out of your seat and rushing you through the computer-generated canyons of city streets, nor a mountain encircled with stars, nor the opening song pouring into the theatre like a Dolby wave getting you in the mood for love, violence, or deceit.

You do not care about any of this, but by stumbling in late you have missed something vital. You are an onlooker still, and you wish to be a participant. You must catch up.

Let us start with the Candy Girl. We already know how she gets to work, that she wheels her bicycle onto a train and then off a train and cycles to her employer's front door, and that in so doing she is inclined to become impatient with pedestrians who get in her spinning whirring two-wheeled path. But what we don't know about her is that she is easy company, immensely easy to be with, although the twenty years of her life have been far from easy. Her skin testifies to this. Small round red marks on her forearms, legacy of her cigarette-smoking father. And finer fainter marks, like the tracks of a caterpillar, on the inside of her arms and perhaps on her legs and other parts of her body that we cannot see.

She has a hard road behind her but, even so, her good nature has remained intact. She is a good girl, and good to be with, and Gest believes herself lucky to have even a limited amount of time to work with such a person.

And what of Gest? You might assume, looking at her and her beauty, that she has not always lived alone. If you look at her apartment, high above the tops of the grimy city trees, you would deduce that she has not lived here so long either. There is a lot of floor space, and not much furniture: a large scratched table in the kitchen, a couple of chairs drifting in the hallway, a mattress floating in the middle of the bedroom floor. And in the work-room nothing to sit on except for two high stools.

No, it seems as if Gest might be here temporarily, waiting for the spring to slide on out of the city before she herself moves on. Not always here, then, although always perfect, and the Candy Girl is slightly in awe of this. On some days this leads to her doing certain things, such as sucking her stomach in

(don't suck your stomach in! begs Gest)

or sucking in her cheeks, hoping to make them less childish and more concave. She has heard of movie stars having their back teeth removed so that the line of their jaw is cleaner and their faces thinner.

The things those stars do! the Candy Girl says to Gest. Although you could be one yourself, the way you look.

And then she blushes, so that her creamy child-cheeks become tinged with the same colour as her pink satin leggings. I'm sorry, she says, the Micro is always telling me that I make too many personal comments.

I don't mind, assures Gest. But please, relax!

Telling someone to relax is useless, of course. Self-consciousness stiffens the bones and shrinks the spirit. Now the Candy Girl sits bolt upright on her stool, neck in a parallel line to the wall: her blue eyes roll towards Gest helplessly and if she could remove teeth, or a couple of lower ribs to make her waist more Victorian, she would do it! She would do it right now, regardless of the fact she has just dismissed the follies of Hollywood.

Gest realizes her mistake and amends her plea before the Candy Girl can snap in two from effort.

Don't suck your cheeks in, OK? She turns to the window to give the Candy Girl some time. Or your stomach! And she looks out the window with assumed vagueness.

Oh, this is much easier! The Candy Girl is quite used to following exact orders: as a child she has scurried to obey her shouting father, as a teenager she obeyed the laws of the urban jungle, and now that she is a grown-up and lives with a man – well, even though now she does pretty much what she likes – still she likes to please.

Is this better? she says, and she sits more easily on the vinyl cushion and hears it puff air comfortably from under her pink satin arse. Her body expands again to take up the amount of air it is used to and her skin softens: she is a balloon with the tension sighing from it so that it becomes slack and – yes, relaxed.

Much better, approves Gest, and she thinks how much she likes this girl and how fortunate that is, for there is no one else in the world who could do what the Candy Girl is doing here and now. And at this moment the sun stretches its left hand into the workroom, flexing five long fingers over the ceiling, experimenting with stripes of light.

What is it, exactly, that the Candy Girl is doing here? Even she is not sure, not yet. This is not her usual kind of job, nor will it be for any longer than the allotted time. (Have you signed a contract? This is the Micro, who might one day make a good manager although at present he labours on building sites, striding shirtless against a blue sky with his fine torso on display and a wolf-whistle on his lips, ready to fall at the drop of a hat at the sight of a tight arse in a small tight mini-skirt. Hot-blooded and half Greek and full of general lust, he is nonetheless devoted to the Candy Girl, and so – Have you signed a contract for this job you are doing? he had asked, only last night.

Of course! The Candy Girl is indignant. She is not stupid, although she may have done stupid things in the past, and she stalks away but the Micro puts his hand up her skirt and pulls her back by the elastic on her knickers and makes her laugh and then makes her strip for him and sit astride him so they end up in bed, no more questions asked.)

Gest doesn't talk much when she works. Her face looks straight at the Candy Girl's face but it is as if she is seeing something else. Sometimes she simply sits and stares, and during these times her eyes are so black and direct that the Candy Girl feels as if she is being drawn in with a pencil. An ear there, a spike of hair there, and what about a nose in the middle of the face? If the Candy Girl got up off her stool unbidden, she might fall down because of Gest not having given her legs at that time, or leaving her with one foot missing.

Although Gest's eyes have the power of strong black lead, her hand holds no pencil. For today at least she just

11

sits and looks, sometimes turning and walking out onto the balcony to look at the trees and the top of the radio tower appearing over the rooftops opposite. There is a seriousness about her that stops the Candy Girl's usually ready tongue – but perhaps she has no tongue, or no mouth yet anyway, for it is possible Gest has not seen these into being.

There is a time, the Candy Girl speaks inside her mute mouthless head, *for speaking. And a time for keeping secrets.* She remembers her mother on her knees on the kitchen floor, in front of the oven. *There is a time to weep, and a time to laugh*, the mother is saying, putting her head in the oven and spraying the grease-covered walls vigorously with a brand of oven cleaner no longer made. *There is a time to break down and a time to build up*; and as the Candy Girl remembers these words her mother shrinks to the size of a pin and disappears right into the oven, leaving only a tiny cough behind her.

Gest has been saying something.

I'm sorry? The Candy Girl does speak now, although it is an effort to force out the words after being so long in her head.

It's time for lunch, says Gest again. And when they go to the kitchen it is quite different, for now Gest becomes chatty. She asks the Candy Girl about the Micro, when they met (two years ago) and how they met (at a party, on a boat).

On a boat? Gest looks intrigued.

A wedding party on a boat, confirms the Candy Girl. (She had been a bridesmaid at that wedding and had carried a passion for pink satin with her ever since.)

Why is he called the Micro? Gest is interested. I have a thing, she hesitates, about names and their appropriateness.

It's Greek for the small one. The Candy Girl blows

12

on her hot tea. He was the youngest of eight children, you see.

And is he, Gest looks curious, small?

Small? The Candy Girl laughs; she has heard the story so many times, how the Micro was the youngest son but grew like a bull, all shoulders and muscle, so that by the time he was eleven he was bigger than all his brothers and by the time he was twelve he could wrestle his father to the ground.

And now, as she tells this – as she thinks of the Micro, so big, so beautiful! – her insides swoop at the thought.

You love him. This is a statement from Gest, and she puts water in the kettle and flicks a lighter and puts it to the gas. She turns to look at the Candy Girl and at that moment she is a beautiful magician with purple flames leaping from her fingertips and around her hands. Shit! she says, pulling her hands out of the gas and the fire, but her face remains smooth and calm.

I— The Candy Girl catches her breath at Gest's beauty and bravery, and also at the number of answers she could give to this statement. But Gest's face is not only beautiful, it is as pale and oval and impenetrable as an egg and although the Candy Girl could tell any number of things – will tell – for now Gest remains sealed and so does the Candy Girl. There is a time, a time for cracking and a time for withholding, there is a time.

At any rate this is a satisfactory conversation to be having in a kitchen with more tea on the way and biscuits to come, and the Candy Girl feels fine. I do, she hurries to reassure, I do love him!

That's good, says Gest. She remains at the stove and for a second the light from the window seems to throw a shadow on the side of her neck. The Candy Girl looks again but Gest is moving now, opening a packet of biscuits and putting them on the table still in their plastic tray.

13

The Candy Girl reaches and crunches, a little guiltily. The Micro, she confides, tells me I have to watch my weight.

But you're not fat! Gest's black eyes search up and down the Candy Girl, like what they see. She is speaking the truth: the Candy Girl is not fat, is simply sturdy like a tree.

The other thing is, continues the Candy Girl, sometimes he drives me mad around the house.

And now Gest laughs out loud for what could be the first time in four days. She laughs and the sun reflects in the window of the building across the back courtyard, glints on the small earring in her right ear giving her a starry lobe. My ex-husband, she says, used to walk around the house with a toothbrush in his mouth.

Why did he do that? It is the Candy Girl's turn to be intrigued, not least because her employer has had a husband.

He thought it saved time, shrugs Gest. He would walk around fast with a toothbrush in his mouth doing all kinds of things, checking the water gauges, putting out the bottles, even sitting on the toilet. As if doing it all with a mouthful of foam saved time! And after all that, you know what? He still had to finish cleaning his teeth.

The Candy Girl gives an immense laugh. Biscuit crumbs fly from her lips, land on the table like pollen. Why— she splutters and sprays. Why do so few men die in their sleep?

Gest doesn't know. The Candy Girl takes a deep crumby breath.

Because, she says, not many men can do two things at once!

And now they both laugh, Gest and the Candy Girl. One of them (the Candy Girl) puts her head down on the table and her big shoulders shake, and the other one

(Gest) throws her head back showing a smooth white throat. Both laugh uproariously at the joke. As the Candy Girl raises her head, eyes streaming, to look at Gest, she is filled with familiarity. For a split sun-filled second she feels as if she has seen Gest before: long before, not in this phase of their existence, and not in this apartment. But she cannot think for she is busy laughing. This is a funny joke! And it will not be the last time that she and Gest will sit at this scratched table, with the veneer rising off the wooden base and the scorch marks made by hot pans and hot mugs of tea. But it is the first time they have discovered that they often laugh at the same things.

So they are off to a good start, then. Go now: leave them alone, leave them laughing in the kitchen over-looking the shared courtyard that is lined around with yellow dumpsters for household rubbish and green bins for recycling. Leave them and go out of their story, back into your own street. Eat a kebab or a pizza, catch a bus, go home for a while and listen back to what you have heard.

The spring

There is an apartment, which is hers for now. Its front windows are on a level with the tops of the trees, and its back windows face another apartment building. This is. This is all.

Day by day there is more green outside. Although it is still cold, so that the opening of a door can bring back the time when you were a child, being lifted from the car in the early creaking vinyl hours of the morning with the air biting your face through the rug wrapped around you – there is still that, but spring is here and the trees below the white windows are the first to tell you that. They are confident.

The strange thing is that, although dogs and children now run freely in the streets, although gutters have become mini water-races carrying balls of bright plastic wrappers, although the shopfronts are lowering their plastic protective hoods and opening their eyes again, there is already an odd sense of decay about the year. Spring has arrived, but it is already sick.

Imagine that one day a relative – an old aunt, say – arrives at your door. She has come for a visit, out of duty or a long-ago fondness for you, or merely from a desire to travel by night train, sleeping in a carriage that smells first of disinfectant, and later of warm odorous bodies, and later still of coffee and buttered croissants. The arrival of this aunt had been announced many weeks earlier but at that time you could not comprehend that this mooted distant Tuesday, existing only as a code on a paper ticket 08/05; TU 14 JU, would in fact become real. That you would see your aunt in the flesh, smell her powdery skin, hear the crackling of nylon stockings worn under a creased tweedy skirt. And that you would then remember how it used to be and what she used to represent, this aunt: your own visits to an unknown city, the weight of your small suitcase dragging red on your fingers, the climbing of folding steps into a plane where, soon, you would be looking down on the unreal landscape of clouds. *There is a highway! There are islands!* (Even then you sought similarities with the everyday and the familiar: even from the magical air, seeking out security.)

This was what your aunt used to mean to you: pillars of cloud, eardrums that cracked with excitement, and a

16

new waking every morning in a dim new light. But now it is the other way around. You are not arriving at her door, she is arriving at yours: anticipated and only recognisable because of that.

For she is lined now, stands low to the floor with her shoulders sloping southwards under a dull fluffed cardigan. She shuffles into your hallway and bends to remove her shoes, and you see how her toenails are thick and ribbed, and that the flesh under the nails is marked with leaking yellow stains.

In just such a way, the spring has arrived into Gest's street. Long awaited but it has not arrived with a bound and a leap; instead it has come crawling, crawling over the rooftops. And at night it settles heavily in the eaves of Gest's empty building, waiting resignedly for summer.

Often it lies in the courtyard at the back of Gest's building, lingering long into the evening. On the fifth day Gest opens her window to an air smelling of sweet decay. When she leans out and looks down, the smell rises six floors up to fill her nostrils, seeping from the swollen ill body of this unrecognisable spring.

Yes, before it had even appeared, the spring was dying.

Not a noticing man

He was not, begins Gest. He was not a noticing kind of person. And how do you miss someone who never sees you properly?

Go on, prompts the Candy Girl. She goes to the stove for coffee.

How do you miss a man who can wake every morning beside you in a room with an east-facing window so your face is lit with a glare, such a glare and a flare! that you might as well be on a B-grade movie set, with a slapdash gaffer caring nothing about lighting but only about the last broken cigarette in the pack in his back pocket, thinking nothing of lighting but only of the fuck he had had the night before in the middle of the night and still half asleep so he hardly remembered the coming and felt simply the emptied-out, something-missing feeling on his second waking?

And still, in spite of this glaring B-grade light, the man beside you does not see you?

How do you miss that person (Gest rests her pale face in her hand), that person who has looked at your face a thousand times before – several thousands of times – and still he does not see that you have a birthmark, small but noticeable, under your left ear? That left ear which has lain on a pillow beside his own ear for ten years, only two feet apart; that ear that has lain listening for the moment when he will turn towards you, a low growl in his throat like a dog, and then the almost inaudible rush of hot blood from his heart to his cock that stiffens and lifts the papery sheets with a small white sound.

He never noticed *that*? asks the Candy Girl, and she stares in an amazed way at the brown brush-mark of freckles under Gest's left ear. For she had noticed this two days earlier, even though it was only the fourth day of work and Gest had turned so quickly from the light that the mark might have been nothing more than a shadow cast by the brick towers of the hospital next door.

Yes, the Candy Girl is simply amazed. That anyone, let alone someone married to this near-perfect, beauti- fully blemished woman, could have failed to notice the birthmark on her neck for ten years! Not notice its attractiveness due to its uniqueness, the way it pulled the ear slightly down towards the collarbone, sucked the skin in and then expelled it slowly like heavy brown weed on the surface of a pond.

How does it make you feel? asks the Candy Girl, and she not only asks, she sings the question. *How does it make you feel?* because using the lyrics of a pop song often helps her to hide awkwardness.

How? The truth, now. It had made you lonely. Because of his inability to see you properly, you had stood at the mouth of a cave, feeling your feet go numb and your hands lose their warmth. You felt loneliness, cold and deep like snow, unable to be melted by ten years of being held close against someone's shoulder. Better by far to be held at arm's length than crushed against the shoulder, better to be pushed away, to be balanced precariously on the tips of the fingers. (Do it! Dare to look! Hold wife or husband loosely and lightly to avoid suffocation. Risk eyeburn, stare into their flare. Do it!)

And now Gest begins to laugh.

What? asks the Candy Girl, and she pours the coffee holding the pot high so the liquid arcs from the spout and spatters on the table: piss from the penis of a man who has never noticed his wife's blemishes, or noticed them too late. What is funny? she asks mildly. Are you laughing at me?

Not at you, says Gest. At this. She holds out a matchbox for the Candy Girl to see. I found it at the bottom of a carton last night, she says, looking at the box designed long ago with safety in mind. It is an over-sized box in bold reds and yellows, the colours of traffic lights and reassurance and the clear-cut games of childhood. And – *Strike away from wife and children*, it instructs.

The Candy Girl not only laughs at this, she roars. She

sits down and roars with laughter, elbows planted in the middle of the small black coins of coffee, currency of friendship and also of something more complicated, perhaps a shared guilt at drinking a beverage that requires children to work in cramped, hot conditions where the rising of the sun brings the promise of split fingertips and pounding heads, and its clanging fall sounds like the turn of a key in a shed door. (Gest has asked the Candy Girl if she would prefer tea but no, she has asked for coffee because of getting a headache if not taking in a good dose of caffeine every morning.) She, the Candy Girl, has never been locked away every night in a shed with twenty other workers, nor has she been forced to piss in a corner of the room that she sleeps in, but she has lived through things that might make the phrase *Strike away from wife and children* seem less funny.

Even so, in spite of the guilt and the suppressed memories – well, even so, the Candy Girl laughs along with Gest. She puts both hands to her head so her hair bursts out between her fingers and when she looks up her face is as red as the matchbox, as round and red as the end of a matchstick, and she seems to be all face, and her face seems to have jumped into the middle of the table, jostling aside the messy spattered cups and the woven-cane pot-stand with the burnt ring in its centre. Now the Candy Girl is simply one large red laughing face, able to see the funny side of a serious old-fashioned matchstick company directed by men who found it diffi-cult to kiss their wives on the lips, to open the soft lips of their wives' mouths and slide in a tongue, or to put a hand on their wives' shoulders as they stooped in front of sewing machines or stoves, but nonetheless remem-bered to prohibit the raising of a hand against womankind.

The Candy Girl has a rare and enviable quality, made rather than born: she has learnt how to laugh even when conflicted. It is not certain exactly where she learned how to do this, though it is possible that her sharp sense of perspective was gained at the moment when she looked at her best friend and companion, almost like a younger brother to her, lying in a dim hostel room with mucus streaming quietly from his nose, and saliva streaked with the bright frightening laughter of blood running from his mouth, while, outside, the dusty hills turned away suddenly to reassert their foreign status.

Gest does not know about this piece of the Candy Girl's past yet, but she has already noticed and appreciated how the Candy Girl can laugh, and for so long too! continuing for what might be a minute and a half before stopping, at which stage her face recedes to its usual size and colour, the freckles on her face sit back down again, and the table rearranges itself into some kind of order.

Is it worse to be not noticed, the Candy Girl asks then, or is it worse to be criticised? There is a real seriousness to her voice that has been put there by personal experience because once the Candy Girl had been told that her arse was like the trunk of a car. She had not known how to take this comment, had fielded it with an unusual awkwardness and returned a clumsy reply, but now in Gest's kitchen some years later her mind goes back to that day: a day in another city when motel blinds had been snapped up so that whisky could be poured, and the late afternoon had bounded into the room and onto the bed to sit down hard and heavy on the Candy Girl's substantial buttocks. She had never wanted to be skinny, her elder sister was the thinnest and most unhappy person she had ever known, and to tell the truth the Candy Girl had had more attention paid to her arse than most, for it possessed a fine thrust and curve to it especially when clad in the three-quarter satin pants she had favoured since she was twelve. But

21

this comment had been a backhander, thrown over a shoulder as the rim of the glass smacked against the mouth of the whisky bottle, and there had been a sour smell in the room as if all the meanness in the world had lain for years on that mattress and the room had been shut up for all that time, just waiting for the Chevrolet to pull up outside with the Candy Girl in the passenger seat.

The trunk of a car, she confides in Gest. That's what he said and I never saw him again. But afterwards I couldn't help thinking. She pauses. Was he right in saying that?

Not right at all, reassures Gest.

Oh I don't mean that! and the Candy Girl shifts on her chair, on her debated arse. I just meant his words. Don't you normally say 'the back of a bus'?

I think that's used about people's faces, says Gest. Not necessarily their arses.

And they laugh again.

Serious now, chides the Candy Girl. Is it worse to be criticised or is it worse to be ignored? But this is an impossible, an unanswerable, question for someone who has always been physically perfect apart from one small brown mark just below her left earlobe, not to mention someone who has been involved in the movie industry and has consequently suffered from quite the opposite problem: that is, an excess of attention from everyone but the person mattering most.

Gest throws the matchbox from hand to hand, tilts on her chair. I just wasn't noticed, she says lamely. She takes a match out of the box, strikes it into an afternoon so bright that the flare is barely visible. She squints through the white glaring room, through the glass panels in the kitchen door to the dim hallway beyond. On the other side of the hall there is an archway set into the wall, no more than a faint dark smear on the dim buttery white paint. She can see no further. She drinks her coffee. She is silent.

Ha ha ha ha

Ha ha ha. They had laughed uproariously in those days.

In fact, he paused, I think you laugh too much. I think you need to be stopped. Then he had taken hold of her laughing chin and kissed her so hard (to stop her laughing) that she felt his teeth clash against hers. She had liked this, his breath, his hands around the sinewy bands of her throat vibrating like cables after the great laughing roaring bulk of an elevator has gone past.

That was at a time when they had had no pillows. (Although Gest has little furniture now, at least she has somewhere to lay her head. And – *Wherever I lay my hat*, sings the Candy Girl, *that's my home*. Busily, she pulls up the top satin sheet to hide the semen stains from the night before when the Micro had pulled his large, beautiful, spraying cock out of her so as not to get her pregnant. *Wherever I lay my hat, that's my home.* So the Candy Girl sings and straightens the bed, and thinks about sex the previous night and then about riding her bike to the station to catch a train to get to another suburb where her employer's apartment waits six floors up, so sparse and empty that it reminds the Candy Girl of the living room at the rehab centre where she had once spent a burning shivering tear-drenched six weeks of her life.)

No, in the time after they were married, Gest and her

23

husband had not had a single pillow to their name, although they had thrown a large flamboyant wedding party in a red-velvet club in the middle of the city. No gifts! they had said, but of course people had brought gifts, for reasons less to do with generosity than with the fact that the bearers of the gifts wished to express their own personalities through their choice of the quirky and unusual so that then the entire champagne-fuelled room would laugh *ha ha ha* and the gift-givers would flush with the pleasure of public recognition. Because of the diverse nature of their friends, Gest and her husband had ended up with a spare room full of oddities that in no way went together: a box of vibrators and crotchless underwear (Gest's friends), a jumbo-size carton of golf balls (her husband's friends), two hundred cut-price blank video tapes (hers), a tartan car rug though they had no car (his), and so on. Not a single person had given them china or bed linen, although Gest's mother-in-law had contributed her second-best sewing machine so that shirts for her son could be made and not bought by Gest, who had never in her life managed to master the art of threading up a machine (where the fuck does the under-ground cotton come from? she would shout in rage and frustration. Your mother can just go and shove a camel through a fucking needle's eye!)

Money had not been the problem. They had had some savings at that time, more than enough to go into a low-ceilinged stuffy department store and buy two oblong foam pillows. But most of their money had been made by Gest, and her husband would not touch it, at first due to male pride and later because he chose to view it as unclean.

Hardly a Jewish attitude! she said to him, but much later, after they had pillows to burn but not so much cash to do the same. Dirty money, she had mocked –

but this was much later, during the grey autumn time when love had been driven underground and boards pulled over its resting place and hammered down with such phrases as: Shylock would despise you; your mother would disown you; and your brothers would shoot you at dawn for being riddled with scruples.

As is always the case when people have known each other for many years, there was a small centre of truth at the heart of these accusations, although their hard colourful coating was pure exaggeration. But now only two solid facts remained from those earlier laughing times:

(1) He would not spend her money on pillows, nor she spend his.
(2) And so they had none.

Didn't he, the Candy Girl hesitates. Didn't he notice you properly when he was, well, you know.

And here, do you notice that the Candy Girl looks slightly gauche? Even though normally she would talk about sex as casually as rent payments or the weather? But this particular query is different, more intimate than general, and made fraught because of the social implications. She and Gest are employee and employer after all, even if they have spent a good part of the previous afternoon laughing together.

And if you had no pillows, now the Candy Girl rushes on to cover her lapse, didn't you get a sore neck?

Had she? Gest is not sure. She remembers lying back afterwards, toe knee spine neck back of her head sharing the hard hurt of the mattress. Blood running into her brain because of the lack of pillows and the way the floor sloped slightly down towards the window. And her body flat as the blade of a knife, straight as a road-marking

25

down the middle of the bed, cutting it in two. And he hovering somewhere to the side of her, and the sound of water running in the gutters outside.

How are you feeling? he had said, and he said it with tenderness and listened to her answer carefully, speaking and listening with far more concentration than when he fucked her (they had fucked in those days with fierceness, paying no particular attention to each other's frailties, for at that time they had still held the conviction – her as well as him – that the human body was unbreakable).

I feel all right, she said; and she had. In fact that whole phase of their lives had been all right: living in their ground-floor apartment in the meatpacking district, with an old bed and no pillows.

We used clothes, Gest remembers now, to save our necks.

That was what they had done, living there in that meatpacking apartment, with its low windows at the back that had to be kept closed to keep out the flies. The spray of water sluicing the cobbles misted the glass so that, outside the bedroom, it always seemed to be raining while at the front of the house it was fine. After a while they had started using sweatpants and T-shirts to place under their heads. Folded into squares they made headrests of the type that the Japanese would have approved of. With several weeks of use they became low and flat, good for the neck and back.

The Micro will only sleep on feather, says the Candy Girl confidentially. There is something she likes, something daring and at the same time comforting, about discussing bedroom habits with a beautiful ex-movie-star who is paying her money to do a job.

After a while Gest and her husband had become quite used to resting their heads on low flat piles of cotton sewn cheaply in cavernous warehouses in Malaysia for what Gest hoped was a liveable wage. The clothes became slightly stained and oily from the natural excretions of their hair, and after many nights there grew up circular traces on the grey sweat cloth which never came off.

Sometimes Gest used these clothes for other means.

For instance – I can't go to bed, she would say.

Why not? her husband asked, his shoulders dropping, and as Gest saw this she felt the bones and sinew of his shoulders as if they were her own, felt their pressure bearing down on her body, pressing her into the bed.

Why not, he said. Why can't you come to bed? He walked disconsolately about the room, looked out onto the high wall around a yard stained with blood. Sometimes they heard the high-pressure hose through their early morning sleep: hissing, washing small bones down through the grates that led to the sewers that led to the sea.

I can't go to bed, Gest paused, because I'm wearing my pillow.

So you are, he said, looking at her grey cotton legs. And he laughed at this *ha ha ha*, in spite of his disappointment.

Ha ha ha ha. Gest walked in her grey sweatpants to the kitchen, away from the pressure in the bedroom and the expectation that she would do something she had never liked doing but had once done for money and was now expected to do for free. She walked away and made tea – jasmine tea, so the kitchen became a pale pink room. But when the window steamed up and she opened it, the blood smell rushed in and the fragrance of the tea wilted and died.

In spite of his shoulders that dropped and his expectations that fell like a guillotine blade on the back of her neck, she had loved her husband. He listened closely to her as she lay flat on their one sheet, a black fitted sheet that never did fit properly, straining at the corners and pulling along the edges like the skirt of a woman determined to believe she is the same dress size as ten years before. Sometimes it cracked when it was being put on the bed, that sheet, as if it was about to split, but they had no money to spare for sheets for the same reason that they had none to spend on pillows.

She lay there on the straining black sheet and he listened to her saying yes, she did think they should have a child, but not perhaps for a year or two. He loved her but he had somehow failed to notice the small brown patch below her left ear, whereas she loved him and watched him closely at all times. When she looked at his beseeching mouth (a child, just as soon as he had finished his training; a child would be perfect) she would observe the way his lip hitched up on the right side, showing a small glimpse of pointed teeth. And from the outside corner of his eyes tiny lines pointed the way to his ears: *this way for quality listening!*

What did she notice about his hair? That it looked better after love-making: more casual and rough, after all the work put into it fourteen hours earlier in front of the mirror had rubbed off on the black sheet, or on the grey makeshift pillows. His hair stood on end after love, making him look like a bird, beaky nose, enquiring, tilting, mouth opening wide: and did she love him, and would she like a baby?

Yes, she would, and she loved him more than she had thought possible, considering the chequered chessboard of her family history. But even then, in spite of his crooked mouth and strong nose and the deep brown eyes that looked right past her imperfections – even then there were disagreements and things she was expected to do, less inviting even than being taught how to thread up her mother-in-law's sewing machine to make cheap shirts for her husband. Things he expected her to do, while knowing that she didn't like them.

A blow job! she echoed, and she would make a face. It sounds like something you should wear protective clothing for and charge for by the hour! Fellatio! she would say, pretending to stick her finger down her throat. It sounds like the name of a character from a bad and ridiculous opera!

The fact remained: for her the act itself was no joke. Going down on him made her gag – she was six years old again and in the doctor's surgery, being told to open her mouth so they could see her tonsils, and the rough wooden stick holding down her tongue was being pushed too far back by an inept nurse. *Gag*! She would open her mouth and stick her head forward and cough, a hard dry cough, so the nurse pulled the stick out too fast grating the surface of her already rough dry tongue, and strands of saliva trailed embarrassingly through the air, spider webs in the wind, coming to land stickily on her chin.

This was how it was with him. Accepting his cock unwillingly between her lips, feeling him push himself further and further into her mouth until he reached the very entrance of her throat and –

Gag!

I don't like it, she said, lying on the black sheet, listening to the gates outside swing and whine in the wind. I don't like it, she said, hearing a child-whine in her voice. I won't.

Although you did it in your movies! (This was always his answer.) So many times in your movies, with other men!

But that was only pretending, for Christ's sake! Gest looked distant although the room was dark. That was only pretending to give head.

This was not true. Before she had married her husband and even afterwards, under the hot eyes of many lights, she had taken other men's cocks between her lips, had held other men's cocks in her mouth and sucked them, feeling the fish-tug of their flesh moving independently of her tongue, and afterwards she had turned her back on the cameras and spat repeatedly into a bucket.

For Christ's sake! she said, rolling away from him and hearing the tight sheet crack under her. You think directors want to have Aids suits slapped on them?

What do Aids suits (he tried to make light of it), what do Aids suits look like?

Like Armani (she was playing along), only more expensive. She hoped this would be the end of it, and she moved to the wall, laying her hands flat against it, pressing through the rough plaster and the wooden struts and the pink fibrous insulation, right through the brick to reach the cool black air on the other side. Now she could feel the chill on her wrists, and the tips of her fingers absorbed the death cry of cattle and the scream of the pigs as they sank onto the bricks flooded with crimson.

But his hands were warm and they reached for her, from behind. Come here! You must, because you are loved by me! And the rough ropes of his love hobbled her, tying her hands, pulling her back from the huge night outside into the small closed bedroom. I love you! He turned her around, pushed down on her shoulders, begging her. He pulled her head into his hot dark smell, her nose was crushed against his pubic hair.

She coughed, choked, hard and dry.

God yes, he said. Oh yes.

She gagged.

More to the right, he said, more to the base, yes, yes.

She did what he asked because, at that time, she had loved him. That was a phase only, a phase of life in which they had loved hard and fucked often, and had no pillows and only one sheet (he was finishing his studies and didn't like to use her money, even though he liked her to give him blow jobs).

When had this sparse, spartan, abattoir-apartment phase ended? Had they willed it to a close, pushing it out the door, slamming that door and choosing another one? There were no memories attached to the day when they had first bought pillows, but when they had the pillows were not of foam, they were of real feather of the sort demanded by the Micro who placed importance on such things because of growing up on a hot noisy island where most of the people he knew were more likely to work in a factory stuffing pillows with feathers than to use them on a bed.

The Micro is a sucker for luxury, says the Candy Girl. He's worked hard for it. She twirls the shiny blue bracelet on her wrist. A present, she says modestly.

A present, agrees Gest. She has started to repeat the Candy Girl's words, realizing that straight repetition can often be taken for an answer. Her tongue can do this job, the job of parroting, leaving her mind free to work.

Those times, those pillowless days steeped in darkness and saliva and blood – they had been all right. There had been only one sheet to smooth when you made the bed, and the taint of the abattoir had hung around your head, even after you had stepped on the bus and were being carried away into the day. Looking at your shoes, planted amongst many others, you couldn't shake the feeling that you had walked through rivers of gore and your hands felt unclean, smeary. But those times were all right, and all-rightness should not be underestimated.

Ha ha ha ha! She had fallen against the cold window, laughing, and felt the glass like a kiss on her cheek, and he had looked at her consideringly and told her she laughed too much. He had taken hold of her cold glass chin and almost shattered her teeth with his kiss.

Now it is Gest and the Candy Girl who laugh, holding their mouths open against the world, keeping it at bay by expelling small hot bursts of air. Times have not been easy for either of them, and still are not: but nonetheless they appreciate the comedy in this strange, sour, magnificent, unruly and tumbling festival that is life.

Ha ha ha. There they sit in the nearly empty room. Today Gest is behind an easel, sheets of white paper hanging like flimsy sails and blowing before her gusty laughs. Often they are at the smallest things, these laughs, and she could not always explain out loud what is funny, but this is irrelevant for the Candy Girl joins in anyway, in spite of having little idea what she is doing here in this apartment, in spite of the spring chill outside that makes her nipples stand out on her large dimpled breasts. No, the Candy Girl has no idea as to why, exactly, she has ended up sitting on a stool most days, often naked; and in the hours when she isn't sitting for Gest, she is kept busy cleaning chisels or sweeping up dust and debris from the floor. But she has been well trained – has had to train herself well – to make others as well as herself feel good. Choruses are easy, familiar refrains express emotions that everyone can identify with: *loneliness, lost love, false loves and true, red roses, moonlight, hitting the dusty trail.* And laughing has a similar appeal, bringing with it companionship even if real understanding has not yet been reached.

The Candy Girl has a great laugh, one that starts in her soft white-bread belly and rolls up through her throat and eventually eclipses her broad smile and thunders out into the room. (This, in spite of having seen too many bad things for her years! For she has seen the grinding poverty of the small leaning houses lined up along the

32

polluted Duoro river, and the crumpled page of the diary left behind by her best friend after the ambulance drivers had taken him away: pages that detailed in a scribble his Five-Year Plan which included the aim of Growing Up. And she has seen the spatters of blood mapping another, a different, country on the flat white front of the refrigerator: her father's last and desperate apology for never having amounted to much. But still the Candy Girl can laugh.)

The phase in that pillowless apartment, with its windows sprayed lightly with water as if with the tears of slaughtered animals, heads flung back, eyes rolling? At that time Gest and her husband had slept on a broken bed. They had found it out the back of the abattoir, lying beside metal drums that were blackened inside from the fiery burning of waste. The slats in the base of the bed were splintered like a ribcage, and several of them pointed jaggedly upwards so that Gest and her husband cut their hands as they carried the bed inside, quickly and surreptitiously, as if it was treasure that they had found instead of just so much of another man's junk. Quite obviously junk, too, for it had been there for four days before they got up the nerve to take it, and in that neighbourhood you could cough so that your eyes flew shut for a second and when you opened them again it was to find that, in that shutting, coughing second, something right in front of you had gone.

They had tried to mend the base of the bed but had run out of wood and patience, and so ever after the bed had two slats that remained broken and two that were missing. It was like a boxer knocked down but not out – it still did what it was supposed to do, could hold the weight of a mattress and had kept a voice of its own. They heard this voice in the minutes before love-making escalated to fucking, before they lost contact with all the world except each other, and their eyes became blind except to each other's eyes. In those minutes they heard the voice of the bed, a hollow groaning voice of metal and wood, weakened but determined not to give up.

They had fucked and fucked in that phase, there on the broken bed. Sometimes, hearing the frame groan under them and him groan on top, and her in the middle of the two like a sweating glossy whore, Gest had wanted the whole bed to splinter underneath them. To break down like the late days, like the tail end of a year when October gives way in a rush to November, and November tumbles into December, and the structure collapses under the weight, the remembered unbearable weight that is three hundred and sixty-five days and nights. Then they would lie quiet among the stolen matchwood, splintered and cut. The wood would pierce their bones and their skin so that for days afterwards they would be marked – marked by pilfered slatted bedroom furniture, and by love. He would listen and she would look, and at that stage they were all right.

Drawing the line

Chameleons are magicians. They are showy and are to be admired for this, but when it comes down to it they have only one trick. Zebras, on the other hand, look obvious but in fact they are far subtler. Zebras are masters at the art of disappearing; they can melt into shadows before another animal could even smell the musky scent of a lion downwind, blending into the sunlit stripes thrown around them by the arms of low gnarled trees. Simply by standing still, zebras can disappear faster than butter on a hotplate, can flee without moving their legs. Although they have been loudly patterned by nature, they have the gift of utter quietness. Such is the paradoxical nature of the zebra.

Because of this zebras are, by and large, survivors. Their expertise in camouflage (born, not made) could allow them to survive not only on sun-hardened plains but also in city streets.

Gest glances out of the high window, down to the cigarette-strewn grass verge between the tram tracks.

What are you looking for? the Candy Girl enquires. Are you expecting someone? (By now, though, after seven full days, the Candy Girl is beginning to realize that Gest expects no one but her.)

In the streets of a city such as this, with its lines thrown by lamp-posts and high brick chimneys and striped radio towers and pedestrian crossings, zebras could easily go unnoticed. They could dance through shadowed train stations lit through dusty glass roofs, criss-crossed with iron girders, in much the same way as the Candy Girl had some weeks earlier. Flamboyant yet able to go unnoticed: unless, that is, Gest was roaming on the same path, hungry, alert, restless.

There she is! There is the Candy Girl, Walkman on her head like the hundreds of people around her, face as blank as the next person's, eyebrows straight to match her straight striding arms, matching the person beside her and the person beside that. Loud floral pants, high platform shoes, bright hair in need of retouching. Colourful, yet retaining the ability to go unseen through the jungle-city. Such is the paradox of the urban zebra.

What's down there? The Candy Girl moves her bright

shiny haunches off the stool, stands (on her high blue velvet hooves), and peers towards the window.

I thought I saw an animal, Gest sounds vague. An animal between the tram tracks.

A dog, most likely, says the Candy Girl with a grimace. That's one thing about this neighbourhood, no offence, like wolves some of them.

There had been an instinctive recognition when Gest had glimpsed the Candy Girl's face, one of the herd, moving with the herd. She had not needed to think: she had been hunting for weeks without realizing it, and she had moved swiftly. So that before you knew it, it was a week on and here was the Candy Girl safely in captivity.

Now Gest frowns. She moves her stool a few feet further away from the Candy Girl.

I'm sorry. The Candy Girl makes a face, showing large square front teeth. Did I get too close?

There is one difficulty with zebras. Although one running zebra may look much like another, every zebra ever born has different markings. Each is unique. This is the secret paradox of the herd-loving, camouflage-melting, safety-in-numbers zebra.

Stand back. Gest must try to see the Candy Girl as a type, although of course she is not for how many other people are there whose overriding ambition is to run a uniform shop selling white clogs to pharmacists and blue aprons to butchers? Gest has singled the Candy Girl out from the teeming city specifically because of the way she looks (no one else has come close), but now she must step back from her prey, not so far as to allow escape but far enough for the possibility. One step, two, and more and more, until her back is pressed against the wall and the vivid unmistakable face in front of her blurs, becoming a suggestion only: the familiar outline of a nose, two eyes, a mouth. So far back that it could be the Candy Girl, or another person alto-gether.

Shall I move? The Candy Girl is anxious, anxious to please.

No, you're fine, says Gest. Again, she thinks she sees a movement out of the corner of her eye but when she turns, quickly, there is nothing there except the budded tops of the spring trees, which are completely still.

Stay where you are, she says, as the Candy Girl begins to shuffle. I'm the one that must move, to get a different angle on you.

She narrows her eyes so far that her lashes come right down over her vision, put feathery stripes over all she is looking at. Now the Candy Girl's face could belong to another. This is better. But there is sweat pouring down Gest's shoulder blades and her eyelids flicker with the effort.

To select the quarry for its uniqueness: then to transfer that unique quality to another. This is the paradox, the difficult paradox at the heart of Gest's task.

The mother-in-law

Gest's chosen profession is not only hard for her now, it has been hard in the past. But for her husband, it was excruciating. Her career path was chequered, extraordi-nary: and her husband, though utterly worthy of her love, was the most ordinary of men.

An artist! he had said, and his usually level voice became high with fright. Are you sure? Are you sure this is what you want to do?

Neither had he been happy with what she was doing for a job when they met. Name any man! he would say. Name a single man who would want his wife to be on show to the world.

Gest could have named a few, but then the world he spoke of was not the world of tabloid press and society paparazzi. No, when she met her Ordinary Man Gest was on show for the raincoat wearers of the world, for the enjoyment of flashers and backseat gropers and art-house aficionados. But once she had decided to closet herself away from all those eyes, to exchange her French-maid's aprons and crotchless knickers for blue overalls and workmanlike gloves, her husband had seemed even less happy than before.

It was not his fault, this worrying away like a terrier over people's occupations (and more specifically, the occupation of his wife). He loved Gest – that much was certain. In the beginning he loved her in spite of what she did, and later in spite of what she began to do. She had an undeniable talent for looking beautiful and doing so without clothes, but she also had a remarkable talent for art: this surfaced slowly and emerged triumphantly to launch her into a less lucrative but equally worrying world.

No, the Ordinary Man was not to blame for his obsessive interest in what people (and particularly his wife) did for a living. His mother had talked about career choices for as long as he had been able to listen, and he in turn talked a lot about his mother, at first because he was unaware he was doing it and later as a conscious ploy to make Gest realize. If mothers must work (he had nothing against this, for hadn't his own mother been widowed at an early age, and hadn't she worked to raise four boys and give them a good education?) – if mothers had to work, they could at least make their career choices sensible ones.

Do you think that art is a wise career choice for a mother? he asked. Most ironically, he had begun pleading when he saw Gest turning down suggestively titled contracts with sub-clauses denoting a minimum number of cleavage shots. Do you think art is a sensible choice for anyone, let alone a mother? he would say. And so on, and so on.

Even now Gest is still slightly puzzled about this.

Wouldn't you think, she says to the Candy Girl, that a man so obsessed with motherhood would be glad about my change in career? Wouldn't you think (she looks at the Candy Girl with retrospective surprise) that a man would be relieved to take an artist to his mother's sixtieth birthday party instead of a porn star?

Although the Candy Girl is young, when it comes to the intricate ways of men's thinking she is as old as the hills. He became obsessed with your porn career, she suggests, *because* of his mother.

Because of? In all her years of looking back, Gest has never seen things from this particular angle.

A lot of maternal fantasies, states the Candy Girl, are satisfied by porn movies. On this day, the ninth, she looks like a Madonna herself, though a dishevelled one. Her creamy face is still slightly flushed from some skirmish she has had on the journey here (an argument, a run-in, with a ticket collector who has been harassing her on the train: perhaps she should not wear such tight tops, perhaps she should report him? She had been talking about this before she had even stepped inside Gest's hallway).

He certainly seemed a little hung-up on his mother, agrees Gest. I don't know if there was anything Oedipal about it, though.

Oedipal? The Candy Girl looks vague, pulls her top down over her stomach and smoothes it over her breasts.

I don't know about Oedipal, she says, but I do know men. Men suppress.

But my husband was such a very *ordinary* man, objects Gest. So very straightforward.

And now the Candy Girl's breasts swell with knowledge. The straightforward ones, she says, are the most loyal to their mothers. They are Peter Pans, they never want to leave.

She has a point here: all men are sons, and always will be. There had been four boys in the Ordinary Man's family, and no girls to fill up the house with sharp corrective gossip and dismissive tosses of the head. The Ordinary Man's small mother had given birth to four lusty boys, all of whom remained at home until they were over twenty, growing tall and strong on their mother's kosher meatball recipe which could never be surpassed by another woman's. Four males born within four years of each other, living within four thin walls hung about with medical diagrams of the human foot. For, in between the mincing of meat and chopping of onions, the Ordinary Man's mother had been a chiropodist, the best in the region. Locals suffering from corns or painful ingrown toenails would force their boots onto their scarred swollen feet, put those burning feet down hard on the pedals, and drive long miles down tree-lined back roads to get to the stucco house fronted by a small sun-porch that masqueraded as a clinic on Wednesdays and Thursdays and even on those days smelled of meatballs and gravy.

Meatballs! exclaims the Candy Girl significantly. The Micro's thing is squid rings, deep fried in batter. But it's the same thing; it's mother worship.

At first the Ordinary Man had not realized how much he talked about his mother but once he had had this pointed out to him he saw that it not only annoyed Gest but also intrigued her. He would lie in bed and make

40

her laugh in a dark breathy way under the sheet by recounting various pieces of maternal wisdom, sayings that sounded like the beginning to a bad joke but that had, in the past, been taken seriously and even now proved often enough to be true.

There was, for instance, *Never trust a waiter with eyeglasses*. This was one piece of advice to have dropped from the pursed wrinkled lips of the Ordinary Man's mother, which had been picked up by her sons and passed along to their respective wives. As one of these wives (the least conventional in a respectable bunch of teachers and nurses) Gest had found, against her will, that this advice was worth listening to. Though it was likely that first the Ordinary Man and then Gest had become hyper-aware to the faults of short-sighted waiting staff, simply because of entering restaurants with these words ringing in their ears. *Never trust a man wearing eyeglasses to serve your food*! And whenever they had scoffed at this warning and disregarded it, several mistaken meals had followed: stringy tofu which turned out to be chicken, bills brought to their tap-water table on to which expensive bottles of sparkling water and champagne had been added, and so on. Soon Gest and the Ordinary Man found themselves lurking at the doors of restaurants, peering past framed menus hung in front windows to check out the levels of myopia within.

Eyeglasses, proclaimed the Ordinary Man disappoint-edly. They would leave, reluctantly, dragging their feet to find a restaurant that employed only those with twenty-twenty vision.

After some time, though, confides Gest to the Candy Girl, I began to wonder.

Wonder what? This is the sort of talk that brings the Candy Girl to life, roses opening in her cheeks, soft thick eyebrows raised in interest.

Why, Gest had started to wonder, did her husband's mother use the word 'eyeglasses' when no one else she knew did? And why, moreover, did her husband quote this old-fashioned word rather than paraphrasing his mother's saying to bring it in line with modern usage? These were not important questions in themselves, but the fact that Gest began to ask them meant something: the start of irritation. This was inevitable, of course, just as rain follows a drought and a dry period comes after a monsoon. But inevitability has never made things easier to cope with.

Both Gest and the Ordinary Man were reasonable people, not about to throw open their doors to a problem sent their way by a sharp nod from the Ordinary Man's mother. And so the new phase in their marriage, ushered in by a short thin woman in a faraway town, began gradually. It was a slow creeping rather than a deluge, but one day there it was, right in the middle of the bedroom floor, its importance able to be judged by the increasing sharpness of Gest's responses to the old-wifeish sayings of her once beautiful, downtrodden mother-in-law.

She was beautiful? The Candy Girl does not usually interrupt, but this fact is another brick in the wall of her beliefs about men's maternal fantasies.

She used to be, says Gest. Though hard work and widowhood wore her out and eventually drove her to the grave. But not (says Gest, with a laugh and a sigh) before she established a veritable Bible of family sayings. And I'm sure her four sons are saying them still.

The Ordinary Man had also sensed the start of irritation; he was not stupid, far from it, although at times it had suited Gest to think of him in this way. But he was not about to give up on his boyhood so easily and, perversely, he began to step up his quota of quotations.

42

He would start seemingly innocuous sentences with the words *As my mother always said*, and these beginnings were the crack in a shoe that rubs the flesh to a state of rawness.

My mother says! Gest repeats, groaning. It used to drive me crazy, I would block my ears and hum.

An infantile trick, the Ordinary Man had said about this, disapprovingly, even though his behaviour was equally infantile. For not only did he continue to quote motherly wisdom to an unwilling Gest, he began to walk around the house singing these gems under his breath, often through a mouthful of stripy white foam.

Always buy shoes half a size larger than your foot, he would hum, first making sure Gest was in earshot. This line was particularly annoying for how could Gest, experienced in porn and art only, argue with a chiropodist over such a thing? How to compete with a small invisible expert in shoe sizes who had laid down the law sternly and gravely with a biblical ring in her voice, as the steam rose off her unsurpassable meatballs?

Soon the beginning of the Ordinary Man's conversations – *As my mother said* – was an instant irritant. The name of the woman whose stringy loins had pushed the Ordinary Man out into the world: her name, to Gest, was soon like sweaty plastic casing strapped onto a bare foot. And the main content of her husband's conversation was, to Gest, as a red rag is to a bull.

Never sleep with the windows open, sings the Ordinary Man carelessly, *until four weeks after the last snow*. He glances over his shoulder to see if Gest is listening, sprays toothpaste over the coffee maker or the stereo, spits and rinses and repeats the charade. And Gest has no choice but to meet the challenge, sliding windows up all over the house only two days after a heavy snowfall, so that she wakes to freezing rooms and shivers her way to the bathroom in her underwear.

Yet still the Ordinary Man plays on, hammering out the lyrics of his childhood over and over again, though it is obvious that his life is becoming more difficult because of it. Because of the two women he loves, his one-time beautiful, possessive, autocratic mother and his beautiful diffident stubborn lover, who stand facing each other in opposite corners of the ring, he must simultaneously play the roaring crowd, the referee, the person who rings the bell to announce the next round, and the bell itself that gives forth a clarion cry: let the battle begin!

Oh it is hard for him (even Gest in her irritation sees that) and he himself knows that he should stop, but there is a stubbornness in him that prevents this. (He passes this stubbornness to their child, so that both have a mutinous determined need to finish whatever they are engaged in regardless of the consequences.) And so for many long months the Ordinary Man continues with his line *my mother says*, so the flesh of Gest's mind becomes rubbed in the same place for so long that it becomes raw and inflamed.

And what does your mother have to say about art? she shouts one day, when the debate over her profession begins again. What does she say about that?

The Ordinary Man looks desperate, defiant. (Of course his mother has, at one time, made a pronouncement on the position of art in society.) He looks over his shoulder as if seeking reassurance, takes a deep breath and then rattles off something about work, sustenance, and walnut cakes.

About *what*? The Candy Girl starts to laugh, though the story has her spellbound.

According to the folklore of that household, says Gest, there was one great cake of life. Work was the flour of the cake, the great sustainer. Entertainment was allowable in smaller quantities—

The flavouring, supplies the Candy Girl.

But art! says Gest. Art is nothing more than the sprinkle of walnuts on top.

A sprinkle of walnuts? The Candy Girl's laugh rolls out *ha ha ha* like a bowling ball in an alley.

An optional extra, affirms Gest, as at the end of a recipe. If desired, sprinkle with nuts. According to the maternal Bible of the Ordinary Man, I was about to enter an optional profession.

You became a walnut! Now the Candy Girl roars.

I became a walnut, instantly, says Gest. I fired my agent that night and no one was happy except myself.

What did the Mother-in-law think you did before that? asks the Candy Girl interestedly.

We told her I was an actress, says Gest, and she wanted to know Shakespeare or musicals. So we told her I acted in movies, and then she wanted to know if she could see my last film.

What did you do? The Candy Girl is on the point of exploding with laughter, but just in time she remembers that her main task today is to keep still as a stone, so she sits up and stiffens her spine and tries to stop her stomach from quivering.

What did I do? Gest thinks back. Stuff with pearl necklaces, eating strawberries off other actresses' breasts, that sort of thing. Tricks that men want to think all girls do when they're alone.

Now the Candy Girl does guffaw. First she leans against the wall, and then she has to stride around the room, gasping for breath, bent double.

What? says Gest, mildly. You asked me what I did.

I didn't mean what you did in your *movies*! The Candy Girl laughs. I meant what did you tell the Mother-in-law?

Oh! says Gest. She gives a laugh too, but just for a

second she has remembered the feeling of pearls being slipped between her legs, and she moves to the edge of her stool and holds on to the seat, puts her feet down on the floor to steady herself. It is not a bad thing, the cool hard milkiness of a string of pearls sliding between your thighs, being worked higher by the fingers of another actress you know and trust: yes, it is quite all right to know the intense dark, the complete secret dark of an oyster shell, and then the prising from rock and the sudden opening to daylight, the sharp and beautiful surrender.

What, she pauses, did you say again?

But when the Candy Girl repeats the question for the third time, the answer is gone. Gest has lost her grip, times have blurred and excuses have blended into others, and besides, the Ordinary Man's mother had died shortly after Gest's transition from porn princess to something other. Such a death had made things easier for the Ordinary Man and Gest, at least for a while: he had lost his embarrassment over her taking up a trivial occupation, and she was no longer regularly provoked and could therefore pretend that their love would last forever; and meanwhile the soothsaying, irritating, strong and steely mother lay rotting quietly under a gravestone in a small town with a stooping spire, her teeth fragmenting and falling into the back of her throat, her once-wagging fingers crumbling away to dust.

There was a relief in her passing, but it was the complicated relief that lies under the surface of many deaths. And there was, too, a sense of guilt. Guilt about stories never asked for and tragedies not listened to, lying too late under six feet of heavy clay. It was undeniable that, crushed under that gravestone, were large measures of strength and integrity, not to mention wartime secrets kept close in the heart of a small indomitable Jewish woman who had lost her husband and had never told how.

As for the gravestone itself, it was carved out with tasteless gold italics and required regular scrubbing with a wire brush to keep away the moss. The Ordinary Man took it upon himself to do this, driving every second Saturday for two hours, rain or shine, to the village cemetary. When he left, he had asked Gest to do this for him, but she had not driven that way for some time now. Today, talking about it with the Candy Girl, the guilt grows again and she pushes it away. No! There is no possible way she can think about these things for longer than a jumbled second – something about pearls and the dark pubic hair of an actress, something about emaciated hips, sunken chests, stories suspected and never told, and warts on the feet.

And what about the guilt felt over not taking more interest in the past of a small stooping woman, a chiropodist and sage who had forged through life slaying short-sighted waiters with her sharp tongue and helping cripples to walk again? Gest cannot afford to add to the guilt she already carries, that lies on her chest at night and sucks the breath from her in the way that, in fearsome folklore, cats do with babies. She shakes her head, crams it all back to where it came from, and looks sternly at the Candy Girl.

Let's work, she says.

Song titles

And who could say what the Candy Girl's real job was? To all extents she appears in the apartment every morning like the *right tool for the job*: useful, essential, like a hammer or a drill or a pack of long sturdy nails with which it might be possible to create something new out of this old life. A tool, a connector, and Gest's right-hand woman: but presumably this is not what she has been put on this earth to do.

According to the contract drawn up in Gest's firm blue hand, this job will last fifty days. Perhaps forty-nine if Gest works faster than expected, or fifty-one if she drags the chain. But once the Candy Girl has jumped down six flights of stairs, step by thudding step, has thundered across six landings and onto the black-tiled floor of the entrance hall for the last time, once the heavy double doors to the building have fallen closed behind her, once the street has taken her back into its hot dry mouth, then these days might become little or nothing to the Candy Girl. Perhaps the time spent in Gest's high apartment will sink fast into the lime-green marshy past, along with all the other odd jobs the Candy Girl has done in her short but lengthy life. The haircutting and the babysitting, the drug dealing and bar tending, and the exercising of racehorses down a wet shining beach. Her memories of Gest may expel a few bubbles every now and then, *blup blup*, but after a while they will disappear without a trace.

Perhaps.

But what does the Candy Girl really want to do, once the fifty days are over and she has finished here?

My main aim – she stops. My main *commercial* aim, she corrects herself, is to reopen the store, and I will run it like it's never been run before!

Like it's never been run before, repeats Gest automatically, but the zeal in the Candy Girl's voice inspires respect. The store in question is a uniform store once owned by the Micro's sister and now temporarily closed; and Gest has no doubt that the Candy Girl will make a go of it, even in a neighbourhood where it is not considered necessary to wear a pink tunic and a white cap when serving ice cream: might even be considered pretentious to sell such things, an offence to the tough tradition of the street, punishable by broken windows and human shit on the doorstep every second morning.

But this is only one side of me, stresses the Candy Girl. She runs a finger down the middle of her body, dividing left side from right, and commercial from the other. In a way it's a matter of family duty, she says.

The Micro's beautiful raven-haired sister had tried to make a success of herself in this city, selling Working Style to the workers: but months after the grand opening of the shop they were still resisting her neat window displays: the long white trousers matched with natty checked waistcoats, flanked by carefully polished chainsaws and gleaming soup ladles. They had resisted, too, her charm and politeness, taking one look at her shop's tidy, carpeted interior and grunting in scorn. And so the Micro's oldest and most beautiful sister had succumbed to depression, had bent under the grey skies of a climate tending towards humidity rather than heat. After a while she had stopped opening the doors of the shop each day, and one morning she had been found hunched under the counter with a crucifix held to her fine breasts and tears streaming down her perfect face, and her glossy hair all matted up with salt and fear. And so the Micro's

49

sister had been taken back to the island where once she had ruled supreme, princess to pauper and then back again; and the shop had remained shut up for some months now, the pink tulips in the garden display turning to reeking brown pulp and the windows covered in graffiti.

I will rescue it, says the Candy Girl stoutly. The people must be educated (sounding like Mao). They must be taught! (with the missionary's ring of authority in her cry). Taught to look the part, that is what they need!

On hearing these words the Micro, who had been looking at other women for a while now, had been moved. Moved by his girlfriend's loud and shining voice, he had come over to her and given her a smacking kiss on the cheek, and promised the moon and stars to her in that moment. When you're ready to open, he pledged, I'll build you a new counter. Once your fifty-day job has finished, I'll build you some shelves.

Commerce, repeats the Candy Girl now, is only one side of me though.

What is the other? queries Gest.

Art is the other! says the Candy Girl. Surely it is the same for you? But so certain of this is she that she hardly expects an answer.

The work I do here is not for money, agrees Gest, although it will earn some. It is my heart work, there is no question about that.

Exactly. The Candy Girl speaks with satisfaction, though she hears only the word *heart*. This is hardly surprising, considering what her own passion is; the word 'heart' has been used more than any other in the history of song, and *this* is the Candy Girl's real job, this is what she longs to do every minute of the day, with a hunger that leaves her only when she is fully absorbed in the present, making love with the Micro or taking the first mouthful of steak smothered with thick peppery barbeque sauce.

The Candy Girl is a singer. Her art side, her heart side? It exists to sing.

To her, with many years of karaoke experience under her belt and her shoes hot from treading the boards of downtown bars, singing is the most important thing in the world. Just watch her fix her carefully typed lists to Gest's floor with tape, see her gyrate her large hips in the middle of the kitchen as the kettle starts to creak and groan over the flame, complaining about having to work while the others in that room are having a break.

At such moments, in such breaks, the Candy Girl opens her mouth ready for song, lets her lower lip fall, and sheds her cardigan as deliberately and carelessly as the magnolia tree sheds its heavy petals. Strong wiry wool spliced, spiced up, with metallic gold: this is her cardigan, and it falls onto the linoleum floor and the Candy Girl hardly notices for she is away now on one of her songs, her mind in a hushed recording booth in New York or a swimming smoky green bar in Kyoto, although her eyes remain firmly fixed on the here and now, on the written words of her songs that lie like a rope under her hands, leading her across the uncertain waters of a memory still cluttered with small bobbing anxieties. Anxieties such as how she had splashed out on Planters Punches last night when she should have ordered beer, for instance; or how her arse had been pinched yet again by the ticket inspector on the way to work and how she had not been totally offended, not *totally*, although she had scowled and sworn in an outraged way so that people had looked up from under their headphones and out over their newspapers, and then she had changed carriages ostentatiously at the next stop but mainly, to tell the truth, because she liked the smell of sausages being fried on that platform, the smell of cracking skins and spewing flesh being turned by the cheerful black teenager with sight in only one eye who might have been sixty years old considering his stoicism in the face of stigmatism, and also because all the other stations from there on smelt the same (piss, dank concrete, dog, and dog shit) and so her carriage change was not strictly or even principally because of an objection to the ticket inspector's firm and friendly crab-thumb closing in on her dimpled satin buttocks – simply because of these things, the cluttered mind-journey, the years of knowing what she ought to feel while not quite feeling that thing, because of the years of practising how to live or at least survive in a city, the Candy Girl has to tape her list to the floor in plain black and white and train her eye on the title of what she is singing because God knows, when the time comes to perform there will be worse distractions than ticket inspectors and the faint ache between her legs, the small dampness growing at the touch of an unknown finger and thumb, yes, when the time for performing her songs happens for real in a downtown bar there will be no reluctant lukewarm kettles and no known face in front of her, but instead beer bottles with brown open mouths, and people jeering or ogling or talking over her, and the doors to the cold street opening and closing, opening and closing, in the middle of So Far Away from You.

Here they are, her twenty songs, laid out in the middle of Gest's kitchen floor:

1. Walk On By
2. Hungry Heart
3. Here Comes the Rain Again
4. Who's Gonna Drive you Home
5. Ocean Tides

Oh, but she was a hotstepper, the Candy Girl! She *was* a hotstepper, although she might not look it today, wearing her T-shirt that is slightly stained under the arms and her third-best pair of leggings. But as she sings in Gest's kitchen the feeling grows and grows: that if she left the room now and stepped out the door, suddenly she would become as wild as an orchid, violet bright and unreliant on any surrounding domestic foliage; she would shed the baggy socks and the leg warmers before reaching the bottom of the stairs, would leave them lying carelessly somewhere on the first floor landing, and by the time she burst out onto the hot street she would once again be the person she had been in Portugal (this her most exotic and edgy time, the days when she had travelled through that long hot country with her drug-addicted boy-companion, her mind wide, loose, untethered to reality, and her body still unconscious enough to revel in the quick sharp shocks it received and then to take the hours lying semi-comatose in the salty sun as simple recovery time).

When we were young! crooned the Candy Girl, injecting every ounce of yearning into her voice, projecting herself into a future of grizzled greyness and a wisdom achieved by age alone. And Gest? Gest, who is not so old yet no longer as young as the Candy Girl? What is she thinking of as she watches her twenty-year-old employee spending her tea break rendering the songs of an aging rocker with the utmost sincerity?

How does it feel? (*sha na na na*) sings the Candy Girl tenderly, her cup of tea sitting unnoticed on the table beside her, breathing steam into the kitchen, turning the air to an even more sultry state.

How does it feel? It feels sharp, it feels loving, it feels envious. This last is the truth: Gest sits with her elbows resting on the kitchen table and she envies the Candy Girl terribly, even as she sees the marks running in and out of the Candy Girl's large sturdy arms, making it look as if she has, at some stage, lain down in front of a sewing machine at a quilting session in a Northern state where the winters are long and the task of supplying every room of the house with several layers of goose-down seems a permissible excuse for living.

Why envy? Because, because – the Candy Girl can simply walk out of here, letting the door fall *clunk* behind her, letting the apartment close, seal up at her back. She can step over the grating by the front door that wafts the smell of warm lettuce and warm laundry up into the street, and then she can merge right into that street, with no one beside her to point and stare. No one to judge, no one to consider whether she is doing the right thing with her life, whether she has wasted time, or to limit the time that is left to her. And it is likely that the Candy Girl would not allow this, anyway; she has a certainty to her that is shouted aloud in the swinging of her track-marked arms and the stride of her legs.

Walk on by on the other side, sings the Candy Girl without meaning it at all. For hadn't she picked her father up many times off the floor as he lay there comatose from alcohol after beating them black and blue; and hadn't she wiped the blood, so many times, off his own lip while adding a few drops of her own to the mess (from her own cut lip, her own split eyebrow) and dragged him to bed knowing that he would remember nothing – not the beatings, nor the help – in the shamefaced, hungover, grey morning?

Do you see, in the titles selected by the Candy Girl, how many refer to the breaking of hearts? Do you notice how many of these songs turn to the ocean or the sky for salvation, how many seek extinction in the bright hiss of fire or the long quiet embrace of the sea? The Candy Girl has done it. Through sheer willpower she has managed to leave a part of her behind; she is able to enter a world where colours are primary, and songs can solve problems, and if momentarily doubtful she will simply put her shoulders back and front up to her fears, love her man and her fellow human beings and come to this apartment every day with a good grace, because this – her coming – has been agreed upon, although meaning that for a short while she must put her other plans on hold. Perhaps she will forget this short enclosed time, perhaps she will not. But for the time being she is here, body and soul.

Yes, the Candy Girl. She's all right.

The settler's wife

The Candy Girl sees no reason not to have children, although she has spent long days crouched in the small back rooms of damp apartments, dark and made darker by blankets thumb-tacked to the window frames, and she has watched people lighting candles for the purpose of turning innocent substances into dangerous ones. Cough mixture, vinegar, aspirin: all heated through with a flame, ready to be shot into the Candy Girl's sturdy blue veins so her creamy face becomes flushed with desire and her eyes are flooded with forgetfulness.

In spite of this, the Candy Girl sees no reason not to have children. Famine, disease, trains laden with nuclear waste thundering through snow-covered forests: these things do not deter her. On the contrary, they fill her with a stubborn determination. Someone has to counteract the rot, she says.

Consider the strange inversion of weather patterns, the way the world seems to be reinventing itself in a malevolent bid for our wandering attention. In a single second, in the moment when we turn our casual careless backs, we can witness a storm smashing the sky into a black and purple bruise; when we turn back it is to find snow falling on our midsummer heads, and a winter wind kissing our bare arms with a cold and lethal breath. But—

It's never too late to turn back the clock, says the Candy Girl.

And what of the future, when the ice floes in Antarctica give up at last, let go of each other's hands and drift apart so that loneliness floods the world? The Candy Girl has read of this possibility and because of this asserts the importance of family. When it is reported that a tidal wave has swept away the entire coastal population of a small sea-faring nation—

Even so, says the Candy Girl stubbornly, life goes on.

She would be the perfect settler's wife, this Girl. Turn the clock back, since she is adamant that this is possible. Let the glass mouth of the watch hang slackly open, let its hands catch the wind and swing loosely like those of a compass. Let them twirl and spin, carrying the Candy Girl with them to a time one hundred years ago. Watch her now: her lime green aerobics tights and pale pink lace top have been exchanged for a beige-print dress that sweeps the ground when she walks, and her striped hair is mouse-brown.

She walks with a sway so the dress sways behind her in the mud; she is carrying one child on her right hip and another is resting in her belly. Around her are the shouting voices of men and boys; there is the creak of rope and the slap of waves on the rounded wooden sides of a boat. And what is the Candy Girl carrying in her hand, so that her left shoulder burns and her elbow cracks like a mast in a high wind?

The gangplank is rising before her, the curve of her future consists of gaping wooden planks lashed together by rope and soaked with salt water. As she looks down she sees the knee of her firstborn, smooth, pale: his small and dangling foot.

(I once worked for a babysitting agency when I was a teenager, she tells Gest earnestly. I was good with the children.)

She – this Candy Girl, this settler's wife – takes a step. She hitches her son higher on her right hip and sees the sullen grey sea tilting far below, through the gaps between her shoes. The leather strap of a piano accordion carves a welted path into the palm of her left hand.

Later she will sing to her small son as he lies wide-eyed, dark-eyed, in the pitching dark. Her husband is playing cards somewhere in the bowels of the ship, in a room lit to fever pitch by the burn of whisky and the prospect of the journey ahead and the low white breasts of the whore on his knee, intended not for him but for the men to either side of him who have no wife or child, and no newborn on the way.

Sleep comes falling, sings the Candy Girl. She plays a few low notes on the accordion, feels its wheezing breath against her body and the baby stirring inside. *Slap slap*: this is the water on the side of the boat, rising to the porthole, looking into the cabin; inside, a young mother with dull brown hair and a determined chin waits for her husband to finish his last life and begin a new one.

Will he return, this husband? Will he come back that night to the low cramped cabin where his family waits? To be sure he does: his wife has a certainty that draws loyalty from him. When he opens the door, his clothes reeking of whisky and smoke, it is only an instant before his face changes. He sees his son's cheek gleaming in the light from the tiny round window. Sleeping now?

(I was not so responsible in those days, says the Candy Girl to Gest, though I was good with the children. I was still a child myself, she confesses, in those agency days.)

The husband strips off his overshirt, throws his boots to the floor, but leaves on his undershirt, his braces and his trousers. This is the first night of many and who knows what could happen in the pitching of the small hours, as his family sleeps around him, breathing into the dark.

Sleep now my darling, my little dove, sings the Candy Girl in a small whispery voice, lying there in her petticoat on the raw brown blanket. She is almost asleep herself but will go on singing until the baby lies still inside her, and her son's eyelashes have stopped flickering, and her husband's rough chin is resting on her breast.

Leave her there, leave her facing a new life a century ago. Return to the girl who sings on trains rather than boats, who strides through city streets swearing at the drunks and giving change to the homeless: the girl with boldness in her heart and optimism in her eyes. The world may be speeding up around her – it is a wild technicolour blur, it is shopping malls pumping out perfume and music, it is mountains breathing fire and guns spitting bullets into crowded schoolyards. But at the centre of it, she remains the same.

Family is the way, she says decidedly. I will try my best when the time is right.

Gest already knows what the Candy Girl has told her: knows that once, some years ago, the Candy Girl had worked for a childminding agency. Knows the name of the agency, and where it was situated, and how successful it was around the time when the Candy Girl had been fired for using drugs on the job and was replaced by a dime-a-dozen girl with no dependency problems and no second thoughts about leaving a child to cry in a dark room on the first night of his life that his parents have left him.

When the Candy Girl tells her that she had once been employed in this way, Gest contemplates saying: *I know you were*. But even as she considers it the possibility is sinking fast, leaving nothing but a tiny whirlpool on the surface of the conversation: an almost imperceptible roughness, a hollow, a dip, which smoothes itself out in a second and is gone.

The art of avoidance

The spring may be ill, it may be breathing its last breaths over the wide grey-green city, but it has not been softened by its illness. The air is still biting in the mornings when the Candy Girl arrives, and the same in the evenings after her departure. Yet in spite of the cold a window in the apartment building across the courtyard stands wide open, late into the night.

Gest is lent boldness by this. On the night of the eleventh day she also leaves her window open and when she walks into her kitchen on the twelfth morning there is a chill to the floor: a deep absorption of cold like the skin of someone who has swum too long in a dark glacial lake. But at least the dust, she realizes, has gone.

Aren't you cold? This is the Candy Girl, arriving like a bright red leaf blowing in from a bleak street. It's colder in here than it is outside! And she pulls her cardigan around her shoulders, remembering the station whistling with wind.

Cold? echoes Gest, who is wearing a woollen hat pulled down over her long dark hair and has her hands wrapped around a coffee cup. No, I'm not cold. Then, because the Candy Girl is worth making explanations to, she amends her statement. I wanted to air the place out, she says. It feels dry in here, empty; it feels like a tomb.

It does. The dustiness in the building has turned the air in the stairwell into something difficult to climb through, should you happen to venture down to the ground floor to collect your mail from the entrance hall. Nothing has come; no letter. But even without anything weighing down your hand, simply getting back up the stairwell is an effort because of the gathering, solidifying dust that presses down on your shoulders and head. And when you get to your door you find that the mass has risen with you, reaching your landing before you have; and when you step over the threshold of what is supposed to be your home you find that, in the time you were gone looking for mail which has not arrived, your house has been possessed. Your hallway is full of a white chalky substance and you cough, cough and think about turning to the unkind, the fickle spring in the hopes that its icy night-breath will help you.

A tomb! This description is something the Candy Girl can identify with. For, if she pauses on the way up to Gest's apartment to catch her breath or tighten the strap on her shoe, she quickly becomes scared. Such a silence behind the closed doors around her! Such a silence, pressing its ear to the inside of one of those doors, listening for her intruding steps. And if she lingers too long (she fears) the door will fall out towards her, will land at her feet *smash!* and when she looks up she will see the deadly silence running right at her like a bull from a gate, trampling her until she lies gored on the landing, bleeding from her mouth, felled in an arc of smashed teeth and small splintered parts of her own body, unable to get up or walk or say a word, which is exactly what this running bullish silence has intended. And then what hope will she have of continuing on up the stairs and getting to her job on time?

So hurry on, past the doors holding back their secret pasts. Hurry past the entrances to many separate and sealed tombs. Hurry before they get you: it is this and not the seventy-two stairs that makes the Candy Girl arrive a little out of breath at Gest's door.

But I might close the window tonight, says Gest

expressionlessly. Her eyebrows are low, pushed into straight lines by the woollen hat, and she gives a dry cough in anticipation of the dust returning. Although, she says, the weather is supposed to clear. And when she looks across the courtyard – yes! the sky is already cracking itself into pieces, marking out the divisions with long lime-green stripes.

The Candy Girl lightens at the lighter tone in Gest's voice. She becomes bolder; she is curious this morning. Don't you mind being here by yourself? she asks. She twirls over to the kitchen window and bends right out as if she is kissing the Blarney Stone. Her head disappears completely and now only the Candy Girl's body remains – large trim thighs, large satin arse, an exposed expanse of white lower back and a stretched stripy torso, all about to plummet out the window into the six-storey void.

Mind! says Gest, and for once she is not simply repeating what has come before. For the window sill crumbles under the Candy Girl's ribs, and flakes of paint fall – inside the kitchen rather than out – but it is enough, it is a warning.

Mind! she says again. Swiftly, she goes to the window and pulls at the Candy Girl's striped shoulders.

There are five floors below you! The Candy Girl rears back into the kitchen, her face slightly red from a rush of blood to the head. Five floors of windows and not a neighbour to be seen! There is a surprising amount of disapproval in the Candy Girl's voice, considering she has just done something potentially dangerous herself.

What if you had an accident? she says reprovingly. Or what, she pauses, what about fire?

Fire? The kettle screams and Gest's response is covered over in a cloud of noise and steam. She grasps the handle of the kettle, pulls it off the gas so that its scream falls away into silence.

This city, she shrugs, is not designed for fire. There is no way you could escape, from this building or any other.

The Candy Girl looks thoughtful. It is true, what Gest says; although this is a big city it is not yet a high-rise one, but even so there are apartment buildings like this one which raise their heads ten or twelve floors to the sky, and hardly a fire escape to be seen. You're right, she says. (She has never considered this before.)

Gest, on the other hand, has been married to a man practised in thinking ahead. *What if?* had been a favourite phrase of the Ordinary Man's, and there had been conversations late into the night about possible disaster zones and civil crises. Maps had been pored over, cities built on fault lines had been pointed out as places where residents were trained to get under doorways and phonebooks held reams of advice but where nonetheless most buildings still sat on foundations of faith.

Well, what about – begins the Candy Girl.

What about Antigua? interrupts Gest. What about hurricanes, and beach bars with roofs of straw and walls of air facing winds so big that they could flatten seven settlements in seven minutes; what about that for a dangerous situation?

Antigua? echoes the Candy Girl uncomprehendingly. I don't know much about that, she says. In fact, she doesn't even know exactly where Antigua is, although she has done some travelling in her time, has seen backstreets riddled with TV aerials and makeshift washing lines, and has watched locals sitting on ragged balconies fiddling with stolen radios, trying to tune in to the latest football scores.

What if you cut your hand off with a carving knife? she counters stoutly.

Look, says Gest. There is a shortness in her voice. Look, she says, and the word cuts a path right through

63

the steamy kitchen to the door. I don't mind being here by myself, I chose it.

I'm surprised that you're allowed, says the Candy Girl. Does she purse her lips because her tea is so hot that, at first, she can only sip the top layer of fragrant air?

I'm surprised, she says, that you're allowed to stay in an untenanted building. She likes the word untenanted, it makes her feel wise and as if, for once, she will be able to ride her bike to the station and wheel it onto the train and not think (for once) that people are probably looking at her and wondering why it is that, with a figure like hers, she does not wear a longer top or a forgiving skirt instead of clinging satin tights. There she will stand at the end of an empty swaying carriage (*untenanted*) looking at but not seeing the map of spaghetti train-lines on the wall that includes her own pink line, which will carry her and her bicycle all the way to the end of her street. And then – at the end of her pink line, her line – she will saunter to her own gate and into the cracked hallway of her apartment block with its curry smells lurking in the corners and the new girl's washing machine shaking the first floor almost to pieces, and then her key in the door, and then she is going straight to the Micro even though he is watching the match between France and some non-starter, and she will be able to say, *Take me now!* (sitting astride him), and he will be made to want her, straight away, so that instead of pushing her off him and saying, *Not now you tart!* (though in a loving kind of way) he will pull her top off and then her bra and with one last look over her shoulder will mute the TV and put his sucking mouth hard over her left nipple and throw her back on the sofa and then, and then—! This, all this! Simply because of the word untenanted.

But Gest is speaking.

I'm only allowed to stay for a while, she is saying. She

takes a sip of tea too, but she bends her face down to the cup rather than lifting it to her mouth, as if the greying china is too heavy for her.

The steam swirls, parts, hangs around in wisps by the window.

And where will you go then? breathes the Candy Girl. What then?

Gest looks up. Then, she says, the building will be demolished.

There is a sudden brightening in the kitchen, a lifting of the atmosphere, as if the heavy slumping spring has been grabbed by the scruff of its neck and lifted right off the roof of that condemned building, and the humidity outside has been sucked away from its walls *whoosh* leaving white bright airless space. They look at each other, Gest and the Candy Girl, and as they put their cups down with a clatter they hear the sound of machines moving in with vast circular track-wheels, and then the ball is swinging between them and it smashes and smashes again into the side wall of the kitchen, and they can no longer see each other because of the vast annihilating clouds of dust and the rhythmic punches, longed for, feared, longed for, feared, and so on until the floor begins to cave in under the caving walls.

Gest waits for the chaos to subside before she speaks. Then –

I will go first, she says, and then the building will go.

The Candy Girl takes a gulp: is it the hot tea or excitement that makes her eyes water? What will be built here after that? she asks. Maybe a mall!

Maybe. Gest smiles.

It could be the making of this area, enthuses the Candy Girl.

It is true, the area in which Gest lives is not a good area of town – not bad, but still one where you would think twice before walking through a park in the eye-adjusting time before night, when the men who have been drinking on the benches all day start to kick the cans away from around their feet and the dogs become infected with the falling dark and run wild, and the trees gap like teeth against the street lights. In the days when she, Gest, used to go out more often she would pass a couple on the bridge near the station, a man and a woman who begged anyone passing for a bottle of meths (every day this had happened, when Gest went out) – begging for raw burning fluid to put on the recent raw stump of the man's hand, and also to drink; and for all Gest knew they were there still, that couple, with their purple liquid and purpling flesh, but she had not walked that way for many days now. Yet still, there were advantages to this area – the huge open sweep of the railway tracks, for instance, making you hungry for change, making you yearn for a breakfast eaten in one of those roadside places with plastic tablecloths and a waitress who would only ever see you once in her lifetime because you were constantly moving on.

And also, the view of the city centre such as there was one, with the radio tower blinking warnings to the planes to *keep away*, and the jumbled motley collection of glass-sided buildings which were in no way high rises, didn't come close, for although this was a big city it was not one that had given in to the temptations of super-malls or concrete monoliths ruled by ruthless business directors or vast underground walkways lined with shops selling suitcases and scarves. It was a big city but still a tentative one, and it had a hidden heart: secret inner courtyards where the weak spring could lay its head, and back alleys where the cats scratched and fought.

But you like this neighbourhood, don't you, says the Candy Girl. Although she phrases this as a statement it is more of a question, for she does not really know where Gest has been living before, before she had approached the Candy Girl on the bridge, stopping her on her way to the greengrocers to buy some dark blue plums, and asking her to do a certain job for a set length of time.

Like? says Gest. She feels a new guilt growing inside her, a guilt like a dragging blood-pain at the way she has taken to repeating words rather than replying. How few people realize this! And so she has become like a criminal who, having gotten away with something once, finds it is possible to repeatedly carry out the crime and go unnoticed every time. *Like*, she says again.

Sure enough, strangely, the Candy Girl is satisfied by this. And your old apartment, she goes on, does your husband still live there? This is as close as she has ever come to asking about the past, and she twiddles the fringe on the teapot warmer.

No, says Gest, he has gone to another country. (And this is as close as Gest has come, today and for many days, to giving a proper answer.)

Even so, the Candy Girl reverts, you shouldn't be up here on your own.

They finish their tea then, one lifting her cup to her mouth, the other dipping her head to her cup. They are quite different, these two, but there is a certain harmony between them, and evasion is only evasion if it is minded by the other person.

Of love and coffins

Falling in love. It is almost impossible to look back on your own particular version of this and define exactly how and why it happened to you. There are so many possible reasons for one person to end up with another and often, when thought about years later, these reasons have become blurred and unclear. Sometimes love happens simply because one person is standing so close to another, another person who is so unintelligent, so unseeing, so likely to see you wrongly! to see you as that person you have never wanted to become (your mother, perhaps, hair smelling always of pale meat, legs sprawling with thin red veins) that, quickly, you turn to the first person and cry: How do you do, and what brings you here, and would you like to come home with me and spend the night between my legs, and then, after that perhaps, the next ten years?

And so, before you know it, you have been shackled, although not unhappily so, and in fact your legs do sprawl with a red spideriness late in the afternoon when the sun stares unforgivingly onto your balcony as you sit there sunning yourself in supposed bliss. There you are, waking every day beside someone you could hardly say you had picked: picked, perhaps, as you might pick a tomato from a bin outside a supermarket, with the evening rushing towards you along a four-lane road and the low light dazzling your eyes, making you reach out blindly and touch the skin of the tomato, cradle it for a second in your hand, feel the weight (about right) and the skin (blemished in one place but otherwise smooth) and think, this will do. Then suddenly, lo and behold, you are married to a middle-weight, passably smooth-skinned tomato! And this is your life.

But my falling in love (Gest starts the story for the Candy Girl, who today is slightly red-faced and puffy around the eyes: trouble with the Micro?) – my own moment of falling had nothing to do with a sidekick friend.

Oh? says the Candy Girl, with a small sniff.

No, there was no secondary other who might show the Ordinary Man in a more attractive light (Gest continues quickly). He was quite alone, caught in one of those sudden suburban moments when it seems as if the street has been recently cleared ready for a film shoot.

What was he doing? The Candy Girl is more than willing to be distracted from the moment when the Micro had shouted at her and slammed his fist against the bedpost, making the pillows jump in a nervous kind of way.

What was he doing, that Ordinary Man? (Gest tactfully avoids looking at the Candy Girl.) He was standing in front of a shop peering into its depths, cupping his hands like binoculars around his eyes. And as I came closer (Gest keeps her eyes turned away from the Candy Girl) he leaned towards the window like a fascinated birdwatcher, but of course he was not looking at birds.

What was he looking at?

He was looking at coffins.

And now the Candy Girl gives a huge jump, in the same way that her morning pillows had jumped under the Micro's fist, and a shout of startled laughter leaps from her mouth. Coffins! She can hardly believe that a man lucky enough to marry Gest, sensible enough to enjoy waking beside her every morning, brave enough to have a child with her, stupid enough to leave her and go to a different country – she can hardly believe that this larger-than-life man had been caught staring at wooden boxes constructed for the purpose of housing dead bodies.

What did he do after that? she asks.

He turned when he saw me (says Gest) and he stepped back from the window with a flush in his face. But even as he was laughing and flushing he looked past me once again, very quickly, as if there were a magnetic field inside the shop pulling at his attention. *I was just realizing*, he said (these were his very first words), *I was realizing that the way in which a person dies is always less important than the way in which they are afterwards remembered. Think of the Romans.*

I disagreed (says Gest). Just think of the Romans! I said. And I stood on that hard pavement outside the coffin shop and reminded the Ordinary Man of emperors falling onto the swords of slaves who would then become free to choose their own particular deaths. Even through the soles of my shoes (says Gest) I could feel the chill of the pavement and when I looked down, needing a rest from his eyes, I saw that leaves from the nearby poplar trees were blowing around our ankles. Thin rattling leaves that had been reluctant to let go of their branches until their last flesh had disintegrated, and even then, after the inevitable fall, still they hung around the living, their rustling and shuffling movement on the pavement a semblance of life.

But think of the people who know they are about to die, the Ordinary Man had said, returning from images of purple robes and bloodstained blades to the modern-day street. *Think of the people who come to a shop like this to deliberately pick out their own—* and he had paused, staring in at rows of caskets lined with satin and balanced on the springy wheels of trolleys. *To pick out their own monstrosity in which to lie*, he finished. He was still so close

70

to the shop window that, when he glanced in, there were reflections in his eyes: brassy handles, and the decorative embellishments jutting like wings from the sides of the coffins.

I tested him then (says Gest's voice). I asked if he thought that the choice of a minimalist coffin was any better. Perhaps something streamlined to enable an easy gliding into the other side: something simple in stainless steel, or a sturdy, oversized and expensive cardboard box? He ignored my sarcasm.

You have to admire them, he said. *At least they have the courage to impose their own bad taste to the end.*

A tram roared past us (continues Gest's voice) and it flicked light and dark over our faces, that tram, spraying us with the shredded bodies of the ghost leaves. The Ordinary Man asked if I would have a coffee with him and I said yes, but as we left I could see. It was an effort to make himself move away from that window, an effort to leave.

Was he always that strange? (This is the Candy Girl, marvelling at someone so different.)

But this is the thing! (Gest also sounds surprised.) He was not strange at all, he was completely normal! He simply had a tendency to stand in front of things for a long time, wondering who in the world could possibly buy them. (Although she sounds dismissive, there is a catch in her throat as if she sees and regrets the lost possibilities of what that most Ordinary of Men might have become: an undertaker, a gravedigger, a grave taker of lives and love.)

He saw no more and no less than the average person, she says. He was truly an ordinary man.

It is typical, says the Candy Girl. Because she is remembering the headboard with a crack running through it, there is a crack in her voice too.

What is? asks Gest. What is typical?

That we always hope for more than the average, says the Candy Girl bravely. That's our own mistake. At this point she must drop her bracelet and slip down off her stool to retrieve it, so that she is able to turn her back for a moment. But when she turns back to Gest her eyes are streaming red.

Oh, says Gest. Oh.

It is such a long time since she has had to comfort anyone, such a long time since the Child came thundering down the hallway chased by his dreams, trailing the black shreds of nightmares from his bare heels, that she hardly knows what to do. Should she tell the Candy Girl to cry it out, or should she tell her not to cry?

Don't, she says. Don't.

But the Candy Girl is wiping her eyes, and clipping the blue glass bracelet firmly back on her rounded wrist. I'm fine, she says stoutly. Fight with the boyfriend, that's all, and we have work to do.

Possibly the Ordinary Man is standing, even now, in front of a shop window. Standing with his back to a hot dry world where the light is unreliable and shimmers, sending waves down the middle of the street so it is impossible to see clearly from one side to the other. What might the Ordinary Man be looking at now? wonders Gest (though she is concerned about the Candy Girl and whether she has been hit that day). What might the Ordinary Man be looking at? Tractor parts, desert boots, car tyres, racks of foreign newspapers, musical instruments. He is in front of something, and he is looking at something. This is as certain as Gest can be, for today is an uncertain day.

You're right. She goes over and strokes the Candy Girl on the arm. Work is important and sometimes it's all we've got. In spite of the hotness around the Candy

Girl's eyes, her arm feels cool to the touch. It is covered in small light hairs and lies against her stomach in a comfortable, comforting way.

Now Gest leans forward and kisses the Candy Girl on the mouth. There is a small intake of breath: from her? She can hardly tell because, even as she feels the hardness of another person's front teeth against hers and tastes the brown acrid two-hours-ago coffee on that other person's tongue, she realizes what she is doing.

I'm sorry, she says, and instinctively she turns and strides back to her own chair, wiping her mouth with a rag. As if the Candy Girl is a leper! Now Gest can only taste turpentine and shame, and she gags into her cloth. I'm sorry, she mumbles, wiping and gagging.

It is the Candy Girl's turn to comfort. She comes over to Gest and reaches out with her brilliant-blue glass wrist, as if she is the employer, as if she is the hirer of workers who come and sit in a nearly empty room for hours on end not knowing but trusting what they are there for. There, she says, holding firmly onto Gest's shoulders and stroking her head half buried in a dirty paint rag. There, she says tenderly, like the mother from a down-home television series where bedroom lights are put out at the end of every half-hour slot and owls cry through the warm dark trees.

Gest raises her face. She hardly knows what she will say. I miss him, is what comes out.

The Candy Girl nods in her new motherly capacity. You might be ready for a new man, she suggests. You're so attractive, even without make-up, even in these old work overalls! You just need to get out more.

But it is not the Ordinary Man to whom Gest refers, not even the first ideal version of the Ordinary Man standing in the autumn street wreathed around with the glamour of death wishes and the rich dark smell of polished oak.

Who, then? The Candy Girl is almost afraid to ask. Who is it that you miss?

(But Gest cannot say his name.)

Whisper it. Say it once, for me.

I miss the Child.

The space between

At one time or another, this city had been ravaged. Perhaps at one time the great muddy river had risen up in anger and roared through the streets, picking up bystanders as if they were dolls and flinging them onto its grey back, and doing the same with planks of wood and trees and dogs and the tiled roofs of houses – so that by the end all were clashing along through the city, all dashed together in one vast chaos of shrieking colour. And after the river had quietened its rage, realized its mistake, and slunk back between its banks the city was left unrecognisable: a flattened muddy wasteland, a bald head strewn over with muddy strands of hair.

Yes, this had almost certainly happened at one time in this city's history.

At one time or other this grey-green city had been razed. By flooding, or perhaps by the sharp whining dislike of one race for another. Did that razing take place over months, or was it years? It is hard to tell, hard to keep track of the days when your calendar is hung on a wall that suddenly, like a frightening malfunction of the heart, splits down the middle, allowing the roof to fall into your kitchen. At any rate, there had been days and weeks of panic and fear. Of quick silver splinters falling from the sky, of running for a cellar or any hole in the ground that might offer shelter for exposed heads and breaking hearts.

And when the blanket of noise had been drawn away from the city, and the blood-orange sky had faded to white, little was left. Banks and town halls, parks and benches and tulip walkways along which lovers had scuffed their hopeful toes – all the carefully planned, meticulously planted flagstaffs of human existence had been snapped and lay strewn on the ground.

Yes, this had happened, more than once, to this city.

At one or more times, this city had been ravaged and razed and then had rebuilt itself. Each time it had picked itself up from the earth, shaken off the debris left by flooding or bombing, storming feet or stampeding ambitions; and it had given a deep sigh and started once more to recreate itself. Strangely enough, each time this happened – and it happened in different ways, depending on the whim and will of different mayors and town planners, and on which particular architect wanted to experiment with glass, sandstone, or steel – one thing remained constant. While brand new buildings stretched their arms up and out, and new glass windows winked, and stones were relaid one by one in the plazas over those too tired or old to go on, there was a space in the middle of the city that always remained empty.

It was a difficult space to fill, regardless of what was around it. It sat on a slight rise in the ground, unusual in this pancake-flat city with no natural vantage points to speak of. The ground tilted in the way that a globe might be set on a brass axis: you felt that you had to stand with your head on one side, and at a distance, simply to get a grasp on that space.

Besides this, there was the fact that all the winds

75

gathered there. From every corner of the country they rushed in, early in the morning or late in the afternoon, so that even when the sun was shining it was not a pleasant place to sit. Shelters made of plexiglass proved useless, unless you liked to sit in a scratched transparent box where your voice had no resonance and fell with a thud to the concrete floor. Strategically planted trees bent and stooped to the superior forces of the winds. No matter how closely buildings nudged up to the space, closing their shoulders around it, still the winds pushed on through to meet in a rushing whirling mass.

Various inspections had been made of the space. It had been festooned with red tape, criss-crossed with measuring equipment, rolled over with small council wheels, and dowsed with sticks. An exact measurement seemed out of reach: records showed vastly differing estimates, violently differing opinions, and an inability to decide on whether the space was the right size for a plinth (too big!) or a police kiosk (too small!). Seats had been put there and taken away again, water features plumbed and stopped up again.

A few years ago an archaeologist had delved into the earth under the space, had extracted a neat cross-section layered with worms and small pebbles, and in its centre a tiny, age-bitten, charred and blackened coin. Had there once been fire on that space? Perhaps a house struck two centuries ago by a bolt of lightning, melting bones to beds and fusing eternal sleep onto eyelids?

Yes, this could have happened. This could quite possibly have happened, on this very spot, this consistently empty space. It is not a good or a bad place any more, it is simply there, silent, waiting. In fact its day of reckoning is not far off – perhaps thirty days, perhaps forty? At that point something will be rolled on in, placed here with ceremony, feted with wine and with ribbons, praised by crowds and criticised by critics. Someone is working right now, in this very city, towards the filling of this spot. But, for now, the space waits.

Go a little closer to it. For the best way to experience the space is not, in fact, from a distance. Try approaching it in the following way:

Walk boldly into the space, arms by your sides, until you are right in the centre. Narrow your eyes against the wind.

Let your feet stand. Allow them to stand until the rocking, tilting sensation settles to a kind of balance. Stand a little longer until you are perfectly, absolutely, steady.

Raise your head now. Look through the gap in the tall buildings to your left, where you will find a clear view of the western horizon.

Watch and wait. Soon you will see the wheeling of birds against the sun. And soon their wings will catch the light, glow for a second, and burst into flame. In that moment – when the birds are on fire – you will hear the call of the boats on the river. And then you will belong.

What is it called, that place? What name have the locals bestowed on it, over its many long years of existence in the heart of their city?

It has become known simply as: the space between.

Bodies

The Candy Girl has never been particularly good at staying still. Yet by now you may have noticed that part of her job is to remain in suspended motion, and to hold poses, for long periods of time. She wavers, scratches her nose, apologizes.

Wouldn't you rather, she looks at Gest dubiously, get a proper model?

Her body is unusual. She is big for a woman: probably right through puberty she had grown faster than her classmates, would squirm in the changing rooms and during gym class would head for the back of the line, cringing as the wall of backs in front of her got sparser and less protective. Then next minute, against her will, she would be forcing her heavy body into a run, eyes fixed on the basketball hoop mounted on the back wall, bare boards falling hard under the balls of her feet. And then she is placing her running steps four-three-two – one, and jumping. And *clunk*! the bottom of the spring-board is hitting the floor and she is landing clumsily on the grey leather top of the vault, and people snigger.

Wouldn't you rather—? she says to Gest, dubiously. I mean, look at me.

Perhaps later in her teenage years the Candy Girl had refused to try on clothes in communal dressing rooms where the bored attendant watched the customers undressing, and the customers sneaked glances at each other in the full-length mirror, and the cheap floor was littered with tiny discarded tops and skinny denim flares.

The Micro says I should stop eating garlic bread, she says. Forty-five grams of fat in one piece, he tells me.

But the Candy Girl is not fat. She has grown into a tall, big, straight person, a tree person, and her legs and arms have retained the natural shape of childhood. They are like those of an oversized boy, sturdy, sure of themselves, unselfconscious when they are doing what comes naturally: holding tight to the handlebars of a bicycle when crossing tram tracks, for instance, or holding a microphone, or holding on to someone when saying goodbye as if that person is the most important person in all the world. This is a gift and a blessing, and not something that anyone can achieve by trying.

Wouldn't one of your movie-star friends sit for you? she asks, doubtfully.

No, says Gest. I have no friends, no friends from that time.

Well, if you're sure, says the Candy Girl. You're the artist.

You are the only one I want, assures Gest. No one else will do.

The eleven-second rule of life

In 1902 a mild-mannered English physiologist, with the last name of a common garden bird, made a breakthrough discovery. Two years after the world had tumbled into the twentieth century Ernest Starling discovered that hormones were a little like adrenaline. Like adrenaline, hormones could be carried around the body via the blood stream.

In a mere eleven seconds, Starling found out – in the

time it takes for blood to rush from your heart to your feet – you could be delivered a hormonal message not able to be ignored.

And so, from the early days of the twentieth century onwards, it was possible to believe in a sudden falling. A falling in love, that is. In eleven seconds – such a small space of time! – you could fall out of love with one person and in love with another. And in a way (thanks to Starling) you could not be held responsible for this. Blame your hormonal heart, blame your messenger-blood.

Gest looks sometimes at her thin ridged wrists. When she has been working for some hours, the veins in her wrists stand up like desert sand blown into long lines. There is traitor blood in those veins, or so she thinks. Those veins, that blood: simply by passing some small flat molecules through her body, they had split her life in two.

She had believed she loved her husband, the father of her child. Of course! She had loved him long before the birth, for many years. Ever since she had seen him standing in front of a shop window, mesmerized by satin interiors and the shiny, overly regular grain of imitation wood, she had loved him. But then she had had the Child, and everything had changed.

It was not his beauty that had made her cry. She held him and he was a lightweight, an onion-weight, in her hands. Small, imperfect, slightly scrumpled like a sheet of paper dragged from a wastepaper bin.

He is, she gulped, he is really—

He's beautiful, the nurse agreed.

But no, he was not beautiful. Not then, not until later after he had lost the hospital taint and gained his own personality, becoming fierce and golden. Why was Gest crying then, if not at his beauty? Because she had spent

80

her life avoiding cliché and now she had stumbled. She had committed the unavoidable crime, the ultimate cliché, she had fallen in love with her baby and because of this, in the short space of eleven adrenaline-ridden, hormonally driven but coolly objective seconds, she loved her lover less.

Things had progressed by this time. They had moved from the abattoir apartment, there had been a growing-in and a growing-up period. They had found a new place to live (it would not have been healthy to bring up a child breathing in the last blood-air expelled from the lungs of dying animals). They had moved to a new apartment in a different area and they had bought pillows (it could not be good for a child to have parents who lacked conventional bedding).

They had moved to a new place, a place where the Child could have a room of his own rather than sleeping in the drawer of an old bureau beside his parents' bed. There was even a small dark space there, more of an alcove than a room, which Gest could use as a work room. That is, she could go in there and no one was allowed to interrupt, but since there was only an archway between her and the rest of the household she could still hear everything, and if anyone passed they could glance in at her. But nonetheless she was considered privileged to have her own space in which to work, while not having the actual privileges.

Artists are like women, the Ordinary Man said at that time, after her occasional complaints. You can't live with them, and you can't live with them!

Other people seemed to find this funny. And he, the Ordinary Man, told it as a joke, mainly against himself. But Gest was unamused. She tried to work in her alcove protected by her curved invisible door of air, but she felt the possibility of interruption like a constant ache in her

81

kidneys, thought it was the cold, wore a rug wrapped around her while she sketched but still felt it layers deep under the tartan scratch.

And the energy flickered on, skittering from room to room, creating odd jags of exhilaration and the occasional belief that they would survive. The Child grew lusty and strong. He headed the Triumvirate during that time.

On other days there were flares of bad temper.

You always, the Ordinary Man would begin an accusation. You never! (These were the two possibilities: you always, you never.)

Which is it? Gest would say. If I always and I never, then what are my options? She would wave her paint-spattered hands in front of her. Painted into a corner, she would say in exasperation.

They became weak, exhausted by each other's predictability. Soon there were stress fractures running down the middle of their relationship. But the Child continued to grow in strength and glory; there was a certain sternness to him that emerged as soon as he could speak.

I am busy, he would say. I am busy, give me some time here!

Gest was busy too; commissions had started to come in and the phone rang many times a day. But when she shut her eyes, she could remember little of what she had drawn. She couldn't help it, went in search of the Child, and her heart would twist at the sight of his small intent head.

I am trying to watch TV, he said without turning his head. Please don't interrupt.

Gest turned off the television and gave him her pencil to draw with, because at that time she could do less with it than he could. He became focused on that, instantly, and she feared for the sound of the car parking outside in the street. This – the entrance of a third – fractured their world.

But the Ordinary Man had become interested in her work, and was pleased that she had left the movie game. (You always seemed distracted back then, he would say. You never took things seriously, at that time.) When one of Gest's drawings was reproduced on the cover of a national magazine he hired a babysitter from an agency for the night. The girl arrived looking vague. Her eyes were a little bloodshot, but there was something responsible about her wide shoulders and her sturdy hips.

Gest and the Ordinary Man drove to a car park in the centre of the city, and then took a lift up eighteen floors to a restaurant high in a tower. This was a radio tower, and at a hundred and sixty-two metres was the highest vantage point in the whole city. The only thing above their heads was a flickering red light warning the planes to let the diners eat in peace, and below them the city lay in a dark circular mist.

The restaurant revolved, so that twenty-five or thirty times they passed an old man playing an electronic keyboard on his stationary platform. Stairway to Heaven, We Could Be Heroes. His voice and the ever-changing, ever-the-same view over the edges of a white tablecloth: these things helped. But there remained a non-specific dread in Gest that increased with every small forkful of rolled beef; soon she felt bloated by fear.

There's something about that babysitter, mused the Ordinary Man. You'll think I'm crazy but she looks a bit like the Child.

Gest's hands went to her mouth. Not crazy, she said through her fingers and then she picked up her fork in a controlled way. But around her golden wine was tilting in glasses, chairs were moving backwards and forwards, potted palms swayed. The Child! How was he, and what was he doing?

Do something for me, would you, said the Ordinary Man. He leaned low over the table, hair lying back from his forehead in dark waves, olive skin washed pale by the lamp light.

What? Gest had said faintly.

Go to the bathroom, he said, and take your knickers off. Bring them back to me. His teeth were sharp, his nose even sharper.

She hadn't: something had happened, the waiter had stepped up from behind a tree to take the dessert orders or there was a request for another song from the tireless old man on the keyboard. The thing was, the Ordinary Man was trying. He was trying hard to turn the clock back: to slice eleven seconds out of the past.

The Child had an air of authority about him at that time. Both his face and his limbs were rounded and firm.

I'm extremely precious aren't I? he would say. He would force Gest onto her knees on the carpet and sit on her back, like a professional jockey. You are precious too, he would say kindly, pulling on her hair. (He was not only authoritative; he could be immensely kind.)

As Gest and the Ordinary Man continued to diminish each other, the Child developed his own independent life. It was hard to imagine him in the years to come talking to girls about his mother, or starting his sentences with the words *As my mother used to say*. Already he was quite detached, chatting on his toy phone for several hours a day, making plans for the rest of the week.

Gest began to feel always tired: far more tired than she had when she was on set all day, dressing, stripping, faking orgasms, simulating ecstasy. She would go to the pouch that hung on the back of the bedroom door and comb her fingers longingly through the cool white pills. This was as far as she went, most times.

I'm extremely precious! At just the right time the Child would put his head around the bedroom door, and smile at her reassuringly. Then he would give Gest a kiss on the ear that made her head ring.

She kept drawing – drew more than ever – but to herself at least she seemed to be talking less and less. There were days in that energy-crisis time when she would be undressing for bed and she could not remember a single word she had said all day, not to people in shops, or friends on the phone, or even around the house.

Tell me another story about the Cultural Revolution, the Child ordered.

She could not remember having told the first one.

Some poor teachers, she faltered, were made to walk through the streets wearing dunces' caps.

Dunces' caps! The Child is aghast. And what else?

Some other poor people, Gest hesitated, were made to kneel on glass.

Don't tell the Child those things! The Ordinary Man burst into the room, his face red. They are utterly inappropriate!

Gest's face flushed up, reflecting his own. He asked for it, she said in her own defence.

The Child lay back on the pillows unperturbed. Tell me about the Little Red Book, he wheedled. And this is how it went, for many months.

Gest had thought it was the neck scarf, which only goes to show how absurd, how absurdly fallible the human understanding of love is. For how could she have thought that one small piece of red fabric around the neck of her husband had been what ended her marriage? But today, on the sixteenth day, she is forcing herself to remember back, think clearly.

85

She had been away somewhere, that was it. She had been away on a plane, to a gallery in another city, for the media had recently spotted a tie-in between her former career and the pornographic element in her drawings, and the curators had also gone for this.

And so she had come to the arrivals gate, talking to a girl who had found out what she did.

I could never be an artist, that girl had said. I don't have the imagination. (Or something like that.)

Then Gest had said goodbye to the girl and rounded the edge of the barrier to find the Ordinary Man unexpectedly waiting for her.

You're blushing! he said. He sounded pleased.

Where's the— Gest looked and blushed again. Where's the Child? (This, in itself, a clue.)

With a sitter, he said.

By now the blood had rushed all the way through Gest's body up to her face and then back down again; she felt it settling heavily in her feet.

With that same sitter? she said. From the night of the radio tower? She was cold, the warm panic had left her, and around them people were emptying away, dispersing to shuttle buses and to cars, leaving a squeaking expanse of floor too big for the two of them.

No, not that girl, said the Ordinary Man. She's gone away, Spain or somewhere.

He tried to hand Gest his coat but she wouldn't take it, and he picked up her bag (she tried to take it) and as she started for the exit she asked the question, thinking it would be easier to sound casual while in motion.

Why are you wearing, she paused, that scarf?

I've had a sore throat all day, he said earnestly. The Child must have picked up something at nursery school and brought it home with him.

He coughed then, coughed away behind Gest to let

86

her know she should ask more. But she couldn't bear to look around at him, to see the edges of the paisley patterns shining white, swirling in the floodlights of the car park.

It's really quite sore, he said, coughing again. He seemed not to notice that Gest was shivering.

It had not been those seconds that had counted, of course not: it had not been the unexpected seeing, the terrible sight of him smiling at her over a knotted scarf, a semi-rakishly tied scarf as if he were trying to star in the worst sort of erotic movie. It was not that partic-ular rush of blood that changed things, although for many years Gest had pinned it to that short interval in a half-empty airport hall in her home city. The end had come long before that, it had come in the eleven seconds when the streaky dark Child had been handed to her, as she lay in her hospital bed still stained with sweat from the birth. With one great swoosh of the heart her blood had turned and begun to flow in the opposite direction.

It is only now, on the sixteenth day, that Gest realizes this. Wisdom sometimes falls slowly, twisting this way and that, like a paper dart before it lands.

The kitchen window

She is no voyeur. But it is impossible sometimes, living in a city, not to see into the lives of other people.

She feels the passing of time like a heavy hand on the back of her neck, making the base of her skull burn and her ears sing in an aching underwater way. Perhaps it is because of this that she is sleeping less?

There is a long-time cavity of pain behind her eyes. During the day it lies quietly enough, unnoticed. She has had it before, once or twice, even in easier times. (It's the fluorescent light, the Ordinary Man had said. It's the strip lighting. This was the reassuring voice of the Ordinary Man, heard only occasionally now down the long length of a phone line.)

But it is different. It is different now. These nights, when Gest lays down her head and waits for sleep, she feels the pain hard and intractable under her eyelids, coiled like a snake. (She has had it since. She has had it since before this story began.) And when the snake breathes in, it swells and forces her eyelids to open again, so that her eyes as well as her mind are exposed to the dark.

It might be a storm, this night. All the long day there has been a muttering outside, a low groaning underlying the groan of the trams. And the light! The light has been odd and unreal, making the trees throw their leaves down in a temper on the street. After the days of chill it has been strangely hot, so hot that it has been hard to work – even the Candy Girl has been slightly snappy.

Gest has clung to the fingernail edge of politeness all day (she is the employer, politeness is her duty, just as it is the Candy Girl's to turn up at her door every morning). After the closing of the afternoon door she steps out onto the balcony. From her high platform she can see the Candy Girl weaving and flashing her way through the crowds. (I'm sorry for being so snappy! This was the Candy Girl, who had also felt the tension, turning as she left and grasping Gest's hand.) Now her apologetic pink back is merging with the distance, although today it is more difficult for her to cycle speedily to the station because of the way people's shadows are taking advantage of the strange light and staking out the pavement in a long, mean way.

Six floors up, Gest is left alone. Left with the half-dormant pain that stirs and mutters with the air.

She eats cold peas straight from the can. Then she sits for a long time in the kitchen looking vacantly out into the hallway at the blank archway: a curve leading to nowhere, filled with nothing but an old shoe rack and some random screw holes.

She sits there on her hard kitchen chair – for how long? Perhaps an hour, perhaps two, cradling a tepid beer and staring at the cracked paint in the archway, waiting for the heat at her back to fade.

Although it is late when she gets out of her chair, the heat feels even greater. In bed even a sheet is too much to bear on her skin. She kicks it off and lies naked.

Still, too hot. So hot it could be midday, except the clock by the bed is assuring her, in a luminous voice, that it is not midday, it is midnight and time for sleep.

Gest lies. She lies on her bed, bare back to the mattress, naked stomach to the ceiling, and concentrates on her breathing. But in spite of her concentration and her quietness, the pain wakes up. It stretches, raises itself on its elbows. (Remember me? it says, and Gest remembers, although once she called it by a different name.)

She opens her tired eyes, looks at the window to see a night world full of movement. Clouds are racing against a bright blue sky; it could be day except that the clock tells her, in a voice as authoritative as the Child's, no! It is not day! It is the middle of a storm-dogged night. And there is the moon pretending to be the sun, swiping at the buildings, cutting them in half with its sharp shadow sword.

Gest gives up, gets up, and goes to the kitchen. But

she is wary of turning on the light. There is too much happening outside; it does not seem wise to attract attention. No fluorescent light, then, but when she lights the stove the gas flame is as blue and strange as the night sky. It leaps out around the element like the bright irrepressible hair around the Child's face.

She sits at the table with her cup of tea and presses the heels of her hands against her eyes. (It's the strip lighting, says the Ordinary Man. No other artist I know works under such harsh lighting.) She will force the pain back. This is how it goes, this is how it goes away, pressing with her fingers until pink and green dots fall like rain behind her eyes.

There is lightning then. It comes through her fingers and her thin paper lids. She goes to the window, though she is no voyeur. She is simply waiting for the next lightning, the thunder, the lightning.

It is a TV set. *Flick flick*. The blue erratic light of a television behind the high window in the building across the courtyard. Most of this building, like Gest's own, is empty (this is not a fashionable area, there are dogs that bite and people who kick cans in ragged parks). But there is someone in there, in that room, emulating a storm. Gest feels angry for no particular reason except perhaps – it could be – that she has wanted to be the only one up at this time, waiting by herself for the sky to let its breath out, to let her relax, and let her sleep.

But instead! Instead she must stand here in her hot dark kitchen while someone else watches a porn movie at a time of the night when no one but watchers of porn would be up. *Flick flick*. No sign of a watching head, no curtains, no secondary light in the room: just the ice-blue migraine flicker that steadies itself for a second and disintegrates again.

For a time Gest stands there naked. The clouds draw

90

back and clear away, the sky dims, and there is no other light except for a paler moon and the luminous, mesmerizing flicker of an unseen porn movie playing in the window opposite hers. When she returns to her bed two hours have passed. And now the snake submits. It lies down now, allows her to sleep.

Pick a name

Pick a name, any name.

This is how the game had gone. Made out of paper folded into triangles, smaller and smaller so that suddenly, instead of a sheet of A4 in your hand, there was a paper blossom. You stood in the schoolyard, the scent of white bread sandwiches hanging around your head and the sweat of a boy's warty hand still drying on yours, and you said:

Pick a name, any name,
and pick an occupation.

You remember more now that you are spending so much time alone, as if suddenly the cracks in your head that have been filled up with so many years of talk, so many days of putting out the bottles and paying bills and passing on phone messages, have been cleaned out with a blade. Channels are freed up again so you can drift back into the past more easily, and it takes only an instant before you are back in the playground feeling the grit between

91

your toes, niggling at you, reminding you of homework to do and the too few hours before the next school day.

Pick a name.

I pick Gardner.

That's not a name, that's an occupation!

The white folded paper had whisked backwards and forwards, working its odd origami magic to predict your future, although you already knew all possible outcomes because you had created them yourself on the kitchen table at home with the seat of the chair pressing red marks on the backs of your legs, breathing heavily, holding your tongue between your teeth and a green felt-tipped pen in your hand, writing in slightly shaky green letters because it was your future, after all, and therefore important.

Veterinarian, hairdresser, make-up artist, chef.

In this way the occupation section was taken care of. And in the number section, that told you what age you would be when you got your first boyfriend and when you married and when you died, you mostly wrote down numbers that were multiples of four because, although you had been told that the world was round, you preferred to think of it as having four corners as they did in the Orient, where city walls were built in squares, and the length of those walls was also divisible by that magic favourite number, four.

In the name section you wrote Gardner, because you had seen a movie that ended with a second of silence as a tribute to someone of that name, and at first you had thought that the director of the movie – a movie that was too old for you, you had walked into the theatre on high borrowed boots with shaking ten-year-old ankles – yes, you thought that the maker of that rushing wild Vietnamese movie featuring small-breasted naked women had bequeathed his work to a mild-mannered man wearing thick canvas gloves and tending the gardens of Beverly Hills, a man who took up a dark green net and skimmed leaves from the tops of turquoise pools though living himself in a small unassuming shack in the dry hills behind the lush city. Afterwards, as you sank back in your seat and waited for the ushers to leave before you did, you thought about it further and, because you were good at spelling, you realized that the dead person to whom the movie was dedicated was Gardner by name – this was not their *occupation* – and you decided then and there that your first-born would be called that, knowing you would be told the exact birth date of this child by the folding paper game in your hand (you were confident that it would be when you were sixteen or twenty or twenty-four), and then you were certain about all things, even though the dissenting voices dropping from the climbing frame onto your stubborn head told you no! Gardner was a job!

Just think of the control you had then. Entire paper futures able to be screwed up if you didn't get exactly what you wanted.

How appropriate! said Gest, when she and the Ordinary Man were trying to remember how to fold the paper in the right way so that they could play the game with the Child.

What, the Ordinary Man hesitated, is appropriate? This was the way he now dealt with Gest, approaching her hesitantly, from the side, as if hoping that something in her profile would remind him of how she had first appeared to him.

Screwing up your paper future! Gest looked directly at the Ordinary Man (this was the way she now dealt with him). Because pretty soon you learn, she said, your real future gets screwed up whether you like it or not.

The Ordinary Man had laughed; he assumed she had said this to be funny, but his laugh was slightly uncertain. Then he bent his head again over the paper origami game and he wrote down *doctor* and *fireman*: sensible choices of career for a firstborn and a male, for their Child.

(He never thought of writing *porn star*, says Gest, even though he was sitting right next to one at the time! She and the Candy Girl laugh at this *ha ha ha* and their eyes crinkle up at the corners, though today Gest's eyes are bleary from the broken night before, from the television across the way and the snake of pain and the gas flame, and she is tired also by her own inconsistency – by the fact that at one time she had participated in the making of those movies, watched by her unseen neighbour, and now she stands naked at her kitchen window and burns with resentment at that neighbour's lascivious midnight activities.)

On they had marched, the two of them, Gest and her most ordinary, loving, and loyal husband. Shoulder to shoulder they sat at their table and worked out how the paper needed to be cut because of not being an exact square, and their fingers had become dashed all over with orange and gold like the pollen from the frangipani flowers that had fallen on the paths of their honeymoon hotel and had been gathered (by him, by her) and presented, with slightly bruised petals, to each other in bed at night. When their new version of the old paper game was complete, they played it often with the Child, who liked it because of the way it gave things their proper place, neat citrus segments meting out his destiny.

Folding back flap after flap, he crowed with delight at the orange words telling him that, at the age of twenty-two, he would be driving a tractor and married to a dentist.

He liked sureness, the Child, and he liked centrality: in a way he was predestined to like these things, born as he was on the dot of midnight, on the cusp of Leo and Virgo, arriving smack bang into the middle of his parents' shared life. It was because of this that, when Gest called him by the title seeming right for him, he felt pushed to the periphery and rebelled. Don't call me the Child! he said, as soon as he could speak. Don't call me by that name, it isn't polite.

Isn't polite! Gest laughed. His objection seemed strange, for she thought quite the opposite: that bestowing a title on a person was the best of compliments. In most lives, after all, there is only one of each kind – one husband, one window-cleaner, one gynaecologist, one hairdresser – and to be *the* one carries with it an undeniable importance.

But orderliness and respect were important to her child. And so to his face Gest called him by his real name, but secretly in her head, and when he was out of earshot, she continued to call him the Child.

It was not that she hadn't thought about what to call him before he was born. In fact she had spent much time on the issue of names: many long swollen afternoons spent trawling through name books, through Latin and French dictionaries, tomes of poetry and drama, dictionaries of derivations and quotations, in an attempt to find exactly the right name for her son. *Her son*. Already before he arrived she could feel his fierce face pressing against the walls of her stomach, impatient to burn his imprint on the world. She laid her hand on her front and felt her palm scorching, lifted her palm. It was not easy, the responsibility towards someone who was not even born yet.

He had turned out just as she had sensed he would be: a small sun trailing fire and light behind it. Sometimes when he came into a room Gest could barely see him through the white glamour that surrounded him; she would peer behind him for the door that he had come through, trying to see if he had closed it properly. And when he dropped his school bag on the floor it was a small chunk of burning rock fallen behind his fast feet.

Aphrodite

Picture this: a rocky headland in Turkey, wrapped around with blue sea. A rocky headland wrapped around with waves as blue and rough as the eyes of a suckling baby, and swathed in legend.

It was here, forty miles from Gokkaya Bay, four centuries before Christ was born, that a temple was raised to Aphrodite, the most beautiful goddess of them all. The temple has since vanished without a trace, as has the sculpture inside. But should you sail around this coastline with the cliffs glowing in the setting sun, you will notice the empty space there, and at the sight of the empty space something inside you will shift and move. Excitement, or grief? These are at times indistinguishable; both cause a knife-twist high up in the stomach, close to the edge of the heart.

(She is so—! begins the Candy Girl, and then cannot go on. She is so—! she tries again and falls silent, for

96

she cannot explain. She cannot explain the mystery that is Gest, she cannot explain the beautiful woman who stands in front of her every day, at times appearing unable to raise her eyes from the floor for minutes on end.)

Here, by the port of Knidos, an ornate temple was raised to Aphrodite. It stood high and long on the rocks that forced themselves into the mouth of the sea, and various priestesses were appointed as protectors of the most beautiful woman in the world.

For how long was Aphrodite forced to stand here, gazing with stony eyes at the far horizon, pretending not to notice the peering, the nudging and the shuffling, of her male worshippers? For how long did she close her ears to the murmuring of sightseers, coming from all corners of the Mediterranean map to be admitted into her presence, to gaze at her proud nipples and the proud curl of her lip?

(Exactly what, asks the Micro, are you doing there every day? Do you even know what you are there for?

I do, says the Candy Girl, slightly evasively. I am there as a model.

But for fucking what? says the Micro. Exactly what are you a model *for*?

For art! says the Candy Girl.

You earn more by singing in a bar, says the Micro. So exactly fucking *why*?

Because of her! says the Candy Girl in surprise, for this is a far easier question. Because of what she is like, she explains.)

Once you have climbed the marble steps of Aphrodite's temple, forehead wet with anticipation and the white stone burning around you, you find yourself in a kind of pleasure dome. A pagan Garden of Eden, where you are offered wine from a chilled cup that clings for a moment to the heat of your lip, then spills its cool green contents onto your hot tongue. This is the saliva, the juice, of Dionysus, here to ready you, to steady your nervous stomach and your anticipatory loins for what you are about to see.

You are in the shade of a garden with fountains echoing the distant voice of the sea. Now you are offered small erotic offerings – marble goddesses, all thighs and breasts and parted lips – to hold in the palm of your hand. But the feelings they arouse are nothing more than a faint shadow running before a boat.

A sweet-faced girl approaches, with a tray of sweet-meats in one hand and a silver pitcher in the other. With the raising of an eyebrow, and the outstretching of one white arm, she motions you to a seat where you may eat and drink, resting in the shade of rosebushes so vast that they are more like trees. The scent dropping around you is sweeter than honey. But it is not as sweet – you are sure of this already – as what you will soon see, that which you have travelled so many lurching miles over land and waves to view. (*Pruvan neta olsun!* These, the words of Turkish sailors, setting sail under a vast red sun, tipping rough raki down their throats. *Keep your prow clean!* This toast, to guarantee a safe journey.)

At last you are beckoned to the gate of the inner sanctum, where you are appraised by the level stare of priestesses. Young girls, these, younger than yourself, hundreds of years younger than Aphrodite, yet still able to hold out their hands for silver coins, to determine whether you have paid enough to see merely the front of their goddess (three small coins) or the posterior view (an additional three).

And there you are, at last. Inside. Above your head the curved stone ceilings hold back the midday sun. Around you the walls exhale cool grey breath on the back of your neck. And before you stands the goddess who governs all, for she is both beauty and love.

(What did she do for a living? The Micro is curious. Before she employed you?)

Nothing has prepared you for this. Her self-contained chin, the slope of her shoulders, larger than life but more delicate than the bones of a bird, lightly traced with lichen. No rosewater is more perfectly scented than the smell of her stone wrists, no *peynir* more crumbling than the enticing spread of her toes, no taste of crushed cumin and cinnamon more full than her rounded womanly stomach.

(She was a star, says the Candy Girl reverently. The world was at her feet.)

Aphrodite. She was the first female nude in history, and her sensual power made men through the ages become weak at the knees.

And it so happened

And it so happened that on the twentieth day, though she was unaware of this fact, the Candy Girl went running. Tears streamed from her eyes for it was very early in the morning and the air was still in cool layers, had not yet resigned itself to the fact that it was all of a piece, had not settled down for the day ready to provide an homo-geneous, duller-than-ditchwater, unnoticed environment in which other city dwellers could dwell on that, the twentieth day.

Slicing through the air. These are the Candy Girl's elbows. Arrowing, narrowing their way through the stub-born leftover layers of the night. Elbows, heels, and a song in her head. What is it? It is Uptown Girl, by Billy Joel.

And in fact the Candy Girl is uptown: she is running by the river where the white ducks are scattered on the water like confetti, and downtown is a long way away (the Candy Girl has taken a train to get here, standing in her tightly laced running shoes surrounded by swaying yawning commuters who have felt compelled to get early to their clean imitation-pine desks, or compelled to leave their grease-fumed argument-infested boxy apartments as quickly as possible: it's all the same to these people travelling uptown, from downtown, with sleep still smearing their eyeballs, but the Candy Girl is alert: she is going running).

Although she is a girl and although uptown, she does not qualify for the lead part in the song she is listening to, through one good earphone and one that cuts out every time her left foot smacks against the ground. For she was brought up, the Candy Girl, on a white-trash diet of sliced bread and fried eggs, and she had walked through her childhood days with a latchkey round her neck. At school she was confronted by the shiny trinkety hearts and butterflies, studded with fake diamantés, that belonged to her classmates, and her with only a key! – a key to the door of their house, for there was never anyone to let her in when she got home from school – but by God, she had an imagination, and a quick tongue for defence, and so there was a story that she told many times, with variations: that the key hanging low and heavy between her small peaking breasts was the *key to Buddy Brady's heart*. And who was Buddy Brady? (There were sometimes disbelieving sneers at this point.) Oh – airily – just some boy, just some broken-hearted boy whom the Candy Girl had left behind at the age of seven when her family had moved further up the coast. (No, really, who was Buddy Brady? In fact he was that character with the fantastic black quiff in the comic book found by the Candy Girl's oldest brother in the toilets at the dance school where he cleaned. The Candy Girl's mother had cleaned for a living and so had her oldest brother, and her three sisters eventually took to it as well, though the Candy Girl herself showed a talent for waitressing being a natural performer. The rest of her family, though, had all ended up scrubbing other people's bathrooms and polishing corporate corridors with heavy industrial cleaning machines – and fucking good at it they were, if the Candy Girl said so herself! You might almost think that cleaning was in the blood, when you looked up from your eggs of a night and saw them sitting around the dinner table, shoulder to shoulder, still in their smocks and their overalls. If you pricked any member of her family with a fork, the Candy Girl thought then – diving her own fork into the very heart of her runny egg – if you pricked one of their strong veined arms, sludgy pink cleaning fluid would ooze forth. Bright yellow yolk pours forth over the Candy Girl's tin plate, flooding through the mounded beans. And if you ran a pin under her family members' toenails, the Candy Girl thought proudly and defiantly, as she crammed rust-coloured yellow-stained bread into her mouth – under their toenails you would find not dirt or skin but the gritty granules of strong scouring powder. Such was the destiny of her family – such was their fate, or their necessity, whatever you like to call it, following on the heels of the day when their father's boots had squeaked over the cracked but clean linoleum for the last time, after the view of his departing alcoholic back had darkened the well-scrubbed threshold for the last time in many years.)

All this history is held in the Candy Girl's own veins,

all lurks under her own toenails. A past cannot be simply left behind in bed alongside a snoring partner, it cannot be sneaked out on and escaped by going for a run along a river one spring morning. But it can be elbowed aside for a while by other things: the optimistic lyrics of a wide-eyed curly-haired no-longer-listened-to songster, or the sight of a steel bridge curving up and over a river with a train fixed tightly on its back. And so on the twentieth day, it happened, the Candy Girl ran and did not consciously remember her latchkey past, thinking mainly of the moment.

On this morning, strangely, the past was also coiled beside the bed of the Candy Girl's employer, living not so far from the station where the steel bridge will deposit its clinging train. Out of this train will pour strap-hanging newspaper-gorged commuters, like a long sigh from an open mouth; they will stream down the street and over another bridge, past two brick towers belonging to what looks like a hospital, and there – just there! That is where Gest lives, and where she is now waking on the twentieth day, though unaware of just what day this is.

Why has the past been lying so doggedly at the side of her bed since the moment she closed her eyes the night before? See it there? See it anticipating the step-ping of her bare feet, its long body coiled into rings, its tail in its mouth, waiting, waiting. But the alarm clock rings. Get out of your bed! it orders. And, startled, Gest swings her long perfect legs over the side of her mattress – but the other side from where the past is lurking. Her perfect long feet reach for the cool floor and take her weight, and her naked body strides, still half in sleep, across the room. (Perfect body, breasts large and firm, arse smooth and skin creamy in the deep shadows thrown across the otherwise clear floor by the brick towers of the hospital next door.)

She looks at herself in the bathroom mirror, backlit by a frosted glass window. She stands square on to the mirror: sees chest, ribs, shoulders, pointed chin. The skin around her eyes is paper thin, the colour of flour: it is dough that has been stretched and rolled thin by a chef working on her face for the nineteen previous days and nights.

Suddenly she hears a voice coming through her left ear. It is broken, disjointed from struggling through the static of many long years. Chin! it says. Up!

Gest stands still, hears only water swilling through the pipes (how long before they cut the supply? Will it last the time?)

Chin up! says the voice, booming loud and clear now in her right ear. Chest out! it booms. And Gest realizes who it is: the director, *her* director, her favoured, favourite director of porn movies, and especially those she starred in.

There had been an interview once with this director, published in a male magazine. His answers had blown off the glossy pages with good-humoured scorn, and in the accompanying photograph his scruffy greying hair blew back in the wind of an off-set fan. He had provided a different slant to the usual full-frontal straight-up approach of this magazine, an angle never achieved before or since in such a dull tits-and-arse publication. And besides he was the only person ever in its history to be given a double-page spread while remaining fully clothed.

The interview had read as follows:

Q: Do you ever lust after your starlets?
A: Lust after my own porn stars! Are you mad! Why the * would I want to * one of them?
   (Most expletives, as you will see, were later deleted

103

by the magazine's editor for, although visually explicit, like most of its counterparts it was prudish in the extreme when it came to the matter of language.)

Q: Come on, you must want to take at least *some* of them to bed.

A: I'd rather take them to acting school.

Q: Have you ever had a hard-on when working on set?

A: Not a * ing hard-on, a *ing hard time! They're all prima donnas and a pain in the *.

Q: Why do they call you, ahem, the Pope?

A: Because of my golden rules.

Q: Which are? (ahem)

A: No sex before marriage. No condoms on set. And I tell them this on the first day of a shoot: to think of me as God's mouthpiece.

And so, in this sparring vein, the interview went on. But in spite of being determined to thwart the salivating journalist, the director meant what he said. He really did see his naked girls as actors, while not thinking much of their acting skills, and although he was not keen on condoms he insisted on the wearing of thongs whenever possible to help the cameramen keep their minds on the job.

Because of these things, and the fact that he genuinely liked his work and the people with whom he worked, the Pope was immensely sexy. He would sit over a late-night whisky in a small late-night bar, his paunch resting against the table, his balding scalp gleaming in the dim light, and his booth would be crammed with beautiful girls trying to get his attention. They would sit on the backs of the high seats or on the table itself, their long shining legs sprawling open and often revealing that, since the end of work, the obligatory G-strings had been discarded and would not be replaced that night.

The Pope remained unmoved by this. Move your fat arse, would you? he would say amicably in his loud rough voice, and he would peer around legs and low hanging breasts to see if his wife had arrived. He would sit back with a resigned sigh. Women! he would say. And you accuse us of having a problem with timing! Then he would laugh *HA* like a great patchy magpie, and pinch the nearest starlet's cheek (the cheek of her face, never of her derriere) and he would tell her not to worry about her career, that soon she would be too old to take her kit off and that would be an end to it.

There is something endearing about a person who can shrink youthful self-importance down to size with one sentence. There is something seductive about watching your anxieties being punctured one by one with the repeated stab of a cigar in the smoky red air, whisky fumes drifting around your head and a rough tweed arm around your shoulders. Even Gest, at one time, had thought she might be in love with the Pope, although she was already engaged to a man met in a poplar-lined street, who had bought her coffee and later a large diamond ring.

Why is the Pope speaking to her now, hollering down the years from his lofty position as the most famous soft-porn director of all times? Why, after so many inter-vening years of silence, does he bellow at her as she stands in the bathroom? It is a long time since Gest has seen the Pope: not, in fact, since a party in a cliff-top villa built high above a black volcanic Italian town.

He is speaking again into her left ear, her faulty ear, her cutting-out receiver of the distant-past ear.

Put! Shoulders! Back! Pull! Arse! In!

Gest has already put her chin up and stuck out her concave morning chest. Now her buttocks tighten instinctively and she says, uncertainly (although on many occasions the Pope had proved to have a great deal of insight) –

I have doubts.

Doubts? the Pope says with a roar in her right ear, as the hot water roars in the cistern. It's not worth a fucking penny, my beauty, if you don't have doubts.

I am scared, she says. But she whispers this into the soft bristles of her toothbrush, muffles it with foam, spits it out and rinses it down the plughole before it can be heard.

The Pope continues to talk her through dressing. Put your knickers on! Wear good shoes! Stop snivelling! Gest goes to the kitchen, wiping her eyes, not daring to look through the door of her waiting work room. From the fridge, she takes a vacuum-wrapped sponge finger filled with mock cream (Insert it in your mouth! orders the Pope. Just kidding!) This is all she can stomach: the softness of the sponge is the closest she can get to eating nothing, and she swills her mouth out with lukewarm water from the tap.

The phone rings. In her bedroom the past stirs, raises its head triumphantly. But it is only the Candy Girl. I'm running a little late because— she pauses. Because I've been running.

Running? Gest doesn't quite understand, but she needs more time anyway. For now she must go, alone, to her workroom and stand under the tall white doorway, must take a deep breath and somehow force herself into the room.

If you can't stand up for yourself, lie down! says the Pope. And take your underwear off while you're at it. HA!

Gest also gives an unwilling laugh, puts her hand on the handle of the door.

Chin up! says the Pope. Chest out!

106

And at this point Gest knows even the Pope cannot help her any more because they have come full circle. Here they are, back at the beginning of her memories, and there is no impatient confident tweedy arm to push open the door, only her own slender bare one, and only herself to stare down the work: snake-charmer, lion-tamer, faith-keeper.

When the Candy Girl turns up, puffing, rushing in with a rustling sound of water and trees and plastic lunch-bags, all is quiet. Gest is absorbed, looks almost surprised when the Candy Girl apologizes for her lateness.

When I got home from the park, explains the Candy Girl, the Micro was awake. She appears unable to sit still, there is an energy running through her that makes the chrome legs of her stool spark and gleam.

Can I ask you something? ventures Gest, picking up a pencil.

Anything! beams the Candy Girl.

Would you mind keeping your lips still? asks Gest.

Of course! The Candy Girl snaps her mouth closed. But her voice cannot be stopped, it pushes at her lips from the inside and parts them again and pushes on through. And even though the Candy Girl's face registers dismay and guilt, her voice continues of its own accord.

I think the Micro was going to ask me something! her unruly voice says.

Oh? Gest does not want to spoil this moment: it is only the twentieth day, after all; she can afford a few minutes.

I think – the Candy Girl leans forward and clasps her hands. I really think that the Micro is going to marry me.

Marriage! If Gest could see through walls, if she could see through the wall into the adjacent bedroom, she would witness an alarming sight: the past rearing up, glittering, raising its head to the sky, shedding silver scales on the bare floorboards.

That's, Gest stammers, wonderful.

Is it? She doesn't know, looking at the faint blue traces of fingermarks on the Candy Girl's upper arms. But how can she not respond to the Candy Girl's excited hands, clasped so hard that it looks as if her fingers might never disentangle from each other again. And now the phone rings again, and she answers it, and it is the Ordinary Man.

It's the middle of the night here, he says. His voice is far fainter than the Pope's, even though he is speaking from the here and now. I just called to say—

Quickly, Gest takes the phone and mouths *excuse me* to the Candy Girl and leaves the room. For only now, after many hints tossed at her from the minute of waking, she has realized: today is no small day hidden in the middle of many insignificant others. Happy Anniversary! the Ordinary Man says, as happily and politely as if they are still husband and wife. And Gest must echo the words back to him, and then chat about different weather conditions and differences in time, while the unspoken topic (the differences that have led to them being no longer husband and wife) lies between them.

So this is why you have visited me, says Gest, after she hangs up. She leans weakly against the kitchen window, still holding the phone in her sweaty hand. Straighten up! says the Pope, by way of answer. If you have good tits, for God's sake show them!

Although there is no one in the kitchen to admire Gest, her straight spine and her perfect breasts, she stands up straight out of habit. When she turns to glance out into the courtyard, the glass behind her is slick with sweat from her bare shoulders.

On that day, ten years ago, the Pope had spoken at the

wedding ceremony. I have never seen a finer couple, he had said, nor a more fuckable one. (The crowd had laughed at this, but many of them looked in a hungry way at Gest and the Ordinary Man, sitting there handsome in their white.) I can only say, the Pope rocked back on his shiny leather heels, that it is our loss this fine couple has chosen, from this moment on, to fuck only each other.

At this the Ordinary Man had turned to Gest, sitting on her white throne beside him. He had taken her by the throat, quite roughly, and kissed her so hard that the room fell silent and then cheered. It had been an odd assortment of guests: beautiful bra-less girls who later became topless, men with diamond buckles at their waists and crocodile-skin shoes, professionals in dark suits with neat ties knotted under their chins, and – well, all kinds of people who became progressively drunker on champagne and eggnog.

Eggnog? queries the Candy Girl, after Gest has gone back in and told her what today really is, after all.

We chose a Christmas theme for our wedding. Gest's voice becomes wispy, white and cool, although the morning outside is humid. And my bridesmaids—

Were they, um, actresses too? asks the Candy Girl avidly. (She does not like to say the word *porn* aloud, out of respect for this special day, although she whispers it quietly to herself as she treads off down the stairs at the end of the day.)

Actresses, agrees Gest, all eight of them. Instead of flowers they held tiny Christmas trees in their hands, and there was tinsel in their blonde hair.

All of them blonde? The Candy Girl's hands go up to her own hair (tigery and bold in some places, in others faded to mouse). She ruffles it up in the way that the Micro likes.

All blonde, agrees Gest. And the Ordinary Man wore

a white suit and a white satin tie, and looked like a rock star. (Strangely, the Ordinary Man's quiet well-modulated voice has already gone from her head, although it is only ten minutes since she heard it talking of differing seasons and degrees of heat: the Pope, speaking ten years ago, is easier to hear.)

And I say to you all, the Pope proclaims to the room, since most of you are in the esteemed business of taking off your clothes and being filmed in flagrante − (the crowd roars again; some of them have already left the room and are making love in the luxurious bathrooms down the corridor, heads thrown back over marble basins, slim thighs braced against marble benches) − I tell you all, the Pope warms to his theme, there will come a day when you realize that your time in this erotic game is up! For life is a big playground, my friends, and our trade is only swings and roundabouts.

Explain! the crowd shouts.

You − says the Pope, spinning on his heel to wave at the tiny-waisted big-breasted happy bridesmaids with tinsel in their hair − you will lose your figures from drinking too much eggnog.

Or, he says, turning back to the room, counting on his fingers:

− your husband will get jealous and demand that you find another job

− you will have a child and decide you must remain clothed in front of cameras

− you will come to the realization that life has changed and so have you, and you will let others do the dirty work.

Had these things happened? Gest stares at the Candy Girl now and there is a mist between her eyes and the Candy Girl's face. Was she not involved in dirty work right now? Work that makes her sweat and lie awake at

110

night, bringing with it a burden so heavy that by night-fall she can hardly walk?

But the Pope is smiling kindly at her and her new husband, and is kissing them on both cheeks. His face is as rough and unshaven as always and his breath is laden with alcohol, but his eyes are clear. Blessings on you, my children, he says; and he is only half joking. And my papal gift to you, he says, is my very own recipe, The Kentucky Comforter!

In fact Gest still knows this recipe by heart, although she has not made one or drunk one since the Ordinary Man walked out of her life. She remembers the way that the Pope had danced with his wife, a large middle-aged woman with wide feet and a laugh that rang around the room whenever the Pope whispered something in her ear. When Gest and the Ordinary Man went out into the street, followed by a clamouring, glamorous, scantily clad crowd, the Pope's wife had held Gest's hand as she sat in the reindeer-drawn sleigh.

How do you do it? said Gest, slightly desperately, over the gilded side of the carriage.

The Pope's wife had not needed to ask what Gest meant: she had winked at Gest through the dark and the tinsel and the confetti falling like snow through the warm balmy night. There is no secret, she said into Gest's ear, and her voice was happy and sad. Just hang on and hope.

But it can happen? asked Gest, looking sideways at the Ordinary Man's quiet happiness.

Of course it can! said the Pope's wife, and the last thing Gest saw as the sleigh pulled away was the Pope sweeping his dumpy overweight radiant wife into his arms and kissing her all over, while all around them glamour girls in red Santa hats cavorted to the tune of O Tannenbaum.

Are you OK? the Candy Girl asks now. Her voice

creeps through the mist, finds its way to Gest. It must be hard on a day like today, she coughs embarrassedly, with your ex and your kid so far away.

Hard? says Gest vaguely. She goes over and throws the balcony doors open. It's so hot, she says.

Strange for spring, agrees the Candy Girl, also walking over to the doors to sample the outside air. It should be cooler for this time of year, she says, and she sounds almost reproving, as if the world has disappointed her by not conforming to seasonal expectations.

(But what can we expect, thinks Gest, when we create midwinter weddings in spring and drive reindeer through the city streets?)

Do you need a rest? the Candy Girl asks. You look a bit peaky.

Gest wipes the film of sweat off her top lip. Perhaps I'll lie down, she says. Just for a few minutes.

Her bedroom is empty: nothing lies on the floor except for discarded underwear and shoes. Chin up! she hears, faintly, as she lies down with her left ear to the pillow. With her right ear she can hear the Candy Girl tiptoeing heavily down the hall to the kitchen, and the clink of glass against the tap.

The Kentucky Comforter, she says into the pillow. Two parts sweet-potato juice to one part bourbon.

And so it happens that the twentieth day, which is also the day of a near proposal for the Candy Girl, slips towards midday. And so it happens that the twentieth day, which is also the eleventh anniversary of Gest's failed marriage, reaches its cusp and falls on into the afternoon.

Two level teaspoons of demerara sugar, recites Gest against her pillow, and three leaves of mint.

Four! corrects the Pope.

Four leaves of garden mint, says Gest obediently. Tear

them, to release the flavour. Her mouth moves awkwardly on the rough cotton, almost hurting, like a kiss from a whiskered mouth.

Shake with ice, and strain frothily into a highball glass. Garnish with extra mint.

Her grandfather the imbecile

Her grandfather had been an imbecile.

He had not approved of women, and because of this – because he thought women were to be disapproved of, on account of their foolishness – his wife had turned into an imbecile also.

(I was brought up in an imbecilic household, intones Gest, in jest. I was brought up by a well-matched pair, a pair of matching imbeciles.)

At mealtimes, her grandfather would do the daily crossword in a chilling silence. If his wife or granddaughter ventured a word – if they coughed, even, or scraped a fork too loudly on a plate – he would slam his newspaper down on the table and leave the room, whether or not he had finished eating. Things vibrated in his wake: the tablecloth shook, plates rattled, the water in the glasses tilted, and the walls themselves began to undulate before Gest's eyes. Then her breath would start rushing in and out of her ears, and the only thing to do was get under the table and hold on tightly to its wooden legs, while looking fixedly at the carpet to avoid the sight of her grandmother's own thin legs, her ashamed ankles and knocking knees.

Gest's grandfather was an imbecile, but one with an extraordinary amount of power. His rage was astounding and his arrogance even greater, and whenever he became arrogant and angry spit flew from his lips and his face became purple and mottled.

For most of his adult life he had worked in a bank which employed no women; there were no female secretaries, and no women answered the phones or cleaned the floors or counted out the wads of notes. Neither did this bank encourage female customers: only the boldest would step through its shiny oak doors, only the bravest and most stylish, those who carried hats and purses and possessed the confidence to request their own bank accounts. The grandfather's world was a particularly hierarchical one, in which women were stupid and homosexuals filthy and children beneath notice and animals dirty, and if he was forced to deal with any of these pestilences in a more than superficial way – well, then saliva would start to fly so the floor became speckled, and the shouting purple cheeks swelled in Gest's vision until she had to close her eyes and count backwards from a hundred, fast and concentratedly, so the day did not splinter into matchwood around her.

Because the grandfather's wife was considered foolish by her husband, not surprisingly she had turned into a fool, a woman who tittered with laughter at the sight of someone slipping on frozen ground and spinning, falling, toppling like an ice skater.

There's nothing funny about that! growled her husband, Gest's grandfather. And Gest's grandmother – who had taken on the task of bringing up Gest because of the fact that Gest's mother had been killed in a car accident two weeks after giving birth and Gest's father was too grief-stricken to cope with anything let alone a baby daughter – would bite her lip and quickly agree

114

that, no, of course nothing was funny, her words slipping out quickly and dully over her stone lips, adding to the already huge pool of irrelevant, unacknowledged, past agreements.

Although the grandmother sometimes made the mistake of laughing when things went badly for other people, she grew anxious when a child dropped a cup of milk on her floor. In that household there were only plastic cups that always seemed faintly unclean, carrying with them a lingering smell that reminded Gest of the bottles filled with acrid yellow piss she had seen when her uncle was in the cancer ward of the hospital, and because of this – to avoid the feeling that she was swallowing urine and might catch cancer – she held her six-year-old breath when drinking her daily cup of milk.

(This was difficult, she tells the Candy Girl later.

What was? asks the Candy Girl, only half listening because reading a magazine article about how to flatten your stomach by raising your legs to a ninety-degree angle and stretching your elbows towards your knees.

It is difficult to drink without breathing, explains Gest, and that is why I often spilled my milk.

The Candy Girl decides to try this method of drinking straight away, with all her attention. There is something obliging and immediate about the way she does such things, something immensely reassuring about her willingness to *try things out*, thereby keeping the hands of the clock moving steadily forwards instead of sticking, standing still. She stops thinking about pointing her legs and elbows skywards, and she reaches out for the bottle of lukewarm water sitting beside her, evaporating in the sun, unscrews the hot blue plastic top with a quiet hiss, takes a deep breath and tries to drink. But it is only a second before she starts to laugh *ha ha ha* into the neck of the bottle and she must pull it away from her red mouth before she chokes.)

Back in the days of the imbecilic grandfather, though, it had been no laughing matter. He had such a temper that when a piss-plastic drinking cup was dropped between small sandalled feet – falling, bouncing on the linoleum, cascading white fluid from its bad-smelling plastic mouth – his wife would instantly move between him and the child, brandishing a mop, apologising, reeking of her own brand of fear. As for Gest, she would rush away to crouch between the stove and the fridge, still holding her breath, and her lungs would fill up with some unnamed emotion until there was a haze before her eyes. The fridge offered a kind of shelter, harbour from the milk storm, flat white water to soothe her fright, but before her lay the tempest. And from this she was protected only by the humming motor at her back and, in front of her, a frightened imbecile (a woman, once) with a foolish mop.

He was a bastard, declares the Ordinary Man protectively. And what about your father? They are lying in bed, Gest and her liberated husband, with their fingers linked: elbows propped on the hipbones, hands pointed in pyramids towards the ceiling.

My father? Gest pauses. He was the nicest man.

The Ordinary Man pretends to take offence. She must kiss him, kiss his cock even while talking of her father, her mouth moving against his foreskin, his cock moving involuntarily against her lips.

He was, she mumbles quickly, the nicest man *apart from you*. She knows this is a lie, even as she says it like a prayer into the hot human dark: her father had been the nicest man she had ever known, and no man in the world can rival a father. He loved me, she says, more than I could bear and so he died.

116

The Ordinary Man pulls at her hair and lifts her head up, telling her not to blame herself for her father's death. (Later, of course, he makes it clear that he considers Gest to blame for everything that has ever gone wrong in the history of mankind.)

But Gest does, she does blame herself, and as she lays her head on the dark sheet she feels the guilt so strongly that she must bite the sheet. She grinds her teeth through the black cotton, tastes dried semen and flakes of skin and the faintest grit of undissolved washing powder. She bites and bites at the edge of the sheet and, out loud, remembers that her father died because she was away in another place.

Not *because*, the Ordinary Man corrects. *While* you were in another place. That is what you mean.

While, or because? These are interpretative words that lag after the facts, their tardy dragging feet bringing neither certainty nor comfort. What were the cold, the hard facts? They were as follows:

Gest had loved her father more than anyone else in the world but, by the time she was old enough to recognize him, he was already unrecognizable. That is, he had once been a big man but after his wife's death he had shrivelled, become shrunken from grief.

The father had seen Gest once a week only in all the years of her growing up: most of her passage from small dark frightened child to tall dark watchful teenager had been missed by him. Oh, he loved her! She could tell this by the way he looked at her with tears in his eyes every time he left her. But he was no good for her the way he was, or so he believed, and so every week he had left her behind to be taken care of by two ageing imbeciles. Was it surprising, then, that as soon as Gest was old enough she had shrugged her lean and gorgeous shoulders and moved as far away as she could get?

She had taken work as a barmaid in a small roadside town, a fun, mad and bad place where people moved on so fast that morality never got a chance to dig in its claws. And after several months of working there, in that small-town juke-box bar where regulars drank till they dropped but never cared to know each other's names, Gest had also become infected by carelessness. She had not taken enough care, had not held the memory of her frail, fragile father carefully enough in her alcohol-soaked head.

Because of this, he became sick. That was it, that was her interpretation. At some time while she was pouring endless bourbon and cokes her father had become sick, though of course he had always been frail. Of what was his fragility born? Of having been left, bereft.

Left? By whom?

First by his wife, who had disappeared one late afternoon in a maelstrom of metal. A hard sledgehammer sun breaking the windshield, splintering it with a dazzling fist, picking up handfuls of glass and flinging them into the motorway. Limbs and other body parts flying too: legs and arms, hands outstretched as if trying to catch the shoes soaring from severed feet. The unbroken windscreen of a truck lying on its side, covered all over with bright shards of metal and bright sprays of blood. This, for the father, was the beginning of the end.

And who had left Gest's father after that?

Well, Gest, of course! Early on for the house of the imbecilic grandfather, and later for a small bar with brown beer-soaked carpet and long green pool tables that stretched before her like runways, promising escape.

So there they are, the unarguable facts. Gest in another place; her father frail in mind and then frail in body. Whether or not Gest's leaving had any part to play in his death – the death of the nicest man she had ever known, up to and including her husband – this is impossible to say.

Thus he had died, one bereaved person passing the condition on to another. Although when they called Gest in the middle of the day so as not to interrupt her schedule (they thought she was working in a pharmacy, she had led them to believe this, and so they believed now they were calling in her lunch hour) – yes, when they called her as she lay, still tangled up in hangover sheets, they said only that her father had gone into a decline.

A decline. Gest grinds her perfect white teeth into the black sheet as she repeats the word to the Ordinary Man. That was the word they used, the most archaic of words.

Archaic? queries the Ordinary Man into the blank dark room. He understands the definition but he does not see, now, the insult of using such a ridiculous, polite, and old-fashioned word to a hungover teenaged Gest lying in her ignorant bed.

And so she had learned about her father's death by instalments. While she was standing by her bed pulling on her knickers still lined with the mucus of lust from the night before, caused by the barman with the dark red hair who had pulled her against him behind the door and slid his hand up under her shirt so her nipples had become as hard and spiked as mountains and she had to go back to serve men who would only look at those nipples – while she stands by her morning bed and pulls those stained silky twelve-hour-ago-slippery knickers up her long thighs and over her flat hips, there are tears in her eyes and her father is in a decline. He might still make it, or so the phone call goes.

Before she leaves the room, skirt half zipped, overnight bag fully zipped, and dark hair in a tangle of regret (the barman is still lying in her bed, pillow pulled over his head to shut out the midday sun, one leg hanging loosely to the floor, and even the sight of his long-toed ridged foot makes her want to stay, in spite of her declining, shrinking, slipping father) the phone rings again. The barman mumbles. Gest snatches it up to hear that her father has just slipped to the bottom of the declining slope. He is now in a coma.

The barman kisses her goodbye, hard even through sleep so her lip begins to bleed. By the time she is boarding a plane the blood is dry; it is a crusty scab by the time she gets to the airport of another city, once her home, with a large free sky and many green spaces although it has since become small and despised in her eyes. Her bitten lip is scabbed by this time, and her father is dead.

He died – Gest laughs to the Ordinary Man, but not with any humour – my father died in instalments. But do you know something?

What? asks the Ordinary Man, nervously but also with a new certainty in his voice, for he now truly believes he is on a par with the dead father.

He had been dead all along, says Gest in a loud voice, into the dark. While I was sweeping and fucking and sleeping and waking, my father was already cold.

And now the Ordinary Man is somewhat surprised, but more by the Machiavellian manner of breaking the news than that a teenage Gest had been pushing the limits of her body and testing the resilience of her heart in the hours during which the body of her father was slackening and his broken heart slowing its beat to a standstill. When he speaks, however, the surprise in his voice is stitched tightly around by resentment: he does not like to hear about Gest fucking other men, even though this was years before she knew of his existence.

What was he like? he manages to say. He is referring, of course, to Gest's father, though for a moment it seems as if he could be speaking of the red-haired barman who had penetrated Gest on her narrow bed before falling into a heavy sleep, the barman who even in sleep could kiss Gest so hard that her lip was still bee-stung at her father's funeral several days later.

My father? says Gest. He was the nicest man.

She rolls onto her back, still holding the sheet in her mouth, takes hold of the black cotton edge with both hands and runs it out fast and roughly between her front teeth so that once again, all these years later, she tastes blood. In retrospect she is surprised that people (by which she means herself) do not die of grief at such moments, when truth and deception are revealed at one and the same time. The extent of both is enough to close the lungs forever, the impact of both great enough that the lungs might collapse inwards like flowers into a sudden darkness.

Say it again, though of course it will change nothing.

My grandfather was an imbecile. My father, the nicest man.

The porn star

By now the Candy Girl feels as if she knows Gest well enough to ask. Besides, her legs are tired – she has been sitting still for a long time here on the twenty-second day – and it is easier to ask someone a potentially sensitive question if you are wandering around the room and looking out the window.

Gest does not take offence, however. On the contrary, she seems to see the Candy Girl's question as quite an ordinary one.

When I was eighteen, she explains, I was spotted by a talent scout working for a modelling agency.

The Candy Girl is not at all surprised by this. If someone has sleek black hair and skin that can pick up a nuance and throw back a mood: if someone has eyes as black as satin sheets and legs as smooth and long as skyscrapers, it stands to reason that talent scouts and model agencies will follow.

After this, says Gest, I did some lingerie modelling for billboards. (The Candy Girl catches her breath at the beauty of a Gest who is fifteen feet tall and standing on the side of a motorway.)

And then, continues Gest, I went for a film audition that turned out to require nudity. And after that it happened. I became a porn star.

Yes, a porn star! The Candy Girl's own eyes are not black but they become satin-shiny at this. She hops back onto her high stool and stays obediently still, her chin turned towards the door, but her satiny eyes dart constantly sideways to look at Gest. She is impressed, she is happy that her employer has such a colourful past, and happy to hear about it.

Only soft porn, assures Gest, and only for fun. It was trash for the masses.

But it must have been difficult. The Candy Girl tries not to move her lips when she speaks; she is not sure if Gest is working on her mouth at that moment but she talks far back in her throat, just in case. All that deep kissing, she says in an odd, lipless voice.

It's easier to kiss, Gest laughs, than to learn four pages of bad dialogue.

What about your husband? says the Candy Girl, and

as she approaches this topic her already slow voice becomes slower, and tentative. This is only the twenty-second day, after all, and there is a thin circle of untested ice around Gest that makes the Candy Girl tread cautiously. What did your husband think of it all? she queries, carefully.

He hated it. Gest puts down a blade with a clatter. He hated the fact that other people might have seen me naked with neither of us knowing.

But wasn't he proud of you? The Candy Girl is slightly puzzled, thinking of how the Micro likes her wearing short skirts and low tops in public. Wasn't he proud of your work?

Maybe of my movies early on, says Gest. At first he never watched them, he just liked the thought of them. And then later, when we were—

Fucking? breathes the Candy Girl.

When we were estranged, corrects Gest, after that he would watch my movies over and over again so he could tell me how much he hated them.

Not true, states the Candy Girl. All men like porn. It's a genetic thing, not offensive.

All men like porn— Gest pauses. Except for porn that their wives star in.

Ha ha ha. This is the Candy Girl, roaring with laughter. She no longer takes care to keep her head still, she rolls it back against the wall so her throat shows bands of quivering muscle. *Ha ha ha*, she laughs and Gest laughs too, though believing what she has said. She remembers the stony face of the Ordinary Man as he watched a slapstick scene: Gest and two other actresses (supposedly cloned by a mad scientist) bursting out of a birthday cake, wearing nothing but some strategically piped white icing. That's disgusting, the Ordinary Man is saying remotely, trying to pull his eyes away from the six luscious breasts (two of them belonging to his wife) and three pairs of tight gleaming buttocks. That's disgusting, he says, fast-forwarding to resist temptation. You shouldn't make light of cloning.

It did become a problem in the end, shrugs Gest. She picks up her tools again and the Candy Girl bites her lip to stop the laughter that is still bubbling up inside her, partly from relief at a topic broached after so long.

It was a problem, says Gest soberly, at parties.

Certainly there had been a problem that particular evening, in spite of the fact that it was some months after Gest had left the world of cakes and body oil and high stiletto heels. Although the party had not been his the Ordinary Man had stationed himself by the punch bowl and appointed himself master of the ladle (a good way to have unexpected conversations, he said) so that he was not there when Gest was approached by someone who seemed to think she looked familiar.

He was a telephone engineer, this man, and Gest hardly knew what questions to ask about this, but she was adept at turning a conversation by now, could swing it with one breath as easily as a weathercock swinging in the wind. And so she led the engineer, lamb-like, away from a possible discussion of why Gest might look familiar to him and steered him instead into the middle of a conversation about his own life's work which turned out to be about regional systems and computer design.

Gest needed something more visual to grasp this (always hung-up on the visual, the Ordinary Man said later, when he could no longer complain about her porn career and needed to pick on her art). And so finally she got the telephone engineer to describe the fact that the systems he worked with were linked to those grey metal boxes that you see but never notice on the side of every city street.

You never notice them, he agreed, until you're *worked in the field*. His voice rang with certainty as he said this: he had the glow of one who had been born into a trade and had turned it into a profession, and was therefore happy for life.

(Across the room the Ordinary Man lifted a large dripping ladle and poured a generous orange glassful of punch for a fellow psychologist. He looked animated: perhaps he was having his own unexpected conversation?)

And inside the boxes, the phone engineer explained to Gest, are hundreds of coloured switches.

Oddly enough (and when Gest repeats this to the Candy Girl they almost begin laughing again) the phone engineer's name was Cord. Although, he joked, I mostly deal with cordless. Can you imagine the bad old days when you had to talk tethered to a wall socket? Talk about a time waster!

It was true, what he had told her; for not many minutes after that someone walked past and said hello to him.

Hey, Cord! that person had said, and not a joking kind of person either: a large man who looked impressive in spite of the fact that there was a flake of pastry caught in the side of his bushy moustache, and when he said the name *Cord* this flake lifted, almost came free, floating to the floor as lightly as a eucalyptus leaf on a Portuguese hillside; but before this could happen the impressive pastry-man passed on by, giving Gest an approving nod and also the information that, although Cord had learnt enough to make a joke out of the fix in which his parents had landed him, he was serious enough when it came to telling the truth.

But now Cord was again looking intently at Gest. And—

You really do look familiar, he said.

As bad luck would have it, the Ordinary Man had just

put down his ladle and finished off the kind of unexpected conversation that as likely as not he had most days in the hospital staffroom, although over a bubbling water cooler instead of a sparkling punch bowl. Now he was behind Gest, putting his hand on her shoulder, just as Cord the phone engineer, unknown to the Ordinary Man until this moment, was saying how familiar his wife looked. And of course, as the Ordinary Man intuited instantly and correctly, Gest had never met the phone engineer before this evening.

There was never any easy way of telling men why I looked familiar, explains Gest to the Candy Girl. There had certainly been no easy way to tell pleasant Cord, whose fiancée was hovering happily over the buffet holding a forked-tongue cheese knife in her right hand even though she was left-handed to avoid clattering her solitaire diamond against the stainless-steel knife handle.

I don't think we've met, said Gest abruptly. She was usually more practised at deflecting such comments but she had been taken unaware by the lemony hand of her husband on her shoulder.

Maybe I fixed your phone line once, in the days when I was still doing repairs? said Cord, continuing to peer at her. Could that be it?

Gest said that it could, and that it probably was, and she said so quickly to avoid embarrassing him. For in front of her stood a pleasant man who had taken the time to give her something new, something new to notice when she walked in the streets, so that now when she passed the closed sentry shapes of grey metal fuse boxes the smell of cream cheese rolled in crushed walnuts would come back into her nostrils, and when she took a second look at the louvred doors of the boxes then she would see straight through them to a balled-up bundle of colourful wires leading into the heart of the earth and into private homes and back out again, linking people who went to parties to chat and eat walnut balls and those who never went out at all, living instead with their ears permanently, hopefully, trained for the vibrations that happen just before the phone begins to ring.

(She was so well-known that men recognized her? asks the Micro interestedly. What's her name?

But the Candy Girl won't say.)

Behind Gest the Ordinary Man is rigid with anger. The smell of lemon becomes stronger now, leaking from his fingers like acid, and Gest's throat is sharp and aching from breathing in his hurt and annoyance, her eyes water with the effort of trying to protect her husband's hurt pride at having a wife who once took her clothes off for money, revealing the beautiful body that is now fully clothed but nonetheless stands right in front of an engaged man who, at some time, has watched her cavorting on screen with no clothes on at all.

We must go, says Gest to the phone engineer. She puts her hand up to her shoulder to touch the smarting fingers of the Ordinary Man, but they are gone. He is gone. He has gone to talk to a smart-looking woman with deep red hair standing like a beacon against the green curtains, and Gest is left with a slightly better knowledge of the engineering world and a much better knowledge of the tangled human wires below the surface of every party conversation. As she watches Cord she sees the knowledge dawning in his eyes; next week he will marry his happy knife-wielding blonde fiancée with her pink-lipstick mouth who will never know that now and then, when she is out with girlfriends, her husband rents porn movies and wanks on the sofa accompanied by the low moaning of women like Gest, now retired but who still has a body to die for, and whom he has now met and talked to and will fantasise over when he fucks his fiancée this very night.

(Tell me her name, demands the Micro. Are you scared I'll fall in love with her?

She's too old for you anyway, says the Candy Girl, marching to the fridge. She takes out a bottle of milk and drinks from the bottle, puts it down and repeats herself. She's too old for you, and she has a kid.

You're jealous, says the Micro. Had he said this to any other girl it might be true, but not in the case of the Candy Girl who doesn't have a jealous bone in her body. The round glass mouth of the bottle has kissed her, leaving her top lip imprinted with a milky half-circle, and now the Micro wants to kiss her also.)

And so it went on, says Gest, and her voice sounds sad. He trusted me less and less, and there was always the issue of what to tell the Child when he grew up.

All boy children like porn, says the Candy Girl quickly. Especially porn their mothers star in! But her joke has a hollow ring to it.

(Couldn't we watch one of her movies together? This is the Micro again, wheedling, persistent, coming up and pushing the Candy Girl against the open fridge so the chill rises under the back of her too-short T-shirt and makes the hair on her arms stand on end. Bottles clink behind her, the freezer box cracks, the Micro leans against her in a state of wanting, wanting his girlfriend as well as all those soft images of mouths and cunts and pink nipples looking as if they are swollen by lust but that are simply erect because of being filmed in a draughty unheated warehouse, with lighting men and cameramen hired by the hour.)

When did he get over that jealousy? asks the Candy Girl. Your husband? She is anxious; this is not really the side of the story she has wanted to hear.

When he took himself away, I suppose. Gest sounds uncertain; had the jealousy ever left the Ordinary Man in the way that love had?

128

He took himself away? The Candy Girl's eyes are no longer shiny from excitement, they are shiny from anticipated fear.

Yes. And Gest takes her feet off the rungs of her stool, and puts them down *crash* in a pile of tools so that the Candy Girl hears only disjointed phrases falling into the middle of clattering hammers and chisels.

Felt unneeded, says Gest's voice. Went and fell. In love. Someone else.

This is bad enough, but it is not this which makes the Candy Girl press the palms of her hands hard against the wall so that the small stucco pinpoints might hurt and distract her from what she is hearing.

He took who? she breathes, and a tear falls now, round, perfect, on her rounded pink breast.

Gest stops shuffling and swivels straight ahead. Her mouth is in a perfectly straight line: no quavering, no lift in the corners. She has had time to perfect this.

He took the Child, she says.

The Portuguese story

If you have read the Candy Girl's story you will know that once, long ago, she had gone to Portugal, lucking her way to Lisbon, working as a roadie for a band.

Lisboa, she called that city situated in the south, where the long secretive lips of the sea led into a wide-mouthed harbour, and green palm trees leaned over narrow streets. *Lisboa*, just as the locals said it; and when the Candy Girl told stories of her time in the Portuguese north where she had ended up, drifting up the coast with her new-found, dying friend – well, when she spoke of her time in the towns of the north then she would say 'Por-to', with a break in the middle of the word like a bridge of two halves. And simply by the way she said this, you knew straight away: the Candy Girl had loved that country like no other, and part of her had died there, in a white town by the sea.

It is on the twenty-third day that the Candy Girl tells Gest about Portugal. First she speaks of the clear and windy air for today, here, there is also a wind, and when Gest opens the window the wooden frame knocks on the white wall leaving small bruises on the plaster. *Knock knock*, and the Candy Girl speaks.

It was under the bridges of Porto, she says, that I found the boy.

She does not explain but Gest knows what the Candy Girl had been doing under one of those bridges, on a night so hot and close that just to breathe in made your lungs feel as if they would stick together and not separate again, so you might never expel the dark foreign voices and the cloying call of the boats on the river.

After this, the Candy Girl begins to speak rapidly. Words pour out of her, the windows rock in the wind, and Gest hears how the Candy Girl and the Drug Boy had made their way up the coast from Porto to a beautiful village, overlooked by a cathedral high on a conical hill. Why had they ended up here? Simply because they had hitched a ride with a couple, a middle-aged English-speaking couple who, sixty miles into the trip, had figured out that the girl and the boy they were giving a ride to were at best carrying drugs to sell, and at worst were addicts themselves. And so they had been dumped uncer-emoniously, that boy and girl, on the outskirts of a sublime, quiet, beautiful coastal village but they had enough cash in their pockets to get a room in a cheap hotel. And this was all OK, until the third morning when the Candy Girl, waking up restless, had forged out into the day and had returned an hour later to find her best friend and companion all but dead. And hadn't she then flushed hundreds of dollars' worth of white powder instantly, unflinchingly down the toilet in that holding-breath time between the closing of the phone line and the opening of the hotel-room door, through which marched foreign ambulance drivers who smelt of breaded octopus and had scant sympathy for a crying girl looking as if she had been out jogging, though it was more likely she had been doing a drug deal in the eucalyptus grove above the town while her friend (this boy, this half-dead, soon-to-be-dead, boy companion and friend) lay dehydrating in an airless room where the harsh sound of his breathing drowned out the sound of the sea. But it was true: the Candy Girl had been running, and in fact when the ambulance arrived she was still wearing her battered pair of running shoes and a sports bra with a dark V of sweat, making it look as if there had been a migration of birds between her cooling breasts in the time it had taken her to look up the emergency number in the stained phone book and realize that dollars were value-less and white powder meaningless, and decide that, after she had seen her beloved travelling companion and friend buried with city money in a small plot down by a grimy river, she would move to a city where she was known by no one except the eye of God and she would begin a life in which she would truly help people to connect with God or others in the world or simply themselves, and never again would she put herself in the dangerous, knife-edge, seductive situation she had been in that morning: knees lifting high under the fragrant eucalyptus branches, headphones on, drums beating loudly in her brain, and with every step taken her mind focused on cheap perfume and candle flames and how many more minutes until the first fix of the day. And this, just as the only person she truly loved at that time took his last, searing, semi-conscious, regretful but full of relief, breaths of air.

Had her boy companion met his death in the way everyone had expected? The tediously predictable way, suffered through by so many of their friends? No, it had been no overdose, but a tumour that had been growing inside him for many long months. A tumour that had been eating him up, this boy, and had left him skeletal: flat hips and a flat squeezed sounding voice, though even the Candy Girl had thought this was simply an effect of the drugs he took.

(There was a tumour inside him, she tells Gest, as large as a tennis ball. Larger than that, she says with a tear in her voice, and it tore him in two.)

After the ambulance men had taken both the boy and the Candy Girl to the hospital, and after she left alone, she had walked home along a long road, small sharp pieces of gravel flicking into the backs of her shoes and piercing the soles of her feet. She sat in the hotel room for many long hours until the day slid away into darkness and then, at last, she got into the bed where she had found the boy lying that morning. And she had taken up the position in which he had lain: face pressed into the wall, back turned on the room (when she had seen him there, the sharp steps of his spine reminded her of the hundred shallow steps she had recently run up to get to the dome soaring in front of her). So she lay in the bed with her forehead pushed hard against the cracking wall, feeling the prickle of dried blood on her feet, and then she pulled the thin sheet over her head and slept, with the last particles of the boy's skin and the smell of his death-sweat drifting into her lungs. So that during the night she breathed in the last remnants of the boy, and in the morning he was gone.

After waking to a completely empty room, the Candy Girl had pulled on her running shoes once more. Pulled the laces tight, pulled the door shut, and headed out of the room into the bright new day. This time she had run, not upwards, but straight along the side of the main highway as fast as if the devil was following her. It was not beautiful, but it had been necessary: the hard tarseal under her feet, the green trees far above her, the hot cars panting on her as she ran.

After hearing this story to its end, Gest is able to look at the Candy Girl from a distance for the first time in weeks. So many days have been spent observing her in detail that somehow Gest has lost sight of the whole. She looks at the Candy Girl's serious face, the stillness of her body suggesting a mountainside, a cathedral, a stoical permanence built up over years.

That is a very sad story, she says, softly.

Yes, it is, says the Candy Girl. I still dream about him sometimes.

Now there is silence. Gest would like to offer something but the Candy Girl appears to need no sympathy. Running, singing, crying, fucking: whatever she is engaged in, there is a solidity to her that will keep her upright.

The silence stretches on, the need to say something grows. Do you think you will be around for the unveiling? offers Gest, at last.

The Candy Girl looks confused. Unveiling? She turns her mind away from Portugal, thinks of Catholic girls in bridal gowns, has a vague memory of a story told to her at school about Salome and her seven layers of gauze.

I mean the unveiling of the work, explains Gest. When

133

it is finished there will be a civic opening, with guests.

The wind slams the window frame into the wall so hard that both Gest and the Candy Girl jump. Gest gets up to shut the wind out and, when she turns back, she gives a start for the Candy Girl is right behind her. That is, she says uncertainly, if you care to go to such an opening.

Care to go! says the Candy Girl, beaming. If you want me there, of course I'll go! She stands squarely in front of Gest, whose eyes are stinging from plastic fumes and the story she has just heard. She stands there in the middle of Gest's chaotic workroom, surrounded by tools and debris and dust, and she is so close that Gest can see the rise and fall of air in her breast.

Of course I'll come! she says. Wild horses wouldn't keep me away. She stretches out her pink wool arms as if she would invite the whole world along with her.

Gest's sigh falls into a suddenly windless room, and it sounds almost like relief. She looks at the Candy Girl for minutes on end as if she is trying to memorise her: a saviour in a pink cardigan, a hand-knitted survivor.

The Red Queen hypothesis

When had her body started to hurt? At the same time as her mind, or sometime afterwards? It is hard to remember exactly when the rain began by the time your clothes are soaked through and the hems of your trousers are dragging with water.

Gest sits in the echoing front room listening to the

Candy Girl's footsteps fade away, getting fainter as they tread down the stairs, heading for the cracked black hallway and the world outside. Her leavings are gentle but inexorable, as all leavings should be (her arrivals the opposite, being as bombastic and sudden as the first sun over the rooftops.)

They have worked late today and the room is already dim. The red and white striped tower stretches its long neck to peer over the houses and into the room. Its blinking light splits the growing darkness around Gest.

When had the pain started? But this is the kind of question that a person like the Ordinary Man would ask, or someone treating Gest in a professional capacity. The only answer Gest can give herself is passive. At some time in the past, her body and her mind had begun to hurt. And since then, since then—

But she must sit on the floor to avoid the peering, craning eye of the tower.

She shelters under the window sill. The sensation in her leg is too undefined to be called pain. Holding it stiff and bracing it against the wall makes it hurt, and so makes it better. To put a name to things, even if that name is pain: this helps.

Gest knows she must move to the kitchen. For in that room, she remembers, there had once been the ringing of a phone: a starting point, and she must backtrack to the time when things first began to crumble. But tonight it is strangely difficult to move. She ends up crawling out of the workroom and along the hallway, feet dragging behind her like the legs of an amphibian more used to dwelling in the sea.

At last she is here. She is here in the past, and sure enough the phone is ringing. But when she gets out of her chair to answer it, her feet have become unreliable. They twist under her, she almost falls.

I'm calling to see if you're all right? It is the Ordinary Man. He sounds all right himself: substantial, his feet planted firmly on the ground. It is Gest's feet that are losing touch with reality, her soles that are finding it difficult to register the touch of the floor.

She does not tell the Ordinary Man about this phenomenon. Why should she? They are no longer married, she can no longer expect him to listen to the small physical problems that once they would have shared. Apart from the sudden unreliability of her feet, apart from the pain in her leg that makes her lean heavily on the kitchen bench while she talks, apart from these things she is OK; she reassures the Ordinary Man of this, and they have a brief conversation. For instance:

When is your opening next month? asks the Ordinary Man.

This is a fairly normal question, and one that Gest tries to answer. But the calendar is tacked to the wall some distance away, and on her way to the wall Gest encounters a chair. She sinks down into it, and stays. There is no hurry.

A voice is talking quietly in the background, at the other end of the phone. Gest identifies it as the Patient; even without the background voice, she would have known that the Patient was present simply by the quickening of the Ordinary Man's tone, and the way the phone grows hot in her hand from receiving long-distance guilt.

I was just calling to see, the Ordinary Man pauses, if you want anything?

Gest begins to say something but at that moment the line cuts out. I do want, she says dully into the dead line. I want to talk to the Child. But the line hums into her ear, the receiver lies greasy and guilty in her hand, her feet prickle. He does not call back. They did not call.

And after that day Gest's feet had never been quite

136

the same. The blood-prickle had begun, as if the flow from her heart was erratic, disrupted, like – like the cutting out of a phone line, to be frank. She tried transferring this sensation to some other part of her body. Her wrists, for example: she tried to transfer the dizziness to her wrists but this didn't work. The feet are extraordinarily important, after all: they can hold the key to someone's character, relate in every way to the rest of the body. Take the Child, just as an example.

The Child had always walked in the most extraordinary way. He had been born with unusually long arms and unusually long feet and, as if to compensate for this, as if to shrink his limbs to a normal size, he would hunch his shoulders up towards his neck, draw his arms as far as possible into his shoulders, and draw in his thumbs. This brought his hands as far as possible from the ground, and as for his feet, from the moment he could walk you only needed to look at his summer sandals to see that his toes were never given a moment of relaxation: they too were pulled in as tightly as they could possibly be, retracted as far as possible into the Child's feet like the head of a tortoise into its shell.

And so the Child walked with his hands held at an absurd old man's angle and his toes clenched inwards, holding himself back, resisting his natural ease. Gest grew irritated at the sight: she could not deny it. Why could he not flail along like the other children? Why was he so conscious of his body, why could he not splay like a spaniel, play like a—

But when she saw his intensity, his burning intent and purpose, her irritation melted, and her heart became fluid and ran away inside her.

So Gest's feet: they had been the first clue. And when had they stopped carrying her out into the street? When had she stopped going out?

Gest, sitting in the same chair as where she once took the prickling, cutting-out, never-finished phone call, reaches out for the can of beer on the table, snaps it open.

She slips the silver ring from the can onto her thumb, marries herself temporarily to the past. (She is able to take her time: there is no hurry.)

And now it is the Ordinary Man's voice again, but not down a phone line this time. He is standing in a different kitchen, their shared kitchen, arguing furiously over his rights to the Child.

You were a porn star, he is saying. A porn star, for God's sake.

Never a star, says Gest, splitting hairs.

Do you really think, asks the Ordinary Man, that any judge would give custody to an ex-fucking porn star? Do you really think any judge – do you, really? (He had always fought hardest, insulted most strongly, when he was at his most scared. Men are like that, the Candy Girl would have said with simple wisdom, had she been around at the time of this argument, had she been there to help instead of high as a kite at the bottom of a Portuguese valley, and incapable of phrasing a coherent sentence let alone offering sense.)

And now, says the Ordinary Man, you're a fucking artist. Do you think that sounds any better when it comes to a custody battle?

The ferocity of his attacks had made Gest realize what she already knew from sitting in her listening dark door-less workspace. She realized the ferocity of his love for his child.

You work away a lot, she said weakly.

You can't cook, said the Ordinary Man.

You never change the sheets, said Gest. So if you get him he'll sleep in the same sheets for the rest of his life.

This had gone on for many months, this tiring, tiresome game of verbal table tennis, where one of them would fumble and drop the ball, and the other would stamp in victory, and the first would recover their balance and the volleying would start again. Quick, hard, brittle volleys, ending with one of them forced up against the wall, hand drawn back so far that it smashed into the plaster and came away smeared with blood and paint.

It was a game, though, with very little purpose. You can't cook, you never. You put work first, you always. You made money by taking your clothes off. You ran off with another woman. When it came down to it, they flung none of these poisoned arrows over the heads of lawyers and across the sterile courtroom. The Child had been slipping away from them while they shouted, he was getting lost in the battle, and one of them had to catch up with him.

Gest had thought, was fairly certain, that it would be her. The Child loved them both, it didn't matter so much to him, but she loved the Child more than life itself. This was another thing she had believed at the time: she really believed that if she didn't get to push open the Child's bedroom door every single morning, lifting it on its hinges to avoid the brushing noise of the carpet, if she didn't get to hear the Child breathe every morning of his child's life, she thought, her own lungs would forget to draw breath and her heart would wind down and would never start up again.

Her leg hurts as she sits at the table. Her neck hurts. She raises the can of beer to her mouth, only to find it is already empty. Yes, she had thought it was impossible to go on without seeing the Child every day. (She stretches her neck again, hears it crack. Her feet press down hard on the rung of the chair, she is grateful for the hurt.)

139

But of course she has gone on, seeing the importance of her task. This is what has saved her.

In the apartment across the way the man is sitting again, low in the window, partly turned away from her to make the most of the fading light. For the sun is creeping backwards now, pulling the high roof slowly up in front of it, drawing the roof like a shadow-sheet up to its chin.

And now the man, that watcher of midnight porn, catcher of evening light, gets up and seems to look straight across at Gest, though because of the sun his face is turned to a white mask and Gest ducks away, moves her chair behind the window frame.

The silver beer ring is cramping her finger. She pulls it off so that her knuckle cracks, and the chair cracks under her as she moves. *There is work to do.*

Tell me the story again! demands the Child, sitting bolt upright in bed, in Gest's head.

Not the Chinese Revolution again, Gest says warily. She waits for the Ordinary Man to bolt into the room.

Tell me, beseeched the Child, about Alice. About Alice, the pink birds, and the Red Queen.

So through the looking glass the two of them had plunged into a fiercely anarchic world where errant knights had their heads chopped off on the whim of a neurotic choleric queen. Flamingos were seized and held upside down, flinching away from the prospect of having their brains dashed out against hard yellow croquet balls. The Child cowered under his sheet as blood sprayed across the white pages, and the Ordinary Man looked in approvingly.

That's better, he said. He had never understood the Child's horrified fascination for the Cultural Revolution. (Where the hell did he hear about that? he had asked, looking accusingly at Gest.) Good, the Red Queen, he said, with a smile and a nod.

It is as savage a tale, said Gest, as any period in history. She did not really approve of editing the world, even for five-year-olds. The Red Queen, she said, is no better than the Red Guards.

But the Ordinary Man had always seen fiction as a safe realm and history as dangerous; and he withdrew, satisfied. Considerately, the Child waited until he was out of the room before speaking. Off with her head! he cried, giving a bray of laughter.

The final shadow falls into the room like a guillotine. Slowly, slowly, the reading man reaches one arm back to pull his window shut against the night air. *There is no hurry!* But Gest no longer believes this. She gets out of her chair.

What were the words of the Red Queen? What was it she had said, about the evolutionary race? Gest's task may be keeping her moving, allowing her to stay afloat; but it is also the enemy, hot, breathing, at her back. The days are in danger of eating her up. And—

It takes all the running you can do to stay in one place, says the Red Queen maliciously.

There is every hurry. It is the twenty-fourth day.

Pissing

Have you ever tried this?

Put a small cup with a rounded bottom under the mouth of a tap, but not so close that the tap is enclosed in the cup: just a short distance away. Now turn the tap on, firm and strong, so the water has no breaks or bubbles

141

in it but becomes one long, strong, flexible penis of water arrowing into the china bowl.

You will find that the cup sends the water back up in a perfect curve, mirroring the curve of the tap itself, inverting its shining shape. Only when the water hits something else (the wall, the hand you are using to control the tap, the side of the sink) will it break and splash, spraying the kitchen with a fine mist.

If you try this, it will inevitably remind you of something. It is like a variation on pissing. It may remind you of the way you hover, hold yourself above the seat of a public toilet to avoid sitting down and picking up germs. See? Your piss pours from you in the same long strong stream as the water from the tap, though probably not as clear as water, depending on what you have eaten or drunk in the hours before: red beet turns the urine pale pink, asparagus makes it a true piss-yellow, and green tea offers a faintly dingy hue.

Try the experiment with the cup and the tap once again. Try it ten or twenty times more, and you will find the effect is always the same: the hiss of the tap, the unbroken arc, the inversion. It is reassuringly human in its banal, its utter predictability.

A discussion about cups and water may seem a diversion, when this part of the story rightly belongs to Gest and the Child. But in the early days, when the Child was learning to use a toilet and Gest was bored by the training – so bored she became! with the racing for the bathroom and the long intimate chats as the Child, his trousers pushed down in baggy folds against his shoes, sat and confided in her about the movement of his bowels: so bored was Gest! she thought her face would split open with yawning, and blood vessels would burst in her eyes. Well, in those early dull days, she and the Child began their own pissing game.

142

The idea was basically role reversal. Gest would stand on a small plastic stool bought for the Child so that he would learn to urinate standing up like a real boy and not like the oddity he was (oh, the brightness of him, the sun blinding from his eyes so you blinked under his gaze). If he used this plastic stool, or so the Ordinary Man believed, he would grow up to be like any other man: that is, unable to urinate in front of other men if self-conscious or scared, able at times to piss like an elephant, splashing the tiled walls of the urinal for minute after loud minute, and at other times unable to tell if he wanted to pass urine at all until his fly was open, his penis was in his hand, and he was poised over the toilet.

Gest knew that the Child would grow up to be no ordinary man, had known this from the moment he had scorched out of her leaving her with a raw, a scarlet burning between her legs so severe that she thought she would die of it, had seen only white bright light for minutes on end, believed this was the last she would see, and that she would never even set eyes on whatever had brought her to this state of pain. But she had, she had forced her eyes through the blind light and out the other side, and when she looked down at her messy bloody boy her eyes already had the sharp vision of convalescence: all things were made new, cut with a knife-edge, lit from the side in an unexpected way so that the boy's cock seemed bulbous and huge, and his balls monstrous, and Gest was surprised almost to the point of crying out, because only days before she had read an article about passive gentle men fathering girl babies and aggressive men fathering boys, and naturally enough she had assumed that the Ordinary Man, with his low well-modulated voice and his habit of standing still for minutes with a toothbrush in his mouth while observing the street outside, would have given her a female child.

Was it because of this (no ordinary beginning, no ordinary boy) that Gest found herself, a couple of years later, playing a role-change pissing game with the Child? Whatever the reason for it, they had a fun time. Gest would take off her knickers and leave them on the bathroom floor and then, naked from the waist down, she would stand with one foot on the plastic stool, facing the toilet in a cowboy stance. Standing astride the bowl she would piss directly into the water, aiming the stream of urine out of her as hard and true as she could, and sure enough this worked as well as if she had a penis.

After this she would put her knickers back on and sit on the washing machine, cool whiteness against the backs of her thighs, and then it was the Child's turn. He would sit on the toilet, tucking his small penis neatly out of sight, and they would chat away together about their days like a couple of girls in the school lavatories: they would talk of his nursery school and who had hit who on the head with a plastic spade, and then of her art and the search for a certain acrylic paint that would provide a strong but unobtrusive background.

Some days Gest would pick up a compact mirror and touch up her eyelashes with an electric blue mascara wand, and then she would give both mirror and mascara to the Child so he could do the same as he sat there, pissing like a girl, defying both his genetic make-up and his father's wishes, and looking all the more beautifully masculine because of it.

Suddenly the Ordinary Man would be opening the door, looking horrified while trying not to. Gest! he would hiss. Do you have to sit there half naked? Gest, do you have to encourage him with make-up? Gest, why did we buy the plastic stool; and why are there urine splatters on the tiles around the toilet bowl again?

He worked on not being angry, the Ordinary Man,

because this was part of his job. When working in the field of psychology it is important to remain calm in the face of disaster – even personal disaster such as being confronted by your wife and son gazing at you with complicity, through brilliant-blue eyelashes, in the closed piss-impregnated air of your own bathroom. But then the Ordinary Man was not angry or aggressive by nature. He had been raised without the presence of a dominant male unlike Gest whom, as we know, had been brought up by a raging imbecile obsessed with controlling the world by the completion of daily crosswords.

As Gest sits on the washing machine listening to the small splash of her son's piss, a memory comes to her, strangely touching: her grandfather bending over an old wringer washing machine, wearing only his shirt. His reddish balls had hung small and abject beneath his smallish cock (even at this stage, though the only cocks Gest had been near were the runty specimens of early adolescents, she knew her grandfather's cock was nothing worth staying in a marriage for). There he stood, believing his shirt hid his genitals from eleven-year-old Gest, and, as he forced the wooden wringer out of its holder with a grunt of satisfaction, his inadequate, ignored cock swung under the swinging tail of his shirt. There was a German word Gest had learnt from an immigrant girl at her school; it meant tail but could, apparently, also be used for a penis, and she whispered it now under her breath, relishing the sour power it gave her, using the slang of German pig-dogs to refer to her grandfather's dangling appendage.

Most of the time, Gest's angry bullying imbecile of a grandfather was nowhere near the washing machine: this was a woman's domain and he had left the washing to Gest's grandmother along with many other chores: ironing, cooking, covering up, pretending he was right

145

when he was wrong, and forcing others to do the same through sheer self-preserving desperation. In spite of all this, he had eventually left his wife, citing the fact that he was tired of never having a lucid or an adult conversation.

There was something in this, for not only had Gest's grandmother abandoned her wits when she married, she had also abandoned the language of her birth. She had bitten out the tongue she had been born with – a tender but responsible tongue that had seen her through a whole eighteen years with never a trip-up until, that is, it had been taken to a foreign altar and forced to say, with a stilted and uncertain sound, the life-changing words *I do*. And after this her old tongue had shrivelled up from shame and a new one had grown, but this one had never worked properly and it stumbled over words longer than one syllable, marking her out as the imbecile her husband believed she was.

Only when the grandmother was alone with Gest did it become apparent she was aware of her loss. I miss the sun, she would say as she stood at the sink, and her eyes would cloud along with the washing-up water. As the dishes cast off their shreds of meat and their potato tumours, becoming pristine and newborn again, the grandmother would become muddied and soiled with memory, her hands lingering too long in the sewer sink. She would raise her hand to her forehead to brush away the long strands of hair that her husband would not allow her to cut. *I miss the bright sky*, she said, *and the noise in the streets*. Now turnip sinews would be hanging from her eyebrows and Gest became irritated at the sight, but the grandmother was focused on a time more than thirty years earlier, and no turnip eyebrows could shut out that vision.

Suddenly, with her wrinkled hands in and out of the

filthy water, the grandmother would start to speak another language – her old one – and Gest would become alarmed, sitting there on the draining board with her arse full of water. Stop it! she would say sharply to her grandmother for, although she was always being told by her grandfather that she knew nothing, she knew at least one thing, and that had been taught to her by the grandfather himself. She knew that this abandoned language marked their family out as poor, as underprivileged and stupid and not worthy of having a white-painted gate (which they had) or a well-kept lawn mowed by a person who was not a relative (this was something they also had).

But the grandmother would not stop. It was as if some blockage in her throat had dislodged itself, letting the past pour out, spewing forth in a stream of regret and sickness. She would not, or could not, stop.

Stop! Gest would scream in rage and panic, and one day she raised up a wooden spoon that had been lying beside her and she slapped her grandmother in her babbling, betraying, mouth. The wood was wet, it smacked damply against the grandmother's lips and teeth, and small drops of water that could have been saliva flew back into Gest's own face.

Then there was silence in the room, and just in time, too, because they heard a key in the door and the sound of heavy breathing as boots were unlaced and placed firmly with toes to the wall, *one* and *two*.

At such times Gest thought she might piss with nervousness, and when she got down off the bench she would brush quickly at the back of her damp skirt and smell her fingers, checking that the only smell was of lemon soap and nothing worse. Sometimes it was soap, sometimes a more acrid smell: the smell of piss, the smell of embarrassment, love, and fear.

147

The child in the snow globe

And all day that day, the sky was white. Its brightness was unearthly. There was a winter glare to it even though the world had long put winter behind it and had kept no memories of snow.

On that day Gest felt under more pressure than usual. The limited number of hours left to her, the creeping, too-slow results: these are the things that are preoccupying her, causing her to wake in a bed of sweat, clinging sheets wet pillow wetness under her hair. On that day she felt under pressure and under surveillance; it was as if the huge white sky was pressing down on top of her building, and the light on top of the tower was looking directly at her.

Have you ever noticed how often surveillance brings guilt in its wake? Walk through the nearly empty customs hall of an airport, for example, and you will soon come face to face with this uncomfortable fact.

Nothing is your fault; at any rate, blame is irrelevant. It is simply that your suitcase has been slow to appear on the luggage carousel and after you have claimed it you must then open it and partially unpack to find your winter coat, for you know that the streets of the new grey city outside will be even colder than the kidney-chilling air-conditioned plane.

You balance your suitcase on a row of metal seats and find your coat, pull out some boots and an extra pair of socks, and put them on there and then in the emptying straggling exhausted luggage hall. You close the suitcase up again, close your coat against the harsh overhead lights (by now you are feeling slightly ill, and in need of a bed) and suddenly you notice. You are the very last person left in that hall and so you must pass alone under the cold watching eyes of several customs officers.

This is surveillance, and the emotion that follows is inevitable. Nothing can be done. Whether or not you have illegal substances in your possession is irrelevant. Whether you have impregnated the pages of your paperback book with liquid cocaine; whether you have swallowed a condom crammed with tablets that is even now distending your belly, and making your lower intestine flame with resentment; whether you have a canister of white powder pushed securely up your anus: these possibilities are irrelevant. Because after surveillance will follow guilt, whether or not you have done wrong.

Hot guilt, flooding through the system, following in the wake of watching. Is it this that makes Gest run through her hallway, bent double, with a strange cramping knot in her stomach?

In the bathroom the child in the snow globe is waiting for her. It sits in its usual place on top of the bathroom cabinet, and the tap is dripping beside it as it always does. But today, the snow child's mouth is moving.

(How beautiful! This is the Candy Girl's voice. Ever since entering the apartment on the first day, ever since taking her first piss in Gest's otherwise bare bathroom, she has liked the snow globe with its round walls and the gilt child inside, brandishing what could be a small crusading cross, or a star. Is it — she returned to have a closer look and her voice pealed back through the doorway like a bell — is it a Christmas decoration?

But no, it was not, even though one year the Child and the Ordinary Man had decided that the figure looked more angel than human, and had taken it out of its steamy habitat and placed it on the floor under the Christmas tree. Although there were no wings on this

149

gilt figure, its cheeks were certainly cherubic in their swell.

The Child had found the globe in a shop on the outskirts of the city. It was autumn then, another autumn, and leaves lay thickly underfoot, but in spite of the chilly air the shopkeepers continued to put out their tables on the leaf-strewn pavements and one of these had caught the Child's eye. He had rustled over, Gest had followed, and they had gone into the shop.

Inside the dark room had been slung about with kitsch as a cowboy's belt is slung with guns. Beaded bags, glittering necklaces, wreaths of velvet flowers, and – nothing! Or so Gest had thought. Nothing here at all for a three-year-old child! But there, in the middle of the clutter, the snow globe was sitting, waiting for them, and sure enough the Child soon located it and extricated it from the mess and carried it home to rest.)

The twenty-sixth day, and on this white menacing day the snow child's mouth will not stay still. It wavers in its watery surroundings and Gest's eyes are streaming. She retches over the toilet, her hair hangs into the blue-streaked toilet bowl and dips into the foul water. And now she shits her pants. For what reason? Because of the same strong but still unidentified emotion that has made her vomit. Still retching, she pulls off her trousers and sits on the toilet with her head in her hands and her clogged mouth open, and perhaps it is this turmoil that encourages the snow globe into motion before her eyes.

You, says the child in the globe accusingly, you have put me here! Around its resentful head, the fake snow swirls.

(How beautiful, marvels the Candy Girl. How beautiful to look at this first thing every morning!)

IT IS YOUR FAULT, shouts the globe child silently,

staring at Gest sweating there on the toilet. The child is also in a crouching position, its golden bottom is stuck out behind it, and its face is as stern and accusatory as a judge. Gest has no time to protest her innocence: the doorbell is ringing, and she must wipe the sweat off her top lip and the diarrhoea from her arse – that perfect arse that has driven so many men to distraction, that has driven them to masturbation, distraction and despair, but is still capable of shitting uncontrollably even as someone is waiting at the door.

The Candy Girl has sweat between her large breasts, and sweat under her arms. Shall I change? she says. She peers down at herself to estimate the damage wreaked by riding a bike fast through hot white heat.

But almost instantly she forgets her T-shirt, for she has spotted something on the floor behind Gest. Although it is a small thing and the hallway is large, the snow globe throws a long hard shadow towards the front door where the Candy Girl is standing.

Are you getting rid of that? she asks, and there is covetousness in her voice. Is it going to be thrown away? She takes a step towards it, as if it is nothing more than any old ornament picked up casually by someone in a long-ago junk shop.

Gest cannot remember having moved the globe from the bathroom to the hallway. How had it got there?

I don't, she says. I can't—

But she is unable to finish.

You can't what? says the Candy Girl, obligingly step-ping into the breach.

I can't throw it away, says Gest. This is not what she was trying to say, but behind the Candy Girl the dusty stairwell gapes like a parched throat and makes her nervous. She steps around the Candy Girl and closes the front door, quickly, before anything else can come in.

That globe? She attempts carelessness, in case something out there has been listening. I can't let you have it, it's important to my work.

Is it? The Candy Girl looks puzzled, knowing little about Gest's work. But right now she is more worried about something else. Are you OK? she asks, peering closely at Gest. Your face looks a bit hot.

Gest sweeps a hand over her forehead and feels cold sweat on hot skin. My stomach, she says, it's not so good today. She forces herself to walk to the snow globe, pick it up, and carry it into the workroom.

It's gorgeous, approves the Candy Girl. Far too nice to be shut away.

But the globe child is even more fearsome in here: it holds its star aloft and brandishes it like a sword. Do not forget, it says, pushing its voice out through its fat gilt lips. DO NOT FORGET WHAT YOU HAVE DONE.

As if—! Again Gest cannot finish. As if I—

The Candy Girl does not notice, is lifting her T-shirt away from her skin and puffing down inside the fabric so the sweat marks will dry faster. She takes off her flat yellow sandals and a sweet odour of hot foot wafts through the room. Phew, she says. Sorry.

Nausea moves worm-like in Gest's throat, thrusting its sickly wet head into her mouth.

Let's get, she swallows hard, let's start—

Compulsively, she glances towards the table. The glass walls of the globe are still managing to contain the sword-holding child, wrapping it round securely, keeping the water in and the air out. But for how long? Glitter lies around the child's golden feet and ankles like some kind of holy excrement, poured forth into an unreal medium just as swimmers piss into the waters of a bathing beach without guilt because of the disconnectedness to the everyday act.

At intervals all morning Gest glances sideways to see the glitter child watching her. It is caught in perpetual motion, its right arm – that supplicating, resentful, angry arm – held forever aloft. It is trapped. But its mouth continues to move, emitting small watery whispers, spitting out fragments of guilt.

Wittgenstein

(The man stops his car and stretches his arms above his head, laying the undersides of his long fingers along the air-conditioned roof. He is more tired than usual that day, though having driven half the distance he would usually. The hard curve under his flattened aching hands reminds him of the roof of a mouth.

To get from the car to the roadside cafe he has to run. The day breathes around his head, so hot it feels as if his skull will split. He ducks and keeps low, as though running through fire.

But the Mad Greek's Cafe is cool enough, and the wife of the Mad Greek is standing behind the counter with one hand on her curved hip.

Do you want the breakfast special? she asks him.

But it's lunchtime! he says. He is half flirting with her and at the same time assessing whether his shirt is too crumpled and sweaty to go straight into the lecture room when he reaches town.

You can have whatever you want, whenever you want it, she says. Honey. (She's bored and this is what suits her: a half-casual, half-intimate encounter.)

So what is the breakfast special? he asks. He's never travelled this road before but it's easy enough to read people on a first meeting: besides, this is his profession.

We call it Grecian eggs, she says. If you don't like it, anything else you want is on the house.

He goes to sit at a table in the window. Outside the air is thick and shiny, stretched so taut by the heat that he can hardly see his car.

Mind if I join you?

It's the only other customer in the cafe, shuffling over with his plate of chopped ham and eggs. Like the Greek's wife, he's bored, has been driving all morning and doesn't feel like reading. On the brown plastic tray, soaking up slopped coffee, sits Wittgenstein's *Philosophical Investigations*, and this is where the conversation about pain starts.

The other customer can make neither head nor tail of Wittgenstein. How, he says, can someone say that you can't *know* you're in pain, even when you're screaming from it? Utter shit, he says, and he picks the book out of the coffee and throws it on the table, shovels another forkful of ham into his mouth.

The tired professional, waiting for his eggs, dabbled in philosophy a long time ago, back in the days when he would stand gazing into the windows of bookstores whether or not he intended going in. Why is he so tired? On other days he drives twice as far as this, the eucalyptus trees blurring outside his windows so parched and dry that they might burst into flame with his passing. He demurs with the other customer's opinion on the words of the small coffee-drenched Austrian genius; there is something in his theory on pain that is worth considering. Think again, he says.

But before he can think again, the confused customer is distracted by the Mad Greek's wife depositing a second

154

plate of steaming fleshy ham on the table. Both men, in fact, are distracted: by the curvaceous hips, by the right nipple almost peeking out of the stretchy denim top, and the navel which is on display at eye level.

Now that's a sight for sore eyes! This is all the confused customer can think of, right at this moment.

Once the Mad Greek's wife has retreated to the kitchen, the two men are back to eating scrambled eggs topped with squares of pink meat and conversing about pain. If they might leave philosophy and speak personally for a moment, says the other customer, he could tell a thing or two about pain. He pulls a photograph out of his pocket. What is it of? It's the face of his eight-year-old boy who is currently undergoing radiation treatment in the city near the coast.

Leukaemia, he explains. According to the nurses, the boy cries but only at night when he thinks no one can hear. He feels sick all day, his legs feel like they're being stretched on a rack, his lungs are clogged and his hair is falling out. Tell me, says the customer, *that's* not knowing pain!

The Mad Greek's wife returns, her long dark hair swinging over her bare shoulder. She asks them if they want coffee. Her eyes suggest to the tired professional that he, in particular, might like more than coffee, that he would get it if it were not for the fact that both he and she are wearing gold rings on the fourth fingers of their left hands.

Isn't she something! says the second customer, distracted again from his train of thought.

But the crumpled professional man is not particularly impressed, though he has managed to respond to the signals of the Greek's wife in a politely flirtatious way. He is a psychologist, he explains, so not easily taken in by the charades of human behaviour. You married? asks

155

the other customer. Not now, explains the psychologist, but he was once, and for some reason he still wears the ring.

What happened to her? This is male curiosity over plastic coffee cups. No good for you? Turned out a bitch? (This, male sympathy, easy between strangers, easy over egg-stained plates and a second-hand book that will be left lying on the red seat after the men have gone.)

Far from it! says the professional, an odd tone in his voice. She was not only kind but the most beautiful woman you could ever hope to meet.

It turns out he is not exaggerating: if he is to be believed, his wife had made a sizeable income from her beauty alone, and the father of the brave dry-eyed cancer-ridden eight-year-old is impressed.

What in the name of God did you divorce *her* for? he says. And he laughs, in spite of the fact that the book beside him has given him a headache for the past two days. Most men would give their balls to marry one of *those*! he says. He laughs again, though secretly feeling sick to his stomach at the thought of facing his tearless, hairless son once more.

But now the crumpled man must leave. He has a lecture to give. A girlfriend? Yes, he has a girlfriend but on this trip he's travelling alone: no girl, no kid, not even a dog.

So long, then. This is male goodwill, and a handshake saying what words can't.

The professional man leaves money for his bill and a tip that is larger than necessary because of his decency and his slight feeling that somehow he has let the curva-ceous wife of the Mad Greek down. He walks out the door into air swirling with the dry ashen particles of leaves but then turns and pauses to look at the impres-sive window display, at the range of meat cleavers and milkshake makers that the Mad Greek is offering at discount prices. He pauses there for a long time, staring into the window as if in a trance.

The other customer watches him through the glass. How long can he stand there in that heat? he marvels.

Suddenly, the man turns and walks off fast to get to his air-conditioned car.

Is he gone already? There is disappointment in the voice of the Greek's wife. She starts to wipe the table. This yours? she says, holding up Wittgenstein by the cover.

Mine? The other customer looks at the curling pages with dislike. No, he says. It must have belonged to the other guy.

Is he still there? she says, turning quickly, looking out the window.

But the other man has gone already, he has driven away into the heart of the shimmering afternoon. No one has learnt his name; it has never been important anyway.)

The burnt-out room

She has doubts about what she is doing, of course she does. There is nothing unusual about this; often she has stepped away from work before it is ready, winced, and stepped straight back up to it before losing her nerve.

But as the days accumulate under her belt, there is less and less room for doubt. Rainy days, sunny, cloudy days: every one a work day, and they mat together to form a tight wadded ball inside her, hairball in a cat's stomach. And as the mass becomes bigger and denser – fifteen days, twenty, twenty-four, and now twenty-eight – Gest finds herself inhaling deep breaths of determination, and trying to exhale the air of doubt.

She leans close to the Candy Girl. Does my breath smell bad? she asks.

The Candy Girl looks surprised. Does it smell of decay? she says uncertainly. Is that what you mean?

Decay, repeats Gest. Certainly, that is what it tastes like.

She rolls her tongue around the inside of her teeth. Almost always in her mouth is the taste of the days locked away inside her, their collective breath drifting upwards to fill her throat. She is not sleeping much but when she wakes even after a doze the smell seems to have grown stronger in the time she has been off guard.

One thing is growing from another, she says.

I'm sorry? The Candy Girl looks bemused. You've lost me.

If this were true, if Gest really had lost the Candy Girl, it would be a strange and unusual thing. For it is very difficult to lose the people who surround you, even in this large scattered world. So if Gest told the Candy Girl that very afternoon to *get lost*, that she no longer required the Candy Girl's services, it is probable that the next morning the Candy Girl would still come clambering up the stairs, leaving sweaty hand marks on the black painted stair-rail, to make sure that Gest really had meant for her to go away, that she had not simply been having a bad day on that, the twenty-eighth day, and now that it was the twenty-ninth she had repented and was ready to go on with their working arrangement. And if Gest met her at the door and snarled at her that of course she had meant it, what bit of *Get Lost* did the

158

Candy Girl not understand? – it is likely that the Candy Girl would disappear for a couple of days and return regardless, to check on the health of her employer, for in speaking in anger she had acted out of character (Gest is by and large a calm person to work with, a person whose skin rarely flushes with annoyance and whose working hands are steady).

But this is conjecture only: these two have an amicable relationship, and its financial basis keeps it on a solid footing. From the start, in fact, it was stabilised by the exchange of money, even if it is now tinged through with the rusty streaks of trust and friendship.

It is time to let you in on a secret. That night, many years ago, when Gest and the Ordinary Man left the Child in the care of a babysitter? The very first night they had left him with someone else on the pretence of having to celebrate something, but more truthfully to test whether there was any love left between them? It was on that night, more than three years ago, that Gest and the Candy Girl had first met. For this was one of the few times that the Candy Girl was sent on a job by the babysitting agency, and it had turned out to be pleasant enough: one child, small for his age though with large feet, one intense golden boy who had requested a story about Chinese professors kept behind barbed-wire fences and had then gone to sleep without fuss.

The Candy Girl had glimpsed Gest only briefly at the beginning of the night; for some reason Gest had been lingering in the bedroom behind the door and had come out only seconds before leaving, with slightly haunted-looking eyes. But the Candy Girl had not taken in much about her anyway, though she had appreciated the smooth good looks of the Ordinary Man; she was waiting for the closing of the door and the long quiet hours in front of the TV with a tin of good grass, and on the couple's return she and Gest had hardly had time for more than a few words (had the Child cried, had he eaten his favourite chicken crackers?) before the Candy Girl – pleasantly stoned by now, with a broad marijuana smile in her eyes – had been hurried out the door; yes, the Ordinary Man had pressed some crumpled notes into her hot smoky hands and simply rushed her out the door so he could get on with pulling his wife's dress off right there in the living room. (Even when stoned, the Candy Girl could sense a man's desire for sex a mile away.)

Can you smell something? Gest had said, sniffing the air after the Candy Girl's departure.

Only lust, said the Ordinary Man, lustfully. He had proceeded to remove her dress and her bra, hooking them over the antlers of the stuffed steer he was so attached to, and he cast her knickers down on the deerskin rug with its small bullet hole dating from the Ordinary Man's hunting days, and after that he had made frenzied unparental love to her right there on the floor.

Later, Gest had protested about the Ordinary Man's peremptory treatment of the young babysitter, about the way he had pushed her out the door with scarcely a word of thanks; and she had forwarded a small card and some extra money to the agency, so grateful was she to find, after her quick fucking, that the Child was quietly sleeping, wrapped in a warm calm darkness. You could, perhaps, see this early financial exchange between Gest and the Candy Girl as a forerunner to their later business relationship; but in truth it is unlikely that the money sent by Gest ever got to the Candy Girl, for the agency had fired her the very next week for snorting coke in a rich client's bathroom. But he had told her, she protested, to help herself to anything!

So this was where they began, these two, and now they have stumbled into each other's path once again.

But this time they see each other more clearly, and offer help with intimate subjects.

If you're worried about your breath, confides the Candy Girl, I know some really good mouthwash. It's called Ring of Confidence, have you tried it?

Gest cups her hands and breathes into them, then breathes in her own breath. But at this moment there is no taint of the matted days, swallowed too fast and with too little to show for them. She can smell only her own fingers, their dry cracked skin and the tiny plastic splinters embedded under her fingernails.

I'm worried. She tries to explain, feeling that the Candy Girl is owed something, with half their working time gone. I'm worried about the passing of days, she says.

Aaah. This is something the Candy Girl can understand, for hadn't she stood in the bathroom only the day before with the Micro hammering on the door wanting to piss, and hadn't she held up a hand mirror to look at her profile only to notice that the line of her chin was not as sharp as it once was? Bang bang, *hurry up*! It's almost enough, she said, opening the door so suddenly so that the Micro fell into the room and banged his shin on the toilet and swore — it's almost enough to make you go on drugs again.

But Gest shakes her head, for she is not talking about ageing.

I'm worried about finishing in time. All this. She waves her hand at the room, at the debris lying on the spotted sheet, trial limbs scattered about as if she and the Candy Girl have stumbled into a nightmare zone, a place where landmines blow people sky high and their remains tumble back to earth.

Aaah. *Now* the Candy Girl is clear; everything is clear, and her eyes beam across the dim room with the joy of having finally reached clarity. How blue her eyes are! as blue as the silk roses on Gest's father's coffin, as blue as the Child's mood when, crying from shame and confusion, he confessed to climbing on the china cabinet and breaking a bowl.

If that's all, says the Candy Girl. Her voice rings with confidence and generosity, and with what might be love. If that's all it is, she says, I can stay a few days longer at the end. I don't have to start at the shop right away if it's going to cause problems for you.

She stands up and comes over to Gest, who cannot speak for a moment, thinking still of coffins and chairs pulled close to heirloom dressers, and a bowl and a body falling. And what else is Gest thinking, so that she cannot speak? Of how blue and clear the Candy Girl's eyes are, and of what a truly good person the Candy Girl is, something rare in a generation brought up on the promise of temporary highs and hearing more television conversations than real ones.

Are you tired? asks the Candy Girl. Tentatively, she reaches out and touches Gest's shoulder, then draws her hand back before Gest has time to register the touch. Maybe you should work more slowly? she says. Not that you don't always look fantastic! But perhaps you should take it easy for a while?

It is not up to me! Gest laughs, and sighs. It is not me who has imposed this schedule.

It's not? The Candy Girl swings back to uncertainty again. She goes to sit on her own stool again, leans back perplexed against the wall. Can't you change it in that case? she asks.

I cannot, Gest pauses. It cannot be changed because I have signed a contract. The work must be done, and then I must leave.

Oh the *building*! says the Candy Girl, who has spent

162

the past few minutes swinging wildly on the vines of understanding and incomprehension. Now she looks down and back into past conversations, and sees solid ground again. I remember, the building will be demolished, she says. And this is why you must get your work finished.

The hospital has bought the land, agrees Gest.

Lines appear deep in the Candy Girl's forehead, parallel tracks between her thick eyebrows. But I thought, she frowns, that the developer's billboard outside said nothing would start till the autumn?

Gest stands up now and shakes her hair back so that small silvery threads of plastic fall like stars from a night sky. She puts her hand to her mouth, coughs, clearing her throat of dust from the accumulated days. I'd rather not hang on right till the end, she says. But her throat still sounds clogged.

Quite right too. The Candy Girl instantly understands. It's one thing to leave of your own accord but quite another thing to be pushed out by those bastard land-lords, says the Candy Girl fiercely, talking now in the voice of her father with all his hatred of the professional middle-man. Do we have no rights? Do we have no say, are we forced out on our ears because someone else hears the rustle of money? Must we listen in our sleep for the fucking bulldozer at our door? And—

I'm sorry! says the Candy Girl, shocked. She does not like using strong language in front of Gest, during working hours at least.

But Gest has not heard this profanity, for it belongs in the Candy Girl's past. And it appears that working hours are over, anyway, for she is picking up gloves and chisels and throwing them into the old black pillowcase that doubles as a tool sack (*many years since that's seen a bed, I'll warrant*, says the Candy Girl's mother, in the Candy Girl's head).

Come with me, Gest is saying. I want to show you something. Her voice sounds blocked, sticking in her throat and emerging sluggishly into the hot afternoon room.

The two of them walk shoulder to shoulder down the hall, out the front door, and onto the cool shadowed landing. Dust and sand lie around the doormat, spreading out in a half-moon. Where are they going? The Candy Girl is unsure, but she is willing and ready and stays close to Gest's shoulder as they turn and walk across the landing. It's like the game she played with her brother in their schooldays, when one of them was the blind person and the other the leader. The blind one had to keep their eyes open like a real blind person, while staring straight ahead and not being allowed to swivel the eyeballs. To walk like this it was necessary to trust the other one completely, and you had to walk certainly, no stumbling, just like a real and experienced blind person for this was the only way you could fool the world into thinking you were true, that you were really not a sighted person.

Gest the Seer and the newly blind girl mount the stairs. The blind girl looks with unseeing eyes at a low window, stares out unseeingly at an apartment building opposite. If her eyes still worked they would look out and down a level, to where a man sits low in a window, holding up a newspaper: they would see a glass set on the window sill catching the low bloody sun, and a smoking ashtray beside it.

But now, already, they are on the next landing. It feels a little like mountain climbing; there is a pull in the backs of the blind girl's calves. (You'd think the builders would get it right, wouldn't you? says the Leader as if she too feels a burning in the legs. The perfect ratio for stairs was discovered in Roman times, you would think they would learn.) There is something odd about the

Leader's voice: it sounds strained, though this could be because – just as when you are getting closer to the summit of a mountain – the air seems to be getting thinner and thinner.

One more flight, says the Seer, and we're there. The blind one stumbles but does not move her head downwards, she kicks the next step and the next and curses her clumsiness, but she cannot throw off the rules of childhood.

They are on the top landing now, in front of a door with iron bars hammered across the hinges. They are to keep squatters out, explains Gest. But in fact the door is unlocked.

She pulls the bars off and opens the door. There, stretching before them, is a hallway looking just like Gest's own, leading in the same compass direction as the hallway down which the Blind Girl looks every morning – looks, that is, when she is able to see.

Are you all right? asks Gest, her voice sounding less strangely affected by altitude and more normally puzzled. Come and look, she says.

And the Candy Girl is restored: she has been ordered to see. She unlocks her eyelids and rolls her eyeballs around a couple of times to loosen them up, and then she follows Gest down the dusty hall. A few nails stick out of the wall and one catches in Gest's sleeve. Ow, she says.

The hall is a mess, and not only because of the nails. There are small pieces of wallpaper peeling away from the wall, hanging in loose strips like skin. If this were the Candy Girl's apartment, she would stick this skin-paper up again, using small pieces of Blu-Tack.

I use Blu-Tack for most things, she says earnestly, before realizing she has been speaking in her own head. (Besides, she thinks, this is a conversation she should never have started; it is not her apartment, nor her wall-paper; she is in a slightly shabby apartment belonging to no one but the state.)

Somehow, Gest follows. Blu-Tack? she says vaguely. I prefer glue, it doesn't bleed through the paper—

But she stops.

The Candy Girl looks at her with newly opened, enquiring eyes.

Here, says Gest.

There is a door to their right. They turn on their heels, ninety degrees, like soldiers practising drill, and suddenly there it is before them. A burnt-out room.

Everyone has seen images of ships that have sunk to the bottom of an ocean. Luxury liners with round brass portholes dividing water from water, flicked through by silver fish. Closets hanging open, seaweed sleeves trailing out their doors. The gambling room, a homage to green: green felt tables, green algae chairs, hands dealt and chips cashed-in a long time earlier. And in the kitchens slow-motion pans swinging on hooks, and fridges that have somehow remained upright and sealed, keeping secret the ingredients favoured by a famous chef who was snaf-fled from the city and lured to a watery grave. For water, like a camera, holds things back, slows them down, freezes an evening for eternity. A room that has been flooded is suspended in time.

But fire is different. It despises water, preferring its own quick, violent, superior skills. Fire waits for no one, and it has left an empty ribcage, a lung sucked of life, a shell that has flared and collapsed and lies here now, spread before the Candy Girl's eyes.

Gutted, breathes the Candy Girl, in the word that the Micro uses for emotional damage as well as physical. Gutted!

You can see why they don't want people up here, says

Gest. You can; there are gaps in the floor that a person could slip right through, to appear suddenly in the ceiling of the apartment below, tinkling through the shards of the cheap crystal chandelier, hanging for a split second above the television set before – the fall! Such a crashing of glass, such a deluge of limbs and lights and wood interrupting the easy flow of recorded dialogue, disrupting the patter of a late afternoon soap opera so severely that these voices are never heard in the same way afterwards. This could happen, should anyone risk their life by walking across this gaping floor, had anyone been allowed to remain living in such devastation, which of course they had not.

Take care! says Gest – or is it the Candy Girl? – speaking out like a responsible soldier who has come across something irregular. Because one of them has stepped forward to investigate and – take care! says the other one, for even an average-sized human might fall through these gaps in the charred wooden floor: even a strong sturdy tree-person, or a curvaceous woman with perfect porn-star breasts. (Gravity, like fire, is unimpressed by beauty or strength.)

Take care! says Gest, in alarm. It turns out to be the Candy Girl who had tiptoed forward towards the window, with its lopsided remains of a frame and its sharp fangs of glass. And through its gaping mouth the tops of the trees are visible, like leafy tonsils.

Fucking hell! says the Candy Girl, looking around her at the chalky black walls and the ceiling that is partly composed of black plastic sheets. This time she does not even think about apologising for her language, even though it comes directly from her: *fucking hell* is about right, is all you can say.

Gest does not venture into the room, for she sees that the Candy Girl is safe enough, tiptoeing on her large pink feet over the wreckage. To have got as far through life as the Candy Girl has, surviving ambulances screaming through the middle of bright foreign mornings; avoiding knives under railway bridges and walking the long distance across a room strewn with handguns and potentially lethal small plastic packages; to have looked one beloved friend in his rolling eye, seen foam streaming from his lips, stroked fingers through his vomit-soaked hair and still, still to be able to speak and laugh! These things demonstrate a strong instinct for survival. And so—

Watch your step, is all Gest says, as she watches her fellow trooper parade the boundaries of the burnt-out room.

What happened? breathes the Candy Girl. She peers from the window. How might her tiny face appear to the street eight floors below, should anyone glance up to the sky instead of staring into shop windows or down at the stained chewing-gum pavement?

It was a house fire, says Gest. Started by a faulty cigarette lighter. She touches the wall and her fingers come away covered in black. No one would stay after this, she says. The housing bureau wanted to sell anyway, so there were no eviction notices needed, no lawyers. She takes a deep breath. Only me, she says. Only me left.

In spite of the fact that no window divides the outside world and the inside, the air smells strange in here. Had this been a living room or a bedroom? It is hard to tell for nothing human remains: no charred chest of drawers, no singed bookshelves, no futon base or drinks cabinet. Neither does the strange smell give away any clues. However deeply you breathe, using your mouth, your nose or your imagination, there is nothing left to tell you that there might have once been sleeping bodies here, lust against that wall or dreams against that one.

There is no leftover tinfoil smell of TV dinners or musty smell of dull schoolbooks: nothing. No trace.

It doesn't do to imagine too much, anyway, says the Candy Girl. If you did you would never sleep at night.

You're right, says Gest.

I suppose you're so dedicated to your work, says the Candy Girl, that perhaps you can forget all this is up here? So dedicated, she repeats in admiration, although so is she; even the Micro respects this about her, when he looks at her neatly looped handwriting, page after page of copied lyrics waiting to be learnt at odd moments and let loose for the entertainment of a beer-fumed room.

Dedication is one word for it, says Gest, looking down at her cut and broken fingernails while the Candy Girl goes to inspect the bathroom (same size as Gest's, same dirty rim around the bath) and the kitchen (pitted rust-coloured linoleum floor, nothing but the empty hollow of the sink).

There are other words for dedicated, of course. Some would say hardworking, some would say diligent, but neither of these carries with it a sense of vocation. Others would say *obsessed*: at least, this was what the Ordinary Man had said, when he came home late at night to find the Child reading in the bathroom in a blaze of light, sitting on the edge of the bath with his feet planted inside it, and his eyes, running avidly over the lines of his book, red-rimmed, and his face stretched around the edges from tiredness. Obsessed! This was what he called Gest, who was in another room intent on finishing this or that before the day ran out on her (for even then the pressure of time was enormous, as always in the case of the dedicated, the selfish, and the obsessed). Selfish! as the Ordinary Man fumed and raged and carried the Child, now almost crying with tiredness but wanting to reach the end of his chapter, to bed. And then Gest's hands and mind were interrupted, their instinctive link broken irreparably by the shouting, the electric lights, and the slamming of doors.

So why did you stay? The Candy Girl is back from her tour of the apartment, and she is harking back not to Gest's marriage but to why Gest would stay remain in a deserted building when everyone else had fled.

Because I wanted to, says Gest. Because I like to be alone.

The Candy Girl can accept this; over the past few days the Micro has been making her edgy, and she has spent much time lying awake waiting for him to propose, or lying awake waiting for him to come home.

But your child? she says. Asking this question feels as risky as crossing the broken floor, but the light is fading and this makes her bolder. Doesn't your child come and stay sometimes? she asks.

Never, says Gest, turning towards the door. It's time to go, she says.

When they have made it safely back onto the landing, they take one iron bar each and replace them with twin clangs through the metal hooks on the door. As they descend the first flight of stairs their footsteps quicken at the same pace. By the time they get to Gest's door, two floors down, they are almost running. There is a light sweat on the Candy Girl's face and when Gest reaches for the doorhandle her hand slips on the metal.

It feels scary, admits the Candy Girl. Don't you get scared, knowing all that's up there? She is breathing fast.

Gest pauses. Not scared, she says. I get lonely.

Do you? The Candy Girl looks puzzled. But you said—

That I like to be alone, says Gest. But I also get lonely.

Now the Candy Girl understands. Living under so many layers of empty rooms, with layers of emptiness below, hearing no other footsteps except for your own; as far as loneliness goes, not very much would beat living in the way that Gest does.

They step into Gest's own apartment. It looks as if no one lives here either, says Gest, her shoulders slightly hunched. It is true: even in the time they have been upstairs, the apartment looks as if it has been emptying itself. Doorways loom larger and emptier than before, and the shadows have piled new dust up in the hallway. The Candy Girl hurries to put the kettle on, to fill up the air with heat and the smell of boiling water.

Tea? she says, looking with relief out the window towards a more populated world. Look, she says, that man in the apartment is still reading.

He can read for hours on end, says Gest, sitting in a chair away from the window. He reads all day and at night he watches blue movies. At least, she adds, the light from his window is blue.

The Candy Girl is relieved to hear Gest make a joke, and she laughs as she reaches for the old red tin where the tea is kept. Maybe he's watching you! she says, daringly.

Gest doesn't respond, sits on her chair with her hands folded politely in her lap, waiting for the Candy Girl to spoon out tea and put it in Gest's teapot, and light Gest's stove with a match from the oversized red and yellow matchbox. You can go after this, she says. Knock off early.

Are you sure? But this is a polite question only; the Candy Girl is eager to do this because she likes to get home before the Micro, to shave her legs (something she doesn't have time for in the mornings), shave her bikini line, put on clean knickers under a clean dress, and redo her makeup. She doesn't like straggling in grimy from the train, remembers her mother's advice *Don't let yourself go or you'll lose him!* though God only knew that

171

saying this had done her plain gaunt child-ridden mother no good. But still, the Candy Girl looks doubtful.

What about your worry with the deadline? she says.

It's OK. Just for today, Gest waves her hand, we will forget the deadline.

The Candy Girl starts to smile.

Although—says Gest.

Yes? says the Candy Girl. She pours boiling water over tea with a sure, disappointed, resigned hand. Of course she will stay; the Micro and his nights out, his guilty homecomings early in the morning, all this be damned!

Gest falls silent, staring at the teapot that has always dribbled when it pours but has never been taken back to the shop due to some forgotten reason (apathy, tiredness, laziness or an unwillingness to enter into a dull discussion about refunds in a suffocating houseware department).

Have some tea, says the Candy Girl confusedly, pouring and splashing. Nothing has been clarified for her today, nothing has been sharp except the acrid crunch of her sneakers on the burnt floor upstairs.

You can go, says Gest suddenly.

For as the sun creeps backwards out of sight, she has realized: when the Candy Girl is there something in Gest is waiting for her to leave, and when the Candy Girl goes Gest starts the long wait again, watching the hands of the clock crawl around another fourteen hours so that she can start listening for footsteps on the stairs once more.

The sun leaves, the kitchen is plunged into shadow. Go, says Gest to the Candy Girl. She clenches her fists under the seat of her chair, thinks of work. This is all. This is all she has.

Imagination

People say the mind is a fragile thing, and this is true. A single happening can alter you for life, can almost destroy you, simply because your mind is not strong enough to deal with the aftermath. Gest has spent many years married to a psychologist, so has become used to discussing such topics. Late at night she has debated these issues, over cognac and coffee, agreeing with her psychologist husband when he says the mind can destroy, disagreeing with him when he states that, almost always, the mind can be put back together.

Humpty Dumpty sat on a wall! She and the Child are chanting, running along a low concrete rampart beside a canal. Humpty Dumpty had a great fall!

All the King's Horses and all the King's Men! (The Child prances.) NO bloody person could put that Humpty together again! He crows, throwing himself onto the ground, rolling there with his sturdy unbreakable limbs.

No one! NO bloody one! He rolls and repeats. Except (raising his head), except probably Lurie.

Gest also lies down on the hard ground. Don't swear, she says. Who's Lurie? She turns her broken-egg head sideways to look at the Child. Her right ear lies close to the concrete and for a second she thinks she can hear the thrumming canter of the King's Men, coming to pick them up and take them home for dinner.

Who's Lurie? says the Child incredulously, coming to lie on top of Gest so that she can feel his pitying heart beating against hers. Don't you know who Lurie is? He's my friend, he used to be a doctor but then people got scared of him.

173

Why? says Gest, in a crushed voice.

He was hurt, says the Child, and now there is a slight anxiety in his voice. He was in a accident.

An accident, corrects Gest automatically, but she starts to breathe a little faster. What kind of accident? The loose gravel bites into her cheek and she pushes the Child aside, sits up. What kind of accident?

It ruined his face, says the Child distantly. No one liked to look at Lurie after that.

Gest can still feel the slice of gravel on her cheek. She puts up her hand to see if there's blood there but no, her fingers come away just as they were: pink with cold, black with ink, white from holding tight around the key to the front door of their home.

Was he in a car crash? she questions. Was he badly hurt?

There is an unease inside her, low down, like an ache in her kidneys. Why have his patients stopped coming to him? she asks. Can he no longer see, can he no longer talk?

But the Child has seen a large dog in the distance and he wants to hurry away. Come on, he says. Time waits for no man. Quickly, he gets up off the ground and strides out in front, hoping that by using a favourite quotation of the Ordinary Man's he might make Gest move along; he does not like admitting that he is a little afraid of dogs. Lurie isn't real, he says over his shoulder.

Is this a normal thing? queries Gest when the Ordinary Man comes home that night. I mean, other children make friends with invisible tigers, or Martians, or, or—

The Ordinary Man waits, politely, for her to finish her sentence.

But our child has a deformed doctor as a friend, concludes Gest miserably.

He'll forget it soon enough, says the Ordinary Man,

taking off his shoes and settling down with a beer. The imagination doesn't store things for long at that age.

Gest wishes that the Ordinary Man would be more comforting. Just because she has a strong perfect body, just because she looks strong and perfect doesn't mean she is invincible! Not when it comes to mothering – on the contrary. She walks fast, a little angrily, to the bedroom to check on the Child.

He is muttering in his sleep, and through the half-dark Gest can see his small determined hand clenched around the plastic coffee coaster he has recently taken a liking to. I don't want to eat those, he is mumbling. I don't like those beans with the wrinkly skin.

Much as Gest wishes the Ordinary Man might be correct in this case, he is not. Day after day, for many weeks, the imagination of the Child brings Lurie into their house, until there comes a morning when the Child looks nervously over his shoulder as he walks down the hall. While he and Gest get their things together to go to the supermarket, he is bending and straying towards her like a thread of nylon attracted by static electricity.

What is it? asks Gest. What's wrong? She looks on the floor, on the walls, for a scarily large spider or beetle.

I'm just making sure that Lurie doesn't come out, whispers the Child, with none of his usual cavalier tone. I don't feel like seeing him right now. There is a thin nervousness in his voice.

Where does he live? asks Gest, picking up her bag and shepherding the Child quickly out onto the landing.

He lives in the wall, breathes the Child. His eyes are enormous in the gloom and he holds on to the black painted stair rail with both hands. He says he won't hurt us but he's not nice to look at.

You know Lurie isn't real, reassures Gest. You told me that.

He used to be real, says the Child seriously. He was a good doctor before, everyone loved him, before.

Gest, the champion of unfinished sentences, should let this go. She cannot help herself. Before what? she says, and bites her lip.

The Child swings himself towards the next landing, holding on to the rail and using his arms like a gymnast to push himself out and down, two steps at a time.

Before he got burnt, he says, not looking at Gest.

He was *burnt*? says Gest. Have you seen him? Her voice is a half-whisper, creeping down the stairs behind the Child.

Thump. Thump. The Child's breathing becomes louder in the quiet stairwell. Now he is at the bottom of the flight of stairs, and he turns to face Gest. The landing window behind him is a bright white glare, so that Gest can see him as an outline only.

I've seen him a couple of times, says the Child's voice. And in unison both he and Gest look back up, involuntarily, at their black painted front door.

He only shows himself, nods the Child, when you light a match or switch on a light. And then he jumps right out of the wall.

There is definite fear in his voice.

He's not scared! the Ordinary Man declares later. Sure, he might have retained this Lurie. (This, a partial admission that his own prognosis had been wrong.) He's certainly not *scared* by him.

So definite is the Ordinary Man about this that, for a second, Gest believes him. For a second she forgets the wild flickering of the Child's eyes in the hallway, but over the next few weeks she sees his fear return every time she lights a match. Lurie! he hisses, as the match is put to the gas stove and the element bursts into flame. Be careful, Lurie will come out! Then he would run straight to the kitchen door and throw it open with the

176

courage of the mortally afraid, ready to confront the gruesome face of his half-friend.

Don't worry so much, says the Ordinary Man, after this has gone on for some months. (It is a sunny day, he feels optimistic, he kisses Gest and starts to make coffee.)

You don't know! says Gest. How do you know what it's like to be in the Child's head?

A bee is banging against the window, driving itself repeatedly against the glass. The chestnut tree reaches up for blue sky, its crackling bark armpits sprouting green. (It may be sunny, but it is not so, in Gest's head.)

The mind is not that fragile, shrugs the Ordinary Man. (So they are back to this!) A child's imagination can be overactive, he says, sounding like a textbook. But it is rarely harmful.

Gest moves her chair back with a sharpness that leaves marks on the floor. It *is* fragile, she contradicts. It can be harmful. It all depends.

But she sees that the Ordinary Man is not really listening. He has turned away from what is happening in his own household, thinking perhaps of a case he is dealing with at work, or how much coffee he should put in the pot. So much depends, he echoes vaguely, so much depends on a red wheelbarrow. Although his hands are moving with precision, he quotes this line carelessly, like an after-dinner speaker handed an easy audience. He is thinking neither of Gest nor the Child, nor of a disfigured person who supposedly does not exist lurking in their walls, and he pats the coffee down with the back of a spoon, with an absent hand.

How does the next line go? He turns to Gest for both of them know this poem; in the early days they would often lie in their pillowless bed, propped up against the wall so their necks cracked, reading William Carlos Williams to each other out of a bent, covered red book.

But Gest does not want poetry right now. No! she says. This is not what she has wanted at all, this sidetrack in the discussion. And the strong smell of basil in the sealed room, a thick green smell, climbs up her nostrils and clogs her throat. No! she says. Not William Carlos Williams.

Yes, corrects the Ordinary Man, wilfully misunderstanding. You know very well it is Carlos Williams.

We were talking about imagination, contradicts Gest. And childhood.

Were we? he says, leaning on the stove, looking out the window. There is a silence and the coffee pot begins to groan and crack with the heat.

You wouldn't know the first thing about it anyway, says Gest. She does not care if this sounds rude. Child psychology is hardly your specialty.

I do know. The Ordinary Man sharpens up now, stares straight at her. In fact, he says, a colleague of mine (he turns to watch the coffee pot and his back is stiff and offended) — a colleague of mine has written a book on that very subject. She knows more about imaginary playmates and the inside of five-year-old heads than anyone in the field.

The coffee leaps inside the pot, the lid sputters. The Ordinary Man keeps his back turned while he explains that this colleague, an expert in developmental psychology, knows many things that Gest does not. She knows that the Child enjoys frightening himself, she knows that other children dream up far worse companions than Lurie, companions whose hands turn to iron claws at night, and whose spit has the power to melt the faces of humans like acid. These imaginings are nothing for parents to be afraid of (says the Ordinary Man, and he sounds calmer, kindly again) because the children themselves are not afraid.

178

What's more – he puts the coffee pot on the table – my friend says that children will interrupt her in the middle of interviews, simply to remind her that these characters are not real.

Gest snatches the pot up. A mat! she says. There is a brown ring on the wood, and a charred smell. Who is this colleague? she asks. This *friend*?

I'm sorry! The Ordinary Man is looking down at the scarred table. I'll send, he sounds flustered, I mean, I'll sand it.

Whatever, says Gest. She does not really care about the colleague, nor about the burnt table, only about the Child who is presently at playschool and, hopefully, is happy. Laying her head down on the table she hears the wood crack under her ear, imagines it falling, crashing, felled in a faraway forest.

Don't crack your neck, says the Ordinary Man. He is changing, changeable today; he swings in the winds of Right and Wrong, which is unlike him. I'll give you a neck rub, he offers.

He has forgotten his attempt at poetry, he has forgotten where this conversation started, with fire and matches and burnt faces conjured up by his son. Something has thrown him into confusion and the only way out is to be practical and helpful. But even after Gest is sitting upright again, having her neck briskly rubbed by the Ordinary Man, she hears the wooden table in front of her still cracking, perhaps caused by the hot sealed air in the kitchen. And the metal of the coffee pot groans with the effort of holding in its hot blackness, and in the corner of Gest's left eye there is a shadow moving in the hallway.

The smell of basil is too strong, it reeks of urine and human sweat. She pushes the Ordinary Man's hands off her neck, goes to the window, opens it and throws the basil plant out. It takes minutes to hear the end of the fall. A dog barks.

Long afterwards, Gest can still smell the complex mixture of emotions from that day: nervousness and irritation (her), and a guilt (his) that remained unexplained for many months. She walks to her present-day window – another time, another kitchen – and looks across the evening courtyard. Now there is no one with whom she can discuss the power of the imagination: the Ordinary Man has left her and the Candy Girl is heading for a downtown bar where she will proceed to sing her heart out, keeping one eye on the back of the room in the hope that the Micro might appear unexpectedly, holding a beer, ready to be proud of her and her talent.

There, in the opposite window, is the head of the reading man. He is in his usual chair but it is now turned to face Gest and she catches the gleam of his eyes. Politely, he raises his glass to her but Gest turns away.

She switches off the bright humming strip light so that she cannot be seen, and she takes a bottle of water from the fridge. She sits at the table with her back turned to the Reader and the light off, and looks through the gleaming night panes of glass into the hallway.

Sitting like this, you can see nothing except for the shadowy archway on the far wall of the hall, with its unsymmetrical white shoe rack sitting lumpily on one side. The archway is faux, leading nowhere, though once, perhaps, you could have stepped on through it into another room. But since the house has been rebuilt, refloored, boarded up, the arch no longer leads anywhere. Except for you, and your imagination.

Because immediately, having little to work with, your imagination starts up. It is strong, so strong, this part of the mind: and who are we to call it memory? It is nowhere near as reliable as memory, it is a crackling phone line down which you hear clicks, cracks, and then – as unexpectedly as a wrong connection – you are transported to another place.

Suddenly the Child is there, leaping out of the white wall. His bright hair stands out around his face: he bursts out of the dark space between inner and outer walls, his eyes round and surprised, his pointed toes reaching out towards the floor.

You have not had to light a match to make this happen, nor must the match flare and die for the Child to disappear before touching the floor. His arms are reaching towards you: he wants to dive through the glass panels of the kitchen door to get to you, to fall on you, all around you, in a great splintering of longing and love.

Imagination is strong, but it is not strong enough. And so Gest sits and clenches her hands and, through the gleaming glass, watches the untouchable Child soaring again and again through the archway. He bursts through the plaster as if through a paper hoop in a circus. Roughmaned lion, clown, beautiful boy, freak. He is all. He is not there.

Chicken crackers

Don't put me in your paintings! This is Gest, quoting her ex-husband to entertain the Candy Girl. That was what he used to say, she quips. Don't put me in one of your paintings!

It is in that time of settling after the door has been closed for half an hour, and the outside air has become amalgamated with the inside so you would no longer know that the Candy Girl is the one who has recently arrived and Gest is the one who has not been outside for thirty days on end. The stale smell inside Gest's head is becoming stronger: it sits warm and cloudy on her tongue, clings to the back of her eyelids, will not leave in spite of teeth-cleaning and nasal sprays and many strong cups of tea. In fact, she thinks, it is more of a taste than a smell: like when you have held a key in your hand for a long time and at last put it down, and raise your fingers to your lips. It is a metallic taste, a grey and deathly taste.

Don't put me in one of your paintings! quotes Gest, talking of her departed husband for the amusement of the Candy Girl. *I am not Material!*

This morning the Candy Girl has bought a newspaper on her way to work. It lies in wads, half in, half out, of her orange vinyl bag. The dull garish front-page picture is partly obscured, making Gest constantly look over at it and keep only half an eye on her work.

And did you? asks the Candy Girl. Put him in a painting, I mean? The morning paper she has so casually carried in with her is full of horrifying tales: a woman who has skinned her lover, the massacre of an entire village, a train burning in an uphill tunnel with people running from the heat like rats.

No. And five years later, Gest shrugs, he became angry about this. You never put me in your paintings! he would shout.

The Candy Girl laughs and sighs. That's men for you, she says, raising her eyebrows that are a different colour from her streaky hair. Her hair is ginger and gold, her eyebrows dark: she is all the colours of a tortoise, and has its chunky slowness.

At this stage the Candy Girl is told she can abandon

182

her pose and have a rest. She pulls the newspaper out of her bag and shakes it open, lays it out on the floor, front page down, and then takes an orange from her satchel. Digging her long, carefully tended thumbnail deep into the heart of the orange, she begins to peel it, dripping onto the newspaper.

Men don't ever really like what you do for a job, she says. There is a slight weakness in her voice, in spite of the way her strong thumb has dived unerringly into the middle of the orange. They resent you having something that is nothing to do with them, she says, dripping juice and worldly wisdom. (She might have had a bad week with the Micro, but still, you had to eat.)

Maybe you're right, says Gest. But it was only later that the Ordinary Man had wanted more of her attention and, losing this, he had then wanted the Child even more.

I'm sure I'm right. The Candy Girl, her mouth full of orange flesh, nods and swallows. Do you want some? she offers. The citrus smell is all around her head: as strong as, stronger than, glue or epoxy resin. Her ginger hair is hung around with it like a halo; it runs, bleeds into the air.

Oh, no. Gest must force herself to answer. She shifts on her stool. But thank you, she says politely.

Even now she can hardly bear to think of the Ordinary Man's enormous distress. Sitting there on the thirtieth day she is as connected to it as she has ever been. Wave after wave of his long-ago distress crash into the room and break over her as she sits. She pulls her feet up onto the rung of the stool. There is moisture behind her ears and her eyelids are slick, as are the backs of her knees under her overalls. She eases the material away from her legs.

I bought these oranges from that fruit stand down the

road, says the Candy Girl in a chatty full-mouthed voice. You know the man who's always behind the stand wearing his Walkman? Today he didn't have it on and he takes my money and he says, you taking oranges to your sick friend then? and I said no, I'm going to work. And he says, oh really, because yesterday I thought you turned into the entrance to the hospital, the one with the brick towers. And I said no, I work *next* to the brick towers and I'm going to be late so can I have my oranges please?

Droplets of recrimination are running down the inside of Gest's arms. She reaches casually for a rag and brushes them away but more come and more, unstoppable like that terrible story she used to read the Child about the magic porridge pot that kept pouring its hot liquid into the streets so people and dogs began to drown.

So *then* the fruit man says – and now the Candy Girl's voice becomes incredulous. Then he says, don't you think if you were lying in a hospital you might like someone to come in and bring you fruit? and I said, look you can't expect me to care for every sick person in the world now can you, and he says that's exactly the problem with your generation, you don't care about anyone except yourself, and I said just give me my FUCKING oranges.

It is strangely comforting to hear that the Candy Girl talks about this apartment to people outside, even as the recriminations continue to run through Gest's head and out every pore in her skin. *You always, you never.* She puts down the rag, wipes her forehead with her arm, feels the sting of turps.

He thought I focused on my work too much, she says desperately. He said I never paid enough attention to the Child.

The Candy Girl keeps up with this shift admirably, making the leap from present to past and from one man to another with ease. Her eyes look particularly bright this day: perhaps the Vitamin C is working its magic even as she crams citrus segments into her mouth?

But wasn't he at least proud, she says, of your work?

Not proud, embarrassed, Gest manages to say. First of all he had to come to terms with the fact that his wife made money by taking her clothes off, and then he had to come to terms with the fact that his wife was an artist and might not make any money at all.

The Candy Girl roars with laughter. Pips spray across the room, forming a small mosaic arc around her, and she sits cross-legged inside them like a lusty mermaid statue.

Ha ha ha, they both manage to laugh on the thirtieth day, although the sweat of fear and remembrance has barely dried on Gest's neck and the Candy Girl has had a bad week due to the Micro's sudden lack of interest in sex, making her suspicious of where he has been on four, five, and then seven consecutive nights when he has told her – has insisted – that he has just been playing pool. And the twin brick towers suddenly loom into the room, parallel shadows lying like railway tracks between Gest and the Candy Girl, cutting between them just when they could do with some closeness.

The laughter cannot drown out what Gest has been hearing. The noises of the Ordinary Man preparing lunches for himself and the Child, getting food together to keep them going through their long unknown days once they have left Gest to herself, in the quiet apartment.

I don't want those chicken crackers, comes the Child's voice. (This, into Gest's studio, in the early morning.) I don't like them, they go soft.

Not if I twist the bag tight, says the voice of the Ordinary Man.

Although it is a winter's morning and still dark, the

lights are off in Gest's studio. She is supposed to be finding an envelope so the Ordinary Man can post a submission away for her but instead she is sitting here in the dim, listening to the way in which two people communicate when she is not around them. The electric light from the kitchen throws everything into the hallway for her to see: shadow chairs, shadow eggshell mobile, the shadow hands of the Ordinary Man busily stocking small plastic bags.

The Child moves. His silhouette is tinier than Gest would have imagined but his voice is quite loud.

All right, he says tolerantly. Twist it tight.

The Ordinary Man's shadow flips the bag too slowly. The mouth of the upside-down bag gapes open, chicken crackers pour out and splinter all over the floor. There is a cloud of dust from the kitchen like the fallout from the collapse of a building, and then there is silence.

The Ordinary Man speaks. What a ridiculous thing to happen, he says, mispronouncing the word ridiculous which is something he only ever does when embarrassed. And now Gest wishes she had never started listening, had just got on with opening drawers and finding an envelope.

You don't say, corrects the Child, *ridiclus*. He sounds embarrassed too, and Gest presses her hands between her knees so that her fingers crack.

You say ri-di-cu-lous, says the Child loudly, as if he is in school. There is a sweeping sound as his small hands rustle the fragments of crackers together.

Gest waits for the Ordinary Man to assert himself. He has mispronounced a word, and he has been clumsy; but he is also the grown-up and this has to count for something. She waits for him to become annoyed, to put the Child in his place, hears his intake of breath.

Give me those, says the Ordinary Man humbly to the Child. I'll put them in the bin.

Chatter starts up again in the kitchen, the radio is switched on, the light is switched off so that the shadow kitchen disappears. There is busy friendly chatter as both the Ordinary Man and the Child make preparations for their days out in the unknown.

When Gest puts herself back there in that grey morning she sees again the long shadow of the Ordinary Man's love, stretching past her point of vision all the way out the front door into the world.

You can't cook, you never. You put work first, you always. You keep drugs in a pouch behind the bedroom door. But when it came down to it, the Ordinary Man had had no chance. He had stayed longer, endured more – for the good of Gest, for the good of the Child – than anyone could be expected to, even after it was obvious that he was no longer loved by his wife. And then, once he had finally given in and allowed himself to fall in love with another woman, Gest had swooped.

An adulterer. Do you think any judge (quoting his own words back at him) will award custody to an adulterer? Do you?

The guilt and despair in the Ordinary Man's set face as he walked from the courtroom, having heard he might see the Child only one afternoon in seven? This is what now bows Gest's neck, she hangs her head and bends her neck as if waiting, longing, for the fall of the guillotine. She had wanted her work and she had wanted the Child, that was all. She had wanted it all.

There is a moment
when you have been left

There is a moment when you have been left that is
like the moment when a knife slips and runs across
your hand. There you are, standing in your kitchen,
perhaps with the radio on so that you hear a report of
a train crash in some distant area of your city. You go
out your door and turn left onto the street, follow the
road all the way to the railway bridge and jump lightly
over the gate at the top of the steps that is supposed
to be for railway employees only, making you run fast,
laughing quietly but semi-hysterically, sensing the
roaring lights at your back and the bruising night somewhere ahead of you. You jump from wooden strut to
wooden strut, go on and on through the semi-dark
suburbs, through the great glass structures of stations
built many decades ago – and then, at some stage before
exiting the scrubby industrial wastelands into the real
countryside, you will come to the train crash you have
heard about on the radio: a few mangled carriages, one
on its side and two others leaning towards the sky in
a yearning kind of way, and although by the time you
have got there they have been cleared of the injured
or the dead it would be surprising if you did not find
something in one of those split seats – a clump of hair,
a half-empty pack of gum, or simply the gentle slough
of skin that follows in our human wake – that belongs
to someone you have once spoken to, in a chance
encounter or a business transaction, perhaps on a day
when you were buying a kilo of vine tomatoes in a
wind so biting that your eyes could hardly make out
the change through the whipped tears, and you and

that other person were both bent double, folding into yourselves like two pocket knives.

But the train crash is nowhere near you, and you open a can of tomatoes with an opener that is not all that stable, one that spins slightly before it engages with the rim of the can. Already you are planning ahead in your mind, to crush two cloves of garlic hard with the flat of the blade and then put some olive oil in the bottom of a non-stick pan and add the white garlic flesh chopped by you and the red tomato flesh chopped by a machine somewhere in Mexico City, and then sealed up so tightly in its can that you could have kept it for another five years if not needing it now.

You bring the knife down on the shiny clove of garlic but it slips, and the blade runs right across the base of your first finger and diagonally across the top of your thumb.

There is a second when you think everything is as it was. It will all be OK because even though you have watched with your own eyes the sharp steel edge crossing your hand, there is no trace of this: simply a small pink thread bordered on each side with two white lines, much as a train track is flanked by pebbles.

Of course, it is just after this that you realize: he means what he says and he is leaving you. The moment is so strong that the world sways. You lean against the stove or whatever is closest to you: the plywood partition wall of your office, if the news has been broken over the phone, or perhaps your head must be rested on the round carved post of the bedhead, hurting the back of your skull.

You had driven him away with your fury, your furious work habits and your determination to get to the heart of all things, even if only to prove there was a hollow space there. With your furious incomprehension of what

189

he was about, him with his need for routines and his belief that somehow, by keeping the household waste under control and regularly recycling bottles, it was possible to keep a grip on the world. It was your own fault.

There is a myth: beautiful women never get left. The Candy Girl believes this, having seen her own mother – no particular beauty, even from early photographs – working so hard, so goddam hard at her job as a cleaner that she had became tiny and wizened, hardly visible (you would never have thought her capable of bringing the lusty ten-pound Candy Girl into the world, even from seeing early photographs) so her husband had had no choice but to start an affair with a younger woman who was altogether more present, no choice but to leave his wife and family and start a new life.

But you—the Candy Girl looks at Gest. I can't understand him leaving you!

We were so different, hedges Gest. And then there was that habit of walking around with a toothbrush in his mouth. I couldn't stand it.

I remember! says the Candy Girl, from her stool against the wall. Today she wears a high-necked white jumper that crackles with synthetic energy. When she leans against the wall for a quick rest and then sits up straight again there is a series of small scratching sounds as the wall and the jumper yearn for each other, cling on, let each other go.

It made me sick, says Gest. He would even change nappies with his toothbrush sticking out of his mouth like a plastic tongue.

We all have our habits, says the Candy Girl peaceably. There is a pause while she considers hers. I run, she says. Nearly every morning. I buy T-shirts with logos on. And as for my other habits, my old ones, they nearly landed me in jail! Which is not something you could say for cleaning your teeth.

They both laugh at this. There is enough lightness in the air today to laugh at such irritations as past marriages and one-time addictions to drugs: there is lightness, and the fact that it is still only nine in the morning so the streets have not yet opened themselves to scrutiny, and the workers in the high offices are looking forward to lunchtime rather than the crowded straggling commute home at the end of the day.

I also—but Gest stops.

(Had it been your fault? You were dedicated to your work: that was what came between you. He wanted you to need him, you wanted your work, you both wanted the Child.)

She changes what she was going to say. You know how you read about people falling in love with firemen? she says, and she picks up a cloth and smells the meths, so strong that it is more of a taste: the burn, the raw burn of it! vinegar lodging in the back of the throat, cleaning your air passages to a stark white.

Firemen? says the Candy Girl, looking interested. She likes a good story about a strong man, a tragedy or near-tragedy or rescue. What sort of people fall in love with firemen? she asks.

The survivors of fires, says Gest. Afterwards they fall in love with their rescuers.

As a way of thanking them, I expect, nods the Candy Girl. It is reassuring to see that the Candy Girl still sees love as a reward.

Now Gest tells the Candy Girl a story: the tale of a high-profile fire chief, an upstanding member of the community who had narrowly missed out on becoming mayor. He began helping out in a community psychotherapy group where victims of violent crimes were encouraged to re-enact their trauma in order to break through the barrier of fear. Not surprisingly, the fire chief proved most effective when it came to re-enacting rescues from burning buildings: and so effective was he that a burn victim fell in love with him (*showed her gratitude to him by offering her love*). The love was reciprocated so that the fire chief's wife ended up becoming the victim – it was the wife who became the pitied and the scarred one, although publicly maintaining a dignified silence.

The Candy Girl exclaims, comments, and wonders why Gest is telling her this.

Because this is exactly what happened to me, says Gest.

I thought your husband was a shrink. The Candy Girl looks puzzled. Or am I wrong? Were you, in fact, married to a fireman?

No, you are right, says Gest. He was a psychologist, to be precise.

Explain, then, demands the Candy Girl.

The circumstances were different but the love affair happened, says Gest. The damaged-goods affair, the clichéd heroic-rescuer love affair.

Who was she? asks the Candy Girl. Her eyes are wide in horror and alarm.

A child psychologist, says Gest. She became ill herself and ended up having psychotherapy at my husband's practice, with my husband. First she was his patient, and then his affair.

So they had everything in common, sighed the Candy Girl. A sharing of everything!

Including a bed, says Gest wryly.

What was she like? The Candy Girl, who is brave enough to take on surly fruit sellers and walk down alleyways in the dead of night, cannot believe Gest's calm. She is impressed, amazed.

They ended up together, shrugs Gest, and after a while everyone forgave each other. She makes him far happier than I ever did.

I tell you one thing, says the Candy Girl consolingly. I bet she isn't half as beautiful as you.

There is a myth: beautiful women never get left. There is a corresponding truth: even beautiful women get left when they don't sleep with their husbands.

You always, you never, the Ordinary Man said, and there was fear and sadness in his voice. You never. You never.

It was true. For many months Gest had not slept with her husband, not once in those months had she given herself to him. She had expected him to stay, and then he had not. She had been left.

The journey down

There is a certain amount of fear in Gest as she ventures down the stairs to the mailbox area. Seventy-two stairs: this is a long way when you have become accustomed to walking no further than the length of your hallway, with only your own door in front of you.

She notices things she did not used to see: the dust on the ledges beside each black-panelled doorway, a splash of paint on the fourth-floor landing. On the third-floor landing, where there used always to be the low sound of a radio coming from behind the door, there is silence, pressing on the wood like water held back by a floodgate. And on the first-floor landing she can still detect the faintest smell of fried fish.

She runs to the mailbox bent double: she has become used to the rarefied Thomas Mann air of her own apartment. Down here exhaust fumes creep in from the street, because cars are panting outside the windows: rows of cars, each with its own set of windows and its own set of heads, one, two or three, looking straight ahead into an oncoming day that will be the same as the day before, and the one before that.

The blinding numbing effect of routine: this cannot be underestimated.

Gest turns her back on the automatons and reaches for the small key, sitting rusting in the lock of the mailbox. Clearing the mail has become the Candy Girl's task; on earlier days she has arrived at Gest's door with a sheaf of envelopes clutched in her hand like a bunch of flowers. (Here, she beams. Maybe today, a letter from your boy?)

But this morning the Candy Girl will be late. She has asked Gest for time off so that she might go to a high office building in the centre of the city, to sign a contract with the landlord of her future shop.

If I don't turn up and sign, she told Gest, I might lose the premises. If I don't finalise the contract he will give it to someone else, and that must not happen! Because if I get it up and running, she had said with hope in her voice, maybe the Micro's sister will come back and help out!

From this you will see the Candy Girl's faith that dreams can be resurrected, and people return. At the very moment that Gest is reaching for the rusting mailbox key, in fact, the Candy Girl is reaching for the signing pen, hoping to restore happiness to the sister of the man she loves, while also supplying the people of the city with quality uniforms for any kind of imaginable job.

So the Candy Girl is not yet here, and Gest cannot

wait for her to come and clear the mail. She is expecting something, and believes it will arrive today.

It is there. She has been prepared but this is the *point of no return*, as they say in war movies, when the men are positioning themselves on a new front ready to leap from the trenches like baying dogs. It is there, the envelope with its official stamp, the only thing in the white metal box except for a flier from a Thai restaurant four streets away. Four streets away! The pressure in Gest's ears swells, the glass doors holding back the street shiver. Should they break, should the glass shatter, an ocean of exhaust will flood into the building and the cars will follow, bobbing on their own saliva, and Gest will drown.

But someone is coming. Someone is coming across the courtyard from the building behind hers, and she retreats blindly back into her own stairwell and sits on the bottom step. Before her the floor of the entrance hall is covered in dust, marked out by ridged soles and large sneaker prints and the clover-pointed paws of dogs. (Wind whips down the stairwell, cold on the back of her neck, and the windows groan in their frames. The building is already giving up on her.)

There is a word much used in journalism: used, overused and often misused, and Gest cannot help thinking of it now. *Underestimated*. She has noticed before the way in which it is bandied around wildly and wrongly, a favourite of journalists striving for effect and falling into cliché because their jobs depend on it.

The psychological effect cannot be underestimated.

She holds the envelope in her numb left hand. She would rather wait, wait to tear the flap across until the intruder – that is, the resident from the opposite building who has right of way through the foyer for as long as this apartment block stands – has passed safely through the war zone and out onto the street.

195

The footsteps are closer now. They sound strangely slow and uneven, but this could be because of the roaring blood in Gest's ears.

The psychological effect of loss cannot be underestimated.

It should be *overestimated*, the word. This is what the journalists mean, that the loss is so bad it is impossible to estimate it too highly. But then perhaps they are writing quickly, correspondents at the front line fearing for their lives and having no time to think clearly about prefixes, as they crouch there between the four flimsy walls of a prefab building that might once have been part of an Olympic Village. But even when skated over by thin and incorrect words, one thing remains. The loss. It is the only solid thing.

The door to the foyer swings open and a tall shadow is thrown across the grey dusty floor, but Gest is holding an envelope with white fingers curling like those of a dead person and her eyes are seeing other things.

What does she see? The walls of a prefab building still shaking from a recent bomb blast. A shaking building in which once athletes stretched in their early beds, masturbating or not, depending on whether they were due to race that day, and whether they believed that beating off before running robbed them of vital energy. This prefab building, once full of Olympic athletes, now crammed with clicking keys, spinning tape recorders, and the distant sound of machine guns mixing with the clack clack of starlings' wings. By the window is a reporter crouched at the keyboard of a laptop, and he has something in common with Gest: both are conscious of a reluctance ever to go outside again.

The enemy must not be underestimated.

But Gest is thinking of the paper lying in her dead white hand, while the reporter can hardly think at all. The difficulty of making a decision between *overestimate* and *underestimate*, when a negative article is added into the equation! The difficulty and the irrelevance of grammatical correctness when, just yesterday, the journalist had been dropped off in a dusty valley by a Land Rover and seven minutes later had watched that same Land Rover explode on a curving road on the other side of the valley. Lost! Allies, friends, companions in terror: all lost in a blaze of fire and noise.

And now Gest drops the envelope. It skids away from her but she makes no move to retrieve it. She has no need. She knows what it will tell her: that in eighteen days from now, on a muddy site on the edge of the city, the cranes will be gathering their strength. And that on the next day they will begin their inexorable journey, rolling towards her and the empty shell in which she lives, which is the only home she has.

There is a voice now, someone is saying something. The slowly approaching person from the back building is right there in front of her. Gest, who has just crouched by the side of a war correspondent with no dictionary and little hope of getting home alive, and who has lived through the next two and a half weeks in the blink of an eye, finds it hard to return to the present. I'm sorry? she says.

The man from the other building is standing in front of her and asking if she is all right.

Is she?

I have lost—says Gest. I have lost.

Your envelope? says the man, picking it up from between his long suede feet, but doing so with difficulty because of leaning on a stick.

Thank you, says Gest. She takes the envelope. It is so heavy that her hand falls under its weight, and she must rest her head against the wall.

An eviction notice, says the man. His voice is low and

oddly accented so that Gest does not know if he is asking a question of her or making a statement. You live here, he says, with the same unreadable inflection.

I have been expecting it, she says, her head still leaning against the dull grey wall. I have known it for months.

But one is never quite ready, he says. To leave a home.

There is something familiar about the way his hair lies smoothed back from his forehead: dark hair streaked with grey. There is something about the way his head sits on his long neck, and the way his body is angled downwards, his left shoulder sliding into his left elbow, which is slotted into the round harness of his stick. But for now Gest looks at his feet, because she has never seen them before. The left one rests lightly on the ground as if, inside its beige suede shoe, it is wasted and shrivelled.

You are the Reader, she says, addressing his feet. You live across from my window.

I do, he says. He doesn't try to pretend anything, they both know he has often seen her too: naked against the night window, doubled up in pain against the kitchen cupboard, eating peas from a can, drinking beer, staring into an empty hallway.

Do you have anywhere to go, he looks at her levelly, once you leave?

I have plans, she says. She lifts her head, stands up as if hearing a bugle call. I have plans, everything is arranged, she says with dignity. I have work to finish before I go, that is all.

Work! he says. He looks at the watch hanging on his thin elegant wrist. I must go, he says, giving an awkward half-bow, I am due at the newspaper in half an hour.

The newspaper? Gest is startled, of course she is, for during the minutes in which the Reader has made his slow and limping way across the courtyard she has been crouched beside a foreign correspondent, watching the stress pull at the side of his mouth, witnessing the shaking of his fingers as they hit the keys. You are a reporter? she asks. And for a second she is back there, crouching below the window sill, smelling the sweat of fear and duty.

Nothing so exciting, says the Reader with a smile. I am not able-bodied enough for that job.

He balances with difficulty on his one-stick arm and extends his other hand to Gest. The skin on his palm is warm and dry.

I hope we shall meet again, he says, bowing his head.

The tracks he leaves in the dust behind him are lengthy ones – his dragging left foot, his sliding stick – and the door falls heavily shut behind him. There is silence. For a second even the traffic is stilled and suddenly Gest is tempted to follow, to step into the street and walk her old ways, over the bridge, down past the station where the newspaper sellers shout and the dogs bark, and the grit of other lives swirls against her face.

But the envelope cuts into her palm in a reminding way. *There is no time.* There is no time to lose. She must not stop, cannot be distracted from her task and the climbing of seventy-two steps to where her work waits for her. The importance of this can never be overestimated.

She turns and starts up the stairs. Behind her in the hallway the dust lies as heavy as ashes.

Heatwave

Although it is still only spring, a strange heatwave has taken hold of the city. Trees wilt and bend their heads to the streets, people toil to and from work, shopping bags leave red marks on palms, straps cut into heels.

The Candy Girl has a sweat on her top lip. When the Micro places his mouth over hers he tastes the sea, although this is not a coastal region, they are far from the ocean here, with dull plains stretching for miles around and the same horizon staying at the same distance no matter how far you might travel. See the Candy Girl struggling through the thick air on her bicycle, see the way the hospital towers are attracting pollution, a dirty smudge around their tops so they look like crematorium chimneys pouring ash into the air.

Leaves begin to fall onto the wide streets, even though it is nowhere near autumn. The leaves are skeletons, consisting only of white delicate veins and stalks. Their young green flesh has shrivelled, they are turning old before their time.

Gest sits in her high workroom. Perhaps because of the heat she is eating less and less; the insides of her thighs are concave and there is a new transparency to her skin. There is no domineering old man to force spoonfuls of food into her mouth, pinching her nose shut so she must swallow or die. No, she no longer has a grandfather to shout at her for eating food from the container without using a plate. Spoonfuls of yoghurt straight from the carton, forkfuls of cold pasta out of a cold-smelling can: this is what she eats, in the odd times when her mind and her body need a rest from work.

200

There are compensations. As she eats less, her vision is sharpening, she is beginning to see things not normally visible to the naked eye. Sometimes there are flashes of movement outside the windows, though when she turns to look she sees nothing but the hot and empty air.

In Roman days, in times such as this, the low shimmering courtyards of the Emperors had become stultifying from heat. The sun would glance hard and bright off the shoulders of statues and the edges of white marble seats, and men would narrow their eyes against the light. In times such as this even the shaded walkways were no longer pleasant places in which to stroll, and neither the flanking columns nor the shade of the shining orange trees offered relief.

At times such as this – in periods of strange and excessive heat – the rich and the powerful would order snow to be brought down from the mountains and laid in their gardens. After the sweating slaves had departed, for a few hours these gardens would be oases of coolness; then ribcages would expand with relief and lungs draw in air that carried with it the memory of wide snowfields and deep crevasses falling to the centre of the earth.

Gest leans on her balcony and looks beyond the flaking transparent trees to the past. Let us follow her then to Italy, though not to ancient Rome but a more recent time. For she has been there, once, and she has a story to tell.

An unfit mother

There was once an old man (she begins the story in the time-honoured way). An old and much-revered man who had been an architect in those days when architecture was still a noble profession, when there was not so much emphasis on haste and budgets, and more of a desire to get things right. This man loved buildings: he loved them so much, or so people said, that when he talked about interior spaces and how it was possible on entry for the soul to soar, his voice sounded like that of a different man. He could sit for hours debating politics or literature over the sticky-mouthed bottles of dessert wine, cicadas hanging heavily from the trees: his guests would talk him down or talk over him, and he would argue back, and another few bottles would be opened and the moths would hurl their heavy bodies towards the lamps hung between the trees, cracking and falling like kamikaze pilots, and the cats would pounce with low growls in their throats and carry the hot moth-pilots away in their mouths, threading unerringly through the ongoing talk and the feet.

But once this man began to talk about architecture, the world was stilled. Arguments died away, guests stopped filling their wineglasses and polishing their knives with linen napkins: bread lay like fallen columns on the white tablecloths, and the wind sighed and returned to the bay.

(He loves people, said Gest, speaking to her husband at a time when this story was still able to be told in the present.

He loves his profession, corrected the Ordinary Man

during a time when he and Gest still slept in the same bed.

He understands the impact of surroundings, Gest shrugged, on people. The impact of the physical, the way the external can be drawn in with one long breath, to fill up your lungs and seep into your stomach, thread its way into your lower intestine, leak into your blood and your bones. He understands that it is possible for *where* you are to change *who* you are.

He understands the principles of space and light, agreed the Ordinary Man, better than any other architect of his time.)

But what he had not understood, that man (this is Gest, continuing the narrative on the thirty-fourth day), what the old architect had not understood was the way the world had started to change around him. Somehow he had lived most of his life sheltered from reality and when he retired this continued. He moved from the churning Italian city in which he had lived most of his life, he left behind its whirlpool traffic and its shrieking skies, and he moved to a hillside above a curving bay. There he bought a house: the first in which he had lived, in the whole of his long life, that had not been designed by himself. This was, in itself, a luxury, giving him a certain respite from his brain.

He lived there on the hillside for several long years, in a low villa with two terraces on the side and a terrace at the back shaded by grapevines. And from the terrace in the front you could see right across the Gulf of Catania all the way to the horizon, to that place where the sky laid its face down on the water and the two merged as if they were one. This was something the old man partic-ularly liked, such a visible sign of trust in Nature. For this was the way he himself had strived to live, main-taining pure ideals in the midst of an increasingly harsh

203

society. He had been dealt some sharp cracks on his thin idealistic knuckles over time but he had survived the attacks, and therefore he had not learnt — or he had refused to learn — the lesson of his years. And so (summarizes Gest) he trusted in the same way that a child trusts; he opened his house to the world at large, just as he always had, and because of this he died.

How did you know him? breathed the Candy Girl. She polishes an apple on her lime-green breasts as she listens: round, round.

Many people from the movie business, explains Gest, began to visit the house. Directors, producers, stars of the big screen and the small: all came flocking to the villa which soon gained a reputation for being a party palace, a fact of which the old man was unaware. Coke was raked into fat lines on the glass-topped tables. Champagne bottles were passed around, wine was poured over breasts and licked out of cunts. And in the many bedrooms girls lay naked on white fur rugs, paid for by the hour or the night.

At some stage in the hours before the dawn, visitors would stumble down the cliff paths that led to the town below or would depart in noisy red sports cars, the heavy iron gates gliding closed behind them. Back in the villa glasses lay on their sides, and needles lay in the cracks of the bathroom tiles. Discarded thongs sprawled like lizards over the side terraces, silk bras were strung through the vines. But the housekeepers rose from their beds long before the architect did, and these sturdy women would work their way around the mess, talking fast and low in disapproving voices, so that by the time the old architect emerged from his shuttered bedroom and stood blinking in the sunlight, the debris from the night before had been cleared away.

And so, says Gest, the architect could remain happy.

He could remain oblivious, and oblivion is not such a bad thing. (She does not sound sad – more wistful, thinks the Candy Girl, crunching into her gleaming apple so that the juice flies.)

He was happy to see people happy, that was it (Gest goes on). It was like an extension of his life's work. And then there was the fact that, in general, he was not what you would call a particularly aware man, even though he had been acutely aware of certain things: the way that light could be made to fall through a slit window, for instance, forming a cross on a dusty floor; the way a whisper could be whipped into a full and creamy voice by rubbing it up against a domed roof; or the way that it is possible for a sharp roof-line against a clear sky to flush the poison from a man's bowels and the anger from his head, leaving him refreshed and cleansed.

He was aware of these things, but only these (and now there is definitely sadness in Gest's voice). One summer the old man hired a local photographer to paint his villa, knowing that the young photographer was struggling to make a living but was determined to stay in the game. Day after day the young man would come to the house, work all morning and eat lunch with the old man, and then sleep for a couple of hours in the bedroom next to the old man's until the full heat of the day had passed. After the working day was over, the old man would give money to the young one and together they would drink several glasses of Averna on the long terrace tangled with vines. Their talk was equally tangled, quick and inter-woven, for in spite of a gap in years they understood each other, these two. But they would almost always finish by discussing two topics: the fashion industry and the film industry, as the old man had many possible contacts and much advice for the young one. He even suggested—

Here Gest pauses, but only to drink from her water glass for her quick quiet mouth is becoming parched as it nears the end of its story.

He suggested the director you worked with? asks the Candy Girl. She is slightly fearful about what she is to hear; her large square teeth bite her bottom lip, goad it into redness.

The director who took me there, agrees Gest. It was a party of porn stars and rock stars, and the kind old man sat in the middle, shining.

One night after the young photographer had finished painting the outside of the house and was due the next day to start whitewashing the interior – that night, sometime after midnight, he returned to the villa. He had spent the evening in a crack house down in the town; when he left there was a smell in his nostrils, the reek of burning flesh against hot glass. But what to do with this knowledge? How to rid himself of the smell?

He drove fast up the cliff road, tyres screaming, wrenching at the wheel. At every turn he was dazzled by the white remembered flame of the blowtorch that had heated the pipe to a glowing red. Pulling up at the double iron gates he vaulted over them, although they were five feet tall and he had been given the code to open them.

The young photographer ran around the side of the villa. Sweat stood out on his forehead and formed a V on his chest, and drops of it fell heavily behind him like rain. There were burns on his fingers that looked black in the harsh white moonlight, and his black eyes were sockets in his white face.

Now the scent of clematis is filling his nostrils – nothing but cheap perfume. He trips against an earthenware pot and half falls on it. Its thick fleshy leaves crush under him, smell of human excrement, sweat. Dirt under his finger nails, fire in his lungs. Nothing to do but throw it all behind him and keep running.

And he is at the front of the house, standing in front of double shutters closed to the night like eyes.

The young man kicks his way into the room that during the day is his; he finds an empty bed. Sweat flies. Next he is standing outside the slatted door of the old man's bedroom and he runs at it, hard, and crashes into the breathing darkness.

The old man is in bed, lying on his side, his thin shoulder lifting the sheet and letting it fall, slightly crumpled, around him. At the crash of the door he sits up, only half conscious. Perhaps he makes a sound? It is possible that he says the young man's name. But before he can do another thing the young man is pulling a gun from under his jacket, and the next moment he blows the old man's brains out.

For a second the Candy Girl can hardly speak. Sitting there on her stool, she shakes her head and rocks back and forwards, holding her green cardigan arms tight around herself.

And you knew, she manages, you knew him? The poor, the poor old man?

I had met him, says Gest quietly. And now the afternoon sun draws away from her, pulls itself quickly back into the street so the bright pool in the middle of the room shrinks to nothing, revealing faded paint-spattered floorboards.

I had met him just once, says Gest dully. He sat in the middle of that noisy wild party and he told me not to be afraid of growing old.

OH, says the Candy Girl, and then she says: How did you find out about the—?

But she cannot say the word, and she sits there turning her apple core round and round under her gnawing front teeth like an otter chewing through a trunk. The apple core breaks: small black pips fall, bounce, under her stool.

I read about it in the paper, says Gest. He was famous enough.

She still remembers the moment: the black and white facts, the blurring. She had been out of the movie industry for some years by then but when she had read the article filed from Rome she saw as clearly as if she were there again the heaving throbbing party and the still white head of the architect, talking to her about old age and the cleanest and most efficient way to pull a freshly cooked prawn from its shell. Tears came fast into her eyes as she read about the bloodshed at the foot of Mt Etna and those tears fell onto the newspaper, streaking it blue and grey.

When the Child ran into the kitchen to get a drink, he stopped short and then shouted loudly for his father.

Come quickly! he had shouted, and had then reached in a business-like way into the fridge to get the orange juice (his mother was in tears at the table, but there was no sense in dying of thirst). Come quick! he had commanded in a shout, and he had buried his muzzle in a musty orange glass and breathed loudly at the rim, not only with thirst but with concern.

By the time the Ordinary Man came running into the room, Gest was on her feet and wiping her eyes, and the newspaper was nowhere to be seen. It was soaring, that paper, from the high window; its damp pages caught the wind clumsily and disintegrated into shreds in mid-air.

What? asked the Ordinary Man, alarmed.

That old architect I met on Sicily? said Gest. He's dead.

She had submitted to being hugged by the Ordinary Man, who explained to the Child that his mother was sad because a friend had died. The two of them had made it up to Gest in their own ways: the Child had created a card laden with glue and thick with glitter, which for many days shed its red sparkling sympathy all over the house and stuck to their skin (red eyelids, sparkling creases of elbows, shiny cracks between the toes). The Ordinary Man did his part by keeping phone calls at bay. Gest is mourning (he had said, in his pleasant polite voice) for an old acquaintance.

This was true, Gest was. But her tears had been as much for the young photographer, waking to a lifetime of barred windows and echoing gates, the burns on his fingers a reminder of what he had done in pursuit of a short oblivion. And the paint in the rims of his finger-nails a reminder of kindness lost, and every night a life-time of silence to be faced. Whereas the old man had at least gone out violently, gloriously, in a spray of scarlet and noise, with the same sudden force as the flinging of a newspaper out a high window; and who could say that he was not the better off of the two?

The one left behind, says Gest to the Candy Girl, is the unfortunate one. But she can only say this now. At the time she had had other reasons for the guilt felt at hearing the Ordinary Man keeping the world at bay, giving her time to recover from a sudden shock. She was mourning prima-rily for the wrong man, for the murderer rather than the murdered, and this was bad enough. But her instinctive flinging of the news back into the world, only hours after it had been retrieved from a noisy street corner? This action had been to save herself. From recriminations, from the tiresome endless discussions that she could no longer stand.

For this is another thing Gest has in common with the Candy Girl, though it has taken thirty-four days of greetings and tea-drinking and farewells to be ready for the revelation.

I have something to tell you, she says, looking directly at the Candy Girl. I took drugs as well.

The Candy Girl starts.

Crack, says Gest, heroin, speed, all. All the time, back then.

Such an expression on the Candy Girl's face! Such a joy, a surprise! Such a love a fellow-feeling a guilty delight a nostalgia bordering on lust. She looks at Gest under lowered lids as if they are now partners in crime.

They were OK, weren't they? she says cautiously. Those days. But as she looks over at Gest her striped hair falls over her face in a coquettish way and apple juice shines in a thin line on her chin.

I had to stop when I became a mother, says Gest, also cautiously. She feels she must underline the differences between them: unlike the Candy Girl she has undergone years of censure and she cannot forget this, in spite of the shared radiance falling on their heads.

Of course you did, says the Candy Girl instantly. What kind of a mother would stay involved in that kind of thing?

An odd feeling rises in Gest's throat as she sees the Candy Girl's simple straightforward standards. A mother does not do drugs: a girlfriend must sometimes allow herself to be hit for the good of a relationship: an employer should not open herself up to an employee for reasons that are purely selfish.

Excuse me for a minute, she says in a professional, perfect-employer manner. She leaves the room and crosses the hallway, and closes the bathroom door and locks it. Then she kneels in front of the toilet bowl and hangs over it, elbows on the hard rim.

The world has turned against her. The one person she talks to daily has just sided, albeit unwittingly, with the one person she used to talk to daily: the Ordinary Man, who at first could hardly bring himself to discuss the subject (through disapproval, through fear, through a respect for private space) and then had never seemed to shut up about it.

At first, when he found out about Gest and the habit she had brought into their marriage, he had been unfailingly polite. He had said:

I would prefer you not to have that in the same house as the Child.

This was what he had said: I would prefer you not to. And he had spoken in a reasonable voice, and the way he had spoken so objectively had made it seem as if the Child was not a part of them at all. As if the Child was not six months old (or a year, or two years) but was a grown-up person with certain rights quite separate from theirs and equally important, who was just not able to speak for himself yet. And the way he had said 'that', referring to the small pouch hanging smudgily on the back of their bedroom door, bestowed a gravity on it which meant that its very existence infringed those equal and important rights of the Child.

Keeping it in full view, too! he had said, as the years went on. As the Child had grown older, and Gest had left the pouch hanging untouched on the back of the door, he stopped sounding reasonable and polite, and began to sound angry. Angrier and angrier with the passing of time, so that after a while he sounded as if he would like to hit the bedpost or the door where the pouch hung, which perhaps he would have done had he been brought up like the Micro, used to expressing his anger in real punches rather than verbal ones.

How can you leave it there, he would say, in full view of everyone!

But he would not move it himself, and for some reason neither would Gest. There was a reluctance in her to put it away and she would say:

211

In full view of who? We are the only ones who ever go into our bedroom.

Not only us, he would say meaningfully. What about the FUCKING CHILD? His cursing was not in any way aimed at the Child, whom he adored and (like Gest) would lay down his life for. His anger was solely directed at her, and at how he now saw her: as an unfit mother.

What he seemed unable to understand was that Gest had only ever been an occasional user, and by the time the old architect had been shot through the head by a drug-crazed local she had become almost a non-user. A non-user of drugs, while a full-time – a devoted – artist, and a full-time and devoted mother. Even as she worked a part of her mind was always attached to the Child, and it had been this way ever since he had been born. She felt the tug of him as he slept in the next room, the rise and fall of his small chest pulling at that part of her mind that belonged to him and him alone: and his breath ran out of the cot and under the closed door, up her legs and her spine to run cool and shallow along her arms as she worked. Why, then, had she kept the pouch with its black smoky insides, and the peppermint tin with its sharp illegal white breath in her top drawer?

As part of herself and a reminder of what she had once been, before becoming willingly, unwittingly, trapped by love.

As it became clearer that his protests had little effect, the Ordinary Man stepped up the pressure. He had said: What if the police come? (They hadn't.) What if the drug squad comes? (They didn't.) What if one of your dealers needs money and turns up to blackmail us, or releases our address to an addict who breaks in and steals all our possessions? They hadn't, didn't, wouldn't, no one came and nothing was broken or stolen, and Gest's past stayed safely there: in the past. But still the Ordinary

Man went on, driven by fear, although not one of his predictions happened. In truth, his fear was that they would prove to be inadequate parents, that the Child would die in his sleep because they hadn't checked which way he was lying, that one of them might let the Child fall down the stairs so that his head cracked wide open on the banisters, that they might become bored with their marriage and one of them would have an affair and set the Child a bad example thus blighting his adult emotional life, and so—

What if, what if? he said.

What if you shut the fuck up, shouted Gest one day, and she pulled out a drawer and took up handfuls of cutlery and threw them at the Ordinary Man's head as if she were a knife thrower in a circus. The cutlery soared past him and hit the wall, didn't stick into him or on the wall, slid in a slippery rush down to the floor.

There was a sudden silence.

Not al dente, said the Ordinary Man, who did not always lack a sense of humour. Better put them back in the drawer for a while.

They had laughed at this *ha ha ha* in an approximation of their old way: but there was an ironic sound in the middle of the knife-roar that Gest did not properly interpret until later. The thing was, she and the Ordinary Man had proved inadequate parents. They had fallen apart and in spite of their care and their fear the Child had fallen somewhere between them, so he no longer belonged safely to two people but only to himself – a burden for any five-year-old, however gruff and responsible he might be. Falling like a newspaper, tumbling through the crack in their marriage, arms outstretched like paper wings.

And so (says Gest, finishing the story as a good storyteller should) the young photographer was given a life

213

sentence, and my husband never knew it was crack cocaine that was responsible for the death of the old man, and the old man had told me the truth when he said that growing old was not the worst thing in the world.

What is? asks the Candy Girl, like a schoolchild. Black pips shaped like teardrops lie glistening at her feet. What is the worst thing in the world?

What I did – Gest sounds confused, as if she has never meant to go this far. What I did to the Child, she finishes in a low voice, and as she does so she drives a chisel hard into the palm of her hand.

What did you do to him? asks the Candy Girl, and because she has seen her employer for thirty-four days in a row, has cleared her mailbox and brought her fruit and heard her piss and made her tea, she comes over and put her hand on Gest's shoulder. Oh what did you do? she asks, anxiously.

But blood is dripping, pouring, from Gest's palm.

Sweet Jesus! says the Candy Girl in alarm, and Gest pushes her chair back so sharply that the Candy Girl's hand falls to her side like a stone.

Sorry! Gest drops the chisel, now rimmed around with red. Sit down, she says. I'll be back in a minute.

Behind her a trail of small scarlet coins stretches across the floorboards to the door. For a second they lie in perfect sealed circles, then they break up in the wake of Gest's hurrying feet.

Stories of sleep

There is an oddness about the Candy Girl when she arrives the next day. She shuffles her sneakered feet in the hallway and refuses morning tea. No biscuit, she says politely. But thank you anyway.

The heat grows. By mid-afternoon it is so intense that Gest's fingers are swollen and she can hardly hold her tools. The Candy Girl looks as if there is an immense pressure inside her. She shuts her mouth tight trying to hold it in, but her top lip becomes large and puffy with the effort.

Do you want to take a break? offers Gest.

The Candy Girl stands up and paces the edges of the room. She goes out onto the balcony but the doors swing wide in the hot breeze, and Gest's drawings are blown all around the room. After the doors are closed and the room is sealed up again, there is a moment of awkward silence.

It's the Micro, blurts out the Candy Girl. I think he is having an affair.

Suddenly tears are pouring down the face of the ebullient, the cheerful, the optimistic and indomitable Candy Girl. She stands like a large wounded animal, making no sound, but her shoulders shake and tears pour heavily onto her T-shirt, fall on the floor of the workroom.

Have you slept? Gest, who is now existing on four hours a night, has smelt exhaustion on the Candy Girl from the minute she stepped in the door. No, the Candy Girl has not slept, not much at all; last night the Micro was out again until dawn, though where he wouldn't say.

You could rest now. Gest hesitates, sees the Candy Girl needs direction, leads her to the bedroom.

It is a long time since anyone but Gest has been in here, and she looks at it with new eyes: sees the black sheet knotted at the window, the dust lying in streaks on the floor.

The Candy Girl hardly looks around. She takes off her shoes and lies down on her side on the mattress, eyes open, staring at the wall. She curls her legs up and points her feet towards the end of the bed, so her big toe emerges from a hole in her sock. Her nail is painted with silver spangles.

Gest bites her lip. Do you want me to stay? she says diffidently.

She pulls the sheet-curtain out of its knot, shakes it down over the window so the dusty white afternoon is shut out. The room is dim now but when she turns back to the bed she can see tears running fast down the side of the Candy Girl's face and into the pillow.

Could you talk to me about something? The Candy Girl's voice is thick and clogged. She wipes her arm across her face so her wrist becomes streaked with wet mascara.

What about? asks Gest.

I don't mind, comes the Candy Girl's muffled voice. I don't want to think any more, I'm tired of thinking. Tell me anything.

Gest lies down beside her on the edge of the mattress. I could tell you, she stops and thinks. I could tell you stories of sleep.

Are they stories you told your Child? asks the Candy Girl, with a snuffle.

When he was small, agrees Gest. When he really believed that the day he had lived through was the only one there was so he didn't want to close his eyes on it.

216

Kids! says the Candy Girl. She pulls her legs up even further so her knees touch her chest. There is a large expanse of back visible between her T-shirt and the waistband of her leggings, and Gest can see the red imprint of elastic on the soft white skin.

Rest now, says Gest, and she moves closer and puts her arms around the Candy Girl from behind, strokes her hair. Do you know about dolphins? she asks.

What? The Candy Girl knows little about these creatures, and even if she did her lips would be too tired to say so.

Dolphins are like human mothers, says Gest, with a small laugh that vibrates against the Candy Girl's back. They can stay awake even while they sleep.

The Candy Girl reaches back over her shoulder, takes Gest's hand and strokes it. Her fingers move carefully over the bandage covering Gest's palm. Is it sore? she asks, in a small worried voice.

A dolphin, says Gest, has two sides to its brain. If both fell asleep at the same time the dolphin would drown.

Have to keep swimming, murmurs the Candy Girl. Have to stay breathing.

Shhh. Gest reaches over and puts her fingers on the Candy Girl's lips. I am the one who is doing the talking and you are the one who is doing the sleeping, she says. Do you know why cats twitch in their sleep? Do you know why horses doze standing up? Do you know why babies kick in the womb?

Soon the Candy Girl's breathing is slow and steady but Gest leaves her arm around her hot neck. She can feel the Candy Girl's pulse beating against her own: feels their hearts get in step and slip out of time for a few beats and then get back in step again.

They lie there curled together for a long time in the darkened room, while the afternoon toils its hot and weary way across the city. Once the Candy Girl turns over and moves closer into Gest. Once their lips touch, and their tongues lightly move against each other.

Did I sleep? asks the Candy Girl. Outside the evening is lying against the curtained window, soft, tolerant, warm.

You slept, says Gest, and she fetches the Candy Girl some water and smoothes her hair away from her face.

And did you? says the Candy Girl worriedly. She reaches for her sneakers, ties the laces and becomes more like the person she usually is: responsible, business-like, taking care. We have done so little work today! she says.

I rested. Gest shrugs. I have not been sleeping well, I needed rest.

They go out into the hallway and look at the shadows of the thirty-fifth day. Tomorrow they will start again, and the Candy Girl will not cry in front of Gest, and underneath the bandage the wound from Gest's chisel will be one day closer to healing. They walk towards the front door.

Have you been out today? (Is the Candy Girl asking because she suspects Gest does not go into the street any more?) It is so hot out there, even the Micro—she stops. Even those who are used to hot climates find this weather hard.

Gest bends to pick up a dust ball, as soft as human hair. As my husband's mother used to say, she begins, before also stopping and correcting herself. As my *ex*-husband's *late* mother used to say, she says, only bad things happen to you outside.

The Candy Girl looks concerned, then thinks that perhaps this is a joke. Ha! she says uncertainly. As she steps towards the door, she remembers something in her bag.

Here, she says. A note for you, I forgot.

The envelope is heavy and beige, pock-marked like

218

skin: there is no name written on the front, and the flap on the back is blank.

Someone from the back building gave it to me, says the Candy Girl. I would have asked him what his name was but—she pauses. I was a bit upset this morning, she finishes bravely.

So you were, says Gest. At the door, the Candy Girl turns to shake hands, as if Gest has not told her stories of gentle mammals and seen the imprint of elastic on her lower back, and as if they have not lain for most of the afternoon in each other's arms. Goodbye, she says seriously. Until tomorrow.

Gest waits until her footsteps have echoed away into the empty bowels of the house. She reads the letter standing up, leaning against the front door. It is hand-written and on one page only: an invitation to meet in the courtyard not the following day but the one after that. It is not signed but in the stoop of the letters and the three-pronged tilt of the letter *M* she sees again the Reader, standing in front of her talking calmly about her future, leaning on his stick.

Game of numbers

Here we are back in the past. Back in a time when Gest was perfect, at least in others' eyes. A time when the Ordinary Man was secure in love and therefore imper-vious to temptation, and the Candy Girl was as high as a kite on the steps of a Portuguese church, and the Child was at the centre of everybody's story.

Here he is: striding bold and irrepressible into the room. His bright uncontrollable hair stands out around his face. Even when he is stern, even when he tells Gest and the Ordinary Man to stop laughing because he is *being serious here* – even then his face shines in a hidden kind of way, as the sun sweeps temporarily behind a cloud.

Some would say that these four characters – Gest, her husband, her child and his sitter – were bound together from the minute that the Candy Girl wandered in a soft marijuana haze into the lives of the small triangular family. That since then their fates have been bound together in some way. Witness the Child fall asleep in his bedroom holding the Candy Girl's hand while Gest and the Ordinary Man drink hopeful champagne toasts in a high revolving restaurant; witness the Ordinary Man losing the Child in a bitter divorce only to reclaim him months later, or Gest spending an afternoon on a mattress beside the rounded and tear-stained form of the Candy Girl.

But this configuration depends largely on where you choose to begin and end. For a lot of the time, while the Candy Girl was travelling and singing and losing her heart to a manly man, there were three rather than four. Father mother child: for many people three is the luckiest of numbers.

Here we are sitting and singing, driving in a car out of a flat city. Along city streets, past an empty tilting windy space, through the narrow ankles of office buildings. Passing under the shadow of a radio tower, and emerging into sunlight: quiet here, green-gold, late afternoon on a weekend day. The Ordinary Man drives, carefully but fast, intent on reaching a hill with a good sunset (even when it comes to the vagaries of Nature, he feels partially responsible; he believes he must be the Provider).

220

Because he is concentrating on the road he lags behind in the song, mostly mouthing the words or voicing only one in a line like a slow but dutiful studio audience following cue cards.

Gest sits with her feet up on the dashboard. She has taught the Child this song they are singing, a repetitive ditty good for driving, so long it can stretch for miles on end and so mindless it can be started again and again. (How does Gest sing? In a surprisingly small voice, for one who appears so strong and perfect: in a small breathy voice, but a tuneful one.)

The song is the well-known one that details the demise of the Ten Green Bottles. The Child sings lustily, strapped into his small car seat behind the driver's seat. Occasionally he boots the Ordinary Man in the back, such is his enthusiasm for the song.

Ten green bottles, hanging on the wall!

(Mind your feet, says the Ordinary Man patiently.)

And if one green bottle should accidentally fall – at this point the Child raises his voice to an excited roar – *there'd be nine green bottles, hanging on the wall.*

The speedometer clocks up the miles, the bottles fall. The Child counts their falling in a rich deep voice as if appreciating each crucial moment: the lurching and teetering, the fall itself, the intake of breath, and then, oh—! The crashing, the smashing and the shattering! Green glass everywhere, and the Child right there to chronicle the noise and the chaos, breathing from the depths of his small important diaphragm like an opera singer.

Perhaps, Gest murmurs to the Ordinary Man, this is what he will be? Perhaps he will be a star and will sing in the great concert halls of the world?

As long as he remains in *that* area of entertainment, says the Ordinary Man wryly. I certainly hope he will not follow in your particular show-biz footsteps. The Ordinary Man is most appealing at these times, detached, dry but not without sympathy, just as he was when first discovered in front of a windowful of coffins, commenting on the comedy and pathos contained in one set of overly ornate brass handles.

And if one green bottle, cries the Child, *should accidentially—*

Accidentally, corrects Gest.

Accidentially fall. The Child sweeps on with magnificent disregard, retaining his glamour and his authority. He might as well be on stage in an ancient amphitheatre, separated from pedants and the populace by rows of blinding floodlights.

There'd be two green bottles, hanging on the wall.

(Why are the bottles hanging? asks the Candy Girl, as Gest tries to relay to her how sealed, how safe and vibrant this particular afternoon had been. The Candy Girl does not know this song, nor does she understand it, and this bothers her slightly as it is part of her job to understand lyrics. But the green-bottle song will never be added to her repertoire, it would not be capable of holding the interest of a beer-drinking audience for even one second, in spite of the subject matter being bottles.)

And soon after that, says Gest, there were only two of us. Or so it seemed. Just like the bottles, only two left. She speaks vaguely, as if she has not been telling the story to the Candy Girl, as if suddenly the Candy Girl is nothing more than a piece of the furniture. For Gest is no longer where she has just been, in the car with her singing child and her driving husband, heading for a hilltop, racing the sun. She is somewhere between that day and the present, has moved on into a greyer time when the Ordinary Man, having given up on her, was busying himself falling in love with the Patient. Nothing like Gest, this other woman, being far more manageable. Ginger-haired, pale-skinned and not without a frail attraction: but she had never dropped her knickers in front of a camera crew (the thought horrified her! she submitted to leaving the light on while undressing, but for the Ordinary Man's eyes only). Nor did the Patient throw cutlery at the wall, nor had she ever licked cocaine off the fingers of porn directors, nor (though having two boys of her own and being an expert in developmental psychology) did she love any child with such a passion that to witness it was frightening. If truth be told, the Ordinary Man's new woman was a far better match for him because less of a challenge; and only occasionally after the divorce did the Ordinary Man turn into the wrong street and walk for some way without realizing that a secret part of him still longed for a kiss with a hint of bite to it, longed for two long beautiful lioness legs to stride towards him, two hands rough with paint spatters to hold his face, and the sound of his Child – their Child – breathing in the bed between them.

How loudly the Child had breathed! (Gest holds her breath now, remembering the way the soft puffs fell in front of the Child like a safety net before him as he ran.) Wherever he was in the house he had almost always been audible, breathing through his mouth and his nose at the same time; when he came into bed in the morning the traffic could hardly be heard over his huge, roaring nose and mouth.

At first, as Gest has said, there had been three of them (in the car, in the bed) and then there were two. In the diminished days the Child displayed a new kindness, not always present when the Ordinary Man was around. Though he came to Gest's bed before the sun was up, he acknowledged that Gest was tired and would allow her to continue sleeping, for another short while. He counted these minutes on his fingers, reciting the numbers in a loud whisper. *Ten nine eight*: he stretched his left hand up towards the ceiling, fingers spread, palm wide. *Five four three*: this was the right hand now, so both small starfish hands were held aloft, and Gest would open the slit of an eye to see the Child's stern and concentrated face, his arms held high, commanding the room like a miniature conductor.

And he breathed so noisily, remembers Gest out loud, I can't understand why we didn't hear him, that night.

What night, says the Candy Girl softly. She is afraid of asking, she is afraid of breaking Gest's train of thought (she is afraid).

Usually, says Gest, he breathed so loudly we could hear him before he was in the room! But not that night.

Perhaps, she thought later, he had held his breath from the time of opening his bedroom door to the time of opening theirs? And then when he saw what was happening there on the bed, he had simply stopped breathing altogether for a minute or two? Because when Gest reached for him he felt a little cold around the edges, his wrists cool in the creases and his ankles like ice.

Look, he's four! the Ordinary Man reassured her. He'll forget it, he'll get over it! And anyway, he continued, it's time he learnt what goes on between a husband and a wife.

But this was not what had primarily worried Gest. It was more selfish than that (perhaps the Ordinary Man had been right when he accused her of being an unfit mother?). The most disturbing thing for Gest had been that, at the moment she looked up from being fucked by her husband to see her child watching them, her soul had been laid bare. Nothing in her past, nothing at all, had prepared her for such exposure. Not having her pubic hair shaved in front of a roomful of make-up artists, not lying in front of several cameramen caressing another actress's breasts while a bronzed and rippling Latin American had stroked her arse. None of this had made her vulnerable! It had all been a game.

But even now part of Gest relives the moment when, lying face down on the bed with the Ordinary Man's cock inside her, she had turned her head on the pillow and looked straight into the Child's eyes.

Sweat pours down the inside of her arms, running thin as piss, and she drops the blade she is working with. It falls into the shallow plastic tray beside her, cleaning fluid spatters. Shit! she says.

In this way, at that time, she had been laid bare. She had been made modest for the first time in her adult life. Having escaped her domineering grandfather and her cowering grandmother – by sheer determination, by perfect looks, a certain talent and a perceptive talent scout – she had strode away so far and so fast that soon, without realizing it, she had reached the point where nothing could embarrass her.

Strangely, she had been grateful to the Child for this, even as the Ordinary Man was springing off her and grabbing up his dressing gown, even as Gest reached for the sheet with one hand and the chilly confused Child with the other. Stroking his cold bright hair, she should have been thinking about what to say but she let the Ordinary Man babble some nonsense and she remained silent. All she could think at that moment was that in some way she had been redeemed by the Child, he had restored her to a normal human state of modesty—

And so I was grateful to him, she says to the Candy Girl.

I hope you don't mind me asking you something. The Candy Girl is hesitant, she is on her knees mopping up the splattered turpentine and seems to find it easier to ask the question with her face to the fume-ridden floor.

She is worried about Gest and the absent Child, about their apparent lack of communication (no letters, and the phone hardly ever rings). And she is also aware of the way time is hurrying on towards the day when she will start selling starchy white uniforms in a shop instead of coming here each day to be a life model, and this will mean no longer having the opportunity either to ask or offend. She keeps her face down, and she speaks quickly. Where is the Child now? she asks.

The Child? echoes Gest, as if she has not just been talking about him, as if she has not just shared the most intimate of confidences about him with the Candy Girl.

Yes, where has he gone? The Candy Girl sits back on her heels and pushes hair from her eyes with her wrists. The rag drips in her hand, acidic, corrosive.

But in the time she has been looking at the floor-boards, Gest's face has become a mask.

The Child does not live—Gest looks away. The Child is not living in this city any more.

And when he recounts his job she falls

She must go to meet the Reader. In his elegant hand-written message, passed to the Candy Girl to pass to Gest, he has politely requested her presence in the court-yard. No matter if he is a watcher of blue movies in the blue and secret hours, he is nonetheless an elegant and polite person and Gest respects this as she looks around her increasingly squalid apartment.

Would you like me to take some of this trash out? offers the Candy Girl every day as she leaves. Empty tins are piled up behind the kitchen door, juice bottles are left standing where they have been finished. When the Candy Girl walks through the apartment with her sturdy stride, a clanging rattling noise starts up: the sound of debris from the last thirty-seven days.

But Gest says no.

I could take the glass out for recycling, proposes the Candy Girl.

There's no point, says Gest. The bulldozers will make a hundred, a thousand, times more mess than what is here.

I suppose that's a plus, says the Candy Girl. At least when you leave you don't have to clean up after yourself. She is newly adept at looking on the bright side: for the last two nights the Micro has stayed in, giving her back rubs and talking over plans for the shop; perhaps he has simply needed to make sure he is with the right girl before settling in and settling down?

After the door closes behind the Candy Girl, the light is still hard and bright. Gest, walking in bare feet, avoids the sharp triangles of sun falling through the doorways. She paces the hallway three times, up and down, wipes her palms on her overalls and ties a scarf over her hair.

The Reader is already down in the courtyard. Gest can see him from each landing window as she descends the stairs, getting closer. Now she sees the top of his head: his hair is thinning slightly. Now a dark red line is visible woven through the tweed of his jacket, now the end of his stick, planted firmly on his left side, glints silver in the sun. He is waiting: he is waiting for her.

He greets her. You got my note, he says, stating the

227

obvious as if he realizes Gest needs time to adjust: eyes, breath, the whole of her inside self.

Such a day! she says. The sunshine is hurting her eyes.

He gestures to the middle of the courtyard, to the sandy play area with its red iron see-saws and gold iron swings. Shall we sit? he says. You look a little tired.

I would like to rest, agrees Gest. But she remains standing squarely in the sand. And what about you? she says. Are you also tired? Did you stay up late last night? There is a challenge in her voice.

No later than you. He is secretive but honest; sure of himself, reticent. There is a reason for him asking her here.

Sweat trickles down under Gest's scarf, wetting the roots of her hair. I am so hot, she says. She cannot hide the desperation in her voice as she looks up at her kitchen window; her need to be there seeps through the surface of her sentence. It is cooler in my apartment, she says. I live on the shady side.

He nods.

But you know that, she says. You see me there. The denim of her overalls feels rough on her sore leg, burning, hurting. She goes to sit on a swing, feels the chains hot under her hands.

I merely wished to talk to you, he says. Before it is too late. Too late to get to know you. And both of them look up, now, at the windows of the condemned building: at Gest's workplace, living space, home.

I have so little time, says Gest, and again there is desperation in her voice. She tells him what her work is and where it is to be placed, and he raises his left eyebrow, impressed.

I am not surprised that no one has managed to do anything with that space, he says. It is a challenge, it has a presence of its own.

But I will fill it, says Gest, looking stubbornly at the ground. I have fought for the commission, my work will go there or nowhere. I must succeed.

And you probably will, says the Reader, looking at her closely. There is something about you, your face. An expression that I recognize.

Gest pushes back on the swing, bracing her legs hard against the sand. (*There is something about your face. You look familiar.*) Why are you always watching movies? she asks in an angry voice. Why do you watch movies so late at night?

The Reader looks surprised: at the turn in the conversation, at her anger. It is part of my work, he says mildly. He turns his head away to look up at his own window, and his lip curls slightly, following the uneven tilt of his body.

What kind of work? says Gest. She swings back to earth, drags her feet in the grit.

I am an obituary writer, says the Reader calmly. I write out the lives of famous people, so of course I must know what they once did, and what they were capable of doing. Even though he now knows what Gest herself is capable of − a flash of anger, a sullenness following the anger − he shows no sign of wanting to leave her.

The sand is filling Gest's shoes, working its way between her toes. Into her nostrils there rises the hot musky smell of the desert: she sees rows of camels lined up outside Bedouin tents, scabby flanks rising and falling, dry skin layered over water-skin, and set into their flat cheekbones are heavy Virginia Woolf eyelids falling on the long afternoon.

But the Reader, writer of the rich and the dead, moves in front of her and she is back in the urban courtyard, with buildings on either side of her. I am sorry, she says, looking up at his tall leaning body. I am sorry. (She is

229

not only apologising for her anger, but for accusing him of being something he is not.) I thought you watched— she pauses. Movies for pleasure, she finishes lamely.

But I do! says the Reader, and he laughs. It is pleasure! he says. It is most pleasurable staying up all night watching Kubrick or Buñuel, and still getting paid for it.

You are lucky then, says Gest.

Perhaps lucky, he replies. His face is gentle and long, not unlike a desert camel's itself. Or perhaps we are born with an instinct for what it is we must do, he says. In which case we have simply to discover it, and luck is irrelevant.

But a sad job, she says. The sun is swept over by a mass of grey cloud, and her shoulders prickle in the sudden chill. Surely you are made sad by it, she says.

Not at all, he shrugs. Not sad at all. I am a privileged man, in spite of being run down by a tram at the age of twenty. He raises his stick, brings it down with a thud in the sand. Being that close to death at an early age, he adds, is a kind of privilege.

How is that so? says Gest, speaking with some urgency. Please tell me how.

It prepares you earlier than most, he says, for what is to come, and this is a rare and sobering thing.

So it has helped you with your job? asks Gest. With writing of the dead?

In a way, he says slowly. Though what I do is little different from your own work, I think.

The sun bursts out from the cloud, Gest closes her eyes against the brightness and sways. How is your job the same as mine? she asks faintly.

You are an artist, he states. You make something new from what you already know, so you are also creating stories.

You think of your job as storytelling? she says.

Exactly that. The Reader leans back on his stick. And like any kind of storytelling, obituary writing comes with its own rules.

What sort of rules? Charity to the dead is all Gest can think of.

No charity, corrects the Reader, counting this point off on the first finger of his left hand. Definitely no charity. And now he leans back against the climbing frame, hooking his stick over the metal bar. Charity is death to the obituary writer. Although he uses this metaphor deliberately, and deliberately lightly, he does so without a smile. He is the opposite of the Candy Girl, his jokes lie still beneath the surface of his words, hardly stirring, barely given space to breathe. Charity is an untruth, he says. It blurs a story and makes it dull.

What then? Gest sits back on the red swing. The metal seat bites through the thin denim of her overalls, sears her thighs. What do you aim for? she says, as the metal scorches secret red marks into her legs.

Tact, says the Reader with a long hard look at her. Tact is a first cousin to charity, but it can still approximate truth. Tact, or code words, he amends. These are the first skills to acquire.

Code words? asks Gest.

Because people are not always trustworthy, explains the Reader, nor are they constant. Stars and performers are necessarily expert at changing their image.

That is true, agrees Gest. They are trained at doing this.

And so I might choose to use the phrase *a colourful embellisher of anecdotes*, says the Reader.

By which you would mean a good liar? guesses Gest.

Correct, says the Reader, with an approving look. His lip curls again, in a kind of smile, but his teeth are barely visible. Now Gest wants to place her fingers into that sardonic gentle mouth, run them around the Reader's teeth, bring them away covered in his gentle, genteel, and most tactful saliva.

Go on, she says. The metal is hot under her legs; she has not looked up to her window for many minutes.

If I said someone was a tireless campaigner for any cause? he asks.

You would mean a do-gooder, she says.

And if I wrote a shrewd businesswoman?

I would say a shrew.

And if I told of the sudden death of a brilliant young writer, the Reader picks up his stick and locks it onto his arm. A brilliant young playwright struck down in the middle of writing his brilliant play?

You would mean that he has killed himself. Gest bites her lip.

The shadows of the hospital towers fall against the Reader's face, lie in twin lines, one on each cheek. You are a quick pupil, he says. Were I able to stay longer, and should you not have a pressing task in hand—He pauses. I assume it is pressing, he says, politely. For I see by the light reflected on my wall that you stay up all hours, meaning that you are either an indefatigable worker or an incorrigible insomniac.

There is no indication in his well-modulated voice, hidden behind its double shadows, that he has seen Gest naked: leaning on her window sill with her breasts against the cool window, nipples hardened against the glass, cunt on a level with the window sill, lick of moisture from a dream still between her legs.

The light, Gest repeats, and she looks at the ground. You are right on both counts, I am both a horrid insomniac and a hateful worker.

You are neither horrid nor hateful. The Reader is grinding his stick into the sand, close to her feet. Besides, he says gently, I do not sleep much myself.

232

It grows between them, that untouched subject, like a mountain of sand, and the wind gets up and blows cool in Gest's face; she could fly from the swing, sand mountain flying in her face, lift into the blue sky. But instead she gets up quietly and stands looking down at the small perfectly round holes the Reader has made at their feet. His shoes are perfectly polished, his trousers fall in neat creases, seams running straight down to the middle of his shoes.

When she looks up at him again he is no longer someone who has given her a quick verbal quiz in the middle of a deserted playground. He is not a desert camel, does not have the power to quench her thirst or carry her long distances on the back of his superior age and knowledge. He is made up of lines and dissected curves, and because of this, because she sees him this way, she knows with a dull certainty: she must leave him, although wanting to stay.

I must go, she says expressionlessly.

And so must I, he says. You'd be surprised, the world is always in a frightful hurry to bury its dead.

I will read what you write, says Gest, from now on. But this is a lie: she will no longer allow the Candy Girl to leave newspapers behind in the apartment, she does not want to know any more what goes on outside, nor does she have the time to learn.

Were you of a different generation, the Reader gives a slight bow, perhaps one day I would write about you. I have no doubt you will become renowned, if only for being the one person in the world to succeed in filling the Space Between.

And then it is over. Gest is thanking the Reader and turning away, and taking her stairs two at a time, though her legs are weakened by long days inside and there is no will in her to return to her apartment, no wish to

233

return to the stale air and the silence. No, there is no reasonable reason to leave this tall linear gentleman of a cripple when instead she would like to cross the sandy courtyard with him, go up the wrong staircase and enter a new room. Enter a room where the air smells of furniture and whisky, lie in a new bed and hear the Reader's stick fall to the floor, crash against the bedpost, and feel the Reader's weight on top of her and his mouth open against her neck, teeth in her skin, tongue in her ear, spit mixing with that of her own sandy mouth.

She closes her door and leans weakly against it. This is all. This is all that she has wanted, on the thirty-seventh day. Is this too much to ask for?

Then there was one

Because of love, Gest had claimed him. She had claimed him, and loved him above all things. Why, then, had the Child deserted her?

There was a simple enough reason: because he was human, that is why. He might have looked like a small golden demi-god, a lion-child vivid of face and bold of heart, who had sprung from the unlikely union of an impeccable suit-wearing psychologist and a beautiful woman with a chequered career path and immigrant blood. But the Child *was* just this: a child, and human, and so he was not as invincible as he looked.

There had been airports, and hotel rooms, and many noisy and prestigious openings. Gest had circulated through these days, talking, laughing, and all the while keeping an eye on the Child standing buttoned into his good clothes, being good. These things (she told herself, time and again) were a privilege. These were good things, extraordinary things that the Child would never have been able to experience had he gone to live with the Ordinary Man, had he been neatly hemmed-up in a neat suburban house with the Ordinary Man and the Ordinary Man's new tidy ginger-haired woman.

And where was it, first, that the world had turned on its head? In the middle of that year, in a hot sultry city, a newly built skyscraper city that floated on a shining glass island. It was there, without warning, that the world had spun upside down, and it had never fully righted itself again.

Here is Gest: newly returned from a gallery and gilded with praise but glad – so glad, so grateful! – to be back with the Child. There is the Child: lying in the huge white pool of a hotel bed, saying goodbye in a dutiful voice to the hotel babysitter who is ushered out the door.

A single image has remained in Gest's head from that hour. One shoe: the thin pink strap of one of her shoes, fastened with a small golden buckle. For when the Child had started to speak she had been unbuckling her thin pink shoe; it is only natural that this image is burned into her memory.

Why—? This is how the Child starts his sentence. He is tossing and turning on the bed, and just as he speaks he rolls onto the remote control so the foreign soap opera he has been watching roars like a tidal wave up and over his voice. Now an unintelligible language is covering a most important utterance.

What, darling? Gest must shout too, to be heard above the noise, and the gold buckle of her shoe drives into her palm. What did you say? (She shouts over the soap opera, while sitting on the floor to pull off her pink gallery-opening shoe.)

The Child seizes up the remote control and, by pressing random buttons, manages to quieten the voices of the screaming housewife, the philandering husband and his shrieking mistress. When he speaks it is into a cold air-conditioned silence.

Why, he says in a small chilly voice. Why are all these bad things happening to me?

Cold shivers run up Gest's back. The hair on her shoulders stands on end like the hair of a cat. She drops her shoe to the floor.

What bad things? she says, in alarm. Did something happen with the babysitter? Did something happen while I was gone?

No, nothing happened with the babysitter. The Child's voice is tiny and creaky amidst the huge pillows. The babysitter was nice.

So what is wrong? Now Gest pulls off her other shoe and is trying to get to the bed, but every step is too slow, like walking through a nightmare swamp. She will never. She will never get there in time. What happened today? she says. She feels as if she is about to cry.

Not today, says the Child. Every day. Every day is a bad day for me. (It is the Child who is crying now, quietly but in a disturbed, a disturbing way.) I am so tired, he is crying, I am so lonely and so tired, and I never know where I will sleep at night. I miss my bed, I miss my train set, I see my father only once a week, I never see my friends. Please let me have my father and my friends, let me have my train, my bed, let me have them every day, oh please.

Gest's pink shoes have been discarded far behind her. She is wading, wading, through grief and guilt, and finally she reaches the bed. The Child, her child, is lying right there in front of her. But when she reaches out he is already disappearing. He is shrinking into the sheets, his flesh fades away under her fingers, and at that moment she knows: she must give him back.

It is as simple as that. Once there were two, then there was one. She must not pity herself. This is the way that many stories go.

The Micro returns

The Micro has returned to the fold. He has decided to give up what or whoever has been preoccupying him for the past couple of weeks, he has come back seeming slightly chastened, and has at last proposed marriage to his Candy Girl. And not before time: Gest has noticed that during this watching, waiting time the Candy Girl's cheeks have become slightly sucked in as if she has been holding her breath for a long time under water, and her skin has been reddening easily, especially around her eyes. As for her eyes themselves, there has been a watery sheen about them whenever Gest has asked her to turn towards the window, which is no trick of the light.

But this morning everything is quite different. The Candy Girl arrives in an ensemble of varying pinks: vivid fuchsia tights, light lolly-pink skirt, and a candy-cane top whose stripes turn to waves as they run over the Candy Girl's large breasts. But nothing, nothing can out-pink the Candy Girl's cheeks (once more perfectly round) and her lips shine as she tells Gest the news.

By next summer I will not only be a shop owner, I will be a wife!

I am delighted! says Gest. She hugs the Candy Girl a little awkwardly and they stand for a minute in the dim hallway leaning into each other, feet further apart than their shoulders in a pyramid embrace.

Well, I am delighted too! says the Candy Girl.

Who can say how many hours she has lain waiting, wedged into the small cracked bath with its dripping hose attachment and its taps smeared around with years of calcium that cannot be budged by energetic scrubbing? Who can say — for no one has witnessed this — if she has cried, lying there as the water cools and becomes tepid, her ears straining to hear boots on the stairs, hearing steps, heart leaping, face lifting — and then, then, the steps going on past the door and up to the next landing? At that moment, perhaps, noticing that her fingers and the soles of her feet have become wrinkled and prune-like, the Candy Girl would have wiped her cheeks so that salt water and bathwater became one, and then heaved herself out of the bath, and dried herself carefully (between her legs, under her breasts, between her prune-like toes) and gone to bed alone, her face turned resolutely away from the clock.

The number of hours, the degree of strain, the clenching of stomach and fists under the hot sheets: such things are not for us to see. And at any rate these factors are now irrelevant, for the Micro has decided to throw in his lot with a good woman, one realistic enough to forgive past transgressions but idealistic enough to dream of outfitting the world. While dreaming of wedding gowns, she will provide chefs with chequered pants, singers with sequins, tradesmen with pocketed leather aprons, and artists with—

But why is the material cloudy? asks the Candy Girl, staring at Gest's work.

She has watched as her arms and legs have been sculpted in clay, has seen them made larger than life, and still more rounded than they are in reality.

(I wish I had thinner legs! She had looked at her thighs critically, at the way they squished together at the top instead of curving away from each other as Gest's did.

You have perfect legs, reassured Gest. Just what I need.

Perhaps the Micro would like me more if—? This was the Candy Girl on a bad and a lonely day, craning round to view the orange-skin dimples on the backs of her legs.

You are sexy, reassured Gest. And I am making your limbs look different from how they really are: larger, less womanly.)

This last reassurance, at least, had been true, for after the Candy Girl had seen her clay arms and legs turned into several different kinds of casts, they were no longer her limbs. They were several sizes bigger, chubbier, chunkier, perhaps even masculine. As they were taken away, limb by separate limb, into the large empty room next door, the Candy Girl had cleared her throat with relief and done a quick belly dance in the middle of the workroom. While Gest was busy dealing with tricky substances such as plastic compounds, the Candy Girl darted quick looks into the broken shards of mirror leaning up against the workroom wall: she was still an entertainer, still a sexy girly entertainer! And she sang a few bars under her breath, something about keys and hearts and first love, to put her world to rights again.

Now, when Gest brings out various limbs and holds them up to the glaring window so the sun shines through them, they are not clear. The light picks up silver-grey specks in them, flecks floating in the transparent plastic.

Did something go wrong? asks the Candy Girl, slightly diffidently. What are those specks? She knows a reasonable

239

amount about quite a lot of things: how to whip up a batch of soda bread on days when the bakeries are closed, how to put one small stitch in the bottom of a fraying zip so it will not suddenly split open in a public place and embarrass the wearer. How to give head to a horny man when she is so tired that her eyes are falling closed and her mind teeters on the edge of unreality. How to comfort a dark beauty from a sunny country who is losing business hand over fist, and losing weight and looks and hope. She knows all these things and plenty more besides, but she has to admit she knows nothing at all about the art of sculpting in synthetic compounds.

To her, though, the grit swirling in the otherwise clear limbs and torso looks like a flaw. She knows that Gest has only eleven days after this one to finish her task, and she senses the urgency that, most days, sucks and roars around the apartment; her anxiety over these things outweighs her diffidence so she speaks more loudly than she means to through the quiet morning room. What are those specks? she says, again.

They are supposed to be there, replies Gest, in an almost absent-minded voice. She puts one flecked arm down on the window sill and turns to the Candy Girl. Do you know anything at all about that man who lives across the courtyard? she asks. The one who gave you the note?

The Candy Girl's relief is huge. The art is all right, and at this moment this is all she cares about. Most people she knows underestimate the kind of work Gest does – people like the Micro and the men working with him who belch and crack jokes and eat sausage for lunch on the construction sites where they work. She is determined not to do the same, and she walks over to the window sill and hovers over the arm, marvelling at the slightly curved fingers that used to be hers but are no longer recognizable as such.

May I touch? She runs one finger quickly and lightly over the wrist – her wrist – which now has a far deeper crease in it, marking the chunky hand off from the rounded arm. She is standing so close to Gest that she can hear Gest's hoarse breathing. There is a break in each upward breath, as if the lungs are covered with a thick shell of dust that must be split open every time Gest breathes in.

It is beautiful, assures the Candy Girl. But Gest is looking at the floor as if in a trance. Splinters of a transparent substance lie in the light hairs on her top lip. Very gently, the Candy Girl reaches out and runs her finger over the left side of Gest's lip so the splinters are dislodged and float away in the soft air. The Candy Girl's finger pauses for a second in the small cleft that runs from Gest's nose to her mouth. Then it moves on to the right side of the lip, and clears that of plastic debris too. The sun is falling on Gest's shoulders, bare except for the straps of her grey overalls. It falls on the Candy Girl's stripy hair that today lies against her neck. It brings them together in a halo. They are safe.

You are so—the Candy Girl breathes in, more smoothly than Gest who is still standing close to her. You are so—! But she cannot finish her sentence.

It seems as if Gest hardly feels the Candy Girl's touch and only vaguely recognizes her voice. I am what? she says, as if in a dream. The Candy Girl puts her hand under Gest's chin and turns her face towards her. Against her wrist she feels the rasp of breath in Gest's throat.

(You are attracted to her! The Micro smirks in amazement and pleasure. You are in love with the Porn Queen!

It is not that! says the Candy Girl decisively. It is not that at *all*! She pushes the Micro away, with his fantasies of his fiancée and a beautiful long-legged ex-princess of porn.

What is it then? The Micro is mocking, standing at arm's length, looking at the indignant rising of her breasts. What is it, if not that you secretly want to kiss her?

She is so different day by day, the Candy Girl tries to explain. She is changing, and I feel there is something I should be doing.

But of course there is! And the Micro comes back towards her, slips his hand up under her tight striped top and inside her bra. Perhaps you should do this to her, he says softly. He takes hold of the Candy Girl's left nipple and makes it grow hard between his finger and thumb. And then, you should do this! He runs his hand between the Candy Girl's legs and she moves into him and twines her legs around his, in spite of her irritation with him, and her distraction, and her concern over something she does not understand.

This is not what she wants! She sounds stern but she kisses the Micro and bites his bottom lip so that he groans and laughs, because this is what they have both wanted for many minutes now and Gest is not there, right at that moment.)

But an odd thing. As the sun plunges behind a cloud, Gest raises her eyes to the window and gives a sharp cry.

What is it? The Candy Girl starts and her hand falls away from Gest's neck. What did you see?

Gest backs away, but not from the Candy Girl, from the window. She leans weakly against the wall and her eyes are completely black. I thought I saw someone out there, she says.

On the balcony? The Candy Girl steps to the glass and moves the flecked arm off the sill so she can peer out. But the balcony is empty, its tiled floor covered only with dust. The air is hot and vacant.

There is no one there, she says stoutly, holding onto the flecked but flawless arm like a weapon. See?

Not on the balcony, Gest closes her eyes. Falling past the window, she says.

The missing

There had been a day, back in those abattoir apartment times, when the phone had rung many times and Gest had been unable to answer it. She could not find the receiver, that was the problem, and as the phantom phone rang on and on she hunted high and low, under teetering stacks of newspapers that slid from the table to the floor, between pots of paint and bottles of glue and jars of cracked dried paintbrushes that she had not taken care of.

Shit! she had shouted at the top of her voice to the empty house, as the phone rang incessantly several times an hour. The reason that she could not find the phone? It was due to the Ordinary Man's extraordinary efficiency. Early that morning, while marching between bedroom and bathroom with a mouthful of striped fluoride foam, he had dealt with a call about a change of clinic times and sometime after that, between spitting and rinsing, he had stowed the receiver efficiently away in his pocket and taken it to work with him.

I can't understand, Gest said, how this can happen.

Allow me some mistakes! The Ordinary Man was exasperated, tired: in one day he had had several patients who, in professional jargon, were termed Jumpers. Though wanting to care more for them – their bitten fingernails, their wild eyes searching for free-falling vertical space instead of imprisoning high walls – to his horror he had found himself wishing for a bridge or a parapet (this was how tired he was, and how disappointed in his own limitations). After this, he had come home to a wife who had spent all day without her main contact to the outside world, because of him.

Give me a break, he had said tersely. It could happen to anyone. Anyone, he added, who *works*. With this jibe he strode over to the old glass-fronted bookshelf that doubled as a drinks cabinet and stared morosely in at the display of bottles as if it were a shop window in which he could lose himself.

He had, however, misinterpreted Gest. She had not meant this, she had simply meant she could not understand the event itself: how something could be heard when it was, in effect, not there. She thought confusedly of how two working halves, once separated, did not work at all: she imagined the black handset, which she thought of as being alive, lying like a dead thing in the Ordinary Man's jacket pocket out of signal range.

It doesn't make sense, she said, ignoring the Ordinary Man's slight meanness. I need that phone engineer to explain how it works, that engineer with the odd name that we met at the party.

You don't need him, said the Ordinary Man, moodily, you *want* him. In the reflective glass door he saw his wife's beautiful puzzled face framed between a half-empty bottle of whisky and a half-empty bottle of gin. You want him, he said (goaded on by insecurity and love) because you're obsessed with trade, and you always have been.

Engineering is not a *trade*! said Gest. But this argument was a ruse because it was true, she was interested

244

in all those who worked with the mysteries of the everyday world: the phone, the television, the water and the gas. Sometimes it seemed as if these people kept the world turning for people like her, once an entertainer and now in a career that some considered even less important, and people like the Ordinary Man whose ability to help others was virtually invisible, being tucked somewhere in the folds of his highly specialized brain.

The gas man, the plumber: undeniably, these people held a fascination for her. I have an interest, said Gest with dignity, in what normal people do for a job.

For once the Ordinary Man did not challenge her on her use, or misuse, of the word normal. You have fantasies about them, was all he said, and he had thrown the phone down on the sofa and poured himself a miserly portion of whisky.

The gas man came today, in fact, said Gest, also making for the bottle. He told me of an explosion, a huge and terrible explosion.

Yes? The Ordinary Man had just remembered this was his real life, and his beautiful wife, and decided to be sensible. What happened?

He had gone to check a leak, said Gest, throwing herself down on the sofa beside the now redundant phone. (She has a story to tell and someone to listen to it, and if another person called right now she would not answer.) He was called to check a leak and he went round straight away but he was too late, because the person living there had turned the light on in the kitchen and BOOM!

Boom? The Ordinary Man grimaced. The room exploded?

The fluorescent light. Gest put her face in her hands. To turn on a fluorescent light is the worst thing to do, or so the gas man says. A room full of gas, a moment of ignition, and then – boom. No kitchen left, no person, nothing.

Poor person, said the Ordinary Man, warmed by the whisky. He could see Gest's nipples through her thin white shirt, he reached out.

The building still stood, said Gest. There was just a gaping hole in its side. But the whole room was gone.

Like the phone, said the Ordinary Man, gone like the phone. He put his mouth over Gest's and talked into her dark throat. The receiver is gone but the phone still rings, he said hollowly. And then they had gone to bed, to their bed with the one sheet and no pillows, leaving behind them images of walls with holes ripped through them and faint blue shimmers in the shocked air.

Had the Child been conceived that night? Quite possibly. But before his birth they had moved to a new place, an apartment on the top floor of a building instead of on the ground floor, all mired around with gutters and mud. There was no outside space in which the Child could play except for a sandy courtyard many floors down, but at least his sleep would not be broken by the sound of stun guns and the cries of animals. His favourite game, anyway, was hide and seek, which could be played perfectly well inside.

Don't look! he would order, and before Gest could close her eyes he would be pointing to the table. I'll just hide there, he would say conspiratorially. Count to twenty and don't peep, and when I say so you can come and look for me there.

There was no point in telling him not to give away his hiding place before the game had started. This was the way he had decided it should be played, with the outcome determined before the game commenced. In this way every game was kept to a minimum of time and fuss. And at times, to further help a witless adult,

246

the Child would deliberately leave a part of his body in full view.

You are not hiding properly! the Ordinary Man would point out, lifting up the tablecloth or dismantling a cushion mountain.

You are not looking properly! the Child would thunder. You must be a seeker! You must be *surprised*! Pulling the cushions back around himself, he would send the Ordinary Man back to the counting corner, once more placing his arm carefully out on the carpet: a small palm, a creased wrist, a rounded forearm. The muffled order would come again: *start looking now*!

At four he had already become as stern as any member of the Red Guard, adopting early the authority of an older generation. So perhaps it was no coincidence that he had latched on to tales of the Cultural Revolution, told to him by Gest's half-crazed grizzled grandfather from his high hospital bed? It is *your* family that has infected him with these notions! the Ordinary Man hissed, while Gest defended herself. The Child has a right to know, she said. He must learn about the difficult balance of power.

(Where is the Child now? wonders the Candy Girl aloud. It seems as if he is hiding still.

The Micro grunts in a sleepy way, pulls her towards him and half snores in her ear. From what I understand he is in another country, muses the Candy Girl, lying close against the Micro's big chest. In another country, perhaps with his father, she says. But he is missed, oh, how he is missed.)

247

The swing and the river

This is an odd occurrence. A boy, aged thirteen. Thirteen years of age, so already in possession of a man's throat, his white face marked out by the downy shape of a beard – this boy falls from a rope swing.

Why a rope swing, and what does he see when he looks down? His dangling feet encased in heavy boots – this is what he sees. The thin bow of his legs trailing up to disappear into his own body; the muddy brown snail-water moving slow and circular as it follows the motion of his rope swing; faces around the edges of his vision, far below and a great distance away, raising vague memories of desks left behind in the city, and the bored snapping of pencils, the flicking of pens, the slapping shut of books with margins full of drawings, of sixteen-year-old breasts glimpsed through white school shirts, and imagined cunts and arses. He's on a school camp, this boy, this faller. This is why the rope swing.

At first he doesn't want to go up to the platform. He has a hard-on: has had no chance to masturbate that morning, has been pulled from his bed too early by a shout from the corridor, and the threat of toast gone cold, and then a one-minute shower behind a curtain that gripped his ankles like sweaty hands. Now his cock strains embarrassingly against his grey cotton shorts; he hangs back behind Addison, he hangs back. And the platform is too high against the humid grey sky, he has no desire to climb all the way up there, grip the rope between his bare legs and feel the jolt in his shoulders and the pull of gravity and the alternative pull of momentum so that he reaches back for the platform with his cracking burning legs. He has no desire. Only a desire for dark, for thoughts of Annie, her soft probing tongue and her breath in his left ear. Only for these dreams and the release that leaves him sighing, after each time older than he was before, happier for a moment before the striving to go on, get on with life, takes over once more.

It goes down, his cock, in time. It subsides and suddenly he is back in life, wants to get up there.

Hurry up, he says to Addison, and his relief is so great that he says it quite roughly: Hurry UP! He pushes Addison aside. Hey! protests Addison. Fucking bastard! But the Bastard cares not a bit for Addison, with his absurd fucking high voice and his repeated attempts to buy friendship by bringing out small wraps of drugs in the long back seats of buses. He cares not for Addison, cared not when Addison was held down in the gym and had a pool cue stuffed up his arse and bled through his shorts (made of the same grey cotton as the Bastard is wearing today), bled onto the hard wooden bench during assembly and had to leave, bent over, red-eyed. One look at Addison at that moment and weakness would have set in; it was the only thing to despise Addison, both then and now, so – Get out of my fucking way, says the Bastard, and he pushes Addison aside so that he half falls against the rough bark of the tree.

Once on the ladder it is easy; he eyes the platform from underneath, blinding slats of sky through the wood. Then he is pushing his head up through the square hole, hauling himself through it, and suddenly he is fifty feet up, head held high, others watching him as if he is ready for a hanging.

Ready for the jump? Ready.

He wraps his thighs firmly round the rope. This is the feeling of dreams: trying to pick up a very small key with huge mitten-hands, waking sweating and frustrated.

Sweaty now because of the climb and the intense humidity, and the green leaves also sweating, hanging close to his face, brushing his ear, right and left – *Annie*!

Now his legs are around the rope and his hands reach high above his head, twist in the loops provided for them, once, twice. He's secure. Thirteen years old, horny, arrogant, yet good at heart, and secure. It's a perfect moment. Only one thing can follow perfection. He pushes off without looking down.

On what day is this taking place? On the forty-first day: and the boy pushes off at the exact moment that the Candy Girl, with the shadow of two towers falling on her back, is pushing on the buzzer of Gest's apartment block. But something has happened, it seems, for she stands for minutes on end (as the boy swings wide out over the grey-green water) and still the front door does not swing open. Perhaps the mechanism linking the door to the apartment upstairs is broken? Perhaps someone has swung on the lever inside, snapping the long connecting cable that runs through the ceilings and inside the staircase walls?

Far away the boy swings on, and the Candy Girl waits on the street. Is Gest also waiting, is she pushing the button in her hallway, sensing that someone is down on the street? Something is not working, something is dead. The lever has been pulled off, the connection has snapped; or Gest is not hearing.

The Candy Girl resorts to shouting. She stands back and looks up, craning her head to see Gest's windows. Higher than these, two floors up, are visible the burnt blackened remains of what used to be a balcony and is now a few charred bars of steel. The Candy Girl shouts loudly, several people look at her curiously, and the florist from next door comes out, sees that it's her and says *good morning* before escaping back into his damp green cave where his soft webbed feet and white hands are more comfortable than in the dry gritty street.

The Candy Girl shouts and shouts. (Many miles away, beside a river, there are also shouting voices, screaming. There has been a sudden fall, a shallow splash followed by what could be the cracking of rock or bone, and above the river a terrible, terrifying fifty feet of absence.)

The Candy Girl shouts, the street waits. (And Addison – even he, with good reason not to – cries. These things are happening simultaneously, although far apart, perhaps even a state or a national border between them.)

And so the world pulls us this way and that, while somehow we remain connected. A man sleeping half a world away stirs in his hot bed, throws his hand against the mosquito net, for he thinks he hears the ringing of a doorbell. And in other seething cities six violent crimes are happening in this very minute, fifty-two cars are being stolen, and eleven houses robbed, glass is falling like a lethal waterfall, kittens are being drowned in troughs, and a boy falls from a great height because of the age of a greying piece of rope. A sturdy girl with panic in her head shouts loudly enough to raise the dead, while her boyfriend is standing high on scaffolding with his back to a vacant wind-swept square: the very square, in fact, where the naked but unrecognizable sculptural form of his girlfriend is to be placed.

Someone is coming through the back courtyard, is in the foyer of the front building, is gesturing to the Candy Girl through the windows. (At this moment Addison wipes his eyes, snot streaming from his nose.) I'm coming! It is a man who carries a briefcase and walks with a stick, iron-grey streaks in his hair, eyes that are kind and tired. He opens the door and lets the shouting Candy Girl in. (The teacher drags something from the river, Addison looks away.)

Thank you! says the Candy Girl. I have work to do upstairs.

You are welcome. And the polite limping man changes his stick to the other hand and holds the door open until the Candy Girl is through, with her rustling bag of groceries and the coloured brochures she has picked up on the way in the hope that she and the Micro might find a cheap honeymoon.

And now the Candy Girl is climbing up seventy-two stairs to the sixth floor (there is blood on the stones, there is mud on the face of the unconscious boy). Now she is nearly in the apartment, and she will enter slightly breathlessly with the news that the buzzer had broken. After that she will be given a key for the next morning and the following mornings, and there will be hot tea in the kitchen before work begins.

The end is nigh

Very early on the forty-second day, the Candy Girl suddenly sat up in bed and said, There is something about the woman whom I work for (and for some reason at this time the Candy Girl did not say her name), there's something about that woman that makes me feel the End is Nigh.

The End is Nigh, she had repeated, and then she had laughed and sighed and fallen back on her pillow, heading straight back into the hazy dream-world from which she had come.

The Micro has been roused from sleep by the Candy

Girl's voice. What did you say? He props himself up on one elbow to find that the sky is still blue-black, though there is the faintest light in the east, and the birds are still silent. What are you talking about? he says.

But the Candy Girl has gone again, back into the place from where she came, and in the morning she hardly remembers this small exchange. The Micro, though: something about the biblical ring of the Candy Girl's phrase has impressed itself on his memory, and he continues to think about it as he showers, emerging from the bathroom with his hair plastered to his head in small wet curls like the pelt of a newborn lamb.

This is the thing about sleeping nightly with another person, it is entirely possible they will catch snatches of your thoughts that would otherwise fall away from you, rolling under the bed to mingle with the dust balls and the light webbed balls of hair, to be swept up later and thrown away. And that other person will carry those loose scrappy thoughts into the next day, or the day after, so when you are in a grocery store absorbed in a daydream of owning a most successful shop, a shop with shining floorboards and clean windows and neat displays of shoes and clothes – well, as you are dreamily pushing your trolley past a pyramid of paper towels, then you will hear:

BE CAREFUL!

and you will say in real alarm, Why?

and the other person will say, THE END IS NIGH!

and then you will both start to laugh, because some-where in your half-memory you will recognize these words as your own, and you will laugh your way through the bright trash-filled aisles to queue up at the checkout, and every now and then you or the other person will whisper, The End is Nigh, and you will burst with laughter again although a part of you, a very small central part, will be clenched like a fist at the betrayal of yourself –

the bringing out of your secret night self into a public place, several days afterwards – and also at the thought of that quiet woman in her high apartment who for some reason you could not give a name to when you woke in the night, and whose face, although you know it is beautiful, recedes from you now.

At least, that is how it was for the Candy Girl, on the forty-second day.

Try to think of disposal as a game

There was a shop that Gest used to go to, to get her films developed: snapshots of the Child, of beaches and swings and birthday parties: all the trappings of a normal and ordinary life. The shop was a pharmacy which had its own photo service, and the counter where you dropped off your films was a do-it-yourself counter, where you never talked to a shop person but instead chose the colour of your envelope (red, yellow, or blue), dropped your roll of film inside, stuck up the sticky gum lips of the envelope, and dropped it in a slot. The ironic thing was that, although you could enter the shop with your small metallic roll of film in your pocket and exit again unseen, minus the film, without having conversed with a single other person, there was no privacy about the process at all. No privacy, in spite of the fact that you had left your film in the close paper dark of a locked counter, and the reason was this.

Once your film had been retrieved from the bin under the photo counter along with hundreds of others, once it had been developed, fairly badly, and put back onto colour-coded shelves ready for collection, it was effectively on display to the world. Any person could walk into the shop, pick up your photos and leaf through them, thereby gatecrashing your holiday, cracking the code of the door to your rented villa, climbing the glossy technicolour stairs and entering the bedroom where the Child lay sleeping in the arms of the Ordinary Man (or perhaps neither was sleeping, for both had slightly self-conscious smirks on their closed supposedly sleeping mouths, as if knowing they were being observed.) And certainly now they were being observed, but this time by an impostor, someone else who was looking at their images, someone who had never actually seen the Child walking on his long scrunched up feet, had never seen the Ordinary Man arguing with the Child through a mouthful of fluoride foam about who had left the toilet seat up (both knew this was something that Gest hated). That impostor, that stealer of other people's photos, was now able to look at the grained black and white arm of the Ordinary Man flung over and around the neck of the dozing Child like a loving noose (a hangable offence, this, to go to the bathroom and dribble piss over the rim of the toilet bowl and not even to try to hide it by putting the seat down).

How did Gest know such theft was possible? Because one day, a long time ago, she had done exactly this. She had gone into the shop to pick up her film and had then found she had forgotten to bring the yellow, or red, or blue slip of paper that would prove the envelope of photos was hers.

I'm afraid I don't have my photo slip, she had said, and the cashier girl, who had been polishing her counter with small bored strokes, licking the ends of her nails to lubricate them against possible snicks in the hope that they would stay perfect for when she went to a club that night, had said, No problem. That's fine, she said without looking up, and she held out her hand for Gest's money.

It was not fine, of course: it was not fine at all. Gest almost complained before she realized that she would then have to go all the way home again, pass through the shadow-gates of the hospital lying flat on the sunny pavement and out the other side, and up many flights of stairs to her door, and ransack bags and drawers to find the slip. So –

Thank you, she said quickly, and she seized up her photos and left.

But after this she was wary, chary of going to that store. And one week later, one thinking thoughtful week later, she returned there.

The polishing girl is there again, but this time she is talking on the phone to her boyfriend. She is giggling, playing with the key to the cash register, fondling it as if it is the boyfriend's belt buckle and all she has to do is reach inside and ping! instant riches and happiness in the palm of her hand.

Gest laughs, in an amazed way, at the worldly naive girl and at her own cunning bird-eyed thieving self. She is here to test the system: sharp eyes, sharp beak, an increasingly sharp sense of the wrong way in which the world is run. She gives one small incredulous laugh, standing there behind the condom stand, staring unseeingly at Billy Boys, Ribbed, Flavoured and Super-Sensitive. (She knows she will succeed, knows that her test will work, but this knowledge does not make her happy.)

It is time. She strides to the nest of photos, to the collection shelf stuffed with coloured envelopes, and rifles through them confidently as if it is her right. As she

256

pushes some to the side, a few fall to the floor and split open, half divulging their innards. (Careful, Gest: thieve, plunder, but do not draw attention to your plundering. Do not disturb the twittering at the cashier counter.)

This one. She has it. A fat packet rightly belonging, not to Gest at all, but to someone with a completely different last name. Now Gest has it in her eye, now in her cuckoo hand: not hers, hers.

It works. The cashier has far more interesting things on her mind than unimportant forgotten slips of paper; she takes the money, still talking and laughing down the phone. Gest feels almost ill with triumph as she half runs towards home. An ambulance shrieks from the gateway beside her door. Gest hardly notices. The many flights of stairs disappear under her piston feet. One landing, two, three, four, and on and on until suddenly she has gone too far, is at the closed attic door and must turn and run back down one flight to find her own home.

The living room is too sunny, blindingly so. The play-room, too innocent. The kitchen smells sweetly of coffee and cinnamon, and must not be contaminated. She goes to the bathroom, slides into the empty hollow of the bath and braces her feet against the taps, legs wide as if for another birth, as if she will give birth to a second Child right there in the stained porcelain gloom.

Slit, slit. Right and left, she severs the packet with her long thin thumbnail. Her left hand is the conspirator, her right hand the propagator, pulling out photo after photo that should never be held let alone seen by her. Soon she is lying back satiated in guilt, lies in a sea of it, places her hot cheek down on a shiny slippery surface. Shots of a tanned man with a towel around his waist, of a woman drinking from a water bottle, a smiling boy holding a baseball bat, a baby holding a yellow rubber duck.

Nothing so special! Her hands dash the photographs about in the bath. Not even high gloss! This way and that she dashes them, creating dull matt waves around her knees. But soon the waves subside and her hands stop, losing the sureness that was only ever born of guilt. *You lie*, they say to her, sotto voce. *You lie. This is another person's past; it is everything special.*

She must hurry, for the Child is due home from his friend's house, will soon be delivered into an atmosphere not fit for a child, let alone the Child, to breathe. The photos are covered with fingerprints; she breathes on them, rubs them with a cloth, hopes for the best, and runs. She arrives at the door of the pharmacy just as the grill is being pulled down by a white-clad woman: a different woman, this, not the pretty girl cashier but an older one with more serious things on her mind than undoing a boyfriend's fly and taking a penis into her hands or mouth.

What is it? She gives Gest a cursory glance.

These photos, pants Gest. They are not mine.

She could get down on her knees on the gum-stained piss-stained pavement, beg for deliverance, but the Child is due home in three and a half minutes.

These—she says, panting.

And the woman snatches them away from Gest, looking at her unseeingly with her timetable eyes. Come tomorrow for a refund, she says. And from this Gest knows. How easy it is to fall into the wrong hands! How easily we can be traded, cut up or trampled on, shat upon, have our faces put on the Internet or our bodies rubbed clean by the spit of someone we have never known. (Later, from this experience, Gest knows how careful she must be.)

Move on now. Move to the present, to a day when Gest is living alone and can no longer expect the Child's footsteps at the door. By now there is no time for photographs, not for taking them or looking at them: no time to sit down with an album and become so absorbed that the scream of the kettle on the stove takes minutes to register. The very act of dipping back into the past is a time waster, and Gest no longer has this luxury.

The Candy Girl is becoming increasingly aware of this. Sometimes she stops on the landing in front of Gest's door and takes a deep breath before going in. For once inside she will be surrounded by the usual hard sense of purpose, pressing into her ears, pushing the air out of her lungs. The Candy Girl respects Gest's attitude to work but, still, it makes her wonder. She is dedicated herself, will sacrifice a party to stay in and copy down the lyrics of a song in her swirly girly violet hand but sometimes, she has to admit, a good laugh and a drink with friends is too much to resist.

The poem seems to be the clue, she says out loud.

What? This is the Micro mumbling through a mouthful of food, but the Candy Girl needs no answer for she is mainly talking to herself.

The poem in her bathroom, she frowns. Stuck up beside the mirror.

The Micro also frowns: he likes to hear stories of the strange porn queen but he would rather not hear about poetry right now, not when he is trying to eat his eggs in peace and catch the scores on the radio before leaving for work.

Oh yes:
there most certainly is
something to avoid

quotes the Candy Girl.

But look at you now: not avoiding.
Turning toward it, dipping into it.
Revelling in it, in fact.

Her voice becomes louder as she says these lines, and it rises and falls in a singsong way. Her eyes, though, are fixed on the Micro's plate and she leans forward over the table and takes the fork right out of the Micro's hand.

Hey! The Micro slaps her on her satin thigh. You'll get, he slaps again, fat.

The Candy Girl's thigh quivers under its blue stretch satin but she munches on, mouth full of pale yellow egg crumbs. She swallows and stares hard at the Micro's face as if a photocopied sheet of paper will appear between his handsome brown eyes and his firm stubbled chin. How does it go after that? she muses. Oh I don't know!

In fact, she does know. Her memory has been so rigorously trained over so many years to remember song lyrics that it works just as well for a poem. Why is she doing this? This deliberate vagueness? She is trying to get the Micro's full attention, that's all. And so she pauses for a long dramatic moment before launching back in.

Taking a handful, or mouthful,
or big swollen eyepopping headful –
and letting it simmer.

Small flakes of chilli fall delicately on her chin. And it has worked. The Micro has become deaf to the numbers chanted out on the sports channel, is wholly focused on his bride-to-be. Christ how he wants her! The neckline of her top is hanging open just beside him and he can see the lacy edges of her pink bra. Her breasts rise and fall with her quoting and her stomach muscles tighten in her seriousness about this fucking poem, but at this minute he still has egg in his mouth. Quickly, he swallows.

Now the Candy Girl is walking away from the table with her fork – his fork – still held slightly dreamily in the air in front of her mouth. I can't remember any more, she is saying. The Micro lunges out of his chair and grabs her from behind. She gives a tiny squeal and pulls away. No, she can't have sex, she's late for work! She grates the teeth of the fork against his arm, leaving a thin line of red chilli and reddened flesh, and the faintest trail of egg. She licks it off, her tongue is warm – but later!

It is mid-morning before she is able to excuse herself from Gest's workroom and go to the bathroom. She must see how the poem ends. Something is pulling at her, drawing her to the words: a goose walking over her grave is how the Micro's sister would describe it, while the Micro would say she has an over-active imagination.

She shuts the door.

Boiling, broiling, brimming –
the opposite way of avoiding,
the wrong way
of escaping rightly.

She flushes the toilet, although she hasn't used it. Not that she has done anything wrong, has just read a poem photocopied from a book and stuck up on the wall, but the Candy Girl is respectful of other people's privacy and doesn't want to give Gest the feeling that she is being snooped on.

What's that poem called? she asks in an offhand voice, after she has returned to her stool. The question makes her feel more honest, is halfway to a confession.

261

What poem? Gest is absorbed in reading an old newspaper, what looks to be the pages where stories are written about famous people who have recently died.

The poem on your bathroom wall, says the Candy Girl.

It's called The Lingerer, says Gest. I hate it.

Why, then? asks the Candy Girl. Why have you put it on your wall?

I didn't mean I hate the poem! says Gest. I like the poem but I hate what it describes.

Why then? asks the Candy Girl again. Because of the fact that she and Gest have now worked together for forty-three days, because they once met in a time when, for both, life was completely different but even then they had been tolerant and respectful of each other's differences – because of these things, Gest understands instantly what the Candy Girl means to ask.

I put the poem up, she looks into the distance, as a reminder not to waste time.

So this is it! This is what she hates about photographs though it is only at this very moment, as the sun bursts through the clouds and the Candy Girl blinks, that Gest realizes. This is why she no longer has time for images, has *taken against them* as her grandmother would say.

They fix your memories, she says out loud. Nothing more can grow.

But with the touch of the sun on her white shoulders, the Candy Girl has stopped thinking about the poem. She is remembering the Micro: there is a residual longing for him that has followed her since leaving him that morning, his lusty hot breath on her bare neck. She does not respond to Gest's statement, and the light in the room has turned her eyes to reflective blanks, shutting Gest out. But then she has not seen what Gest has done in the days before these, in the days before the

Candy Girl had come running, running late, out of the station, bag flying from her big shiny shoulder and had bumped into Gest – wham! – and apologized and run on, but Gest had started after her and said that in fact the Candy Girl was just what she had been looking for and would she consider meeting the next day for coffee and a chat. No, the Candy Girl had not been there in the week during which Gest had walked up and down this long straight street, black hair scraped back in a rubber band, depositing small folded packets in each orange rubbish bin for the entire length of the avenue. Had the Candy Girl witnessed this she would have asked more and understood more: but instead she becomes focused on her muscular lover (which is as it should be) and she dreams the day away and asks if she can leave a few minutes early, murmuring something about getting to the magazine shop to look at Bride.

Gest stands on her balcony after the Candy Girl has let herself out, after she has called goodbye in a voice that ricochets off the walls of the stairwell and bounces off the black painted doors on each landing that lead only to emptiness. Now, from her high vantage point, Gest can see a pair of chunky blue satin thighs disappearing fast into the distance, carrying their owner towards a violent but loving man. And dotted along the road, picking up the sulky orange of the late sun, are lines of rubbish bins that echo the line of the trees. Those very bins, in fact, used by Gest to dispose of her memories of the Child.

Instantly, she is back in those first days after the leaving. They were simply a waiting time, there was nothing at all to be done but wait, and on these mornings Gest would stumble to the window and see only white. White sky, white trees, white ground, and no way of knowing which way was up or down so that going out into the street was like being tipped into silty water: sinking, turning, never surfacing. Strange that other people seemed to have no similar problem (Gest recognized this dimly; wiping her eyes she would see figures hurrying past her, heading to their definite destinations). But when she tried to follow these ghostly figures, hoping to be led in the direction she needed to go – just to the shop, just to the bank, just to the doctor's or the lawyer's office – she would sway and lean against a lamp-post, and have no choice but to stumble home again.

On these watery days, the Ordinary Man's voice came sharply down the phone, cutting through the whiteness like light through a surface only sensed to be above. Hearing what she was doing, or not doing, he spoke even more curtly: he seemed to think Gest should be out there carving her way back into the world, not waiting around leaning on lamp-posts.

Once the whiteness cleared away, Gest's head also became clearer. It was then that she saw the need for action, saw what had to be done. To open the cover of every book, to flick through every magazine, to slice pages from photo albums and empty boxes out on the floor. This was not easy: oh, far from easy! But from what Gest had done in the past, from her stealing voyeuristic long-ago experiment in the photo store, she knew that she must not be careless. She must not allow a careless world to get its hands on what was precious to her. If she could not have the Child, then no one else would be allowed to, and she proceeded to sit on her floor with a blade, eyelids scraping over dry eyes, cutting up photo after photo. She cut them into halves and then into quarters, and she divided the pieces into many separate envelopes so that not one image remained intact, and then she brushed her hair away from her face and trudged out into the world that had regained a pale kind of colour – a sky that stayed up and a ground that stayed underfoot – and she deposited pieces of the past in every litter bin she came to in that long straight street, in a deliberately random manner so there was no way in the world that any person could fish an envelope from a bin and open it in a sunless afternoon bathroom, and put their wrong hands all over the Child's face and body, and pore over his brightness, and so possess what she was no longer allowed to have.

(It's weird! This is the Candy Girl, lying in a tangle of sheets with sweat between her huge beautiful breasts. Huh? says the Micro, blurrily. It's weird the way she has no photos, says the Candy Girl, pulling a pillow over her head.)

The runner

There is a certain nervousness about people when they become the recipients of someone else's bad news. A nervous quality that makes them more like birds than human beings, about to be blown skywards with the first dark wind.

These people are not afraid of the one who recounts the bad news to them, perhaps over lunch on the first warm weekend of spring when tables have been set out on pavements and there is a startling looseness to the day, a blowing leafy feel that loosens tongues and sets elbows back on chairs in a careless manner. When the news is told – even before the pale green soup has been served in white bowls rimmed around like a tidemark of weed in a pool – shoulders are hunched in spite of the warmth, and women reach for their jackets as if to prevent ill luck falling from the speckled sky and onto their exposed shoulders. Elbows are removed from the backs of chairs, wine glasses shake a little as if in sympathy, and the diners at the other tables put down their forks and stare over curiously, and even a little enviously, because of the sudden air of importance that bad news brings with it.

The person who first tells the news, and the one who is first to exclaim: these details will shortly be forgotten, they will become blurred like the address on an envelope left half out of a letterbox by a postal worker wanting to get his work done before the drizzle turns to a downpour. Bad news does not simply travel fast, it seems to travel by itself. It may rely on human tongues and human curiosity for its spreading, but these are only agents, discarded almost before the facts are spewed out onto the white tablecloth. Bad news will get to where it needs to, regardless. It can be heard in the hum of electric wires, it can be seen in the Judas trails of jet planes crossing the sky in a parody of faith, it is tasted in the stewed coffee served to you by someone who does not like your momentary, temporary face enough to make a fresh pot. It's there, all around you, and there is hardly a need to hear the words.

Think of a runner in a war. More reliable than a radio, which is prone to cut out at crucial moments, its signals able to be intercepted. Oh, far more reliable than this! As long as the runner is not gunned down, that is, as he flies across no-man's-land, his boots seeming to weigh no more than the light sand arrowing up behind them, his woollen socks and his thick laces turned to weightlessness by sheer fucking fear. Now he is free-falling down a dirt slope, now pounding over the bodies of men

266

with whom he has drunk beer and eaten beans (his foot slips in the split-open spilling innards of a friend's skull, his laces spray friends' blood over the backs of his bare legs as he runs with his bad news).

He is a reliable runner, this man, following in a good tradition. He has been excused from front-line duty because of a lucky stigmatism in one eye – lucky in this instance, though in the past it has made his pretty fiancée uneasy (at which part of her body is he staring? and which eye should she meet when toasting to the future with a potent mix of beer and elderberry wine?). Lucky, unlucky: excused from front-line fire only to end up right in the middle of it, because of the stigmatism, because of his fast legs and sturdy lungs.

Now the runner is out the end of the trenches, leaving the lines of bodies both dead and alive behind him, and there is only scrubland between him and his destination. Remember the running coach you had when you were fourteen? Remember how he hit your legs with a willow twig cut from a cold winter tree – not unkindly but nevertheless hitting you behind the knees, telling you with the whip and the flick to *use* that empty space you have made for yourself with your outstretched arms, dart on through it like a shark through a hole in a wrecked hull. Use it! and you do, arrowing forward into the dull afternoon with your breath already behind you and the small red lines on the backs of your legs some kind of trophy, for whom you're not sure but you don't have time to think. The runner's mind darts back in time and forwards again; he jumps bushes rather than curve around them as if there is a willow switch behind him.

Jump bushes, and potholes that twist and riddle under the feet. Now a sandhill. (Behind him a friend closes blood-streaming eyes on his last view of the world.) The runner is moving so fast that his body has outstripped his mind and when he spots the sentry box he can no longer remember what it is, although knowing this is where he should be. And when he falls into the doorway he cannot remember what he must say, had he the breath in his collapsing paper-bag lungs to say it at all.

The cruelty of the situation lies in its paradoxes. The runner is reliable, and unreliable: both have led him to near death. Almost blind in one eye, he has taken in images so bright and burning that they will never leave his brain. And as he collapses against the sentry post, having nearly killed himself for duty, it is about to become apparent that his effort was essentially unnecessary. Because it is bad news that he has come to deliver, not good, and had he realized this he might have paused to kiss the forehead of a slain friend or to pick a badge out of another friend's muddied hand. He might have stopped altogether, sinking down in the midst of the warm, mud-stained, bloodied, comforting flesh. Because in his breast pocket the runner is carrying a stained paper in which defeat is announced and retreat is ordered, but too late for the cornered men. The news is bad and because of this it has been known before the runner even took his first long stride. As human minds were deliberating over how to break the bad news it was already out there, seeping into the smoky sky, writing itself large on the smouldering land so that by the time the runner was on his way he was in fact jumping and slithering across vast letters spelling out the very news that is contained in his breast pocket. While the sweat from his chest is tearing through his flannel shirt and soaking the paper, the sweat from his forehead is being snatched by the wind and flung back into a world that already knows what he thinks it is his duty to tell.

This is why no one fears the messenger. He is unnec-essary, seemingly important but utterly irrelevant in a world where bad news travels with its own velocity, is carried on the sour breath of the day.

Who are the people afraid of, then? They are afraid of you. Because it is your life into which the bad news has entered like a bullet between the eyes, exiting the next moment through the back of your skull and carrying with it the shreds of so many things! Ordinary things, like minor disagreements over messy floors or toilet seats or lights burning after midnight. And the not so ordinary: images such as a small hand curled around a silver handrail, or the surprising quality a voice has after a day of absence.

There was some animal foresight in you which had known this would be so, even before you turned the corner on that very hot evening, racing into your street. Under your hurrying feet – hurrying, but still, at the cornering moment, not urgent – the pavement had remained solid, in spite of the extraordinary heat. But the next moment everything had shifted; the ground was falling away, cracking all around you, and the skin on your hands also cracking so that you threw down your bags and left them; and there were stress fractures running through the concrete faces of the buildings on each side of you, and above you the clouds were smoking orange.

It was then, already, that you knew: bad news was yours. In those few seconds the sky had shifted over you and it would never reposition itself in quite the right way again. And people would leave you because of it.

Later you can hardly remember a thing. Who was around to help you at this time? So very many of your friends had flown from you, removed themselves through fear, leaving large blanks in your vision.

Later still, it was you who removed yourself.

The burning child

Gest has been wasting time. In spite of her hurry she has been looking back, and her dreams have been full of the dragging images of war: mud, splintered bones, crackling wires giving out wrong information. When her phone rings, sweat starts up all over her body. (She is expecting the line to be cut off, daily.)

The phone call comes from a long distance away, from a dry red country where trees put down five-metre roots to suck moisture from the rocks, and people wander and wither in the desert.

It is like no-man's-land here. It is the voice of the Ordinary Man, skimming long miles over dusty plains, leaping up to bounce off the satellites, taking its mark from a tall striped blinking tower and arrowing down into Gest's very apartment. (Such is the precision of the Ordinary Man and his communications; so they have always been, although they have become rare by this time.)

It is like no-man's-land here, too, says Gest, looking at the battleground of her workspace, the stumps of discarded hands and legs, the casts split open to reveal gaping innards.

How is the work going? the Ordinary Man says, uncomprehendingly.

It is on target, says Gest. It will be finished in time.

I wanted to check, the Ordinary Man's voice has a hint of awkwardness, that you have somewhere to go. Afterwards.

Afterwards? says Gest. I have made plans, you must not worry. But of course the Ordinary Man worries; he is a man who has always taken his responsibilities seriously, one who has asked his ex-wife to regularly scrub the gravestone of his small and bustling mother because he is no longer living in the right country.

Gest puts down the phone but the call has made her weak, so that for a while she must sit on the floor with her head between her knees. Her thighs have become thinner: they curve out in the middle and back in at the knee joints, encircling a fragile egg-shape of air.

It is time for the Candy Girl to be let in: but she is a necessary disturbance, an invited intruder, because part of the process. She is more curious today, and she asks questions about the end result: how, why, and what will Gest name it?

I have told them, Gest shrugs, to give it whatever title they choose. So of course it will be called Destiny, or Ambition, or Life Force!

Any of those would be grand names, says the Candy Girl admiringly.

To tell you the truth, says Gest, I do not care about names.

The day grinds on, the light outside swells and grows full and then slinks away again. There is no sign of the Reader: his window has been closed all day. And the Candy Girl leaves early once again, for tonight she is performing and as she sits on her stool she is jittery with nerves.

Go, says Gest. You are no good to me if you cannot sit still. But she does not speak unkindly: she wishes the Candy Girl all the best for her performance, although by now it seems unimaginable to be in a crowded bar with alcohol spilling from the taps and people leaning up hard against each other, and the hot lights, and the sweat, and the voices.

She ventures out onto the late afternoon balcony, stands

271

on cracked tiles clogged with ash from the cigarettes of past residents. At one time one of those residents twined red plastic flowers around the metal railings. Long-ago beautiful, they are now filled up with grit and with dust, their stems pitted with cold and bleeding artificial green into the rusty orange railings. Gest sees all these details with startling clarity, in spite of the fading light.

(The Candy Girl is lifting her bike onto the train. And – Fake Plastic Trees, she is humming, pretending insouciance, trying to ignore the growing nervousness in her stomach. This had been one of her old friend's favourite songs – he had liked all Radiohead songs but particularly this one, and he had shouted it out from the back platform of trains rattling through the ridged Portuguese hills.)

The balcony on which Gest stands has grass on it, too, but unlike the flowers the grass is real. It grows raggedly, doggedly, in the cracks of the tiles, six floors above where it should be. And there is moss on the interior walls of the concrete. Gest lays her fingers against it; feels it both slimy and rough, like the surface of a person's tongue.

(*Her fake Chinese rubber plant*, croons the Candy Girl at home in her kitchen. She spoons some yoghurt into her mouth: she has heard that yoghurt is good for settling the stomach, though others say milk products should be avoided before performing. The song she is singing, though, has a puzzling title. For how can you have plastic trees that are *not* fake? She looks around for the Micro. But he is not there to solve this mystery, and the Candy Girl goes on spooning and swallowing.)

Gest straightens up and hears the bones in her back crack; she is aware that, day by day, her joints are starting to grate, bone on bone. But the low sun catches on the edge of the balcony, and she is given a sudden picture:

272

a ravine, wild and unpopulated, and around that ravine are trees, each standing in their own circle of lime-green grass. And high above, large birds are circling, their wings slanted to catch the updraught. This! Oh, this is freedom! No traffic below, no clocks and no consciousness: simply a low searching sun, the deep cleft of a ravine, the whispering grass and seed pods cracking in a hot wind.

(*She lives with a broken man*, sings the Candy Girl in a rich white creamy yoghurt voice. *A cracked polystyrene man*, she warbles: but this is not her own situation! Not at all, not for her, for at that very moment there is the sound of the Micro's key in the door, there is his loud voice calling out for her and his strong sturdy steps heading her way.)

When the light finally disappears behind the high rectangle of an office block there is the sense of a sudden plunge. A falling of the world: this is what it is. The street falls into grey, the buildings sink back into place, and it is evening. Gest goes into her workroom and closes the balcony doors, sits her husk-body down on the floor, sits on a sheet of cardboard to cushion the contact of bone on wood. Outside the concrete is dull again, the plastic flowers continue to decay.

After a time she goes to her kitchen, opens the fridge. There is little in there: not much more than a couple of beers, half a tin of tomatoes, a bar of chocolate, and some coffee in a jar. But again all detail is sharp – the rim of red sludge around the tin, the imprint of the chocolate pressing through the silver foil. And this is a kind of compensation: vision is sharpened by hunger.

Gest eats a forkful of cold tomato flesh and listens to the empty building around her. The fridge swallows, the fluorescent light above her head burns and whines. Gas whispers in the copper pipes that file across the wall in straight lines to the stove. The water in the taps turns

273

and kicks like a baby. Silence can cause a new alertness, a more acute form of hearing.

(Far away, in another part of town, the Candy Girl is on stage, in an old Italian pizza joint under the arch of a railway bridge. Every eight minutes trains thunder overhead making the microphone tremble so that, for a moment, the Candy Girl is fearful it is her own voice that is shaking. But no, the walls of the pizzeria stand firm – their bricks are rough from absorbing the noise of the engines, but they have been here for many years and will be for many more – and the Candy Girl sings on. *My fake plastic love*, she sings, while somewhere still in the back of her head is the quiet afternoon apartment, the sunlight creeping through the dirty streaked windows, the grimy plastic roses tapping in the wind, and the silence of abstracted, distracted thought. *It wears her out*, sings the Candy Girl tenderly, *it wears her ouu-t*.)

Gest turns the light off and sits down at the kitchen table. The window across the courtyard remains dark, but in spite of this she thinks she can see an interior to the room. There are surely paintings on the walls, and no doubt there are neatly labelled tapes on wooden shelves, and a pair of slippers hidden under the window ledge. Just as deprivation offers a more acute way of seeing, so can loneliness bring peace. The gnawing in Gest's stomach, the pain in her leg: these things have subsided, for now. She puts her cold bare feet up on another chair and takes a mouthful of beer, staring through the glass panels of the kitchen door into the hallway.

Suddenly the Child is there, leaping through the white wall towards her. This is usual, this is nothing unusual, though no less terrible for its frequency. But tonight – oh, tonight the Child is different! He is unrecognizable, and Gest sits and stares and cannot move, mesmerized with terror.

His hair, the Child's hair is ablaze. He is ringed around with fire. And what else? What else is different? His face is covered in flame so Gest cannot see his eyes or his nose. Flames stream upwards as he soars from the wall, and his pointed toes reach out and down towards the floor. Gest's sharpened vision has given her this: the Child's flaming face, through which the cavity of his mouth gapes, and there are no teeth in his mouth but a tongue that is dark and swollen, and his scream is soundless.

(*If I could be who you wanted*, sings the Candy Girl. *If I could be who you wanted, all the time, all the time.*)

When it is over, when the hallway is empty once more, Gest puts her head down on the table and stays there for a long time. But the sickening, predictable pain in her leg has started up again, and she must leave her beer where it stands, slide her feet back into her shoes, get to her feet. There is no hurry? There is every hurry. The days are breathing at her back and she dares not stop.

It is the first time her soul has left her body

Today is Thursday. That is, other people would call it Thursday but Gest no longer gives names to things. She sees only in numbers, and today is the forty-fifth day.

In front of her the Candy Girl sits twiddling her thumbs. At least, this is what other people would call it, but Gest has spent so long dissecting the Candy Girl,

275

breaking her body down into separate parts, that she does not see the whole any more. And at any rate, she is not concentrating on the hands today.

The Candy Girl sits, curvily nude, and plays with some long strands of hair she has combed from her stripy head. Water falls past the window. Others would call this, rain.

It makes me want to pee, offers the Candy Girl. That watery noise.

Gest does not hear this confidence, nor does she hear the rain landing in the guttering, splashing on the tiles of the balcony or the leaves of the trees. She hears the silence around the drops in the same way you might hear right through the sound of a helicopter some distance away, picking up the *flack flack* of the blades but not the engine.

Could you turn to the left? she asks. She continues to smooth and sand. The pores of her skin are thick with dust, she has long stopped wearing gloves when she works just as she has stopped wearing protective masks when heating plastic on her stove. (Toxic? This word means nothing to her, though it may frighten other people.)

The day wends its way through to late afternoon, the Candy Girl leaves, and the rain continues but eases. Through the gaps in its falling come small sounds: the gasp of car tyres on the hospital driveway next door, the fall of bin lids, a voice speaking in a foreign language, a bell. The doorbell? It is Gest's own.

She goes into the hallway where she is confronted by the Candy Girl's forgotten umbrella, lying in a crumpled red heap on the floor. She goes to the door. Here you are! she says. You'll be needing this to get home.

But it is not the Candy Girl returning. It is the Reader. His face is lightly covered with water and the streaks in his hair are as bright as silver.

I hope I am not intruding, he says in a tone of the

utmost politeness. But since the other day in the court-yard I have not been able to stop thinking.

Thinking? says Gest. About what? She holds the umbrella at her side like a rifle.

I have been reluctant to disturb you, says the Reader. But in some way I feel that you are already disturbed, am I right?

Gest takes a deep breath. You are, she says. She steps aside and lets the Reader into the hallway. It is the first time for many weeks that anyone except the Candy Girl has been inside Gest's apartment, but the Reader seems to specialize in being unobtrusive. Even though he is standing so close to Gest that she could touch him, it is almost as if he is not here, might just as well be across the courtyard still, safely shut away behind his glass window. The air in the apartment continues to lie quietly in the long hallway, the water in the pipes trickles on.

Would you like tea? asks Gest, but she knows he has not come for this.

The Reader takes a few steps down the hallway. He walks with an uneven tapping sound: good foot, bad foot, cane. When he turns around, he leans his cane up against the wall and looks directly at Gest.

I am concerned about you, he says. I came to see if you need help.

There is a moment of complete silence. Gest's chest rises and falls. Oh yes, she says. I could do with helping, though I think no one is able to do this.

Allow me to try, says the Reader. And now he takes his long raincoat off and, most politely, comes over to Gest and takes her in his arms. They stand there for a while holding on to each other, and then move quietly through the hall, still holding each other's arms as if they are crossing a wide river. They make a small detour around a snow globe, standing like a tiny island of glass

277

and glitter in the middle of the bare floorboards, and then they are at the door of Gest's workroom.

The Reader looks in the open door. Your commission? he says.

The large transparent figure stands surrounded by a circle of shavings and dust. Its right hand stretches towards the ceiling, its open fingers grasp at air.

So that is it, says the Reader. Or nearly it. What will it hold in its hand, when it is finished?

It will hold nothing, says Gest. It is simply reaching out.

Then at last they are in the bedroom after a journey that might have taken minutes, or hours. It is possible from here to see the Reader's living-room window across the empty space, a black square in the dim wet afternoon. And still the Reader holds on to Gest's hand, firmly but lightly, with his warm dry grip.

This room has witnessed both much and little: many hours of wakefulness, a crying girl curled on the bed, a sleep-ridden kiss. The thin sheets on top of the mattress are twisted and strewn.

I do not sleep much, says Gest, gesturing at the disarray. I no longer seem able to sleep.

But the room feels quiet enough now, its walls and floorboards covered with the light shadows of water and glass. After this Gest and the Reader do not speak. They do not speak until after the Reader has gently stripped off Gest's work overalls and knickers, has combed some splinters from her hair and brushed away some dust from her eyebrows and some dirt from her cheek, and then has removed his own clothes and gently lain on top of her and come into her.

Instead of speaking they watch the changes in each other's face, and the rain slips on down the window, moving over their pale flesh with shadowy fingers. The

Reader is as considerate as ever; he moves inside Gest as if somehow knowing what it is like to have forty-six long days built up around your bones, brittle, hard, a semblance of protection but no kind of armour. He strokes her hair during this time, and when he comes out of her he kisses her forehead, and they lie quietly for some time listening to the water outside the window.

When he speaks, he must first clear his throat, but he sounds the same as ever. Are you OK? he says. His voice is the same, quiet, moderate, but he is different. When Gest looks at him lying long and melancholic beside her, she is aware of a change: she is seeing all of him. Not only the side of his head, not just his hand shaking out a newspaper, or his profile blurred by layers of glass and distance.

All, she says in wonder. All of you.

So accustomed has she become at seeing in small parts that she must look for a long time at him, up and down, up and down: head, foot, pillow, foot of the mattress. And her vision is not large enough; her eyes have spent too much time dissecting and narrowing, and now she must stretch them. She opens them as wide as she can, places her fingers on either side of her eye sockets, stretching out her seeing.

What——? The Reader is watching her across the expanse of black pillow. What are you doing? He laughs: a laugh emitting from the whole of his mouth, a luxury to be savoured now, and also later when Gest will be by herself again.

I am trying to see all of you, she says. Trying to take all of you in. For most of the time, you see only in parts.

I see only in parts? The Reader is puzzled.

So masterly has Gest become at the parroting back of phrases while thinking of something else that at first she does not answer. She simply sighs and turns on the bed, pulls the sheet up over her and lies still, looking at the ceiling.

But the Reader's hand is turning her head on the pillow, his long fingers holding her chin. Explain to me, he says. I only see in parts?

I did not mean you personally, Gest manages to say. She rolls slightly away from him so that she can continue (the touch of his fingers has brought tears into her throat).

Imagine this, she says. You are sitting in a bar looking through the window, and outside the window is a low awning, and beyond the awning is an alleyway filled with sun and people walking by. Can you imagine?

I can, he says.

And you are sitting at a plain wooden table. Gest conjures this up with a wave of her hand. And the owner's daughter brings you a jug of sangria and some sardines, and a small box of paper tissues to wipe your fingers with.

I'm there, he confirms.

For as long as you sit at that table, says Gest, the awning hangs at the same level, and this means you can only see the people who are passing from the chest down.

That sounds promising! he says, and for a minute he leaves Gest's imaginary bar to concentrate on Gest herself, raising the black sheet, running his finger lightly over her right breast.

Now you've made me lose, she says, my train! I have lost my train of thought.

We were watching men with broad chests. (He takes his hand away.) Men with chests but no heads, women with full bodies but half a neck, and children – do we see the whole of a child?

We don't, she says, because the awning is low so as to shade the bar completely, allowing the old card-players to see their cards.

280

So what happens when we stand up? The Reader preempts her. Do we see only feet?

Only feet, says Gest. And when we walk out into the glaring white sun we see nothing but silhouettes.

And when we ask a stranger for directions back to the hotel, suggests the Reader, we notice only their hands?

You see? says Gest. We see only in parts and this is our misfortune, we are either too close or—and she hesitates. Or much too far away, she finishes, her voice becoming small.

But you underestimate me. As the Reader speaks, his chin makes a slight grating sound against the pillow for it is evening, and the end of another day. I see the whole, he says, because that is my job.

But you! cries Gest, and she turns away from him and hits the wall with the flat of her hand. You see the whole only because you are the furthest away of all, she cries. You see the dead! She is kneeling now, hitting the wall again and again so that the dull thuds travel through the plaster and brick and out into the space between the buildings, to hover like bats in the high dark air.

Now the Reader is kneeling behind her, although awkwardly because of his bad leg. He is holding her fists and drawing them into her body, pulling the noise and anger back into the safe semi-dark of the bedroom. Gest is held hard against his chest, is made to lie back on the pillows. He will try to explain his work again, although he knows she understood it that day in the desert playground, with the urban wind blowing around their feet and the breath of garbage cans on their cheeks. He'll explain again, which will give her time to get over her hurting fists and her sudden fear.

What is my job? he says, stroking her hair in an absent kind of way. A kind of cosmic cataloguing, that's what you might call it. A morbid microfiche. Forensics for the famous.

Gest puts her face down against his ribs. Although he feels frail and thin, she has never known such comfort.

Seriously, he says, it is a kind of redemption – perhaps the only kind possible. He speaks without wryness now. But I think you know that already, he says. He pulls her head off his chest and moves her up on the pillow so that her face is on a level with his. He kisses her hard on the mouth, missing her bottom lip but getting her top lip (she is not quite back to where she was, not yet.) He takes her under the arms and moves her up the bed a little further (now she is equal with him), makes her lie on top of him (above him, but equal still).

The Candy Girl has sung many times of the difficulty of love. How hard is it, really? How hard can another person pull you into them, closer, closer, so your pelvic bones grind together and flesh is pressed on flesh, knees braced on a mattress which is braced against the floor, floor raised on steel girders above the ceiling of the next apartment down and the next, and so on and so on until it feels as if you are being drawn down *so hard* that you will be dragged through the very foundations of the building, through layers of soft melting tar and cool dark worm-ridden soil and still you twist, on and on, between the tangled far-reaching roots of trees, past rocks, into the hot heart of where it began. Into the burning place, where your hair might be raked from its roots and you would feel nothing, your skin pierced by sharp black-ened wood – nothing – and your organs blister, burst out of your body and, still, you feel nothing. Nothing! Because this is love.

Today is the first day that Gest's soul has left her body. Nothing has prepared her for this, and afterwards the Reader turns his face to the side so she is able to cry a little in private (she is not yet ready to be watched), though after she has done so he turns back and smoothes the tears out of her face with one long hand.

You are the only person, she says to him, and now midnight falls heavy as a moth against the window. The only person—but she muffles her mouth against the edge of the mattress, bites down hard.

He drags himself up in the bed, reaches for his jacket and pulls out a pack of cigarettes. May I? he says, with courtesy and a hint of mockery.

Yes, she says, into the mattress.

He smokes sitting up with his back against the wall: that is, with his back turned temporarily on his own building, his own life, and his mind wholly focused on Gest's problems.

How much longer do you have in this place? he asks. Only a few more days?

Yes, says Gest again. She lifts her mouth off the mattress where it has left a small dark circle like a coin: the payment she must make for wanting to talk, to share the burden. Just a few more days, she says, and the building will be gone.

I have asked you before, says the Reader, but you did not give a real answer. Do you know where you are going afterwards?

Yes, she says, for the third time. The Reader waits but she is stronger now; the moment for vulnerability has mingled with the smoke from his cigarette, risen to the window, and is gone.

A new building here will not be a bad thing, says the Reader, when he sees she will not speak. For the neighbourhood, I mean.

You are right, says Gest. There has been a bad feeling here since the fire.

At least you have had a quiet place to work, jokes the

Reader. No neighbours complaining about noise, no smell of fish in the hallway.

Only the sweet smell of plastic compounds. Gest is also joking, but there is a dusty crack in her voice.

Plastic? the Reader queries. Is that what the figure is made from?

A kind of plastic compound, says Gest. But it will be encased in a glass dome so that no one can harm it.

She sits up beside him, shoulder to shoulder, but refuses his offer of a cigarette. She hasn't smoked much, she says, since her movie days. He tells her he has never seen one of her films: at least, he doesn't recognize her physically.

By the way, he says. What is your name?

Isn't that a bit forward? says Gest. You've only just slept with me!

The Reader laughs but when he hears what her name is he looks surprised, and ash from his cigarette drops on her arm, singeing the hairs. I'm sorry! he brushes it off. Although he is apologizing, at the same time he is thinking of what she has told him. You know that you are famous, he says. But not from your movies.

That depends on what your interests are, returns Gest.

True, I am not a porn aficionado! he admits. Even so I would like to see one of your films. Although after this – he looks at her sitting naked beside him. After this, he finishes, even one of your own porn films would be an anticlimax.

And now he reaches for her cigarette-scorched arm and brings it to his mouth, licks it, and the hot saliva from his mouth increases the burning but she does not tell him so. You are so beautiful, he says. You are beautiful and perhaps you are famous for your movies, but not only for those. You must know that for one so young you have quite a reputation in the art world.

I do? Gest is sure and not sure; she knows the slipperiness of fame.

284

You do, says the Reader, and I have no doubt that you will succeed with that city space where others have failed. That space, he repeats, but once again his habit of repetition is nothing like Gest's: he is not avoiding thought, but burrowing deeper into it. It would be easier, he sighs, to write an obituary for God. He seems genuinely sorry for Gest, that she has been chosen to fill the Space Between: that feared, fearsome, beautiful, unfillable space.

It has been empty for so long, agrees Gest, that even God might find it difficult to fill. Perhaps a nude marble of Adam wrestling with a group of town planners?

The Reader laughs again and as he does so Gest sees his ribs move under his skin. She traces them step by step up to his collarbone, and he traces hers.

You're thin for a porn star, he says.

I used to be curvy, says Gest. I haven't been eating much recently.

Did you have big breasts? he asks, running his fingers over her chest.

I did, she admits.

And did you have an arse? he says.

I still do, she says. What do you think I sit on all day?

You are beautiful but thin, he says. And you have a lot of birthmarks on you.

I have this one. Gest touches her neck.

Yes, says the Reader. And also these.

When Gest looks down at herself, it is true. She sees a number of small fleck-marks covering her arms and hands. From working, she says, in slight surprise. From not taking care.

She looks again, sees the blemishes that her skin has picked up over the days as a person might collect tiny stones from a riverbed. As she herself would have in the days when she was still able to walk out under the sky,

285

when she would walk for miles with a pack on her back and sandwiches in that pack, secure in her own perfect skin and the width of the sky and time that was limitless.

Constellations on your skin, says the Reader. That is what you have. I could make a whole sky out of you. He reaches out for his jacket again and this is what he does: makes a sky from her, maps her out, joins up her marks with a fine felt-tipped pen. She feels the small indigo feet of it storming over her skin, and his hand, driving those felt-tipped footsteps: hard and meticulous, far fiercer than when he fucked her.

Now you are finished, he says, my own work of art. But what is this? he says, looking away from her starry arms. He gestures at her leg but he does not touch it, as if this time he is in fact afraid of hurting her.

That? Gest turns her face away. That was a strange and unfortunate accident.

The Reader strokes her neck with fingers that have written many lives to their end. Is it a burn? he asks.

I was down in the street when the fire broke out in this building, says Gest. I happened to be down below and some metal fell on me.

Do you think you should get treatment? The Reader is concerned. You could go to the hospital next door.

I am too busy, Gest sounds dismissive. And it is not so bad. It was better for a while and now perhaps it is infected. But I have no time for treatment.

Of course, your work, the Reader looks at her closely. It is admirable, he says, the way you focus on your work.

Then, suddenly, from across the courtyard comes the flick of a light – not the Reader's light, for he is in bed beside Gest, but it sweeps from an unknown room into this one like the beam of a lighthouse, making the Reader realize: he, too, has work to do and it is time for him to start. It is time to go back to his room and begin watching

286

the smooth unconcerned faces of those who once revelled in the public eye and have now escaped it forever.

And so it is time for Gest to smooth her hair, to put on a shirt over her green constellation arms, to prepare for the final stages.

The Reader dresses, too, and then leads the way into the hallway. He moves quietly, unevenly, in front of her. The outline of his shoulder blades is sharp through his thin black suit jacket. By the time he turns at the door, Gest has almost forgotten his face.

What did you say? She has not heard him, cannot hear.

May I see you again? His eyes rest gravely on her face and in the dim hallway his face has the stillness of a mask. He reaches for her hand.

Again? says Gest. She holds on to his hand for a minute, and then a minute longer, before stepping back and watching him turn away. The stooped body, the exposed back of his neck, the careful steps down the first stairs. Leaving. Leaving her.

She moves back behind the door but does not close it. Sheltering there, she listens to the uneven tap of his footsteps getting fainter and fainter down the stairwell.

Goodbye, she says.

The day the wind came

On that day (Gest begins) at that time when the evening blurs and runs like paint into night, so if you are out on a tennis court the ball – only a minute before a small

287

point of certainty – becomes a tricky unknown thing, flying and swerving past you so that although you swing your racquet hard and skilfully nonetheless you feel the sickening feeling of the racquet head connecting with nothing, your wrist clicks, your arm brings your body to an abrupt halt, and the ball runs on behind you into the groaning gathering dark: at that indistinct time, on that particular day, there came a huge wind.

It blew through the city like a giant sigh (and now the Candy Girl also sighs, as if in sympathy, her breasts rising and falling with a slight scratching sound, the sound of nipples against thin pink nylon), as if all the sorrows of the world were being let out in one breath.

It blew through the city in that early evening and who knew where that restless, chesty wind was heading? Gest's voice is soft, suffused, mixed with layers of stuffy air and the fumes of melted plastic; and who could say why she is telling the Candy Girl this story at this moment, for it is morning, not evening, and there is not the slightest bit of wind.

Yes, who knew where that wind was heading, or where it had come from? Gest asks the Candy Girl in a musing kind of voice, as if she has never considered this before.

Where does the wind come from? shrugs the Candy Girl. That is the sort of thing only the weather people can know.

It lasted a minute only, that wind, says Gest. A few minutes at most. And so sudden was it that there may have been no official warning, only what people saw blowing up in front of their own eyes.

But now she stops because suddenly the wind under discussion is seeming to rush back at them, blowing in the window, straight through their conversation, lifting papers and sketches off the floor and rattling brushes against the sides of jars. Such are the Pandora habits of history: do not even try to shut the lid down on such a wind.

The trees themselves lifted. (Gest can go on, once the random restless memory-breeze has left again.) It was as if they would rise right out of the ground. They had been disturbed by the wind, those trees, as if promised something better than standing in a dull straight line glared at by streetlights and breathed on by trams. *Come* said the sighing wind (but where to, no one knew), and had the trees listened any longer it is possible that they would have gone, pulling their feet free from the sandy soil, leaving behind the shit nestled in the cracks between their toes and the cum-stains from businessmen and rent boys, the light balls of hair that had drifted down from balconies, the lipstick-stained cigarette butts tossed from the windows of waiting cars, and the trailing promises whispered at midnight by illicit lovers who, for some reason, had never stopped to think that these trees might not be here for ever, might one day depart leaving the secrets of the lovers exposed.

Yes, those trees might have disappeared on that day, caught up in the vast orange mouth of the wind, had not the birds distracted them. Hundreds of birds rising from the bushes, flying out of the bells of street lamps to form vast circles over the street. They rose and rose in rings until the sky was almost black and to look up into it was like looking into the black cone of a tornado.

Black and orange, muses the pink nylon Candy Girl. Not colours you would normally see in nature.

But do you not remember that day? asks Gest, and now her voice is not dull, it is amazed that such a thing could lie forgotten in the Candy Girl's brain.

Last spring? The Candy Girl crinkles her forehead. Twelve months is a long length of time to flip back through, especially if you have had quite a year: learning the lyrics of forty new songs, managing the urges of a lusty boyfriend and capturing the attention of crowded bars, thinking of overheads and rates for a new business, not to mention spending six weeks as a life model for a famous artist.

Last spring – she says again, in a confused voice.

Nearly twelve months ago to the day, says Gest. In three days' time it will be the anniversary of the day the wind came.

But now the Candy Girl does remember! Though at the time she had a bad case of cystitis, had spent the week burning, straining on the toilet, thinking she would go mad unless the medication worked quickly, and no hope of sex, not until it was better: so there had been little time to take notice of what was going on outside the window of the cracked bathroom, in the moist damp flat with its louvre windows open to the spring air. I do remember, she says with relief. There were reports on the radio about roofs flying off houses!

And huge trees fell into parks, says Gest. And a car was lifted high in the air, flying over the motorway and landing on the wrong side.

A miracle that no one was killed, says the Candy Girl stoutly. Thank the Lord.

Yes, you remember now, says Gest, and there is also relief in her voice. She glances towards the windows, but the hard morning light hits her straight in the eyes, so that they water and sting. When she turns back to the Candy Girl, she has to blink several times before she can see her properly.

And the papers also said—the Candy Girl is eager to continue the reminiscence game, now that she is a part of it. But she sees Gest pushing back her chair, pushing her hands against her eyes. Are you all right? she asks, in concern.

Gest doesn't reply. Do you want some water? she asks, instead.

No, the Candy Girl doesn't: she has a full Diet Coke beside her. But thank you anyway, she says politely. When Gest returns from the kitchen there is a light sweat on her face and she is carrying not only a bottle of water, but a small piece of paper. Could you call this number for me when you get home? she asks. And she hands the paper to the Candy Girl. As a favour to me?

Of course! The Candy Girl will do this, and more. But do you want me to call now, she says, from here?

The phone was cut off this morning, says Gest. Please call for me later, and ask them to come and pick the work up from here. Tomorrow.

The work is finished! The Candy Girl looks first pleased, and then concerned. Is it safe to stay here all alone without a phone? she asks. And as she speaks she looks older than her years: her concern for Gest pulls her cheeks in, and responsible lines settle round her mouth.

Safe? Gest looks vague, looks around the room. As safe as anywhere, I suppose. I don't need a phone.

What about the electrics? (In her newly responsible guise the Candy Girl is reverting to the language of an older generation.) The Electrics, she repeats almost sternly, and what about the gas?

The power and the gas? Gest sounds more definite now. I have three more days, she explains, they have promised me that.

It is time for the final inspection of the work: for exclaiming, for poring, for touching and smoothing. This is an odd experience for the Candy Girl, touching her own body while being outside herself. The Micro's sister, she turns confidingly to Gest, would call this a *transcendental experience*. She looks again at the legs that have

291

been modelled on hers. At the chest, made flat, but hers: and the rounded childish chin. Sturdy forearms, creased wrists, fingers held high to the sky: hers?

But it is quite different from me, she marvels. You have made me a boy! How odd it is that people – even the Micro – will walk past this not knowing that it was once me. It is a boy, agrees Gest. But you are there, you have provided the form. And she looks at the Candy Girl as if it is the first time she has seen her. You *are* there! she says, looking from the larger-than-life stylised body to the pink-nylon-clad real one.

Now the Candy Girl is glowing with suppressed pride. It is her! (though a boy) and it is to go on show in the middle of a city square! If only her mother were alive to see! But pride is not one of the Candy Girl's faults, and firmly she squashes it away behind her eyes and rearranges her face into an expression of professional interest. Now tell me, she speaks with the curious yet detached tone of an art critic. What is it flecked with?

It is flecked with ash, says Gest.

Ash? The Candy Girl looks up, amazed. What a lot you must have smoked during this time!

Not ash from a cigarette. And Gest looks away. If you will not be shocked, she says, I will tell you where the ash comes from.

But when it comes to real life, of course, the Candy Girl is unshockable. She has a past littered with needles and candle flames and the underbellies of bridges; she has an old head on young shoulders. No, she will not be shocked; the only thing that sometimes takes her by surprise is other people's meanness.

Tell me, she says without fear.

It is ash, says Gest, from a human body.

You don't say! The Candy Girl is even more amazed, her face lighting up with incredulity. From a body!

292

It is there as a reminder, says Gest slowly. It is there to remind us that our lives are always affected by those who have gone before.

Doesn't the Candy Girl understand this! She understands it with every bone of her body: how the past never leaves us, how our heads remain weighted with the dust of long-ago roads, and our limbs weighted by the years through which they have carried us. Only this week she has had a dream about Portugal, has smelt again the musky eucalyptus leaves, heard again the cracked voice of a friend, felt her feet running heavy as lead, stumbling down a hill *too slow* – and then the waking, sweat running between her breasts, sticking her thighs together, staining the undersheet with faint yellow marks. Yes, she knows.

We are never alone, she says. (This is her offering.)

Gest is pleased that the Candy Girl has lived up to expectations, has not been squeamish, has registered no disgust or dismay. These reactions would be wrong; after all, just walking past the hospital to get to work each day it is likely that the Candy Girl has been breathing in other people, the incinerated particles of human matter poured out into the air, crowding up her nostrils and jostling into her lungs, making the spokes of her bicycle less shiny than they would otherwise be.

I have had the ashes for a while, says Gest.

(She was brought up by her grandmother, the Candy Girl explains to the Micro. Her grandmother was from a faraway country. She was a very sad woman.)

I have had them for a while, Gest says again. But at first I did not know what to do with them.

You must find exactly the right place, agrees the Candy Girl. I buried my mother under a rose tree in a public park, I think it is against the law. But it was her favourite park, she shrugs, so I did it anyway.

293

You must not worry about what other people think is right, says Gest.

I put my mother in a small tin that once held Danish butter cakes because those were her favourites, confides the Candy Girl. She only just fitted.

That is a nice story, says Gest, with a hint of a smile.

But I could tell you a story about the Micro's sister! And the Candy Girl's voice lifts with retrospective amazement. The Micro's sister wears their dead baby brother in a ring! She had him crushed down and made into a diamond – did you know they could do that?

I did not, says Gest.

It cost her half a year's wages, nods the Candy Girl.

That is nothing to keep a life, says Gest.

The Candy Girl turns back to the sculpture, surveys it with her head on one side, a gaudy tropical bird in the middle of a grey swamp. Are you satisfied with it? she asks.

Satisfied? I can hardly say, says Gest. I suppose I would like more time. More time, more skill, just more.

There is such sadness in Gest's voice that the Candy Girl rushes to reassure. Like me with my singing, she says. I would like to sing—oh, so differently!

Gest is silent and the Candy Girl looks back at herself, larger than life, pink flesh transformed into clear plastic through a mixture of heat and chemistry, made from a substance boiled up on Gest's stove in the unseen night hours and flecked with someone else's bones. I think it is a masterpiece, she says solemnly.

And now it is time, although it is only the forty-seventh day, for the Candy Girl to depart this phase of her life forever. After the phone call, Gest tells her, she need not do anything more, though of course she will be paid for the full fifty days.

But I can come back if you change your mind! Is the

Candy Girl reassuring her employer, or herself? I can come back any day, she says, if you need me.

No, says Gest. You must not come back, and I will not change my mind. But thank you, thank you for everything. She comes to the Candy Girl and takes her in her arms. Their smells mingle; green apple shampoo and strawberry lipgloss mixing with clean musky skin, dusty fingers and determination.

It is never easy to watch two people who have become so close saying goodbye. How much, how much to show? And what will become of the short but sturdy twisted rope of their relationship, braided so tightly over eight-hour days and hundreds of cups of tea?

It is not really goodbye. The Candy Girl swallows. Is it? Again she seems to be searching for something: an assurance, perhaps, that although her final pay packet is in her hand, she may at any time be called back to her post. She hugs Gest again. Her swallowing sounds loud in Gest's ear but for a minute their breathing is indistinguishable.

Follow her now, this sturdy reliable girl with her head full of dreams – white satin dreams, dreams of happiness and star-spangled fame. Follow her large kind feet and her big rounded shoulders down seventy-two stairs and into the street. Watch her for as long as you can, until her dark-rooted head and her sparkling pink earrings are lost in the crowd. After this, for her, there will be the train home and the setting sun: these are before her, and a lot more besides. Although you can no longer see her, her resolute face is turned towards the future and what it might hold. A shop full of white aprons and yellow rubber boots, a wedding ceremony joining her to a red-blooded bull-headed man nonetheless capable of lasting love, and after this a party to end all parties, and after this, perhaps, a child.

Look back, if you can bear to

Look back now, and see this: the Child is arriving at Gest's door, his neatly packed weekend bag in his hand. In it are two striped T-shirts, which have been folded into small squares by either the Ordinary Man or his red-haired psychologist, who continues to be made uneasy by the alien vibes that hang around the Child's head after a weekend spent with Gest. Two T-shirts, placed on top of two pairs of underwear; two pairs of socks, and one spare pair of shoes that are oddly large for a six-year-old, oddly formal for a child.

Look back and see this. It is Saturday morning now, and the Child is knocking on the door of the back bedroom. He comes in and gets into bed with Gest, but something is not right. He is hot, his face is flushed, and his golden hair is not as shiny as it should be.

Gest turns, still in half sleep, and holds his hot pyjama-clad body close to hers. She pulls him in to her belly as if she would return him to the womb, keep him safe once more from colds and viruses, from people that shout and dogs that bite and the unfairness of having to sleep in a different bed every second weekend, and carry folded T-shirts in a bag across town. Are you OK? she asks, concerned.

I feel a bit prickly, says the Child. But he is stoic, accepting his impending illness with the resignation of an old man. This will be a snuffly snot-ridden weekend, with a sharp hint of fever.

Showers, breakfasts; the day progresses. Gest works with a casting, her careful pouring accompanied by the sneezes of the Child from the room next door. She sneezes too, behind her mask: from the creeping dust in her studio, from sympathy with the Child. And as always, the bag of pills on the back of her bedroom door is tugging at the weak edges of consciousness. *Come on*, it wheedles. *Welcome*. Its voice is only ever this insistent when the Child comes to stay: this is Gest's own illness, to be fought and overcome not by vitamins but by willpower alone.

See this, if you are ready to: the radio tower blinking its red eye through a blanket of dust that has spread itself over the surface of the late day. For we are witnessing the aftermath of a freak wind: a huge wind which has swept through the city, knocking the tall grasses flat, unsettling the trees and the birds, scattering leaves and paper and people all over this city with the hole in its heart.

The Child has started to whine. It is late on Saturday, he has been playing in his room all day, there is a rest-lessness in his legs and his heart. Is he homesick? He is not sure, because he is not quite sure where home is. And Gest cannot help him right now with this problem, for she is working like a guilty fiend in the next room (a deadline to meet, and this must be cast now). But her son's temperature is rising, and when she goes in to kiss him and promise him fish fingers and oven chips for dinner when she is done, his forehead is sweaty.

Oh she loves him, how she loves him! and for a moment all other commitments are forgotten. She crouches beside him to look at his drawings: a police car, a boat, nothing spectacular, for he has no particular talent for drawing, but beautiful, so beautiful because drawn by him. Tears come to her eyes. Yes, they will have dinner soon and will chat in the kitchen, and then the whole of tomorrow is his (so this is why she has worked like a fiend today). Tomorrow they will walk and talk companionably on the dry path beside the railway tracks, then they will stand on the bridge for ten minutes and count the trains flying underneath them, and whoever guesses closest to the right number will choose the flavour of the ice cream bought from the van by the station (they must always eat the same, these two, each wanting to taste the same as each other; as they crunch the cones they will give each other small vanilla kisses with their cool ice cream lips).

This promise makes the Child happy! His smile wins through his sharp feverish crossness and he hugs Gest, but there is slick sweat on his forehead and in the creases of his arms, and now Gest realizes what she has not thought about all day: that in twenty-five minutes the pharmacy along the road will be closing, and it will not reopen until Monday morning. She looks for a minute at the Child, at the flush in his cheeks and the dangerous shine of his eyes; and she is decided. She must run out now, get aspirin and cough syrup and all the things that the Ordinary Man has stacked in his bathroom cupboard for emergencies such as these while Gest has no such provisions, the only drugs in her household not being fit for a child – a danger, in fact, lethal for a child – and therefore hung high on the back of the bedroom door in a small black pouch.

Hear this: the whisper of the pills as Gest hurries into her room to pull on her shoes. Hear their small whispery promises, offering her an easy evening with all tiredness floating away, and the lifting of worry about the Child (*only a common cold!*); but no, nothing is common, nothing is to be taken lightly when it comes to the Child and his small vivid self. Gest pushes aside her bathrobe hung on its hook to find the pouch, puts her hand lightly on it, slips her hand into it for a second to finger the cool white reassurance inside: the oblivion pills, shining,

shining, in their darkness, never more tempting or more seductive as these times when the Child is near.

She looks at the clock. She must hurry. In twenty minutes the white-coated pharmacist will be dragging the red sign in off the pavement, will fold it away and lean it on the inside wall of the shop with the surrounding smells of cardboard and sharp carbolic soap. She must hurry! But the bathrobe falls off the back of the door and the bag of pills falls with it, its mouth wide, spewing its contents all over the floor. Pills skid and scatter under the bed, strew between shoes and underwear: candy for the imagination, confetti for a dangerous wedding.

Gest swears – *shit!* She starts to clean up, then looks again at the clock. Seventeen minutes. And she leaves the mess and rushes into the hallway but the Child is already there, right outside her door. Can I lie on your bed, he asks, while you go to the shop?

No, you must not! says Gest. Just stay in your own bed till I get back, and then you can move, I promise.

There is a curiosity in the Child's eyes: he notices that Gest is flustered, and there is something lying on the floor beside her foot. What's this? he asks, and he picks it up, turns the small white oval in his sweaty coldy hand, raises it instinctively to his mouth.

No! Gest snatches it away. No, you must not! She puts it in her pocket and shepherds the Child back into the front bedroom. Stay here till I'm back, she begs. Please?

The Child nods, he is obedient, he lays his small damp face on the pillow. But there is a sharpness in his face, a new alertness to his body, and Gest knows (for she knows him as well as, better than, he knows her). She knows he will lie on the narrow divan only until her footsteps have disappeared down the stairwell, and then he will get up again, straight away, to investigate.

See this. Gest's indecision is warring with her haste.

The key to her bedroom door: where is it? Not in the lock, not in the back of the door or on the floor amidst the scattered pills. The hands on her watch are spinning on into the evening. She runs back into the front room. The Child is lying completely still, holding his arm up to the ceiling, flicking an old cigarette lighter into the air as if he is at a rock concert. Click, click: Gest cannot tell if the sound is made by the lighter or is the rough breath in his throat.

Be careful with that, she says.

It doesn't work, he says, clicking without success, without flame. See?

All right, she says. She looks down at him and her heart kicks at the sight of his face: familiar, his own, part of her. I love you! she says. She kisses him, smells his hot sour breath on her face.

And I love you, he says seriously.

See you later, alligator, she says. She gives his hot hand one last squeeze.

In a while, crocodile! he rhymes back. He lies still: is ready to get up in sixty seconds and see what Gest is hiding in her room.

Loving the Child, kissing him, holding his hand: these things have taken another three minutes. Gest closes his door, walks fast down the hallway and then turns and walks as fast back. Very quietly, she turns the key in the outside of the Child's door, fastening him in, keeping him safe. Back soon! she calls, hoping he has not heard the key; and at last she is running, jumping down the stairs, two steps at a time, all eight flights of them.

Look back and see this, if you are able to focus through eyes that smart and sting. Gest, who has made it to the pharmacy just in time, is waiting in a queue. See her heart still pumping in her chest, pumping with love for the Child, and desire to do good for him, and the running of three long city blocks. See her fingers tapping on her unblemished arms, see her perfect breasts rising and falling more slowly as the minutes go by, and the lines deepening between her black eyes as she waits, and waits.

Finally she is emerging from the pharmacy with cough medicine and child aspirin crammed into a paper bag. The street is deserted now, littered only with leaves, and the birds that blackened the sky earlier have disappeared. Perhaps they have settled back into the trees but even so they are oddly, utterly, silent. So quiet is it that, as Gest hastens back along the street, her breathing is the only sound she is able to hear. That, and her footsteps on the flat pavement, fast and getting faster. There is an unease in her stomach that she would like to escape, and she starts to run.

But what is this? Two blocks ahead a column of black smoke is rising into the air, as straight as a tower, stretching for the sky. Gest stops dead. In that second the column of smoke teeters; it topples and falls into the street, disintegrates into a black cloud obscuring trees, tram tracks, all.

Watch Gest drop her bag and pull off her shoes. Watch her run blindly for home, flying across an intersection without looking so that cars scream around her like crows. No shoes, no bag, and what is she carrying? One white pill in her pocket, and a black metal key clutched in her hand.

Look at this scene, if you can bear to, if you can bear the wrenching in your stomach, and the constriction in your throat as if it is wrapped around by a wire that will soon cut and crack into gristle and bone. Look at the sight Gest must witness now, although still one block from home.

Smoke is pouring from the front of a tall building: hers. Dark smoke, gushing from the front window of an

301

apartment eight floors up: her apartment. It is pitch black, this smoke, as black as midnight and blacker than fear. The acrid smell burns its way into Gest's nostrils (it has never left).

Now, for a second, the smoke lifts and clears. Gest can see the Child. There he is, out on the balcony, a small stick figure turning this way and that. And now there, there is the Child. He is leaping from the burning building.

It slows down, the world. Time goes into slow motion so that his fall is long and quiet, and no one sees its violent end. He flies like a small fabric toy, like a toy filled with polystyrene balls: heavy and heavy-limbed, yet light enough to hold in the palm of your hand and small enough to catch in the blink of an eye.

She will never forget it. She will never forget. The blazing window, the high balcony on fire, and the Child soaring from the flames, one arm held high in a desperate salute.

The Candy Girl sings

Yes, but how would the Candy Girl like to sing? She thinks she knows how, when she has space in her head to consider it—when her mind is not full of what she must buy when she goes to the supermarket (lists in her head, the sharp green smell of cleaning products in the air) or when she is not hurrying to the bank to shuffle envelopes of hard-earned cash across a counter so bills can be paid. Such things as these distract, pulling her away from her dreams of singing, as does the occasional quick hair-tug of longing for the old days, the old ways, when she would wait under the damp arches of a bridge inhaling the wet seep of stone, stand in that stage of edginess so her ears began to hear the slow growing of moss through the stone, spores reaching far and hard towards the dim light – she will admit it, there is still occasionally a sense of longing for such a moment of arrival, after a long time standing in a carefully casual slouch with the drizzle falling in a curtain beyond the dank hideout, and then – then! – at last the knife edge, at last something sharp after thirty-five long dull minutes of waiting, and then the recognition of eyes meeting under hoods, gaze as hot and hard as the sweep of a searchlight in a locked timber yard, and the press of palms, the quick shift of paper notes belonging to no one but the state anyway, and the reward of a tiny baby weight in your hand, a small plastic bag filled with powder and zipped across with a fastener-top, pulled across and secured (comfortingly fast) and the quick walk away with quickened breath, and at last the sense of time being thrown wide open again, a whole horizon in front of you where, only thirty-six or thirty-seven minutes earlier, life had been closed as if you were banging your aching head against the hard wooden surface of an immovable door.

Oh, the past distracts, as does the present; but sometimes when the Candy Girl is alone, running along a river path or lying in the bath with her toe stuck up the tap to stop the dripping – at these times she knows exactly how she would like to sing. To Gest she has simply used the word *differently*: I would like to sing differently, is all that she has said. But if made to be more precise, to pin it down exactly, this is how she would sing.

Like an Armenian singer, possessed of a voice more instrumental than human. An instrument, though, bears always the weight of its construction, has been crafted, hammered out in brass or cut from the arms of trees; it has then been sold or given to another person who must learn it, learn to love it and to know it before the possible extraction of magic. Whereas the voice of the Armenian singer, perhaps heard at a festival in a windy grey wasteland with tenement houses looking impassively over six-foot fences and buses groaning past unseen: well, that kind of voice has no learnt quality about it, but instead a born strength and purity so that to hear it is like listening to someone sleeping under your own quiet ear, the only extraneous sound the swell of breath entering the chest cavity and its unhurried release (somewhere under your left ear, moving your hair, letting it sink again in the warm dark). That Armenian voice, in which hope is held in a sliding rise, reaching a plateau and hovering there for many long moments, perfectly suspended – although from here, at any minute, the voice might slip back into exquisite melancholy once more. And either is possible: the captured suspension, or the fall. The not-knowing is the only certainty. This, the only certain space between.

Do you remember that carpet you used to sit on in your grandparents' polished hallway? At six years of age, you would sit tight on that carpet with your feet stretched out in front of you and the backs of your knees lightly touching the paisley swirls, and your legs following the direction of the length of carpet towards the front door. Your hands were flat, placed one on each side of you, your thumbs firmly braced on the rough carpet edge and your fingers sliding slowly, one by one, off the red-purple swirls onto the varnished wooden floor. And with each slip of the finger, *one, one, one,* there was an increasing awareness of the minutes passing. Soon the door will fly open. Soon, soon you will fly!

And it happens. The hallway, the runway, is left behind and you are heading fast out the door. The lawn beneath your rising carpet is a rush of blades that blur into solid green, and then you are in the thin air, tears whipping from your sharp-cornered eyes to form salty lines between your eyelids and your ears.

Now you are above the city, that city you are never allowed to go into by yourself, not without some other, some older person holding on to your hand, pulling your arm up too high, stretching your arm up and up so there is a burning in your shoulder and the seams of your western-gear shirt with its smart pearl fasteners crack. But from where you are now the city is not dangerous; you are holding tight to your carpet, and holding your breath, and the city is nothing more than a painting below you, near perfect but not, like a picture by an artist who is an admirer of Brueghel, who paints similar scenes but modern ones: drowsy workers carrying brief-cases instead of scythes, and bored women with shop-ping bags rather than baskets. Probably at this very moment the artist's other canvases are leaning half finished against cold cracked walls in a studio somewhere beneath your woven tapestry chariot; and the artist himself – a man who knows how he would like to paint when he has the space to think about it, but who is distracted by having to earn a living – is right now walking to an office where he will print out clear colourful maps designed to catch the eyes of tourists who are headed for ice cream carts and T-shirt shops but get waylaid by this artist's clear and colourful maps. At this very minute, as you are looking down at the streets snaking around below you, this artist is striving to reproduce those streets, drawing them with topographical correctness but also

305

with a hint of pen-and-ink quirkiness to them (a cartoon tree, a spire with looping shingles). In this way, the artist hopes, his maps will have more appeal than those of a traditional cartographer, and when they are hung on the backs of bathroom doors in faraway countries it will be possible, for a moment, to gain the magical feeling of stepping back into that city, to feel its dry cracking pavements once more under your bare feet which in reality are planted on a pulled cotton bathmat.

It is this stylised city that you see now as you peer over the edge of your weaving Brussels carpet with its heavy woollen pile and its strong linen back. Not dangerous, no: you are not in peril. For you are high in a light blue sky here, you are far away from grasping hands and the flashing blades of knives, out of reach of angry grey flood-water and scorching tongues of fire. The sounds of the city are too far away to be heard but its streets can still be seen quite clearly, looking larger than they should considering your height. What can you see from this perfect vantage point? Cars parked illegally on the diagonal, breaking up the clean lines of avenues. Pigeons scattered like breadcrumbs over squares, and men zig-zagging between train stations and bars, calculating various factors in their minds: the time of the next train, the number of people queuing for drinks, the length of time it will take for a foaming Guinness to settle in its glass, and the possible mood of the wife at home. (How fast will she lose patience, that wife, how quickly feel justified in leaving the house, walking off with loud justified steps to meet some other man at another bar in another part of the city?)

Is it dangerous, where you are? No, far from dangerous. You are six years old but you are safe, held securely between a layer of cloud and a layer of earth. Below your rough woollen seat, which gives the occasional waver so that you must hold on fairly tightly – now you notice your finger has been bloodied by a carpet tack pulled up, uprooted from that long-ago suburban hallway – below you is the near-picture-perfect city, teeming with life. What is the necessary blemish of the city, what is its flaw that makes it real? There is a hole in its heart, a windswept sloping empty space in its centre: but even as you soar and dip you see the small figures of men placing something right in the middle of that space. You strain to see what it might be – is it a figure, is it a dome? But your carpet dips – *hold tight*! And you are leaving the nearly completed picture behind.

So you soar on over long straight train tracks. Swoop low past windows, where dark women sit at tables and quiet men sit reading. And as you do so, be aware: this is as close as you will ever get to freedom. You are touching nothing, nothing is touching you. It will be this way for as long as your journey lasts.

You fly! Now you lose sight of the city, it slips from your mind and there is only the sky: a clear white-blue, streaked across, crossed like the back of a donkey by dark grey jet trails. You are flying, held up by the Armenian tradition of song: and soon you realize that your carpet is no longer there, it has also been left behind you, but the song holds you aloft and carries you many long miles, so easily that you are hardly aware of the pressure of air around you or your spindly gull-legs that fall, float out, behind you. And all around is the circular horizon, a soft and gentle yellow.

Soon there are mountains, crumpled beneath you like paper. Now a ridged brown sea, and still the singing goes on somewhere inside you, a heartbeat or a breathing, breath in your lungs. Lie there on the air and listen to the singing, to how you would sing in a perfect world. Listen to the breathing and soon you will realize: you are no longer lonely. You have left loneliness behind.

An end to tiredness

There is peace here, in the apartment. This is what she has been left with. This is what she has: what she has earned.

A large space marks out the middle of the workroom: although swept clean, there are some scrapemarks on the floor. Men have taken away the work of fifty days, and although it is gone nothing has fallen.

She looks out on to trees. Their leaves have been scorched by the strange and early heat. They are like skeletons, these trees, all thin backbones and thin veined branches, and their flesh is almost transparent. But looked at through half-closed eyes they make a whole, provide a dry green screen that is safe.

Walk to the other side of the apartment now. Walk to the kitchen window, look out, and see the dazzle of sun on the closed windows opposite. Do not try to see through this dazzle; rest is to be found in reflection.

She is beautiful. Still beautiful, perhaps even more than before: but she is tired. So sit now, wait an hour or two for the light to dwindle into grey. This was the time of day when the leaving had happened. At this time, this grey dimming time one year ago, she had left this building, had left her apartment two floors up from this one and had run down the stairs past this very door and out into the hot street. This – soon – will be the time of day when her heart had been ripped from her body. (She does not mind admitting this now, now she is ready.)

She sits still at the kitchen table. Nothing moves, nothing catches her eye, nothing is falling. The hallway is lit by the reflection of the sun but the wall remains sealed. This is rest. Rest is what she has.

What will she do in this short while when the light has faded? Get up, then, and walk to the stove. Her hands are thin, but they are steady enough. Watch her now, turning on the gas controls, holding them in, taping them in firmly one by one to the front of the stove. And when she puts her ear to the elements she will hear a thin purple sound: the sound of four veins of gas feeding into the air.

Far away, a girl she has known and loved is singing. But here the room is silent; it is waiting.

She sits once more at the table, lays her arms out in front of her, thin blemished skin on cool scarred wood. In this small amount of time – a time during which the Reader will look out his window to see a faint bright-ness in the west, and when the Ordinary Man for the first time will recognize the alien stars in the sky – Gest will bow her head. She may be thinking back, or forwards; either is possible.

Far away now someone is singing about love or death, which are not so very different after all. Here in the kitchen the air is becoming stretched; it shimmers like a curtain, moved by the thin breath of the stove.

And so, when the time comes, Gest will walk to the far wall. (This will not be difficult, after the days she has been through.) Walking steadily in her bare feet to touch the wall, perhaps looking once over her shoulder towards a closed window. But it is getting dimmer and it is time for the light to come, time to flick life into the fluorescent tube that hangs so silently and powerfully above the purple haze.

The kitchen is heavy with gas now, and she will do it. Do it now: flick the switch and with that flick, for a second, see the world blinding and bright. So beautiful and blinding, so bright!

And then there will be nothing more. No more time; this will be all. The fall, and the relief of it.

Acknowledgements

Thanks to Simon Trewin, Jill Foulston, and Donna Coonan for their help and support.

SHOT

Sarah Quigley

A pitch-perfect novel of loss and discovery, *Shot* is the
debut of a startlingly rich and fresh imagination.

Lena has always looked at things a little differently – and
although she has never found life particularly funny, her
skewed vision has meant half a lifetime of stand-up
comedy. But when a bullet whispers past her ear during a
drive-by shooting, it quickly becomes clear that life is no
joking matter.

Suddenly the past is dispensable. Her career, her name, an
ambitious lover, a disillusioned mother and a bumbling
father: Lena sheds them all and heads north, where, in the
frozen wastes of Alaska, her heart begins to melt.

'Joyously unpredictable' *Venue*

'Lovely, ironic prose . . . catches the heartstrings'
Irish Examiner

'A wry and heartwarming tale of love, loss and discovery'
Faces of the Future, *Waterstone's Book Quarterly*

'A humorous and intelligent reworking of the American
road trip genre' *Big Issue*

A RHINESTONE BUTTON

Gail Anderson-Dargatz

Job is a farmer who sees colour in sound: colours like the shifting northern lights gracing the sky of his home town Godsfinger, Alberta.

And even in this community of curious characters – a town where crop circles occur, birds drop out of the sky, a duck waddles around in a nappy, a cook in stilettos flips burgers at the Out-To-Lunch café, and a crazy lady squirts her water pistol at those she thinks are out of line – Job is an outsider.

Then his ability to see sound begins to fade. Job finally knows that it's time to wake up and really listen – most particularly to Liv down at the diner, someone who has been talking to him for some time now . . .

'Few contemporary Canadian novelists can match her ability to capture moments of acutely observed rural life that conjure mood and a way of life'
Toronto Globe and Mail

'Known for her tantalizing titles . . . this is Gail Anderson-Dargatz's story of Job's search to find a life'
Elle

You can order other Virago titles through our website: *www.virago.co.uk*
or by using the order form below

☐	Shot	Sarah Quigley	£6.99
☐	A Rhinestone Button	Gail Anderson-Dargatz	£7.99
☐	Seventh Heaven	Alice Hoffman	£7.99
☐	Cassandra at the Wedding	Dorothy Baker	£7.99

The prices shown above are correct at time of going to press. However, the publishers reserve the right to increase prices on covers from those previously advertised, without further notice.

Virago

Please allow for postage and packing: **Free UK delivery.**
Europe: add 25% of retail price; Rest of World: 45% of retail price.

To order any of the above or any other Virago titles, please call our credit card orderline or fill in this coupon and send/fax it to:

Virago, PO Box 121, Kettering, Northants NN14 4ZQ
Fax: 01832 733076   Tel: 01832 737526
Email: aspenhouse@FSBDial.co.uk

☐ I enclose a UK bank cheque made payable to Virago for £ . . . .
☐ Please charge £ . . . . . . to my Visa/Access/Mastercard/Eurocard

Expiry Date ☐☐☐☐   Switch Issue No. ☐☐

NAME (BLOCK LETTERS please) . . . .
ADDRESS . . . .

. . . .

. . . .

Postcode . . . . Telephone . . . .

Signature . . . .

Please allow 28 days for delivery within the UK. Offer subject to price and availability.
Please do not send any further mailings from companies carefully selected by Virago ☐